James's focus was on Lily. Her eyes were closed, her face tilted to the sunlight. He studied her features. High cheekbones and round chin, the slight downward arc of her nose, and full, lush lips.

He found her beautiful.

He ought to speak to her. Yesterday the words had left him. The feel of her, the scent and taste of her skin, the way she had shivered with pleasure at his touch, made conversation impossible. Words had been unnecessary. Everything important could be said with a kiss, a caress.

BOOK YOUR PLACE ON OUR WEBSITE AND MAKE THE READING CONNECTION!

We've created a customized website just for our very special readers, where you can get the inside scoop on everything that's going on with Zebra, Pinnacle and Kensington books.

When you come online, you'll have the exciting opportunity to:

- View covers of upcoming books

- Read sample chapters

- Learn about our future publishing schedule (listed by publication month *and author*)

- Find out when your favorite authors will be visiting a city near you

- Search for and order backlist books from our online catalog

- Check out author bios and background information

- Send e-mail to your favorite authors

- Meet the Kensington staff online

- Join us in weekly chats with authors, readers and other guests

- Get writing guidelines

- AND MUCH MORE!

**Visit our website at
http://www.kensingtonbooks.com**

Passionate

Anthea Lawson

for Barbara—
Enjoy!

ZEBRA BOOKS
Kensington Publishing Corp.
www.kensingtonbooks.com

ZEBRA BOOKS are published by

Kensington Publishing Corp.
850 Third Avenue
New York, NY 10022

All Kensington titles, imprints, and distributed lines are available at special quantity discounts for bulk purchases for sales promotion, premiums, fund-raising, educational, or institutional use.

Special book excerpts or customized printings can also be created to fit specific needs. For details, write or phone the office of the Kensington Special Sales Manager: Attn. Special Sales Department. Kensington Publishing Corp., 850 Third Avenue, New York, NY 10022. Phone: 1-800-221-2647.

Zebra and the Z logo Reg. U.S. Pat. & TM Off.

ISBN-13: 978-1-4201-0456-1
ISBN-10: 1-4201-0456-X

First Printing: October 2008
10 9 8 7 6 5 4 3 2 1

Printed in the United States of America

Chapter 1

England, February 1847

"Tunisia?" James Huntington paced the length of his uncle's study and halted in front of the wide desk. "I've been back in London barely four months. Is it really necessary for me to leave England again so soon?"

"Sit down, James. Please." Lord Denby waved to a nearby armchair. "Under the circumstances it is both necessary and expedient. Good heavens—what were you thinking? You shot the Duke of Hereford's son in Hyde Park."

"I didn't shoot him in Hyde Park, Uncle. I shot him in the buttock, and he was only grazed. I aimed wide—it's not my fault the coward threw himself into the bullet's path."

"Perhaps that would have excused you in India, but you are in London now. A duel . . ." His uncle shook his head.

"It was unavoidable." James settled into the leather armchair. "That fool said things about my sister that were scandalous and untrue. I had to challenge him—her reputation was in jeopardy."

"I appreciate your need to defend Caroline's honor, but you have placed us in a difficult situation. The Duke of Hereford will not take your public humiliation of his son well. James, your aim was most unfortunate. Young Hereford's entrance to every social event will be commented upon—at least until he can sit down again. Frankly, I need you out of town until this blows over."

James studied his uncle, noting how weary and stern Lord Denby looked in his formal black mourning clothes. His usually neat desktop was crowded with account books and piles of correspondence. It couldn't be easy trying to restore order to an earldom. Grandfather's recent death had left Lord Denby with the title—and an estate in disarray. The last thing he needed right now was a scandal.

James ran a hand through his already tousled brown hair. "I can see leaving London. But why Tunisia? I could simply make a quiet disappearance to one of your country properties."

"You could. But I need you to go to Tunisia." Lord Denby lifted his spectacles and rubbed the bridge of his nose. "This is as much about your grandfather's will as it is your regrettable duel. He chose to tie up a rather large number of loose ends by passing them along to his descendants. One of the most troublesome concerns his residence, Somergate."

"Somergate?" It had been his grandfather's primary residence, the property the old man had lavished his attention and money upon—often to the detriment of the family's other holdings. James remembered the moist warmth of the grand conservatory there, the sharp, earthy smells of the tropical plants. He had been a boy, his father still alive, holding James by the hand and carrying Caroline on his shoulders. James's grandfather had led them through the maze of greenery and bright blooms, speaking the names of the plants as if he were greeting old friends.

James swallowed, banishing the old ache the memory evoked.

His uncle shuffled through a pile of paper on his desk. "We can't wind up the estate until the will's provisions have been carried out—or proven impossible. Your grandfather always claimed he had made an important botanical discovery during his adventures in Tunisia, but had been unable to bring back the specimen that would prove it. His traveling companion,

Mercer, died there, and the journals that documented the expedition were lost. Under his will, whichever descendant manages to recover and publish those journals receives the Somergate estate and his blasted horticultural collection."

James leaned forward. "That's absurd."

"No, that's your grandfather. My solicitor tells me the old schemer left no loopholes."

"What if no one is willing to go chasing across Africa looking for lost journals?"

"Then Somergate goes to Kew Gardens. Such a bequest would no doubt cement your grandfather's reputation among his scientific peers, but it would be disastrous for the family to lose such a valuable property."

Somergate gone. It was unthinkable.

"What does my cousin think of all this?" It was a question that had to be asked—not that James personally gave a damn what Reggie thought.

Lord Denby shifted in his chair. "I have not discussed this matter with him. I realize the odds are long, but this is a chance to have something for yourself. Your father left you little enough when he died, and I would like to see you independent and not beholden to Reginald when he succeeds me. I know how it stands between the two of you."

He didn't, not really. But this was not the time to set him straight. Ever since James and Caroline had been taken in as orphans by their uncle, Reggie had been an enemy—using every opportunity to let them know how unwelcome they were, always reminding them of his own superiority, that they were not the true son and daughter of Lord Denby and did not belong there. It had not been an easy childhood. But it was also not easy for Lord Denby to have a son like Reggie for his heir. James firmed his mouth. Some things were better left unspoken.

His uncle continued, "I would like to see you settled—for my brother's sake, and for your own. Your prospects in London have dimmed considerably in the last twenty-four hours."

Not that they had been particularly bright to begin with.

James stretched his legs out and absently noted a scuffed

patch on his boots. Being back in society was not what he had hoped. It was too bloody passive, for one thing. He was beginning to wonder if cashing in his officer's commission and returning home had been a mistake. He lacked both the temperament and the funds to enjoy a life of empty leisure.

Perhaps Lord Denby was right. Maybe the eccentric provision in his grandfather's will was his best hope—and even if it was no hope at all, his uncle still needed someone to go, if only to prove that the journals had long ago moldered into dust.

But still, Tunisia?

"Assuming I went, what would it involve? I can't see interviewing every tribal sheik along the North African coast. There must be a map—isn't that how these things go?"

"We have this." Lord Denby pushed an inlaid wooden box toward him. "The solicitors released it to me after your grandfather's death."

James took the box. "It must be a very small map." He lifted the lid to find a packet resting on the red silk lining. "Letters?"

"They were penned by your grandfather from all around the Mediterranean. Love letters to your grandmother before they married." There was an uncharacteristic huskiness in Lord Denby's voice. "I find them difficult to read under the circumstances. The top one is most pertinent."

James removed the letter from its envelope and leaned forward to catch the light filtering through the tall Palladian windows. The writing was faded, the letter dated 23 July, 1792.

"There is a description of your grandfather's capture by Berbers and subsequent escape," Lord Denby said. "Look at the top of the second page."

We had made our way west along the Medjerda River, and though only three days' travel from the capital, we came upon one of those untouched places every explorer longs to find. This narrow valley in the mountains, a wild, rocky place, was filled with a profusion of Orchis boryi. *They were in high bloom, rank upon rank ascending the valley until they broke in a wave of splendid purple upon an upthrusting of huge boulders. We camped at the foot of these rock giants where a small spring pooled.*

"What are *Orchis boryi*?" James asked.

Lord Denby shrugged. "Your grandfather was the botanist, not I. Continue. He describes hiding the journals just before they were attacked."

I squeezed into a cleft in the ravine and scrambled up to a rock shelf, concealing the box that held our journals. It was then I noticed the most delicate flower clinging to the walls. It had small yellow petals and it rooted itself tenaciously in the fissures. I had never seen a flower quite like this. If only I could have examined it more closely—I'm sure it was hereto undiscovered. Then Mercer cried out and I went to him.

James was silent. He remembered the story. If he closed his eyes, he could see the old man in his library, a fierce light in his face as he recounted his adventures. The room had been crammed with artifacts from far-off lands. Bizarre carvings of animals, colorful rocks—rough-hewn turquoise and carnelian, even a nugget of gold. And a stuffed owl with glass eyes that always seemed to be watching him.

His grandfather had given him a large, speckled egg from a collection in a glass case. Whatever happened to it? Mysteriously broken, no doubt, when James returned with it to his uncle's home. Nothing important to him had been safe from Reggie's jealousy.

"Well?" Lord Denby asked.

James tapped the letter against his palm. "Why didn't Grandfather return and fetch the journals himself?"

"He loved your grandmother deeply. It was for her sake that he never mounted an expedition to recover his papers. Only after she died did he think of going back. By then ill-health and the obligations of his position prevented such a journey."

James flipped the letter over. "What's this?" There was a rough sketch on the back depicting a narrow vale with a huge rocky escarpment standing sentinel.

"The map—or the closest thing we have to it," Lord Denby said. "I assume it is the rock formation where he hid the journals."

"A sketch? What good is a picture of a valley when you have no idea where the valley is? This is a bit flimsy to justify haring off to Tunisia. Besides, my sister will never forgive me for leaving again so soon."

"Caroline will understand. Especially as it was her tart tongue that began the trouble with young Hereford in the first place."

James couldn't suppress his grin. Caroline was never one to mince her words, and he and his uncle both loved her for it. Lord Denby had truly been as a father to her. For that alone James owed him a debt of gratitude.

He would go to Tunisia.

And if he were successful? He could hardly bring himself to imagine it. But to be master of Somergate—gods, how his prospects would be changed.

"I will need to consult a botanist," he said, drumming his fingers on the arm of the chair. "Someone who can tell me about that purple *Orchis*, and where one might find a whole valley of them. One of grandfather's associates, perhaps?"

"Most are old men. Of those still left . . ." His uncle pursed his lips. "I do recall one. Sir Edward Strathmore. He and your grandfather corresponded regularly. He seemed an amiable fellow when we met. I could write a letter of introduction."

"Good. Send it today."

"You'll go, then?"

James rose, feeling more himself than he had in months. "I will."

Chapter 2

Lily Strathmore touched her brush to the paper, streaking crimson highlights along the petals taking shape on the page. She had finished the technical studies and now was painting for her own pleasure, letting the lush, perfumed warmth of the conservatory transport her into the heart of the flower. She stepped back from the easel and considered the rich red of the *Amaryllis*. Yes, that would do nicely.

"Lily?" Her cousin Isabelle stirred on the nearby chaise. "Do you really think your parents will take you back to London with them? The expedition wouldn't be the same without you."

"They won't if I have any say in the matter. I've only been here a week—hardly long enough to make a start painting your father's new specimens. I'll find some way to stay. I always do." Lily set her paintbrush down and smoothed back her unruly chestnut hair with both hands. "Mother only wants me back in town because she has some scheme in mind—something matrimonial, no doubt."

"London isn't all bad, surely. If you return you'll be able to attend the balls and parties. While you're dancing with dashing gentlemen, I'll be carted around Italy with father's precious roots and twigs."

"At least you won't be required to dance and make

conversation with them. I'd much prefer to travel about the continent with your family. Collecting and painting flowers is far more interesting than trying to impersonate one in a ball gown."

"So you have told me, for the hundredth time. But what about suitors? Surely you have scores of them?"

Lily exhaled. "Hardly scores. And being pursued is not so enviable when it is your mother selecting the pursuers." Lady Fernhaven had an unerring eye for the most placid, staid, and well-bred gentlemen society had to offer. None of the men who had been allowed to present themselves over the last four seasons had made Lily feel even a momentary flutter of emotion. No, that was not precisely true. Not if one classified boredom as an emotion.

"Don't worry," she added, seeing her cousin's serious expression. "When your season comes you'll have a lovely time and dozens of handsome suitors, I promise."

"Do you think so? I will pass?" Isabelle was due to make her come-out next year and cherished notions of London.

"Quite well."

Isabelle's sparkling nature, her golden hair and fair complexion, would be well received by society. No doubt her cousin would have a throng of suitors. Lily did not envy her at all.

She took up her brush again and swirled it in a pan of deep green—the leaves needed more shading to bring the flower out. The delicate brushwork took all her attention.

A gentle hand fell on Lily's shoulder, drawing her out of the world of shadow and tint and back into the conservatory. How long had it been? She looked up to see her Aunt Mary smiling.

"The painting is lovely, my dear," her aunt said. Her gaze shifted to her daughter. "Isabelle, your brother is about to go riding and wonders if you would join him."

"Of course." Isabelle jumped up. "It must have stopped raining."

Aunt Mary took the seat her daughter had vacated and gave Lily a searching look. "Your parents seem set on taking you back to London."

"No doubt Mother has another perfect prospect waiting. Perfect, that is, until we actually meet. With all the men in town, you'd think there would be someone. At this rate, I won't ever marry."

"There is no one? With your younger sister now wed, you are the only daughter left at home. Have you considered what that means?"

Lily set her brush down. "In what way? I don't relish the idea of ending up a spinster—but at least there would be plenty of time for painting. Life without a husband is better, in my estimation, than life with the wrong husband."

"That seems a lonely choice, my dear."

Lily shrugged. "I have come to terms with the idea."

Her hand smoothed her painting apron. She had always thought there would be someone for her, and children, too. But, as her mother so frequently reminded her, she was four-and-twenty—perilously close to being on the shelf. Her chances of making a match that would satisfy both her mother and herself were growing slimmer each day. Yet she could not bring herself to encourage the stuffy, self-absorbed aristocrats she was paraded before. She knew her duty was to make a match that would enhance her family's status and her father's position in Parliament, yet she had always believed that there should be something more.

Aunt Mary studied her. "You realize your sister's marriage changes your own situation."

"How so? Beyond the fact that I will now bear the full brunt of Mother's matchmaking."

A look of sympathy passed across her aunt's features. "You are the last unmarried daughter. Your mother may soon stop trying to see you wed and instead turn her focus toward seeing that you are ready to tend her—and your father—into their old age. The freedom of spinsterhood comes only after your obligation to your parents has ended. That might be very late in your life."

Or not at all. The muscles in Lily's jaw tightened. She had not fully considered it before, but her aunt was right. Horribly right.

Her mother was never an easy person to live with. The thought of playing the dutiful daughter, of fetching and carrying and accompanying her on an endless round of social calls . . . Lily shook her head. It was simply impossible.

"I'd imagined the opportunity to travel, to paint—not play nursemaid and companion to my parents."

Aunt Mary met her eyes directly. "I thought it best that you understand the situation clearly, my dear, especially with your parents' visit coming to a close. They would like a word with you in the drawing room. I expect you'll want to freshen up."

Lily entered the drawing room to find her father standing before the window, staring out at a patch of blue framed by dark clouds. Her mother sat in the wingback near him, hands folded in her lap, waiting. To pounce, no doubt. They were both dressed for travel, Lady Fernhaven, as always, in the first order of fashion. Her sea-green silk walking dress was a perfect match for her eyes—an unusual hue that Lily had inherited.

"There you are, darling. Come in. Your father and I have been discussing your future. You know we only have your best interests at heart. Really, you cannot afford to rusticate out here any longer. Look at you."

Lily followed her mother's gaze down to her hands. Despite her efforts she had not been able to completely remove the crimson and viridian stains the paints had left on her fingers. She curled them into her palms and met her mother's eyes.

"Mother, I came here to document Uncle Edward's new botanical specimens. It's important work. The publications of his papers with my illustrations have been well-received."

Lady Fernhaven's lips tightened. "That is all very well, but you have more important things to consider. Time is not standing still, Lily. I fear soon it will be too late."

Usually Lily had a ready reply, but her conversation with Aunt Mary had been sobering. She looked at the woman before her, tense as a coiled spring, then to her father standing motionless and unreadable. Then past both of them.

Outside, the gardens at Brookdale Manor were awakening. Hardy green spikes of woodland hyacinth poked through the brown carpet of leaves and the thin spears of crocus were well up, bearing their promise of jewel-bright yellow and purple flowers.

What promise did her future hold? None—unless she chose a different course. Spinsterhood would be a marriage of sorts, a marriage to her father and mother—chilling thought. She might not be able to find that elusive someone, but she could certainly do better than these two. Truly, they were partners even less suitable than the gentlemen who had called upon her. As a married woman she would at least be a lady in her own right.

Lily focused back on her mother. "Who is it this time? You no doubt have someone in mind, having eliminated the fortune-hunters and untitled younger sons, of course."

Lady Fernhaven fixed her with a sharp look. "I am sure you recall my dear friend Countess Buckley. We find ourselves with a similar problem. Her son, Lord Gerald Buckley, is a most agreeable young man. The two of you would suit admirably, Lily. He is heir to a very respectable estate and title. You are the daughter of a marquis, a lady of good family and breeding."

Her father left his refuge among the curtains. "I have to agree. We fear you are heading for spinsterhood if you do not mend your ways. At your insistence, we have given you a great deal of freedom—perhaps too much. It is past time to take up the responsibilities of your position in society."

Lily tried to read his face, searching in vain for the understanding she usually found there.

Lady Fernhaven continued. "Lord Buckley is presently sightseeing in America. His mother assures me he intends to call upon you when he returns. They correspond regularly and the situation appears very promising."

"Very promising? Is he kind, Mother? Does he treat his servants and horses well? Will he love his wife and children more than a bottle of brandy?"

"Really, Lily, you do carry on. You are the most particular girl a mother could be burdened with. The Buckleys are a very old and well-respected family. He'll be an earl, for goodness sake."

Lily folded her arms. She knew very little about Lord Buckley, and only vaguely recalled sitting at supper with him—had it been last season, or the one before? He had not left a *bad* impression. He had not left much of an impression at all. She knew he did not spend much time in London, but then, neither did she. Did he also flee a mother who sought to manage his life? Lily was acquainted with Countess Buckley—it was entirely possible.

"And if I refuse to entertain Lord Buckley's company?"

Her father spoke. "Then I hope you had the foresight to pack your valise. You will return with us to London immediately and remain there."

She narrowed her eyes at him—the betrayer—but his jaw was set, his mind made up.

"What about my painting? And the botanical expedition? Uncle Edward needs me."

"We have spoken to him," her father said. "He understands the situation—understands that he will have to find another illustrator."

"You aren't serious. You can't be. It isn't necessary—"

"It is necessary. I'm sorry, Lily."

She turned and began pacing, a habit her mother deplored. Her parents were determined. And united. It was so uncharacteristic of them. No wonder her aunt had tried to prepare her. Now Lily was fenced in by her mother, and her father guarded the gate.

Could any husband be more intolerable than this pair? Maybe she had been wrong to reject all those men. There had been some kind ones, some handsome ones—there must have been. She should have just chosen one and been done with it.

Possible and probable futures swirled through her mind. The room was suddenly quiet but for the coal hissing in the grate, the swish of her skirts and the sound of her pacing feet. Whichever step she took—right now, under the combined scrutiny of her parents—could set her course for the rest of her life.

Which life did she choose?

Lily pivoted to face her mother. "When is Lord Buckley due to return to London?"

Calculation leapt in Lady Fernhaven's eyes. "Sometime mid-season, I believe. June at the latest. What are you saying?"

"I'm not saying anything—not yet." She could not endure the triumph unfolding across her mother's face. Lily began pacing again. "And he has expressed interest in, ah, arranging a union?"

"Yes." Her mother leaned forward in her chair.

Lily's heartbeat sped faster than her steps. Marriage was the only way to avoid becoming a spinster. She shot a glance at her mother. And becoming a spinster was not an option. While she had not anticipated that today would be the day she agreed to wed, there did seem to be advantages. What better way to avoid the pressure to make a match than by making one?

She stopped in front her parents. "If Lord Buckley and I had an understanding, it wouldn't be necessary for me to spend the season in town. It wouldn't even be wise for me to dance and converse with other unmarried gentlemen while he was away."

"Where are you headed with this?" her father asked.

"If I'm agreeable and Lord Buckley is agreeable, then there really is no reason to parade about the salons and ballrooms of London. I might as well continue here, painting." She widened her eyes and looked directly at her father. "Don't you think?"

"Well . . ." He glanced at Lily's mother. "She does have a point."

"No she doesn't. She will just waste the season painting pictures of foliage and then refuse Lord Buckley when he returns."

"I will not refuse him, mother. I'll accept Lord Buckley's suit—on the condition that I can remain here to finish my work, and accompany Uncle Edward's field expedition next month."

There. It hardly seemed possible she had said the words.

"You will?" Exultation flashed in Lady Fernhaven's eyes. "You will!" Turning to her husband, she said, "Didn't I tell you she would come around if only you would side with me?" She rose with a rustle of silk and took Lily's hands, squeezing them tightly. "You will not regret this, darling. Lord Buckley is a very wise choice. If you will agree to his proposal of marriage, then I think you may be spared the rigors of the London season. In fact, you are right. With Lord Buckley away, your absence will be all to the good. We will, of course, expect you back in town upon his arrival."

"Of course, Mother."

Her father stepped forward and took Lily by the shoulders. "We will hold you to your word."

"I know. I intend to keep it." Oh heavens. What had she just done?

He pulled her into an embrace. "We'll see you in town before you go abroad."

"And I will arrange something with Countess Buckley when you visit," her mother added. "She will be eager to renew her acquaintance with you."

Chapter 3

Lily had painted every day since her parents had left, as much as the light would allow, trying to forget the future and lose herself in the swirl of color and shade that had always been her solace. Time seemed so precious now, and she had paid so dearly for what little was left. But today was such a fine day for a ride, Lily had let her cousins coax her away from her easel.

"You're going to grow roots if you stay in the conservatory a minute longer," Isabelle had said.

"We'll have to pot you up," Richard added. "Do come."

It had been fine day for a ride—until now.

Lily clutched at the saddle, but there was no stopping it. It was slipping. Frightened by the sudden motion, her horse shied, tumbling her with a splash into a shallow ditch. Cold mud softened her fall and her favorite green velvet riding habit soaked up water like the rag it had just become. Blast. She should have just stayed in and painted.

"Lily!" Isabelle turned her horse and raced back. "Are you all right? Is anything broken?"

Lily struggled to her feet. "Do I look all right? No. I rather resemble a mop." She set her hands on her hips—her very damp hips—and tried to ignore the clammy fabric clinging to her. "Go ahead. Laugh. I don't find the situation particularly funny."

"Of course not." Richard dismounted and offered his handkerchief. "You may want to—mop up."

Her cousins burst into a fit of laughter. "Sorry, Lily, but you are a sight. We're glad to find you in one piece, though." Richard bent and fished her saddle out of the ditch.

He examined it carefully. "You won't be riding back on this," he said, pointing. "The girth's given way."

Lily gathered her sodden skirts and waded forward. "How do you propose we get home?"

"We could double up." Richard looked at her muddy dress and took a step back. "But maybe I should just trade horses with you—once I catch yours, that is."

She climbed out of the ditch and took the reins of Richard's horse—his very tall, very spirited horse. She glanced up at the beast, then over to Isabelle. "Would you care to ride Hercules home?"

"*Moi*? Oh, no thank you. I'm *quite* comfortable where I am. You'll have to ride astride, you know."

Astride! If she were observed riding in such a very unlady-like fashion it would be the talk of the shire. Lily turned to protest, but a cold east wind gusted up and her teeth began to chatter. Visions of steam rising out of a hot bath tantalized her. Riding astride might be risky, but she certainly couldn't remain dripping here in a cold field.

It took some doing, but with her skirts kilted and a boost from Richard—who, like a gentleman, kept his head turned away—she managed to throw a leg over Hercules's back. She hauled herself into the saddle, wet velvet bunched up around her thighs and showing an indecent amount of skin. How wicked it felt to sit with her legs exposed and splayed across the huge animal's back.

She laughed nervously. "If Mother could see me now she would either disown me or die of mortification. Probably both! Why, just last month Miss Clara Abernathy caused a minor scandal in London when she lifted her dress to mid-calf while descending the steps of the family carriage." Lily looked at the water dripping from her bunched skirts and down her naked thigh. It was outrageous. "Let's take the back way and cut through the fields. We can't chance being seen."

"True," Richard said, still keeping his eyes conspicuously averted. "But Farmer Cottle has his bull out to pasture. It's the meanest-tempered animal you'll ever see."

Isabelle nodded. "Would you rather risk certain goring? Let's ride around to the front gates—it will be faster and we can stay behind hedgerows most of the way. And don't worry. There wasn't anyone on the ride out, after all."

"Very well," Lily said at last, all too aware of the muddy trickles snaking down her legs. "I need a bath now!" She wiped her cheek with the damp sleeve of her riding habit and urged Hercules forward.

The wind was blowing colder when they traded the shelter of the hedgerows for Brookdale Manor's elm-flanked drive.

"Almost home," Lily said, then halted abruptly. Oh no. Why hadn't they risked the bull?

A gentleman was sitting his gray horse before the wrought-iron gates. There was something military in his bearing, a controlled energy that left the impression he could move from repose to full charge in an eye-blink. His lean, handsome face was turned to her, and she watched in horror as his gaze lowered to take in her exposed legs. Hot embarrassment washed over her and she was suddenly, unbearably, conscious of her indecent state.

"Who is that?" Isabelle stopped beside her.

"Someone I'm sure I do not want to meet." Lily yanked the reins sideways and kicked her heels hard.

The great horse reared, its powerful muscles tensing and releasing as it bolted forward. Lily clung to the saddle, concentrating on staying on as Hercules leapt the ditch that ran beside the drive and made for the open fields. Behind her she could hear her cousin's alarmed shouts, but she hardly cared. Her only concern was to remain mounted and disappear from view as quickly as possible.

"Hold on!" The man's voice sounded impossibly close.

She risked a glance over her shoulder. Truly, it must be a

nightmare. The stranger was pursuing her, leaning low in the saddle—and he was obviously a far better rider than she would ever be. Despite her best efforts he was closing the gap between them. He drew his mount alongside, matching hers stride for stride.

"Kick your feet from the stirrups," he commanded.

Before she could protest he leaned in and wrapped one arm tightly around her waist. He pulled her to him and Hercules, who wanted nothing of the maneuver, put on a final burst of speed and ran out from beneath her. She was suspended, clamped against the stranger, his arm coiled just below her breasts.

She must have been held in that most humiliating way for a very short time, although it did not seem so. The stranger brought his mount to a halt, then leaned over and lowered her to the ground.

Lily might have admired his riding skill, if she had not been so angry. But his "rescue" had made the situation a hundred—no, a thousand—times worse. She tugged at the disarray of her skirts as he dismounted and came to stand beside her.

"That was a near thing, Miss. Are you—"

She looked up him. His amber-flecked brown eyes were unnervingly close. "I am perfectly fine. Except for being chased down and plucked from my horse."

He regarded her steadily for a moment, and she had the impression he was trying not to smile. "Then I must beg your pardon. I assumed your mount had run away with you."

Cheeks flaming, Lily lifted her chin. "It was not at all the case. I was only . . ." But how could she explain? Wasn't it obvious that someone who had behaved as indecently as she had would flee the eyes of a stranger?

"Lily!" Isabelle rushed up with Richard close behind. "Oh dear, what a dreadful morning you have had."

"That was quite a bit of horsemanship, sir," Richard said, giving the stranger an admiring look.

"Like someone out of the circus!" Isabelle added. "The way you swooped her from the saddle."

"Indeed," the man said. "Perhaps I should seek out that

profession, since I have been informed I have little prospect as gallant rescuer. My apologies to you all for the manner of my introduction. I'm James Huntington, down from London and looking for Sir Edward Strathmore of Brookdale Manor. Is this his residence?"

"You have found it, sir." Richard offered his hand. "I'm Richard Strathmore. Sir Edward is my father. This is my sister, Isabelle, and my cousin Lily."

"Lily's girth broke," Isabelle explained. "The saddle slipped and took her with it. That's why she was—"

"Isabelle, please!" Lily felt her blush deepen.

"I was only going to say that it was lucky your fall was softened—by a nice muddy ditch."

Lily wanted to cover her face with her hands. Did this man have to hear every humiliating detail?

"I have heard that some people pay dearly to lie in a bath of mud," Mr. Huntington said. "Good for the complexion."

The tension burst.

"Mud baths!" Richard laughed—the wretch—and Isabelle too.

The so-witty Mr. Huntington smiled, humor sparking golden lights in his eyes. It was beyond mortifying.

Lily could take no more. She swept them all with a glare, then turned on her heel and marched back across the pasture, dragging her ruined skirts as she went.

James watched the woman's retreating form. What an odd creature. She had charged off like some kind of bandit-queen, riding astride and leaping ditches. All she lacked was a dagger clenched between her teeth. A dagger she would have used on him when he pursued her, no doubt.

Richard smiled. "You caught Lily at a severe disadvantage, sir. You will find her far more agreeable once she has had her bath."

James doubted it. He did not intend to find her at all—agreeable or not. He would consult with Sir Edward and be gone before the admittedly shapely Miss Strathmore had finished rinsing out her hair. She had a lovely pair of legs and he would not soon forget their display, but his business had nothing to do with the beauty who had sat so brazenly astride her mount.

"Come, we will bring you to the house. Father will be in the library."

"You are most kind. Despite the awkwardness of our introduction, my errand demands that I see him."

After the grooms had taken their horses, Richard escorted James inside and rapped on a mahogany door.

"Hello, Father. You have a visitor. Mr. James Huntington of London."

"Yes, yes, come in." A balding man, shorter than James, with bright blue eyes and a ruddy, genial face, waved a hand lens at him. "Welcome, Mr. Huntington. I received your uncle's letter and have been expecting you. Do sit down."

Sir Edward settled in the chair opposite. "I knew your grandfather—a fine man. We exchanged correspondence on matters botanical. His passing was a great loss for the scientific community—but I'm sure you didn't ride all the way out to Brookdale just to accept my condolences."

"No—although I thank you for them. I need your help locating a valley my grandfather visited on one of his expeditions to North Africa." James reached into his coat pocket for the letter and handed it to Sir Edward. "I would be interested to know your opinion on this."

The botanist took it and began to read. "What misfortune," he said when he had finished. "To discover a new bloom and be prevented from collecting it. That must have been one of his chief regrets."

"That and the loss of his friend, Mercer."

"Yes, yes. Of course."

"Have you heard of the valley, or have any idea where it is?"

Sir Edward shook his head. "I'm afraid not."

Well, James hadn't expected it to be that easy. He settled back and looked about Sir Edward's library. It reminded him of his grandfather's study. The cheerful fire burning in the grate warmed what was clearly a working room—full bookshelves, sturdy tables given over to scattered notes, hand lenses, and stacks of pressed botanical specimens. The north wall was filled with framed watercolors. Leaf and stem, root and petal— all the glories of the plant kingdom rendered in exquisite detail. The vital quality of the illustrations caught his attention.

Sir Edward followed his gaze. "Ah. Lily's botanicals. My niece, Miss Lily Strathmore. She has quite a talent, don't you think?"

"There's a remarkable spirit in her work."

Could it be that the same creature he had encountered had the talent and sensitivity to produce such paintings? It was said that only a fine line separated the artist from the madman—or in this case, the madwoman.

Sir Edward nodded toward the paintings. "Lily captures the essence of the bloom without distorting the proportions or rendering the detail inaccurately. Her paintings are portraits rather than merely technical illustrations. You must meet her before you depart—a charming girl. In fact, you must meet the whole family."

"I would be delighted." James mouthed the polite response. In truth, he would be delighted to find out where the valley was and take his leave, without causing further embarrassment to himself or Sir Edward's peculiar niece.

"Good. You will take tea with us. Now, concerning your grandfather's letter—I am familiar with the *Orchis* mentioned. It is of the Mediterranean *Orchidaceae* family, all terrestrial, you know. The species described in the letter grows in hilly, upland terrain. We need a map." Sir Edward rose and went to a large wooden case. He retrieved a roll of paper, cleared an area on one of the wooden tables, and unfurled the map.

James rose and joined him, securing one edge with his hand. "North Africa. And a good map, too." He ran his finger along the southern coast of the Mediterranean, through Morocco and Algeria, and halted. "Tunisia. My grandfather was here, in the northern mountains."

"That still leaves you with a very large area to search."

James traced a meandering blue line. "This is the river my grandfather followed from Tunis. Local tribesmen might be able to help, but I can't count on it—not with the reception they gave my grandfather and his poor friend Mercer."

Sir Edward pointed. "Don't forget the elevations. The flower grows in the uplands. That should narrow your search considerably. The valley might not be impossible to locate. Think of it, being the first to collect an entirely new species of flower—discovered by your grandfather, no less! Let me just see . . ." He turned his attention to a heavy, leather-bound volume on the next table and paged through, muttering Latin names and nodding occasionally to himself.

James looked down at the map again, studying the mountains. At least he would not have to search the vast southern desert. He would be spared bad-tempered camels and blowing sand.

Sir Edward closed his tome with a clap. "I can find no mention of anything that could be the flower your grandfather describes. Possibly in the *Primulaceae* family, but it is hard to say. You're not thinking of going alone, are you?"

"Actually, I am."

"With all respect, Huntington, that's an absurd idea."

The corners of James's lips quirked up. The man's candor was refreshing after months of the London scene.

"You must take a botanist with you," Sir Edward said.

"I hadn't planned to."

"But my dear fellow. Not only would one be able to help you locate the valley, he could identify the unknown flower and help you bring back a viable specimen. You must take a botanist."

James imagined having to slow his pace to allow some scientist to inspect every leaf and petal along the way. He shook his head. "I'm departing soon. I doubt I can find someone on such short notice. And besides, it isn't necessary."

"Truly, I beg to differ. Will you be able to recognize a valley full of *Orchis boryi* when you see it? A purple flower, yes. But how tall? How many petals? What distinguishes it from half a dozen other purple flowers that grow in the area? Look." Sir Edward returned to the map. "I can already tell you that the southern side of the river will be much more promising—here, where the mountains come sweeping in. That is where you will find your valley."

James met his host's bright gaze. "Are you certain?"

"Well, not as certain as I will be when I get there."

"Are you offering to accompany me?"

"Are you inviting me to go?"

James studied Sir Edward. Not a young man, but robust, the botanist appeared fit to take to the field—although traveling with another person, particularly one of a scientific bent, would mean more baggage, slower travel, more complications altogether. His plan had been to ride light with just a local guide.

On the other hand, with the man's expertise, he might actually find the valley. Not that James imagined himself master of Somergate as a result. Too many years had passed for the journals to still be intact. He wasn't going to cling to a false expectation. Still, it was almost impossible not to reach for the slice of hope Sir Edward held out. If he were going all the way to Tunisia, he might as well do everything he could.

"I need to depart within a fortnight. I doubt you could be ready in time."

"On the contrary! I am already preparing a foray to Italy. This trip will hardly take more by way of logistics. What do you think, Huntington? Will I do as your botanist?"

James lifted his hand and let the map curl closed. It was not, after all, such a difficult decision to make. "I think you will—very well."

"Excellent!" Sir Edward clapped him on the shoulder. "We'd best get to work, then. Think of it—an undiscovered flower, an adventure into the wilds of North Africa. Simply splendid."

James grinned. His host's enthusiasm was infectious, and the thought of having someone along to share the journey lifted his spirits. "How soon will you be able to leave?"

"Two weeks should suffice. You must make arrangements to come stay here at Brookdale. We will coordinate our plans."

Sir Edward's brows suddenly drew together. "Though there is one slight complication I failed to mention. A minor one, I assure you."

"Oh?"

His host blew out a breath. "Well, it's just that my family is expecting to accompany me. It wouldn't do to leave them behind. They are all accustomed to travel—quite useful in the field."

"Your family? And just whom does that involve?"

"My wife, of course. She takes care of most of the details of travel, you see. And my son Richard, and daughter Isabelle, couldn't leave them behind, and Isabelle's companion Mrs. Hodges, very reliable, and—"

"Stop." James held up his hand. "Your servants and dogs as well, no doubt. It won't do, sir. I cannot be responsible for shepherding your family around North Africa—this is not some jaunt to Brighton."

Sir Edward drew himself up. "I believe you underestimate my family. They are accustomed to difficult travel. Why, only last year we went into the Pyrenees for five weeks. Quite off the beaten path. They have always accompanied me. If they are not allowed to come, I am forced to withdraw my offer."

Damnation. Taking along a botanist made sense, and Sir Edward was the only botanist James knew that was willing to travel. The only botanist he knew, period. If there was to be any hope of success, the man needed to be included. But his family?

James thought of the fresh-faced Richard. He had handled his horse well this morning by the front gate, and without aid of a saddle. His sister, Isabelle, had also shown herself to be adept. But riding skills were not enough. In Africa they might well face things more dangerous than a charging artist with bared legs. At the very least, the family would make travel excruciatingly slow.

He turned to Sir Edward. The man's eyes shone with hope and desire. Perhaps the same desire that had led James's grandfather to discover the valley in the first place. James brushed his hair back with his fingers.

If the journals had by some miracle survived, then a delay of a week or two would hardly matter. If they had not, then speed would make no difference at all—except to his sanity.

"Very well," he said. "But your hounds are staying behind."

Sir Edward reached out and shook his hand heartily. "You will not regret it. We will find the valley, collect the flower, and perhaps even recover your grandfather's lost journals. I do not doubt that we will be successful, Mr. Huntington. Not for a moment."

"We are agreed, then?"

"We are agreed." Sir Edward rolled the map and replaced it in its tube. "But enough business—my appetite tells me it is time for tea. Come and meet my niece, whose work you were admiring, and the rest of my family."

James walked with his host to the door of the library then paused. "There is one more thing. It, well, it has to do with the Duke of Hereford's son . . ."

"In the rump!" Sir Edward chuckled as he opened the door. "Yes, your uncle was kind enough to inform me."

Lily's maid helped her peel the green riding-habit off.

"Toss it out, Bess. I never want to see that dress again." It was too much a reminder of that mortifying meeting by the front gate. Lily stepped into the steaming bath and sank down with a sigh.

"What happened, Miss?"

"I'd rather not discuss the matter. Please, bring more hot water from the kitchens."

Lily squeezed the sponge over herself, rinsing until the last memory of mud had left her skin. If only the memory of Mr. Huntington's gaze could be washed away as easily. She lay back and rested her neck on the rolled rim, but could not relax. The humiliation still hummed through her. It simply was not done, to let an unknown gentleman see so much. What must he think of her!

She prayed he had finished consulting with her uncle and

returned to wherever it was he came from. She would feel more settled when she knew he was no longer beneath the same roof. And even better knowing that she would never have to encounter him again.

"Miss? The family will be gathering for tea in a half-hour. I have heated towels for you."

Lily rose from the tub. It would be easier if she could plead a headache and remain in her room, but after her fall that would cause undue concern. Aunt Mary would insist on calling the doctor. No, she would have to join the family. Surely Mr. Huntington would be as eager as she to avoid an awkward second meeting.

Or would he?

There had been an unmistakable flash in his eyes as his gaze had followed the curve of her thigh. It was a look not easily forgotten. It haunted her still, causing the incident to play and replay in her mind.

The tension in Lily's shoulders eased as she entered the drawing room. There was no brown-haired man waiting to turn his knowing gaze on her, only her cousins and aunt, and Mrs. Hodges, Isabelle's governess-turned-companion.

"Come, sit, my dear," Aunt Mary said. "I heard you had a difficult morning."

"Difficult may be understating it. But I feel much better now."

Mrs. Hodges glanced up from her knitting. "A good strong cup of black tea, that's what's needed. Settles the nerves. Straightens the spine." Her words were punctuated with the sharp click of her needles. "A pity the tea-trolley has not yet arrived."

"Well, neither has Father," Isabelle said from her place on the green and gold settee. "Lily, come play cards with me. I am dreadfully tired of playing by myself."

Lily took up her cards, but could not focus on the game. What was keeping Uncle Edward? The clock on the mantel seemed louder than usual.

"Really, Lily." Isabelle swooped up the hand. "If you are not interested in playing, just say so. I have not beaten you so easily in ages."

"Perhaps Richard will give you more of a challenge." Lily glanced to the young man draped in the nearby wingback. Richard seemed absorbed in the magazine he was reading and made no response.

Aunt Mary set down her needlework. "Isabelle, do rouse your brother. He seems to be lost in Mr. Dickens' latest installment."

"Rubbish, if you ask me." Mrs. Hodges frowned. "Horrid novels that fill young people's minds with nonsense. Why, I never have met anyone as peculiar as those characters described by Mr. Dickens. The man is off his head."

"But entertainingly so." Isabelle began teasing the pages from her brother's hands. "Give over, Richard. It is my turn to read."

"Now, Isabelle—" Aunt Mary began, but halted as her husband entered the drawing room.

Lily looked up—her uncle was not alone. Oh no. It appeared Mr. Huntington had been invited to tea after all. Just his tall presence in the room made her feel as though she had been caught in some wickedness. How awkward of him to have come here.

"My dear, permit me to introduce Mr. James Huntington." Uncle Edward led his guest forward. "He is the grandson of my colleague and mentor, the late Earl of Twickenham."

"Please be welcome," her aunt said. "We were saddened to hear of your grandfather's passing. I hope my husband has been of some assistance."

"Your husband has been more than generous." Mr. Huntington made her a bow. "Thank you for allowing me to monopolize his time on such short notice."

Uncle Edward offered Mr. Huntington a chair. "I understand you have already met my children, Isabelle and Richard. And my niece, Lily."

"I have had the pleasure." A hint of a smile touched Mr.

Huntington's lips as he took a seat. "Miss Strathmore, I hope you were not harmed by your fall this morning."

Lily resisted the urge to draw her legs up beneath her, even though they were decently covered in her pale green tea gown. "I am quite recovered. Thank you."

He did smile then, an expression that looked so well on him that Lily almost wished she could forgive his presence. Her gaze lingered on the strong planes of his face. The light cast defining shadows beneath his clean jaw and along the column of his neck. Highlights bleached by the sun shown in his brown hair—burnt umber, yellow ochre—she mixed the colors in her mind's eye.

He raised an eyebrow at her.

Drat the man. She was a painter, for heaven's sake. She looked at things—flowers, landscapes, people. Her gaze had been entirely of a professional nature.

"The tea-trolley, at last," she said, thankful for the distraction. "I find myself quite thirsty."

Aunt Mary poured out the tea. Lily took her cup with cream and sugar, studying Mr. Huntington more discreetly as he engaged the others in conversation. It was as she had thought. He could not be a true gentleman. His hair, for one thing. It was over-long, giving him a relaxed, insouciant air—as if he were just returned from some wild escapade. She pushed a strand of her own behind her ear.

His clothing was equally telling—not in the first state of fashion at all. It was well-tailored and of quality fabric, but hardly something a refined gentlemen would wear. In fact, if it were not for his broad shoulders showing off the coat to such advantage, the garment wouldn't be worth mentioning. And it must be the striped fabric of his breeches that made his hips appear so narrow and his thighs so well-muscled.

Very well-muscled. She felt herself flush. But really, this morning Mr. Huntington had seen more of her than any man should. What was so wrong with noticing the cut of his trousers? Clothing could speak volumes about a person. If she looked carefully enough, they would reveal much about his character.

Lily glanced down at his boots and felt a stab of satisfaction. His boots were not *quite* deplorable. They were, however, worn. Scuff-marks showed through the polish—decidedly not the boots of a perfect gentleman. Oh, he might speak charmingly to her aunt and uncle, he might even avoid comment on the incident at the gate, but his boots did not lie.

Relieved that she had found something worth disparaging, Lily sat back. He had her at a great disadvantage, but at least there was something. He was neither as dashing nor as handsome as he might appear at first glance, and it seemed unlikely that he moved in the same social circles as herself. She let out a breath. After today she would never have to see him again.

They had almost finished tea when Uncle Edward cleared his throat. "Mr. Huntington has brought exciting news. Today he showed me evidence of a previously unknown flower!"

"My grandfather discovered it, but was unable to bring back a specimen," Mr. Huntington added.

"And since he needs a botanist, I have offered my assistance."

"Why Edward, that is wonderful," Aunt Mary said. "It is what you have always dreamed of. Where was the flower discovered?"

Sir Edward drew in his breath and paused dramatically. "Tunisia! Mr. Huntington has kindly invited us to come with him. With your approval, my dear, we shall travel to Tunisia instead of Italy."

"How exotic!" Isabelle said.

Lily set her cup down too quickly. "Not Italy? But . . ." She mopped at the spilled tea with her napkin. This was an appalling turn of events. She shot another look at Mr. Huntington and fought to keep the heat from rising to her cheeks. Bad enough that she had to take tea with him today. Surely her aunt would refuse.

"The Chadwicks have business interests in Tunis," Aunt Mary said, offering Lily the tea towel. "I do believe Lady Chadwick visited with her husband and reported that the climate and population are far more agreeable than that of Egypt."

Uncle Edward gave his wife an encouraging look. "Imagine walking the palm-lined ways of Tunis beneath the domes and minarets. We could explore the ruins of ancient Carthage. Be the first to collect a plant not yet known to science. It is an opportunity that simply cannot be passed up!"

Aunt Mary smiled. "Mr. Huntington, are you certain you do not mind? You could hardly have been expecting the lot of us when you signed my husband up for your expedition."

"In truth I was not, but I need to find the valley where my grandfather discovered the flower, as quickly as possible. I could not delay until Sir Edward returned from Italy. I am grateful that he has agreed to come at all."

"Then, if we are not imposing, I see no reason why we cannot change our plans. Edward would not be able to enjoy himself in Italy knowing he was missing the opportunity to track down a new flower." She took up the silver serving dish. "Tarts, anyone?"

Lily stared at her aunt in disbelief. "Tarts?" This *man* had been here less than three hours and he had completely upended everything. She did not want tarts, and she did not want to go to North Africa with Mr. Huntington and his scuffed boots—she had been counting on studying the work of the famous Italian artists, not riding camels in the Sahara. Not with *him!*

She looked to the others. Only Mrs. Hodges seemed to share her irritation. The matron was scowling and attacking her knitting.

Uncle Edward beamed. "I know we will all enjoy this adventure, and I have taken the liberty of inviting Mr. Huntington to stay with us at Brookdale. We'll need to work together if we intend to depart within a fortnight."

"I am sure we can manage it, my dear," Aunt Mary said. "But remember, you promised to get Lily back home to London before we leave." She turned to Mr. Huntington. "And when may we expect you to join us here?"

He rubbed his chin. "I can wind up my affairs in London fairly quickly. I'll return on Monday, if that is acceptable."

No, Lily thought with a rising sense of desperation. It would not do at all. She glanced at Mr. Huntington. He could upset everything—he *had* upset everything. But what could she say? That he couldn't come because she had behaved immodestly?

And it was a wonderful opportunity for her uncle. If Mr. Huntington truly had knowledge of an uncollected flower, there was no choice but to go with him. Even if his gaze carried the memory of her legs bared to the thigh.

"What a time we have to look forward to, eh, Huntington?" Uncle Edward pushed his plate away.

"I'm sure it will be an experience we will never forget." Mr. Huntington rose. "With your permission. The ride back to London is a long one. It was a pleasure to meet all of you."

His eyes met Lily's and she did not look away. She could not let him see how thoroughly the morning had unsettled her. It seemed a long moment before he spoke again.

"Good day, Miss Strathmore." He inclined his head then followed Uncle Edward out of the room.

Lily watched his departing back, then spoke. "Aunt Mary, do you think it is wise to change our plans? I mean—North Africa! Surely it is far more dangerous than the Continent."

Her aunt looked at her with raised brows. "Lily, I'm surprised. Mr. Huntington strikes me as a sensible man, and his uncle sent a letter recommending him. Besides, weren't you the one advocating that we sail to South America and explore the Amazon basin instead of go to Italy?"

"That's right," Richard nodded. "You said the dangers of headhunters and crocodiles had been sensationalized and that we would be perfectly safe if we wore wide-brimmed hats and slept beneath mosquito netting."

Isabelle leaned forward and snatched Lily's hand. "Isn't it too thrilling? This will be much better than boring old Italy."

Mrs. Hodges gave a snort of disgust. "Italy, Tunisia, Timbuktu, things change so fast around this house it makes me dizzy."

"Now, Mrs. Hodges, you have accompanied us as governess

and chaperone on many occasions," Aunt Mary said. "Surely this trip is not too daunting?"

"Daunting? Hmph. If I didn't go, the whole lot of you would wind up in trouble up to your necks. Someone needs to keep a clear head, and I expect it will be me." Mrs. Hodges returned attention to her knitting, the conversation closed as far as she was concerned.

"It will be high adventure," Richard said. "I wonder if we'll meet any pirates on the way?"

"Handsome ones, preferably." Isabelle released Lily's hand and swooned back against the cushions.

Whatever her overly romantic cousins thought, Lily knew there was no way she could enjoy the journey. This was to have been the last great adventure with her uncle and his family before—well, before she was married to a man selected by her mother. It was perfectly irksome that they would now have a stranger in their midst—particularly the wretched Mr. Huntington. It was a disaster of the first order.

Aunt Mary set her teacup on the tray. "It will be an excellent thing, getting to know Mr. Huntington a bit before he leads us out into unknown territory. My dears, do endeavor to make his visit with us pleasant."

"We can all go riding." Isabelle winked at Lily.

Lily gave her cousin a frosty look and rose to her feet. "I am going to the conservatory."

Why was it she had so little control over the things that mattered in her life? Let Mr. Huntington come if he must—but she would certainly not go out of her way to make his stay an agreeable one.

Chapter 4

Brookdale Manor buzzed with activity. Messages flew back and forth from London, and Uncle Edward dispatched servants to the train station on a daily basis to receive parcels. On the wide lawn, large canvas expedition tents were spread flat, airing out prior to being packed. Watching from her second-floor window, Lily could not help but be caught up in the excitement.

She avoided most of the disarray of packing by applying herself where she was most useful—in the conservatory painting her uncle's newest specimens. She had completed several in succession until it was time to see to her own preparations.

Hands on her hips, Lily surveyed the chaos of her dressing room. Trunks lay open, half-full of morning dresses, satin evening wear, and serviceable cotton for the field. Her lady's maid, Bess, bustled in, balancing a stack of boxes in her arms.

"More hats, Bess?"

Bobbing a curtsy, the maid lost her balance. Lily rushed to catch the teetering boxes.

"Sorry, milady. Your aunt sent these over. She's keeping us all that busy."

"Put the boxes in the corner," she said. "We'll sort through them later."

With only ten days left until their departure, Aunt Mary had matters well in hand. Her role, as always, was to transform her husband's enthusiastic impulses into practical reality. She insisted they pack every element of a proper wardrobe. "After all, we will be traveling in society until we reach Tunisia, and even then will be moving in certain circles. We must dress accordingly." One would think they were planning to be gone a year, rather than a season.

A tap sounded at the door.

"See who it is, Bess," she said, trying to decide if her blue crepe evening gown would fit into an overflowing trunk.

"It's a parcel for you, Miss Lily." Her maid returned, carrying a bulky package.

"Excellent! Set it down on the bed." Sometimes, she thought, the best gifts are the ones you give yourself.

Lily untied the string and carefully folded back the brown paper. Pans of watercolors shone up at her like untouched jewels; a set of new paintbrushes tipped in sable, each polished wooden handle smaller than the next; a perfect gray square of gum eraser; pencils of varying hardness nestled in a metal case. Supporting this wealth, thick blocks of watercolor paper. Lily trailed her fingertips lightly over the textured surface, delighting in its tooth.

She bundled up her new treasures and placed them next to a stack of drawing boards and journals on the window seat. There remained only the delivery of her new folding easel and she would be ready to depart. The thrill of impending travel coursed through her, despite the heavy concerns of the past week.

She had always loved traveling, particularly with Uncle Edward and his family. Mr. Huntington could not take that from her. She had given it much thought. He would be no different than the foul-smelling guide who had led them through the Pyrenees—a necessary, sometimes useful person, but someone to keep at arm's length, especially when the wind was blowing from the wrong direction.

Lily drew a battered journal from the stack beside her supplies and paged through it. This one held her impressions of Scotland—quick pencil sketches of faces, studies of building details, the coach that had conveyed them through the lowlands.

Tunisia would be far more exotic. She imagined sketching an ancient minaret at dawn, or a Berber woman veiled in blue standing beside a hidden fountain.

She was just setting the journal back when Isabelle burst in laughing.

"Hello, Isabelle. What mischief are you up to?"

"Mischief?" Isabelle widened her eyes. "You must have me confused with someone else. My brother, perhaps."

"My mistake. What serious matters have you come to discuss, then?"

"The arrival of the exceedingly handsome Mr. Huntington, of course. What are you planning to wear?" Isabelle bounced down on the bed. "I think one must make an effort to make a good first impression, though," her brow furrowed, "I suppose the second impression must be equally important. It would, after all, be quite impossible to make a first impression now."

As if she needed to be reminded.

Although to his credit, Mr. Huntington had been discreet. Her uncle remained unaware of the incident, and she had received no letter from London informing her that she was the subject of gossip. If the man could hold his tongue, she might yet avoid a scandal.

Lily grimaced. "I shudder at the first impression I made. I can only comfort myself by hoping Mr. Huntington took me for a lunatic. People tend to excuse the insane. You don't suppose he has forgotten the whole affair?"

"I very much doubt he will have forgotten you, Lily. The way he looked at you in the drawing room . . . no matter, he will not forget me either if I wear my blue . . . or no, my yellow gown, although perhaps that is too elaborate. What do you think?"

Lily made a show of looking her cousin over. "I think," she tipped her head, "you will look lovely whatever you choose."

Isabelle wrinkled her nose. "That's no help. But I thought we could, well, coordinate?"

The sound of a vehicle coming up the drive bought them both to the window. A black coach slowed as the driver pulled smoothly back on the reins. The manservant seated beside the driver hopped off, folded down the steps and opened the door.

James Huntington stepped out. His dark green coat hugged his shoulders as he descended with easy grace onto the drive.

"Ooh," breathed Isabelle.

Lily's heartbeat quickened. Drat the man. It was going to be exceedingly awkward facing him again, much less traveling to Africa and back in his company. She leaned closer to the window.

Footmen busied themselves unloading a trunk and various bundles as Mr. Huntington disappeared beneath the portico.

"He's here!" Isabelle turned, gave her cousin a quick embrace and whirled out the door.

Lily sank down onto the window seat. The sight of Mr. Huntington had made her feel rather peculiar. She must still be recovering from the shock of their first encounter. Whatever the case, he was not like that fragrant guide in the Pyrenees. He was not a hireling—he was a gentleman and a guest. Her aunt and uncle would insist on treating him like one of the family. Of all the bad luck.

She took a steadying breath. She could manage. What choice did she have? It was not as if she were some silly young girl. She had only to keep a clear head and pretend they had never had that unfortunate encounter by the front gate.

That evening Lily took extra care with her appearance, directing Bess to style her hair in the latest mode. It's because of Isabelle's expectations, she told herself, studying the effect of her up-drawn hair. The heavy mass of chestnut waves was difficult to coil into the sleek chignon, and Lily sighed as yet another strand escaped to tickle her bared shoulder. She had chosen her green satin gown, but was wondering now if she should change it for something more demure. *I'm turning into Isabelle,* she thought with a wry smile. The green would do quite well.

The chime of the dinner bell sounded through the hall, followed by a quick knock on her door.

"Come in, Isabelle," she called without turning.

"How did you know it was me?"

Lily looked at her cousin's reflection in the mirror. Isabelle's pale yellow gown and burnished hair made her shine. "Who else? I'd hardly expect Richard to come escort me. You are all aglow like a narcissus, cousin."

Isabelle curtsied. "And you are a forest sprite, Lily. That gown is very becoming."

"Well then," Lily said, rising, "let the flower and the fairy proceed to dinner."

There was a tall figure on the landing as they approached. Mr. Huntington, dressed for dinner in a cognac-colored coat, lighter waistcoat, and tan trousers. Lily hesitated, then lifting her chin she marched forward. It was too late to hope he had not seen them.

He smiled, deepening the dimple carved in his cheek, and bowed as they approached. "The Misses Strathmore. May I have the honor of escorting you both down to dinner?"

Isabelle giggled. "Thank you sir, for the kind offer." She set her hand on his sleeve and leaned close.

Inappropriately close. Heavens, they hardly knew anything about this man, and here was Isabelle dangling off his arm like a butler's tea towel. Something would have to be done.

"Isabelle!"

Surprised, Isabelle dropped Mr. Huntington's arm and turned. "What's wrong?"

"Um . . . your hair."

Isabelle's hand flew to her head. "Oh dear. If you will excuse me, Mr. Huntington." She dashed back down the hall.

Lily stepped forward and took his arm. It was fortunate that she had intervened. Her cousin was far too naïve. The girl had practically thrown herself into Mr. Huntington's arms—second impressions indeed.

"Shall we proceed to dinner?" she asked. Mr. Huntington raised an eyebrow, but made no comment. She could smell the faint trace of soap and musk on his skin. His strong hand covered hers completely—odd how she could sense the slightest movement of his fingers against hers. And even stranger how that sensation made her heart beat faster. She glanced up into his amber-flecked brown eyes and for an awkward moment she could think of nothing to say.

"Miss Strathmore," he said finally, "are you well?"

"Yes . . . no . . . it's just . . . lovely weather we are having. Was your drive out a pleasant one?"

His gaze sharpened. "Are you sure there is nothing besides the weather you wish to speak of? You did send your cousin spinning off like a top. I assumed it was because you wanted to converse privately."

She drew in a steadying breath. "What would we have to discuss?"

"I thought you might be concerned that I had spread the tale of our unusual introduction."

"Really, Mr. Huntington." Lily winced inwardly. He had her at a true disadvantage. "I was hoping you had forgotten the incident in the excitement of your preparations."

He looked down the empty hallways on each side of the landing then leaned so close she could feel the heat of his breath against her skin when he whispered, "I have not spoken of it to anyone, nor will I. But it is unlikely I will forget."

A door opened nearby and he straightened. "And the weather was fine for the drive out."

Dinner was the usual informally genteel affair. True to his word, Mr. Huntington made no attempt to bring the conversation around to their first meeting. Instead, he spoke vividly and entertainingly of the cities in the Far East he had seen as an officer stationed there, although Lily was too preoccupied by the encounter on the stairs to do much more than nod or smile when it seemed appropriate. She did manage to listen when the conversation turned to his grandfather's estate. Mr. Huntington's description of its extensive gardens and enormous glasshouse made it sound very much like a grand version of Brookdale.

"I understand that your grandfather made an unusual bequest of that estate to Kew Gardens," Uncle Edward said. "A pity, really."

"Oh," said Mr. Huntington, setting down his fork. "Why so?"

"Because they will destroy it. Your grandfather's collection of plants is the envy of every horticulturist in England, and Somergate is too remote to be attractive in itself. I expect it will be stripped of anything of botanical interest and the property leased out to generate income. There will be a good deal of infighting over his rarer specimens."

Mr. Huntington looked genuinely pained. "Why didn't my grandfather realize this? He devoted the latter half of his life to Somergate. I can't believe he would willingly allow it to be destroyed."

"I think he was rather blinded by his love for the place. He thought everyone would treasure it as he did. I'm afraid there were those who played upon that sentiment. In his correspondence he seemed desperate to see it preserved. Why he thought entrusting it to Kew would be preferable to the stewardship of his own heirs, I can't understand."

After dinner the family retired to the drawing room, where the men drank brandy and Richard went to the piano and began to play. It was there that her cousin was his brightest self. He freed the music locked up in the written notes—chords and quarter notes became living things chasing each other, dancing lightly or growling deep somber tones as the mood took him. His youthful awkwardness slipped away as he sat elegantly upright, in mastery of the instrument.

"Your son plays remarkably well," Mr. Huntington said to Aunt Mary, when Richard paused to search for another piece of music. He turned to Isabelle. "Do you play also?"

"Oh no. Unlike Lily with her painting, and Richard with his talent for music—"

"And father, who can name each and every part of every plant he sees," added Richard.

"—I have no talent."

"Except a talent for dramatic exaggeration," Mrs. Hodges said, looking up from her knitting.

"What about you, Mrs. Hodges?" Mr. Huntington asked. "What is your talent?"

She looked at him over the rim of her spectacles. "My talent is for judging character."

"And for cheerful excess," added Lily, shooting the matron a quick smile.

"Impertinence," she muttered and bent over her yarn, but not before Lily caught a glint of what might have been a smile in her expression.

"What of you, Mr. Huntington?" Lily asked, serious now. "What is your talent?"

A wicked humor flashed in his eyes and was gone before the others noticed. She tried not to imagine what talent he had been thinking of. Something unsuitable for discussion in the drawing room, she was sure. Society had its share of rakes. If Mr. Huntington was one, as she now suspected, he could doubtless lay claim to all sorts of unspeakable talents.

"My talent," he said, interrupting her thoughts, "is for appreciating the talents of others."

"Lily," her uncle said, "I almost forgot. I have had this letter half the day." He fished in his waistcoat pocket and retrieved a crumpled envelope. "From your parents. I apologize for its condition and for the delay. I'm keeping track of so many things, it's a wonder I can remember my own name."

She took the envelope and smoothed out its creases. Had her parents changed their minds, denying her the expedition after all? Surely Lord Buckley hadn't arrived home yet.

"Well? Aren't you going to read it?" Isabelle asked.

Lily broke the seal and read, shifting to keep Isabelle from peering over her shoulder.

"Father tenders his regards. He intends to send a coach to take me back to London." She did not mention that her visit was to include being presented to Countess Buckley. Apparently the two mothers had already begun to arrange the rest of her life.

"You won't be leaving before the ball, I hope," Isabelle said.

"No, the coach will arrive Saturday afternoon."

"That's all right then." Her cousin sank back in her chair.

"There is to be a dance this Friday at the home of Squire

Thomas," Aunt Mary explained to their guest. "Local society will be there. It presents an excellent opportunity to bid our friends and neighbors farewell. If it were not for the ball, I daresay our departure would be delayed by numerous visits from well-wishers."

"You might find it amusing, Huntington," Uncle Edward said. "Not a London crush, by any means, but the food and drink will be excellent. Thomas is known for his table."

"Do come," Richard said. "I am weary of dancing with my sister and cousin."

"And our toes are equally weary of being danced upon by you, brother dear."

Mr. Huntington smiled. "I would be pleased to go as your guest, and relieve Richard of his obligations." His gaze found Lily.

A curious tingle shot through her when she thought of whirling to the music with Mr. Huntington. She imagined he was an excellent dancer.

"Lily," Uncle Edward said. "Will you be finished with the illustrations by Saturday?"

She took a moment to focus on his words. "Saturday?" Oh, yes, when father was sending the coach. "I have almost completed the paintings. A touch more work on the *Anthurium*, and I will be finished."

"Splendid! I'm sure you have done your usual superb job."

"I think you will be pleased." She looked over to the piano. "Richard, now that I am almost done with the botanical work, I was hoping you would sit for me tomorrow. I saw a new style of portraiture at the Royal Academy that I would very much like to try."

"I think I promised Isabelle I'd escort her into the village." He looked pleadingly at his sister. "Didn't I?"

Isabelle grinned. "Actually, he did. I have a stunning gown to wear for the ball and need one more fitting. I'm sorry, Lily."

"It's for the best, I suppose." Lily shook her head in mock disapproval. "Richard does find it a challenge to sit still. You can have him, Isabelle." She looked pointedly at Mrs. Hodges. "There are other subjects to be had."

"Hmph," Mrs. Hodges said. "The trials I endure. Very well, Miss Lily. If you insist, and your aunt doesn't put me to packing steamer trunks." She seemed gruffly pleased with the request.

"After luncheon tomorrow, in the conservatory. I should be ready for you by then."

Chapter 5

Soft light filtered through the brass and cut-glass doors leading to the conservatory. James glimpsed palm fronds and the huge leaves of philodendron inside. When he swung the doors open he was enfolded by moist, scented heat. Vivid memories of his grandfather's conservatory flooded through him—wet pavers, the potting bench, a huge watering can with flaking green paint.

Since returning to England, James had often felt the wash of memory as he revisited places he had known as a child, but this was beyond anything he had experienced. He stood for a moment, eyes closed, flooded with light.

Sir Edward had retired for his afternoon nap, leaving James with a message for Miss Strathmore. It would probably have been wiser to send a servant to deliver the message. The woman was altogether too tempting. It would be better if he kept his mind on his business—he couldn't afford to offend his host by dallying with the man's attractive niece. Not that she was a suitable candidate for dalliance in any case.

Ahead, a brick walkway circled an enormous round planter. Ferns drooped and water cascaded over rocks into a shallow pool. Above him, a huge spiny tree soared two stories, brushing the glass roof and spreading its umbrels over the flowering plants below.

Skirting the pool, James sighted a figure through the leaves. Miss Strathmore was working at her easel, her back to him. She wore a blue apron tied over her dress, emphasizing her waist and the sensuous curve of her hips. Her sleeves were rolled to the elbow revealing slim, strong arms and capable hands.

He leaned his shoulder against one of the great iron columns that supported the structure and watched her. She appeared completely at ease, humming a tune he did not recognize and working the canvas with quick, precise strokes of her brush. Every now and then she would stop to look at the potted flower sitting amid a jumble of art supplies on a tall table. Her humming would stop. Then she would dab her brush in color and begin painting and humming all over again. The warmth of the greenhouse had brought a glow to her skin, and a strand of hair had escaped the pins. Not a girl in a pretty gown, but a woman, authentic and as beautiful as any of the exotic blooms that surrounded her.

Miss Strathmore must have sensed his presence. She whirled. "Mr. Huntington. How unexpected."

"My apologies if I surprised you. I did not want to interrupt your work." That work was revealed now on the easel as a rich scarlet flower, its heart-shaped form limned with light.

She shifted, blocking his view of the painting, and folded her arms. "Is there something you need?"

"Only to deliver the message that your easel did not arrive."

Her frown deepened. "It was supposed to have been delivered two weeks ago. I assure you I will not do business with that firm . . . Mr. Huntington?"

His gaze had swept past her to where a sturdy pair of black shoes protruded from behind the table. He raised an eyebrow. "It appears we are not alone."

"Of course not. That would be most inappropriate." She glanced behind the table, her look softening. "Mrs. Hodges— poor dear. The heat of the conservatory makes her drowsy."

James peered behind the table. Mrs. Hodges dozed on the chaise lounge, her wide chest rising and falling with each breath.

"I hate to wake her," Miss Strathmore said, "but the light

will be changing soon. I cannot very well paint a portrait without a subject."

He looked down the path toward the doors, then back at Mrs. Hodges. The message was delivered. Now would be the time to make his exit, but he could not simply walk away without offering assistance.

"Perhaps I could take her place."

Miss Strathmore considered him for a moment. "Have you ever sat for a portrait before?"

"No. But I would do my best. No napping, I promise."

She bit her lower lip, apparently of two minds. "Well," she said at last, "you will have to do." She pulled a tall stool to a nearby grouping of tree ferns and patted the seat. "Sit here, if you will."

James settled himself. It wasn't as if he had anything pressing to attend to—and she did look fetching in her blue apron.

Miss Strathmore placed a fresh art board on her easel and straightened her apron. "Are you sitting comfortably?"

"As comfortable as can be expected."

"I would like to paint you in quarter profile. Please turn to the right."

He shifted. "Like this?"

She shook her head. "No, back the other way . . . Yes, that's it."

She began to sketch, her pencil sweeping in broad, confident arcs, and her gaze becoming direct and appraising. It traveled up and down, lingering, measuring, judging. Her eyes traced his face, stared deeply into his own, followed the line of his chin to his neck, then down along his shoulders.

James was completely unprepared for the intensity of the painter's gaze. Coming from a woman of Miss Strathmore's attractions, it was . . . disturbing. No lady had ever stared at him so boldly—at least not with innocent intent. He felt uncomfortably warm and wished he had thought to loosen his collar before they began.

As Miss Strathmore worked she bit her lower lip, or furrowed her brow, and all the while her eyes continued to devour him. Her hand traveled over the board as it willed but her gaze never left him. She breathed deeply as she worked, her focus evident in each fluid movement of her body. As the minutes passed, James found it increasingly difficult to remain still. He tried to ease the tension by looking past her to the foliage that framed and shaded her, but he could not concentrate. Again and again his attention was drawn back to the woman before him.

She was not a conventional beauty. Her face held too much strength—a stubborn lift to her chin, the high cheekbones softening into the curve of her cheeks, her nose too prominent by current standards. Standards that celebrated the cultivated looks of a pampered flower, not the willful wildness he sensed in Miss Strathmore. And her eyes. He had noted them before, their depths, the way they shifted color like the surface of a tropical sea. A man could lose himself there.

She set down her pencil and selected a brush. The moment her gaze left him he felt relieved, and oddly abandoned. The respite was short-lived—her attention returned to him almost immediately as she dipped and swirled paint on the palette. She held the paintbrush like a scepter. She was queen here, a queen of color and light, vibrant and passionate. And what would that passion taste like? What would she feel like in his arms? His bed?

He closed his eyes, shutting out the sight of her, and shifted on the stool.

"Are you still comfortable? We could take a break, if you'd like."

"I'm fine." He opened his eyes and tried to look more at ease.

"It's going very well," she said, then her eyebrows drew together. "Wait. You moved. Try turning to your left a bit more." She watched him swivel and shook her head. "No, that's not quite it. One moment."

She stared hard at the sketch then moved to stand in front of him, their eyes at a level.

"I am used to more immobile subjects that I can place at will," she said. "I think it would be easier if I just . . ." She reached out and set her hands on his shoulders.

The pressure of her fingers guided his body to the left. He turned in response, but his eyes remained fixed on her face. She was so close he could smell her fragrance—lavender and linseed oil. His pulse throbbed.

"Now, tilt your head up a bit . . . no, not quite so much."

"Like this?"

"Here, let me."

She lifted her hand to his chin and raised it with a gentle pressure—as if for a kiss. His gaze dropped to her lips, full, and open. If he leaned forward, just a few inches, he could brush them with his own.

Her eyes darted to his, and he saw realization seep into her as the artist gave way to the woman. She took a hasty step back, then retreated to her easel.

James cleared his throat. "Do I have the pose right?"

"Um. Yes. Well enough. We can break soon. You'll be able to stand and walk about then."

He rather doubted it—his response to her had been tangible and physical. He would require a large frond if he were asked to stand before his yearning had subsided.

James closed his eyes and summoned up images of the worst field conditions he had endured while serving in the Queen's army. He would not dwell on the woman before him. He would not watch her eyes as they lingered on his body or recall the smooth touch of her fingertips.

At last she stepped away from her work. "You are free—for the moment."

He stood, twisting at the waist to loosen his tight muscles.

"It is tiring to keep still," she said.

"I ought to be used to it—in the army we were trained to stand immobile and at attention for hours. Though with the amount of starch in our dress uniforms, there really wasn't much option."

She smiled. "I shall have to instruct Richard's valet to starch him thoroughly before I try painting him again. You are doing splendidly. Would you like some lemonade?" She lifted a carafe from the table beside her and poured two glasses.

James joined her, noticing how petite she actually was. It surprised him. She gave the impression of being taller, but her head only came up to his shoulder.

As she handed him the tumbler his fingers brushed against hers. The coolness of the glass contrasted with the warmth of her skin. Miss Strathmore's eyes widened.

She took a hasty sip, then set her glass down with a bump on the crowded table. Several brushes rolled off the edge, tumbling to the bricks.

James went down on one knee to pick them up. He counted two heartbeats, three, before he straightened, offering her the bouquet of brushes.

"Thank you," she said. "I seem intent on making an unfavorable impression, don't I? I assure you, in most circumstances I am perfectly capable of setting down a glass of lemonade."

"I do not think you make an unfavorable impression, Miss Strathmore. In fact, I find you extremely . . . interesting."

"Interesting. Of course." Her lips tightened. "How kind of you."

Damn. He hadn't meant it that way. "Let me say instead that you are talented and pretty. And your eyes are extraordinary."

"I have never heard the word interesting defined in quite that way." She became much occupied with placing the brushes back on the table, but he noted the color creeping into her cheeks.

James finished his lemonade and searched for a safer topic. "How long does this portrait process take?"

"Only a little more work today—the light is going."

He let out a breath. It would not be so difficult, then.

"And I'll need you tomorrow afternoon as well, when the light is better."

"I see." Yet as uncomfortable as it might be, he almost wished the painting would take longer—days, a week even. There was something deucedly compelling about this woman.

"Ready?" she asked.

"Of course." He returned to the stool and tried to recapture

his earlier pose. One would think that after sitting in the
position for more than an hour he would remember how it felt,
but Miss Strathmore did not even pick up her brush.

"More to the left, I think. Your shoulder was even with the
edge of the frond." She came to face him again. James tensed
as she lifted her hand. Her touch brushed his skin, lingered
against his cheek. Her eyes found his.

Without thought he caught her fingers and drew her hand
to his lips. She gasped and he felt her shiver in response. He
drew her forward, and she swayed into him and placed her
palm against his chest. Heat burned into him from her touch.

"Mr. Huntington—"

He brought her closer and her hand slid up to grasp his
shoulder. She was standing between his knees, the curve of
her breasts brushing his shirt.

Mirroring her earlier touch, he set his fingers under her chin
and lifted, tilting her face up. Her eyes were half-closed, her
lips parted, as sensuous as the heady flowers blooming around
them, as enticing and irresistible. With a sense of inevitability, he lowered his mouth to hers. Her lips were as kissable as
he had thought—warm and soft. He deepened the kiss, pressing his mouth more firmly over hers to taste her sweetness.

She let out a sigh. He slipped his arm behind her, splaying
his hand over the curve of her back, and she leaned further
into his embrace, like a blossom seeking the light. Gods. Fire
kindled in him at the press of her breasts against his chest, the
speeding of her breath, the smoothness of her skin. He could
feel the wild pounding of her heart as he moved his mouth
over hers, devouring her with his lips as she had devoured him
with her eyes. It was only fair that she be captive to his touch,
his mouth, to the wild insistence that had gripped him the
moment she had stepped into his arms.

His fingers tangled through her chestnut hair while he
savored her, holding her close against him, warm and pliant.
That same passion he had glimpsed while she painted now
thrummed between them, alive and aware and full of desire.
Her lips were nectar, and he could not drink enough of her.

The kiss was an eternal instant that lingered and flamed like a fire. Only the sound of Mrs. Hodges shifting on the cot sent them hurrying back into the containers of their bodies. James felt Lily pull away. She slipped out of his embrace and stood, eyes wide.

"No," she said, but there was no sound, only her mouth forming the words. She took a step backwards, then without another word, turned and ran.

Lily slammed the door of her bedroom and leaned hard against it. Flashes of heat still pulsed through her and she let herself, just for a moment, relive the taste of his kiss. Her heart had nearly stopped beating when she stood between his knees and felt the delicious inevitability—the warmth of his breath, the first brush of his mouth against hers, the sweet fire of his kiss.

How could she have been so weak?

She pulled off her apron and wadded it into a ball, throwing it toward the bed. She knew where this path could lead— she had been there when she was Isabelle's age.

It had started innocently enough. Her new art tutor was young, and handsome in a quiet fashion. His canvasses glowed with an inner light that was generating interest in society. How proud her mother had been to acquire him as a tutor. How taken Lily had been as they sat in the springtime garden sketching one another. He knew everything, and she was so hungry to learn.

It was not long before their mutual passion for art lead to passion of another sort. Their glances had progressed to shy touches, hand-holding, then a few gentle, stolen kisses. Her body had thrilled in response to his caresses. The first time he had stroked her breast through her gown she had thought she had become a firework, a blazing flower shot into the sky.

Lily had imagined herself desperately in love, but looking back, it seemed she had been in love with the heady feeling of discovering herself desirable. That first taste of a young woman's power had been intoxicating.

And so it went, spring giving way to summer, until a stolen hour in the evening garden had turned heated. He had lifted her skirts and entered her, gasping apologies as he thrust wildly. She had barely understood what was happening until he gathered her into his arms and stroked her hair. They were both crying, and yet her body yearned for him, yearned for a kind of completion she did not understand.

He resigned his position the next morning. He would never forgive himself for robbing her of her innocence, he told her. Marriage was out of the question, their stations were too far apart, he could barely support himself, let alone a wife, and she would come to despise him for taking her away from her world of wealth and privilege. She took his words in, but they did little to shield her from the aching misery that followed. She had never again allowed herself to be so vulnerable.

Until today.

Lily paced to the window. Outside, the early spring drizzle had resumed. Another wagon of supplies trundled up the drive, the driver hunched under his wet cloak. Mr. Huntington must have sensed her weakness. She always lost herself when painting. He had felt her vulnerability and acted the rake. Hadn't he checked to make sure Mrs. Hodges was asleep?

Yet somehow she could not bring herself to believe it. Perhaps it had been the look in his brown eyes as he had drawn her to him, perhaps the way he had tipped her chin up for their kiss. There was a tenderness in his touch that could not be a lie. He was not a wicked man—just a dangerous one, and his presence here was disturbing everything.

In five days her father's coach would come up the drive to take her to London. There she would sit in a parlor and drink tea with her future mother-in-law. Marriage. Would Lord Buckley's kiss inspire that flare of her senses, the feeling that she was truly alive in every corner of her being? She doubted it. He was her mother's choice, after all.

Lily bent and picked up her crumpled apron. What was she going to do? She had encouraged Mr. Huntington. He had kissed her first, but she had kissed him back. What would he expect as they traveled together? She had lost her innocence, but in the years since she had gathered the tatters of her virtue about her. Her future husband deserved what little she could offer. She was a fallen woman, but not a loose one.

Or was she? She closed her eyes and she was back in the conservatory, enfolded in Mr. Huntington's arms, his hand pressing against the small of her back, his lips drinking her in.

She must not let it happen again. She must not give him the opportunity to tempt her. Her only hope was to press on, pretend it had never happened. Lock the memory of his caress away with her secrets. She could manage—she had to. It was simply a matter of immersing herself in her work. She would signal to Mr. Huntington that she was not available, and if he asked, tell him directly that he would be allowed no further liberties.

And she was going to finish his portrait—it really was going very well despite the unfortunate distraction at the end. There was no reason to let personal disaster ruin good work. Sketching him had been effortless, and when she had begun to paint there had been a boundless power running through her—she could not put her brush wrong. It had been heady and wonderful. She had become transported and let her defenses down. It would not happen again.

Lily shook out her blue apron and carefully folded it.

It had only been a kiss, after all. Likely a trifle to him, a passing fancy. Anything more than a cordial acquaintance between them was unthinkable.

Chapter 6

James lay awake, staring up at the dim shadow of the canopy over his bed. He had been unable to find Lily that afternoon, and when she finally did appear at the dinner table she had hardly spoken to him except to say that she required him in the conservatory tomorrow afternoon.

He had not acted in a very gentlemanly fashion, kissing his host's niece, but he could not be sorry for it. She had been so warm in his arms, so responsive. His body still burned with the memory of her.

Of course, it would not happen again. She was returning to London in a matter of days. A stroke of luck since he was not sure he could endure the temptation she presented for the days and weeks an expedition would last. It was madness to contemplate a dalliance. He knew the price if they were discovered, and he could not pay it. He had nothing to offer except the fool's hope of recovering his grandfather's journals. It was best to act the gentlemen for a short while longer, then circumstance would take care of the problem.

He tossed and tangled in his sheets before at last falling into a fitful slumber where past and present twined hazily together. The dream came again—half memory of his departure for India, half odd, disjointed collage.

He was standing at the ship's rail looking down at the dock

below. Lovers were embracing, wives and children waving tearful farewells, sailors and stevedores loading baggage into the ship. There was no one for James—his sister was in boarding school in York and he had not bothered to inform anyone else who might care to see him off.

In the dream, as in real life, the ship cast off and pulled away from the dock. A bell rang, and sailors climbed in the rigging, setting out canvas to catch the offshore breeze. Slowly the people on the docks, and then the docks themselves, shrank into the distance and disappeared. He stood gripping the rail until he was the only one left, staring blindly at the cliffs and hills of England.

This time, the dream changed. A gentle touch on his shoulder, and Lily was behind him smiling, wearing her blue painting smock. Then, in the way of dreams, they were back in the conservatory, Lily again in his arms, leaning into his kiss. She pulled back, looked deeply into his eyes for an instant, then ran. James followed, but the brick walkways twisted and the foliage had overgrown the path—he had lost her and could not find his way home.

The dream followed him into daylight, leaving him with a vague melancholy when he woke in the gray light of dawn. The familiar pain of his old longing had echoed through him all morning.

Now he paused before the cut-glass doors that divided the conservatory from the rest of the house. What could he say to put things aright? What would Lily require of him?

Stepping through those doors was like stepping into a different world. No matter how gray or cold it was outside, here was a paradise of warmth and lush fragrance. Again he had entered this haven of the senses, and there was no way out but forward.

He followed the path past carefully tended plantings and nodded to a gardener pruning a leggy hydrangea. Ahead, he could hear her voice.

"Lord Buckley is presently in America. Mother and I are going to take tea with the Countess upon my return to London . . ." Seeing James, she broke off.

Lily's hair was coiled tightly at her neck, though chestnut strands were already escaping. Her blue apron was drawn over a soberly cut gray gown. She was standing by her easel, speaking to her aunt who was seated on the wicker chaise and holding a portable writing desk. James squared his shoulders.

"Good afternoon, Mr. Huntington," Lily said. "Aunt Mary will be lending us the pleasure of her company as we work today."

"Yes, Lily suggested I catch up on my correspondence here. The atmosphere is lovely, don't you agree?"

"Very much." James flicked his gaze to Lily.

"Please sit, Mr. Huntington."

He returned to the stool and tried to let his body remember the pose. One foot firmly on the ground, the other heel resting on the lowest rung. Shoulders at an angle, just so. He did not remember the leaf that was now tickling his neck, though.

Lily eyed his pose with a frown. She began to move toward him then hesitated. "Come and look at the sketch from yesterday. That should give you a better idea of the positioning."

He rose and rounded the easel for his first glimpse of the portrait. Even unfinished the painting had a vital energy to it, a sense of coming into being that stirred him. Or perhaps it was standing so close to the woman he had so recently kissed.

"I see." He studied the lines of the pose, imprinting them in his mind, then returned to the stool.

Lily rewarded him with a faint smile. "Yes. That's it precisely."

He lowered his voice. "I'm glad you are continuing with the portrait. After yesterday, I wasn't sure how you felt."

A hint of color rose in her cheeks. "The *painting* is coming along very well." She looked directly into his eyes. "I am not in the habit of abandoning my work."

"An admirable quality. Have you always been so single-minded?"

"Yes." Her smile was gone now. "In fact, I find it difficult to work and converse at the same time. Because flowers do not require it, I never developed the ability to banter while painting."

"As you wish."

In silence he watched her begin to paint. Her focus narrowed, her sea-green eyes became more intense as they moved over him, but today the transformation did not catch him so completely off guard. There was more of a respite, periods when she focused on the image on her easel. James wondered what she saw when she looked at him, how the colors spoke to her and then were translated into his face and form. The quiet was broken only by the dip and scratch of Lady Mary's pen and the faint whistling of the gardener somewhere beyond James's vision.

There were times when the intensity of her gaze became too much. Then he stared straight ahead and concentrated on the sweeping lines of the greenhouse—glass and iron imprisoning and at the same time sheltering the lush foliage. Outside the trees were still leafless, but inside was a tumult of green.

The sound of light footsteps on the walkway broke the spell. A maid with freckles on her nose entered and dropped a curtsy to Lady Mary.

"Beg pardon, milady. A man is here with more packages. I think they need your direct attention."

"Very well, Anne." Lady Mary rose, setting aside her lap desk. "Please excuse me for a moment." She smiled at Lily and James, and then led the servant from the conservatory.

They were alone, and the silence between them quickly grew as tense and charged as the air before a lightning storm.

"Miss Strathmore," he said. "I hope I did not cause you distress yesterday."

Her fingers tightened on her brush. "Distress? Oh, no."

"I did not intend to put you in a compromising position."

Her gaze dropped to the brick pavers. "Mr. Huntington, I took no offense. In fact, our interchange had all but slipped from my mind."

"I wanted to reassure you—"

"Please, it is unnecessary. Do not worry yourself further on my account. I've put the incident behind me, and would ask that you do the same."

"How practical." He could not so easily erase the memory of her softness pressed against him, her lips warm under his.

"Precisely. It is the only sensible course. And, Mr. Huntington . . ."

"Yes?"

"You should have no expectations. I do not allow—"

"No, of course not."

"Then the matter is settled."

James regarded her for a long moment. "If that is how you want it to be, then it is settled."

She held his gaze a heartbeat too long, then dabbed her brush and returned to her work, some deeper emotion darkening her eyes. A strained silence fell between them.

"I have ordered up a tea tray," Lady Mary said as she came briskly up the walk some minutes later. She glanced from James to Lily. "It should be along shortly, if you are ready for some refreshment."

"Yes," Lily said, "that would be lovely. Though I am nearly finished."

"Finished?"

"Yes. The work has been going very well. Another quarter-hour should see it to completion."

James was curious to see the transformation from sketch to painting. Though more uncomfortable than he might have guessed, observing her in the act of creation had been captivating. He watched her paint, knowing it would be his last opportunity. It was like seeing any creature in its perfect element—a hawk soaring high, riding invisible currents, or a quicksilver fish darting through water. Time had seemed almost suspended, measured only by the dip of her brush, the beat of his own heart, the graceful presence of the artist before him.

The scent of narcissus filled the air, sweet with an edge of citrus. Lady Mary turned her page over, the rustling of paper like the hush of palm fronds on a tropical shore. He was filled with a quiet regret that he and Lily could not enjoy an easy companionability. The shadow of yesterday stood between them.

At last she set down her brush and took a deep breath. "I am done. Or near enough that you are now free, Mr. Huntington."

James rose and stretched. He and Lady Mary moved to join Lily at the easel.

"Oh, Lily!" Lady Mary exclaimed.

He could not speak at first, only look. His figure was cast against subdued greens, making it stand out strongly in vivid tones of gold, white and warm brown. Behind his shoulder the palm fronds were parted, revealing a shining glimpse of white petals.

She had painted him looking slightly to the left, focused past the viewer as if searching for something in the far distance. The longing he saw there startled him. Was it so obvious? It was his yearning as the ship pulled away from the dock, the ache he still felt when he thought of the happy days when his father was still alive.

But she had not just shown his longing—she had shown his hope. Hope that this mad adventure to Tunisia would succeed, that he could save Somergate and at last find a place he could belong to. Lily had painted more than his physical form, she had described his deepest emotion. It was something he had not anticipated—that her skill had transmuted him to this. His heart contracted painfully. He looked down into her upturned face, seeing the unspoken question there. *Is it you?*

"It is wonderful," he said softly.

Her sea-green eyes smiled into his. Once again he felt the absurd impulse to reach out and gather her into his arms—but there was no place for him there.

Chapter 7

James ignored the buzz of conversation that followed him through the club as he made his way to the back and selected a chair facing the fire. London, it seemed, had not yet forgotten his duel with the Duke of Hereford's son.

Sinking back into the supple leather of the armchair, he accepted a glass of brandy from the waiter. He had come to town for a day to take care of the last details of the journey. Passage to Tunisia was booked and all the arrangements made for loading their supplies and equipment. In all, preparations were going remarkably well despite the extra work necessary to accommodate the Strathmores' entourage.

It was good, too, to be away from Brookdale. To be away from Lily, if he were truthful. James felt more than distracted by her. All day his thoughts had returned again and again to the conservatory and to the painter with the blue apron and soft, kissable lips.

"Well, well, if it isn't my cousin, the celebrated duelist." The taunting voice intruded into James's thoughts.

"Reggie." His pleasure dimmed as he watched his raven-haired cousin slide into the adjacent chair.

"I see you are riding out your notoriety in the bottom of a glass. Capital idea. I'll join you." Reggie signaled the waiter.

"I wasn't aware you were a member of this club. Their standards must be slipping."

His cousin arched a brow. "Since they let you in, I'd have to agree. Look at you, James. You are under a cloud of scandal, you have no prospects, a pitiable income—and your boots are a disgrace."

James glanced down at his boots and frowned. "Why are you here? And more to the point, when will you be leaving?"

"You wound me. I have searched high and low to compliment you on your marksmanship, and all you are interested in is when you might be rid of me. I say, your years in savage India have done nothing to improve your manners." Reggie leaned closer, his eyes dark as coal smoke. "I hear you're being exiled. A shame, but family honor and all that."

"I'm touched by your concern."

"Don't mention it, coz." He accepted a glass from the returning waiter and drained it. "I would have thought you'd be long gone by now, hiding under some rock. Tsk, tsk. Father will be disappointed. You were always such an obedient child. Did they issue you a new backbone in the army or are you still planning to leave town like a good little boy?"

"My plans are not your concern."

James had hoped that after his long absence in India his relations with his cousin could be more civil. They had been at odds since the day he and his sister had arrived as children, orphaned. Every act of kindness displayed by their uncle toward them was taken as a slight by Reggie, and often accompanied by some petty payback—a broken toy, a missing letter crumpled and tossed in the wastebasket before it could be read. It was as if Reggie believed that there was not enough love in the world, or that his father's heart could not expand to include three children in the household.

Whatever his motivation, Reggie appeared intent on picking up where the two of them had left off. If anything, he seemed more hostile than ever. Caroline had shared some of the darker gossip circulating about their cousin. His erratic behavior, disappearing for weeks at a time, the frequent shouting arguments with Lord Denby—and the troubling rumors that he was deeply in debt and financing his excesses by taking loans against his inheritance.

Reggie fixed James with a dark-eyed stare. "As I am the Huntington heir, your plans are very much my concern. Particularly when my sources tell me that since gunning down poor Hereford in Hyde Park you have been tearing about buying tents and pack-saddles and such. Hardly necessary if you were planning to retreat for a few weeks to the country." He sat back and steepled his long fingers. "I must admit, I became curious. What is my cousin up to? Why is he down at the shipping-line offices inquiring about passage to the Mediterranean?"

James felt the familiar cold fire burn through him. "You have no right to spy on me. You're meddling in affairs that are none of your business."

"James, James. If you're planning what I suspect, it is very much my business."

"What business might that be?"

"The absurd quest for Grandfather's journals."

So that was Reggie's game. James took a sip of brandy. "You know about the will, then."

Reggie's mouth twisted unpleasantly. "I have a keen interest in how *my* property is disposed of. Grandfather's scheme to give away Somergate is mad. My solicitor will contest any attempt to transfer the property to Kew Gardens."

"Why don't you go recover the journals yourself?"

"Because I'm not fool enough to believe that the journals can be found. Are you?"

"I am going to Tunisia at Lord Denby's request."

Something like pain ghosted in Reggie's eyes. "Yes, father is playing favorites again. You have always jumped when he snapped his fingers, haven't you? Dutiful and domesticated."

James should have expected it. The fact that Lord Denby had asked him to go to Tunisia to search for the journals would provide one more arrow in Reggie's quiver of grievances. Why did his cousin have to take everything as a personal slight?

Despite his animosity, a sliver of pity stirred. Reggie was a difficult son, compelled to set himself at odds with his father. It had sometimes been easier for Lord Denby to display warmth toward his nephew and niece than his own child. But Reggie was not blameless. James had been away for seven years. It was more than enough time for Reggie to show himself worthy of his father's respect.

"Would you have gone if he had asked you?"

Reggie waved his hand dismissively. "Leave the civilized comforts? Those journals cannot be found. However, I have access to a villa in Italy and an arrangement with a very enthusiastic opera singer. I'm sure she would be eager to meet a rugged, handsome fellow like you. Think James, the soft caress of a willing woman, the sound of fountains in the courtyard. The smooth skin of her lips, her breasts, her thighs. When was the last time you had a truly beautiful woman? Why waste your time in Tunisia when you could spend it so pleasantly in Rome? We could go together, coz, patch up our differences after all these years. What do you say?"

"You play the tempter very well—but I have no desire to share your favorite prostitute. There are better ways to resolve our differences." James set his empty glass on the table at his elbow. "I'm not interested in going to Rome."

Reggie shrugged, though his expression had tightened. "I was merely offering alternatives. As your cousin, it would pain me to see you suffer through this exile alone. Consider it, James. I am well acquainted with the terms of Grandfather's will. It is completely vague on where he stashed his blasted journals. Locating them is impossible."

"That may be true, but I'm going to Tunisia to search for the valley of purple flowers, whatever the outcome. Grandfather's letters at least provide a place to start."

Reggie went very still. "Letters?"

Blast. Could it be that his cousin had not seen them?

"They are nothing important. As you said, the entire quest is a fool's errand."

"I would very much like to see those letters."

James crossed his arms and stared into the fire.

"Damnation!" Reggie slammed his glass down. "I am the heir. Somergate is mine. I will not have it taken away by Grandfather's mad whims—or your scheming." He fixed James with a glare. "I am certainly not going to let you go off to Africa and return with some forgery. That's it isn't it? You intend to forge the journals and steal the inheritance. You have always sought more than what you are entitled to—more than you deserve."

James rose abruptly. "Your company—and your accusations—are growing tiresome."

He could feel Reggie's gaze burning his back as he strode away. Why hadn't Lord Denby told his son about the letters? James needed no favors from his uncle—especially ones that set Reggie at his throat. Well, the harm could not be mended now. Nothing to do but keep pressing forward with his plans, and hope that Reggie would not interfere.

Chapter 8

Lily paused in Isabelle's doorway, smoothing the burgundy tulle skirts of her ball gown. Her cousin sat at the dressing table, surrounded by bottles of perfume, hair combs and strands of beads while a maid dressed her hair into artful golden curls.

"Lily! Do come in." Isabelle sprang up and embraced her. "My nerves are all aflutter. This is my first *real* ball, you know. I need your steadying influence, not to mention your wonderful eye for color."

"Oh, Miss, see what you've done." The maid waved the curling tongs in distress, but Isabelle only laughed.

"I have every faith that you can set my hair to rights in a twinkling, Lucy. You have such a skilled touch. But, Lily, how fine you look." Isabelle skipped back and gave her an approving glance. "That neckline is rather daring—is it the current mode?"

"Mother's modiste says, 'Enough plunge to imply naughtiness without actually committing to it.'" Lily glanced down at her tightly fitted bodice, trimmed with dark green satin ribbon.

"I think she has quite succeeded. You will make heads turn tonight. Especially Mr. Huntington's—which is fortunate, for I have decided that, while quite handsome, he is too old for me. Besides, it is clear he is taken with you."

"Really, Isabelle. He is not." Lily paced toward the window, catching her reflection in the wavy glass panes.

She did look well this evening, and though she did not care to admit it, a part of her wanted Mr. Huntington to notice. The same treacherous part that summoned up his image at night while she waited for sleep. After painting his portrait, she could evoke him in perfect detail, his face and form, the clean line of his jaw, the way his eyes crinkled slightly at the corners when he smiled. Of course, she could do the same with flowers she painted—it was merely the result of gazing so deeply at a thing.

All the same, no flower had ever kissed her.

That kiss still haunted her, evoked by any passing, sensuous moment—the slide of her sheer night dress over her skin, the long, silky strokes as she brushed out her hair, the saturated fragrance of the conservatory.

She turned away from the window. "Even if Mr. Huntington were, as you say, 'taken with me,' anything between us would be impossible. We are going to be working together. A scientific expedition is no place for romantic folly."

"I declare, you are starting to sound like Mrs. Hodges. Admit it, Lily, you find him handsome." Isabelle tilted her head so her maid could fix the last pins.

Lily did not reply. It would only encourage her cousin.

Isabelle pushed aside boxes of jewelry and delicate scent bottles. "Earbobs. The blue or the silver?" She held them up, one to each ear and turned her head back and forth.

"The blue. Most definitely. They contrast nicely with your gown, and match the bows at the bottom." Isabelle's dress was a pale rose silk moiré that fell gracefully from her bare shoulders. The pointed waist of the bodice accentuated the full, belling skirts.

"And, of course," Lily added, "they make your eyes sparkle all the more."

"Do you think they will inspire Charlie Thomas to *finally* dance with me? I hope so—most anxiously. He never does at the Assembly rooms, only watches me with such a wistful look. It is quite sweet."

"More than sweet, if your blush is any indication. No wonder you are leaving the agéd Mr. Huntington to me."

Isabelle's flush deepened. "Well, Charlie Thomas *is* sweet—unlike my brother. Do you know what Richard said this afternoon? He vowed he would never partner Anne Riding again, as she treads far too heavily and yanked him all about last time they danced. Isn't he a wicked one? And poor Anne, she moons after him so."

"He will have a hard time avoiding poor Miss Riding tonight."

"Yes, it would be easier to escape his own shadow. Still, I should like to see him trying to take cover beneath the refreshment tables. 'Oh Anne' I would say. 'Come and try the ladyfingers. They are divine! Dear, my fan has dropped directly beneath the table! Would you be a sweetheart and fetch it for me?'"

Lily laughed. "Isabelle, I think you are the wicked one. Wouldn't you aid your brother?"

"Only if he bribes me handsomely."

There was a knock at the door, and Aunt Mary entered, elegant in a blue satin gown. "My, you both look lovely this evening. Lily, I would like to ask a favor of you."

"Of course, Aunt."

"Would you be kind enough to allow Mr. Huntington to escort you this evening? He is a stranger here, and you know most of the local gentry. It will help him feel at home."

"Certainly." Lily kept her voice even. Spending the ball on Mr. Huntington's arm was not going to make for the most comfortable evening. It was difficult enough maintaining light conversation across the dinner table. His gaze had an alarming tendency to snag and hold hers longer than was proper, making her forget what she was about to say.

Still, if they were to travel in company to Africa, now was the time to establish the boundaries of their association.

The coach carrying their party drew to a halt in front of the gaily lit facade of the Thomas residence. Footmen in green livery hurried to throw open the door and set the steps. As the gentlemen disembarked, the unseasonably warm evening air wafted the perfume of blooming hyacinths into the coach.

Mr. Huntington handed her smoothly down. He cut a handsome figure tonight in his black and white evening kit. Even his shoes were polished to perfection.

As they mounted the stairs behind Aunt Mary and Uncle Edward, Lily kept her eyes fixed ahead, trying to ignore the tension fizzing along her nerves. There was no call to be nervous. It was just a ball, for goodness sake.

The front rooms of the Thomas residence were crowded with people talking and greeting neighbors. It would be difficult to mix paints to match the varied hues displayed there. Bright jewelry adorned the older ladies, amethysts, sapphires, and diamonds glinting and refracting the lamplight. The richly colored gowns were paired with even richer textures—silks and satins, velvet and tulle—all thrown into relief by the starker evening wear of the gentlemen. She did spot one or two bright coats circulating through the crowd, relics of another era—but then, that was part of the charm of a country ball.

Squire Thomas, a tall, lanky gentleman, and his wife, Sarah, greeted arrivals at the entrance to the ballroom. They welcomed the Strathmores warmly.

"And welcome, Mr. Huntington," Sarah Thomas said. "We are glad Sir Edward has seen fit to introduce you to the neighborhood. It is always refreshing to have a new face at one of our gatherings. Miss Lily, so nice to see you again. I must say, the two of you make a handsome couple."

Lily felt warmth touch her cheeks as she dropped their hosts a curtsy. Did they have to carry on so? She was only doing her aunt a favor.

She moved with Mr. Huntington into the ballroom's blaze of light and heat. Three large chandeliers were suspended from the high ceiling, cut crystal sparkling in the light of scores of candles. The walls were lined with mirror-backed sconces holding oil lamps, casting even more light over the throng. On a dais at one end of the room a string ensemble provided music for a swirl of dancers.

Lily and Mr. Huntington quickly became separated from the rest of the family by the crowd. Well, she knew her duty. It was up to her to keep the conversation going. She turned to him, intending to say something light and chatty, but when she looked into his eyes words abandoned her. The weight of the silence grew between them.

This would not do. She was supposed to help him feel at ease. Though he hardly seemed uncomfortable. His hand was laid firmly over hers, relaxed and warm. She was the agitated one, acutely aware of the conversations that hushed then resumed with vigor once they had passed. Young women glanced sidelong at Mr. Huntington and whispered behind their fans. Lily could imagine their talk. *Who is he? What are his intentions?*

"Well, Mr. Huntington," she said at last. "Did you ever encounter tigers in India?" Good heavens, what a foolish question. She braced herself for a long, tedious tale of a bloody hunt.

Mr. Huntington grinned. "Tigers? Far more than you might imagine. They tended to congregate in the ballrooms and parlors of my countrymen."

Lily smiled. "It makes an amusing picture—tigers dressed in formal evening wear. There have been numerous sightings of such beasts in London. Did you escape intact from your encounters?"

"Just the usual bites and scratches. Are there any tigers here tonight, Miss Strathmore?"

"That remains to be seen," she said, not quite truthfully. She had spotted several that would eagerly pounce on Mr. Huntington if given the opportunity. Lily tucked her hand more securely through his arm. She *had* promised Aunt Mary that she would look after him.

"I've been meaning to tell you," Mr. Huntington said after they had strolled on a bit. "You look more lovely than any flower this evening. That gown is . . . very flattering."

"Thank you." She tried to take the compliment lightly, though something in his voice made her feel warm. "You are turning a few heads tonight yourself. The Riding sisters over there have been giggling behind their fans ever since we entered the ballroom—and I assure you, I am not the cause. I have had tea with them on several occasions and never once did I evoke spontaneous fan giggling."

"Fan giggling?" He glanced down at her. "I haven't inspired that since I split my breeches dancing the mazurka in Bombay."

"You didn't." Lily laughed.

"I'm afraid it's true. I had been invited to a ball while visiting and had to borrow formal attire from a friend. Unfortunately, his build was somewhat slighter than my own. I assure you there was a great deal of fan giggling when the trousers gave way."

"Mr. Huntington, if you wore trousers as tight as you imply, the fan giggling began long before you split your seams."

Humor sparked in the warm brown of his eyes. "I believe you are right."

"I frequently am." She returned his smile. "Whatever did you do?"

"The only thing possible. I removed my jacket, fashioned it into a sort of kilt, and finished the dance—although in a somewhat more deliberate manner. Then I escorted my partner from the floor and dashed for the nearest exit. My friend never did forgive me for ruining his trousers."

"I'm disappointed there is no mazurka on the program this evening since it is your specialty." He laughed. "A waltz would suit me just as well. May I bring you something to drink in the meantime?"

"Burnt champagne would be lovely."

Lily watched him move away, relieved that their conversation was going well. The evening was turning out to be civil and amusing—precisely what was needed.

Richard hurried up and took her hands. "Please Lily, dance the galop with me." He glanced over his shoulder. "Anne Riding."

"What? My cousin actually begging me to dance? How the tables have turned. Your sister says you bribe handsomely. Is it true?"

"Yes, but Isabelle's price is too steep—she wants my favorite horse! Please, Lily. You're my only hope."

"Oh very well. You're lucky I am so filled with charity this evening." She let him pull her toward the dance floor. "I'll rescue you and your horse too."

The two of them formed up in the long lines of ladies and gentlemen on the floor. Soon the strains of a lively reel had them whirling about and some of the younger folk made a show of kicking up their heels in the energetic dance. Richard danced well, never mind what Isabelle might say about his skills. When the music finally ended, Lily was breathless.

Mr. Huntington found them as they left the floor and handed Lily her champagne. "I see Richard decided to dance with you after all."

Richard straightened. "Sorry to steal Lily away. She came to my rescue—it was a desperate bit of business."

Mr. Huntington lowered his voice: "Speed and camouflage, they are your best hope. And if you are cornered, turn the topic to a subject that woman cannot long abide—the merits of different fowling guns or an account of your exploits at billiards."

"Mr. Huntington!" Lily said, "I shall hold you personally responsible if Richard ever raises those subjects in my hearing."

Richard, spotting Miss Riding closing on them, gave a muffled groan. "Thank you for the dance, and the advice. If you will excuse me—" He was gone, slipping with surprising agility in the direction of the refreshment tables.

Mr. Huntington turned to her. "Miss Strathmore, I believe this next dance is mine."

"Certainly, sir." It was the least she could do for their guest. Lily took a hasty sip of champagne then set it down on a nearby table. It was making her feel a bit unsteady.

The musicians began marking out the beat for a quadrille, an older, stately dance.

"Shall we?" Mr. Huntington held out his hand.

She set her hand in his, tamping down the rush of sensation as his fingers closed over hers.

He drew her confidently onto the floor and swept her a low bow as the figures began. Turning slowly, they revolved around one another. Lily's skirts grazed his trousers in passing. The measured paces of the dance drew them forward and back, close enough to almost touch, then away, circling a new partner and back again.

Lily could not help meeting his eyes. He held her gaze for a heartbeat. Then two. Her breath quickened and she felt suspended in some quiet, magical bubble that enclosed just the two of them. Everything fell away, and it seemed that time had no meaning beyond the graceful dip and sway, the advance and retreat of their steps. The sleeve of his coat brushed softly against her arm as he passed, a whisper of a touch. The contact made her pulse leap.

Her every sense was enhanced. The taste of the fruity champagne lingered on her tongue, the lavender perfume she had touched to her throat enfolded her in rich fragrance, the sound of violins cast a net of music that drew them smoothly through the twining figures.

Then the music slowed, and it was like waking from a dream. She could not look at him. Tomorrow she must return to London where her mother would talk endlessly of guest lists and wedding gowns and the prestige the union with Lord Buckley would bring.

She stumbled, and in an instant Mr. Huntington was at her elbow, supporting her. His touch burned through the silk of her gown.

"Miss Strathmore?" Concern darkened his brown eyes.

"I'm fine. Just a momentary dizziness." Lily cast about for a place to sit. She needed to escape him, his touch and scent, the sound of his voice. She needed to regain her wits—but he was guiding her through the crowd and out onto the terrace.

Quiet folded about them as they left the ballroom. She took a deep breath of cool misty air to steady herself. The light shining through the doors and windows reached only a few feet before fading into the black and silver of the night.

"Better?"

"The air helps."

He leaned against the stone railing, the planes of his face softened by shadow. Far too handsome—and far too close. She closed her eyes, holding onto the rail with both hands and drew in another breath, trying to collect herself.

"I feel much better now," she lied. "Shall we return?"

"Let's walk the terrace and enter the ballroom by the far doors."

"I really don't think . . ."

"We can avoid the crush that way."

It was a sensible enough idea, though after their indiscretion in the conservatory, after the way she had just responded to him during the dance, the last place she should be was alone with him on a moonlit walk. Yet somehow her good sense had deserted her, leaving behind a wistful yearning, a burning restlessness just under her skin.

Lily pulled her shawl up over her shoulders and set out along the terrace, declining the offer of his arm. She might be foolish, but she was not stupid.

He kept pace with her, hands clasped behind his back. She could have sworn he was grinning.

Lanterns were set at intervals, highlighting a branch here, a bough of evergreen there. Below, a thin mist was rising over the lawns, curling low about the tree trunks and topiary. Lily paused to draw her wrap tighter and turned to look out over the gardens. It was a romantic scene, if a bit chilly. Impossible to paint with any fidelity.

"Are you cold?"

There was the rustle of cloth and then the weight of his coat settled over her shoulders, carrying his warmth, his scent. It was wicked of her, but she savored it.

"Thank you." Her voice was more of a whisper than she had intended.

"Lily." He spoke her familiar name and it was like a caress, his voice deep and close behind her. His hands rested lightly on her shoulders.

She closed her eyes and did not answer. They should return

to the ballroom, but returning was hard, and yielding to the moment so easy. So perfect. She leaned back, letting her head rest against his chest. Immediately his arms encircled her.

With a groan, he bent and set his lips to the side of her neck. Sensation flared from the touch of his mouth against her skin. His hair, soft and cleanly scented, brushed against her jaw, and she could barely keep her balance as he trailed slow kisses up the column of her throat.

His hands settled on her hips and he turned her to face him. The moonlight showed the unmistakable desire in his expression, his eyes heavy-lidded, his hands anchoring her in place as he lowered his mouth to capture her lips. Lily slid her hands up to his shoulders and closed her eyes while the exhilaration blazing through her flared higher. She was aware of every place where she pressed against him. The night chill was banished by the heat of their two bodies.

"James." She returned his kiss with an urgency that surprised her, an urgency that only increased when he slid his tongue against her lips, tracing a hot line along the seam of her mouth. Lily felt as though she could barely breathe—as though she did not need air, only this, the touch and taste of him, to sustain her. He moved his hand to her face and stroked her cheek, his thumb smoothing along her cheekbone and jaw with a gentle pressure, coaxing, opening. Lily parted her lips, allowing him to enter and explore, hot and moist.

She had never been kissed like this. It was thrilling and unexpected and her blood caught fire. She responded, letting her tongue meld against his, wanting to devour him. There was no tomorrow, no ball, no moonlit terrace. Only the two of them, holding each other with such a fierce yearning that Lily thought her heart might break.

Chapter 9

James was almost lost in the surge of reckless sensation. Lily felt incredibly right in his arms, her body molded against his, her fingers clutching his shoulders. Her mouth was sweetness, and fire, and he wanted more. They had minutes, but he needed hours to press kisses over every inch of her skin. Gods, it would be so easy to lose himself with this woman.

The music was still playing, but was it the same dance? How long had they stood wrapped in each others arms? With effort, he broke the kiss.

Lily looked up at him, holding onto him as if he were the only solid thing in the universe. He watched as the dreamy look faded from her expression. She smiled unsteadily.

"A singularly effective way to get warm."

Warm? Did she have any idea how warm he wanted to make her?

Above, a lone cloud ghosted across the sky, shadowing the moon. Lily's smile faded with the light, and she stepped back, pulling off his coat. "Mr. Huntington, we really must return to the ballroom before we become a subject of speculation."

"Of course." James shrugged into his coat. She hadn't fled this time, but the sudden return to formality stung. In an instant the fire had been banked.

The light in the ballroom dazzled them as they entered.

"Excuse me," she said. "I must visit the ladies' retiring room."

James watched her go, then turned away. He could not spend the evening staring at the spot where she had disappeared.

"There you are Huntington," Sir Edward hailed him. "Come, let me introduce you around. There are several people you should meet—and the delicacies at the refreshment tables are starting to disappear. I promised you a fine repast, but we'd best hurry."

"To the refreshments." James hoped he sounded adequately enthusiastic.

"I trust Lily has made your evening more pleasant. She is acquainted with almost everyone—practically grew up here."

"How is it that she has spent so much time with your family? Don't her parents live in London?"

Sir Edward laughed. "Indeed they do, but as you have no doubt discovered, Lily has a will of her own. London is not entirely to her taste—especially these days."

"Why is that?"

"Her mother. She is quite set on Lily making an excellent match—drags her around to all the balls and whatnot. Lily would rather paint. A pity it has to end. Lily's parents have made it clear that her—rusticating, they call it—will no longer be tolerated. They intend to take her in hand, poor girl. Ah, here we are." Sir Edward gestured to the sideboard loaded with platters of meats, oysters, chilled salads, and various pastries. "Didn't I tell you there would be fare to rival London's finest? Do try the lemon tarts. Splendid things."

James took a bite. "Delicious. You were saying about Lily . . . ?"

"Oh, yes. Whisking her back to London tomorrow is part of the new program. Lily's mother sees matrimony as a battlefield, with spoils to the victor. I never understood that, although she certainly married well by her standards. My brother Michael's rise in the House of Lords has increased her matrimonial investment many times over."

James nearly choked on his lemon tart. "Lord Michael Strathmore is your brother?"

Sir Edward nodded. "Yes, although he knows next to nothing about botany."

James cast about for an empty chair. To think, five minutes ago he had been kissing the daughter of one of the most influential men in Parliament. Lord Michael Strathmore, Marquis of Fernhaven. The name was a fixture in the London papers. And Lily, with her paint-spattered blue apron and her botanical illustrations, was his wayward daughter.

It was not good news.

Sir Edward selected another tidbit from the table. "Say, don't these oyster croquettes have a fine flavor? I doubt even Lily's independence will stop her mother this time. Unique as Lily is, she is still a catch, particularly for one with political ambitions. My sister-in-law will have her sights set high, you can be sure." He broke off. "There you are, Charles. I have someone I want you to meet. Huntington, this is Mr. Crawford."

James shook hands with the elderly gentleman sporting a bottle-green velvet coat at least two decades out of fashion. "Mr. Crawford, I'm delighted to make your acquaintance. The weather this evening is unseasonably warm. Are such early springs common here?"

"Common?"

Sir Edward pointed to his ear and nodded significantly toward the older gentleman.

"Are early springs common here?" James repeated.

"Springs? Why back in '08 we had such a spring. The fruit trees were blooming in March. Unseasonably warm, that. There was an abundant run of herring that year off the coast of Cornwall. When the herring come, you can count on a mild winter. Now, in '14 we had just the opposite . . ."

James set aside his plate, appetite gone.

Lily was the Marquis of Fernhaven's daughter. Strike him for a fool. It was a good thing that her father was sending a carriage to collect her tomorrow. If he slept late enough he might never have to see her again. He certainly would not seek her out. In fact, he would go out of his way to avoid her until her mother had married her off to the highest bidder.

This attraction to her was more of a mistake than he had thought—and it had to end. Now. He'd had the misfortune of falling in love with a woman of Lily's status once before, and had no intention of repeating the blunder.

He had just turned twenty when he met Amanda Granville, the daughter of a peer, a man very like Lily's father. James had been introduced to her in the swirl of her first season and they had fallen instantly and madly in love. The two of them had exchanged fervent kisses whenever they could slip away, and she had promised to be his.

Unfortunately her father had very different ideas. How had he put it? *I will burn in hell before I allow a landless, title-less orphan of a second son to marry my daughter.* There had been quite a scene when James had come to press his suit. What a miserable young fool he had been.

You are nothing! You are so far below her it's laughable.

"Amanda, tell him," James had pleaded with her, but she had only sobbed into a handkerchief, not even daring to look at him. Her father had summoned his menservants and ordered them to seize the young man who had the audacity to ask for his daughter's hand. James could still recall the shame of being forcibly escorted down the stairs and tossed out on the street.

If you come near my daughter, or my property, I will have you arrested and flogged. Lord Granville had been in such a rage that he had shouted it from the open window of his study, heedless of anyone who might overhear. *"Drive him away!"* he had called to his men, and to his everlasting humiliation, James had run down one of the most fashionable streets in London chased by servants in Granville livery.

The next day he had used the money left by his father to purchase an officer's commission with a posting in India. Better that than be the laughingstock of all London. Amanda had promised she would follow him anywhere. If his suit failed, they had planned to begin a new life together far from England.

But love was not enough. Love was *never* enough.

Soon after his arrival in Bombay he had read of her marriage in the *Times*—a brilliant match to the Duke of Trentley.

James ran a hand through his hair. Thank the gods he had found out about Lily in time.

Sir Edward had abandoned them for a serving of lobster salad, but Mr. Crawford seemed to take the loss of half his audience in stride. "A spring this early puts me in mind of '27—that was the year of the great sheep blight."

"Indeed." James gave him a hollow smile. He scanned the room behind Mr. Crawford. It was not difficult to spot Lily among the lesser lights. She was beautiful, and spirited, and completely unobtainable.

What to do? There really was only one course. He would dance their final dance, bid her good night, and pray the bitter prayer that he might never set eyes on her again.

"If you will excuse me, Mr. Crawford. I have promised this waltz to a particular lady."

"Ah, go on then, me boy, go on."

James made his way across the ballroom to her as the musicians signaled the waltz.

"Miss Strathmore, I believe this is our last dance."

Lily's heartbeat sped as she gazed up at James. Didn't the man realize how confusing everything became when he stood so close to her?

Fixing a smile on her lips, she allowed him to lead her into the center of the room. The musicians played the opening bars, the violins first sliding then soaring into the notes.

When he gathered her into his arms, she stiffened.

"Relax," he murmured. "It will look very odd if I have to haul you around the floor like a sack of flour."

He was right, drat him. Lily focused her gaze on his lapel and gradually let herself fall into the rhythm of the dance. He was looking at her, she knew, but she could not meet his eyes. She had regained some of her composure since they had returned from the terrace, but now that she was back in his arms she could feel it slipping away. What was it that made her susceptible to the charms of this man when so many others had left her cold?

James swept her around the room in such perfect time to the music that it seemed they were lifted, propelled not by muscle and bone, but by a swell of spirit that carried them. All around them couples swirled in a riot of color, yet the two of them moved together in the heart of the music, alone in the pure, sweet center of the waltz.

She relaxed into the movements—it seemed her heart offered no choice. Hand resting on his shoulder, she felt the play of muscles tensing and releasing beneath his evening coat. His arm circled her, guiding her through another turn. She was floating, and when his thigh brushed hers in passing, she felt the impression burning against the silk, against her skin, for long moments after.

This would never do.

Despite her best efforts, being close to James made her want things that were beyond inadvisable. The thought that had been nipping at her since their kiss on the terrace returned.

She should stay behind when the expedition left.

Acknowledging it made her heart twist, but she had to face facts—in particular, the tall, masculine one that was swooping her around the room. What else could she do? Find a way to get rid of James? Not with her uncle set on finding the flower. She had not seen him so excited in years—and that was saying a great deal.

There would be other expeditions, perhaps, if her future husband permitted. At the very least she would still have her painting, a family, freedom from her mother's matchmaking. She had bargained for the expedition, but who could have anticipated Mr. Huntington?

"Tell me, Miss Strathmore, do you regret not accompanying your uncle to Tunisia?"

Lily blinked up at him. Goodness, could he read her thoughts? "Yes, I'm disappointed, but I see no other option under the circumstances."

"It would be difficult to deny one's parents." He spoke as if daring her to correct him.

"I beg your pardon?"

"Your father is sending a carriage for you tomorrow, is he not? I was there when you received the letter."

"And you thought I was returning home because my uncle was going abroad?"

"I thought your family was sending for you, that is all."

Lily looked away. Could it be that he didn't realize she had been planning to go on the expedition? That might explain his kisses. Well, perhaps it was better this way. She wouldn't have to explain why she had changed her mind, at least not to him.

Wistfulness stole over her as they twirled and turned once more about the floor. This would be the last time. James would go, as he must, and when he returned she would be wed.

The music was slowing, bringing them back to a room filled with voices and laughter. Their interlude was now truly over. It would be best if she remained in England. Swallowing past the tightness in her throat, she swept James a deep curtsy, silk skirts hushing along the floor.

He bowed in return. "Thank you for the dance, Miss Strathmore. I only wish it could have continued a little longer."

James woke early to a soft, gray drizzle. The new day barely brightened the sky and the sun felt immeasurably far away. Thoughts of Lily filled his mind—the way her lovely, mysterious eyes sparkled up at him in unguarded moments, how she felt in his arms melting into his kiss, her passion, her determined self-possession.

He sat up restlessly, pushing free of the sheets. The shock of cool air against his bare chest brought him fully awake.

Lily was leaving today.

He pulled on his clothes and left the room. It was too early for the family to be stirring, especially after the late hours they had kept last night, but the house was awake. He caught the distant sound of rattling dishes and low-voiced conversation as the servants went about their early-morning duties. He padded quietly down the hall and descended the empty stairway. Without intending it, he found himself in the drawing room, its serene greens and golds nearly colorless in the wan light.

The piano lid was closed, the empty furniture waiting patiently. It was a room asleep, except for the portrait of him propped on the mantle. Sir Edward had placed it there for the family to admire the night after Lily had finished it. James could make out the strong lines of the composition even in the pale half-light.

With no one to witness but the empty chairs, he could tell the truth—his life had been undeniably richer and more hopeful since he had met her. Being near her felt like sunlight— even when she was glaring daggers at him. He hated the idea of her leaving.

No. He wanted her—wanted her with him. And if she were just Lily the artist, or even Sir Edward's daughter, that might be possible. But she was not Sir Edward's daughter, even if she seemed intent on playing the part.

Love was not enough. Love and property maybe—but never love alone.

He turned back to the portrait. Could it be different this time? What if against all odds the expedition was a success and he returned as master of Somergate? Would that be enough?

If only he had Somergate, and Lily's heart, and her family's blessing. James laughed grimly up at his portrait. "You have fine prospects, my friend."

The image on the mantle remained silent, heart's longing written large in its eyes.

Chapter 10

Lily stepped out into the rain, following her father's footman to the waiting coach. What a wretched day. She shivered against the persistent drizzle and drew her thick wool cloak more closely about her. Her thoughts veered toward James—the weight of his coat around her last night, the warmth of his arms.

Why was she torturing herself this way? She had made her decision. She must not let herself think of him.

Uncle Edward walked beside her, holding a great black umbrella to shelter them both. "You needn't make any hasty decisions about staying behind, my dear. Take a few days. Post us a letter on Monday. It would be a shame not to have you along." He handed her into the coach.

"I know, Uncle. I will write you." Lily pressed her lips together. She could see he was dreadfully disappointed but putting a brave face on it. She leaned out and kissed his cheek before settling back into the seats. Her maid, Bess, tucked a lap robe around her.

"The foot-warmer is just there, miss. And your aunt made sure we were well provisioned." Bess dug through the large wicker basket beside her. "There's scones and cakes and meat pies and, my, even oranges and a flask of wine, and some fine cheese and a fresh-baked loaf. You'd think we were traveling across the whole of England, Miss, not just up to London."

Lily nodded. Aunt Mary left nothing to chance. How many more provisions would her aunt find necessary to bring to Tunisia? Well, Lily would not be there to find out. She sighed and turned to the window.

The coach swayed as the footman climbed up beside the driver. Lily stared out at the beloved shape of Brookdale and the conservatory, gray and wet now, but still lovely. Still home.

A tall figure near the stables caught her eye. He stood there, alone in the rain.

"Oh," she breathed. Her fingertips brushed the glass.

The driver snapped the reins and with a crunch of gravel the coach rocked forward. When she looked out again James was gone, the sight of him lost behind the stone walls.

The coach arrived at the highway and turned toward London. Lily watched the drenched green countryside rolling past. The expedition would have been dreadful—a constant battle between her attraction to James and her duty to her future. She should be relieved that he was no longer any concern of hers.

It was over. Time to turn her thoughts ahead to London.

She would have to tell her mother about the change in plans—though she certainly would not let her know the real reason. Lily bit her lip. Not that her mother would inquire too closely—she would take her daughter's return as capitulation. It galled, but what else could she do? She closed her eyes and let the rocking of the coach lull her into a fitful rest.

The hours rolled on heavily, with no break in the rain. Bess delighted in bringing forth offerings from the basket, which Lily nibbled at dutifully. At last the horses' hooves rang over cobblestones. She glanced out the window to see that the fields and hedgerows had given way to tumbledown walls and dwellings. They had reached the outskirts of London. Ragged children, like flocks of dirty sparrows, chased after the coach, begging for a few pence. Street vendors called out their wares in strident tones, and the bustle and squalor of town closed in around them.

Gradually the neighborhoods turned to more genteel

dwellings, the people on the street dressed in finer clothing. The coach passed well-tended parks and gardens until they made the turn into Mayfair and drew up to the pillared and ornate residence that was the Marquis of Fernhaven's London home.

It was not the house Lily had grown up in. No, this place was far grander, as befitted her father's advance in prestige and power. Her mother had it decorated, and re-decorated, in the latest mode. It had never felt like home, it was merely the place she stayed between visits to Brookdale. Lifting her chin, she descended the steps of the coach.

Edwin, the butler, greeted her at the tall double doors of the main entrance. Like many men in his position, he seemed to consider smiling beneath his dignity, but his eyes twinkled a welcome. "Miss Lily. Your mother awaits you in the front parlor." He took her cloak and gloves. "Her ladyship, it seems, is extremely eager to have you home."

"Thank you, Edwin. I shall attend her directly." She smiled warmly at him, then turned down the hallway. A riot of color and texture assaulted her. Gold-figured wallpaper draped with emerald-green velvet swags and paintings that were eclipsed by their own carved and gilt-covered frames. There was a new lacquered table with climbing Chinese dragons for legs and a huge red urn filled with peacock feathers. None of this had been here before. Lily shuddered. Mother had been decorating again.

Lady Fernhaven turned from the window and crossed the room in a flurry of damask skirts when Lily entered the parlor. "Welcome back, darling!" She gave her daughter a quick embrace, then led her to the floral chintz settee. "Come and sit. We have so much to discuss. I hope your journey was not too taxing?"

"Mother, there is something I need to tell you—"

"And I you." Her mother leaned forward, eyes sparkling with excitement. "Lord Buckley is amenable to our plans and will pay his addresses to you when he returns to London. Oh Lily, isn't it wonderful!"

"He what?" Her mother's scheme had progressed further than Lily had imagined. She had thought she and Lord Buckley would discuss the matter together and come to some arrangement.

"Countess Buckley is sure he will make you an offer. She told me this in the strictest confidence, of course, but I do want you to be able to dream about it and know your dreams are not in vain." Her mother smiled. "You see, Lily, one can be both practical and romantic."

She stared at her mother. "I had hoped we'd have a period of courtship before entering into the formalities."

"Of course you will, dear. All is ready for our visit to the Countess on Monday. I have ordered you a new dress, one that is quite becoming and shall suit you perfectly."

Lily felt a wave of weariness. She closed her eyes.

"Isn't it splendid? You are going to be a countess!"

"Mother, it has been a long journey and I am feeling very tired."

"Of course, darling. I was nearly overcome by the news myself. Go up and rest. Your father and I are attending a dinner party this evening. Have Cook send up a tray."

When Lily stepped into her room she thought for a moment she had opened the wrong door. Her curtains were now a thick rose velvet, not the soothing green silk that had hung there before, and the coverlet and pillows on her bed had been changed to match. She turned in a slow circle in the center of the room. Where was her art? Her Turner and Clara Pope's camellias? The pictures on the wall had no merit except that they harmonized with the room's new color-scheme.

She yanked the bell-pull, now a length of knotted pink silk.

"You rang, Miss?" A breathless young maid hurried up.

"Where are my pictures? The ones that used to hang in my room."

The maid twisted her hands in her apron. "I knew you would not like it, but Mrs. Hatcher insisted they come down."

Lily set her hands on her hips. "And who is Mrs. Hatcher?"

"Your mother's new interior planner, Miss. She is a fearsomely opinionated woman—if I may be so bold."

"This woman—she told you to get rid of my paintings?"

"Yes, Miss. Most decisively. Said they spoiled the effect of the new colors."

Spoiled her colors, did they? Lily intended to do a lot more than spoil her colors, but first she wanted her paintings.

"I do not agree with Mrs. Hatcher's opinion. I want my pictures found and rehung—tonight! Fetch Edwin immediately and get everyone searching. So help me, if any harm has come to them Mrs. Hatcher will pay dearly."

The maid bobbed a curtsy and scurried away, but Lily scarcely noticed. She was already tearing the offending paintings down and tossing them into a pile in the hallway. She would have burned them, if she had a match and a hope of not setting the house afire.

Another maid appeared at her door, carrying a tray. "Cook sent this up for you, Miss Lily. They're still looking for your pictures. Jeffrey is searching the attics now."

"Thank you, Dora. Tell him that if he comes across my old curtains, he should bring them as well."

"Too late, miss. He's here."

Jeffrey, a bone-thin footman, sidled through the door, arms full of framed artwork. Lily hurried forward. "Gently, now. Lay them on the bed."

"But miss," Dora sounded appalled, "The coverlet will be ruined. The wrappers are horribly dusty."

"I will not shed any tears if Mrs. Hatcher's coverlet is ruined. Let's have a look at what Jeffrey has found." Lily watched as the paper on the first picture was pulled gently back to reveal one of her early paintings—the formal gardens at the old house. She shifted it and glanced at the others.

"These are not the ones I'm looking for." It was work she had done years ago. Her Turner was not here, nor the others.

Jeffery gathered up the pile she had pushed aside, revealing the bottom-most painting. Lily froze. She had not seen this one for years—had tried to forget about it. It was a portrait of a young man holding a paintbrush. His features were even and pleasing, his expression earnest. Robert, her art tutor, the one who had . . . Lily hastily replaced the other pictures on top, hiding the sweet-faced young man.

"Take these away—they are not the right ones at all."

"Perhaps these will do, Miss." It was Edwin, standing at the door with a stack of paintings.

Lily jumped up. She recognized the frames. "Oh, Edwin, I could hug you."

"Please refrain, Miss."

"Then help me hang them."

"I would be most honored. Where would you like this misty one?"

"Right here, beside the bed." Lily felt her spirits rise as each familiar piece went back up. It already felt more like home

"Much better." She turned to the servants. "Thank you, all. You have been so kind."

After they had left—taking the discarded paintings piled in the hallway with them—her dinner suddenly seemed much more appealing. Lily ate some soup and pudding then went to her writing desk.

Dear Uncle Edward,

I have arrived safely in London to find the house completely re-done. It is beyond garish, but at least I have been able to restore my rooms.

It pains me to think of missing the expedition, and of disappointing you and the rest of the family, but it is simply not possible for me to accompany you. Think of me when you are in Tunisia, and write often.

Lily stopped and tapped the end of the pen against her lips. It was not fair. She should not have to abandon the expedition, and her uncle should not be left without an illustrator—and she most definitely should never have kissed James Huntington. Seeing the painting of Robert had reminded her exactly where her feelings for a man could lead. It was a warning, an omen.

"Take your time," her uncle had urged. "Think it through."

But there was no time. If she waited another day to decide she wouldn't have the heart to remain behind.

Lily finished the letter and folded it into an envelope, ready for the morning post. It was out of her hands now.

"Good morning, darling," Lady Fernhaven said as Lily entered the breakfast room. "I trust you slept well. We should speak about our visit to Countess Buckley this afternoon. It is in everyone's best interest that it go smoothly."

Lily took a scone from the sideboard and joined her mother at the table. "Tea first, Mother—please."

"Here you are." Lady Fernhaven poured her a cup. "We have so much to discuss."

Lily would have liked to linger over her tea, but her mother was hovering. She set the cup down half-full. "Very well." So much for easing into the day.

"Countess Buckley and I shared a season, you know. We both had the good fortune to make excellent matches that year— though she did manage to catch an earl. Not that your father is in any way inferior, what with his advance in Parliament."

"Of course not." Lily nibbled her scone.

"The point is, I know the Countess well. She has strong opinions about what sort of activities are proper for young ladies. When she asks about you, make sure you keep your responses demure and to the point. And no need to go into any great detail about your painting—no need at all."

"What, exactly, are you saying? That Countess Buckley does not approve of women painting?"

"Oh no, no. Just that we need not mention the scientific part. I'm sure she has no objection to lovely pictures of flowers— very feminine."

"A large part of my art is botanical illustration, Mother." Lily pushed her plate aside.

"Well, it likely will not matter. I shall keep the conversation moving in a favorable direction. Now, about your hair."

Lily lifted one hand to the unruly knot at the back of her

head. The hair, of course. It was always the hair. She hated that her mother could make her feel so inadequate. "I can have Bess—"

"I will send my own maid to help you get ready. One can't be too prepared for a visit like this."

Four hours later Lily was suitably combed and coiffed, laced more tightly than she was accustomed, and buttoned into the new dress her mother had ordered for the occasion. It reminded her of preparing for her presentation to the Queen. There was the same nervous fluttering in her stomach. She wouldn't be making her bow to the Queen this time, but there was more at stake—her entire future.

She and her mother arrived at the Buckley mansion at half-past three. The butler led them through the grand entrance and down a long corridor—the sound of their heels echoed on the polished marble floor. He halted before an imposing pair of gilt-edged white doors. Lily drew in a breath—not as deep as usual due to the tight corset—and glanced at her mother, noting the subtle signs of tension in the set of her shoulders.

"Marchioness Fernhaven and her daughter, the Honorable Miss Lily Strathmore." The butler held the door open for them.

"Come along, darling," murmured Lady Fernhaven, stepping forward.

The room was dominated by a pair of tall glass cases containing dozens of porcelain figurines: artfully arranged shepherdesses, ballerinas in mid-twirl, fat men in waistcoats, and fairy-tale princesses. Mirrors set at the back of the cases allowed the figures to be admired from all angles.

Countess Buckley rose gracefully to greet her guests—a figure from her own collection come to life with impeccably styled hair and fashionable gown. Older, of course, but as carefully sculpted. Her eyes in particular were a pale blue, like the faintest wash of watercolor. Those eyes—yes. Lord Buckley had those same eyes. Lily suddenly recalled them staring mildly past her as they danced a schottische at the Chadwick's ball last season.

The Countess's eyes were far from mild as she turned an

appraising look on Lily. She did not smile—perhaps she was afraid that such a slip would mar the well-preserved perfection of her face.

"Miss Strathmore. Your mother has told me so much about you. Please, sit, and we can become better acquainted." Countess Buckley gestured with one slender white hand to a grouping of velvet-upholstered chairs.

Lily sat and laced her fingers together in her lap. Her green skirts, edged with creamy lace, settled about her. The afternoon gown was truly lovely. The subtly patterned taffeta was gathered into hundreds of tiny pleats at the waist, which dropped to a point. Overall, it gave the impression of waves—discreet, ladylike waves that knew their place and would never rise and crash onto some desolate, rocky shoreline.

As the countess rang for tea, Lily's mother leaned forward, speaking softly. "Don't worry, darling. I'll take charge should you get in over your head."

"Really, Mother. I'm capable of holding a polite conversation."

Their hostess rejoined them in a rustle of silk. "I am so pleased you could come calling today. We can have a cozy chat, just us women."

Cozy? That seemed unlikely—there was nothing remotely cozy about Countess Buckley.

"Miss Strathmore, your mother tells me you are something of a lady artist."

"Yes, I paint. Botanical illustrations, mostly. Are you interested in horticulture, Countess Buckley?"

"Heavens no. I leave that to the gardeners. But botanical illustration—rather a man's business, don't you think?"

"There have been any number of women whose illustrations have been well-received. Clara Pope, for one."

"I think one should make a distinction between what is well-received and what is proper."

"Lily makes charming flower pictures," Lady Fernhaven said before Lily could reply. "I even have one of them in my drawing room. Roses. Beautiful roses."

"I see. Well, roses are a refined flower, and a worthy subject for a lady artist." Their hostess swept Lily with her pale gaze. "You are actually rather pretty. You have met my son, Gerald? A very handsome man, I'm sure you agree."

"I'm sure." Lily turned her lips up at the corners and hoped it would do for an answer. What could she say? *I'm sorry, but I have only the vaguest recollection of your son?*

The Countess gazed deeply at her for a moment before turning her attention to pouring out the newly-arrived tea.

Lily let the smile drop from her face. So, her painting was barely acceptable? Would Lord Buckley share his mother's opinion? The thought made her stomach tighten.

"And how is your son?" Lady Fernhaven asked. "Lily has been wanting to know. Is he enjoying his travels?"

"Very much." The countess handed each of her guests a cup of tea, her back remaining perfectly straight. "His most recent letter described a great fall of water somewhere in the state of New York—the name escapes me. He intends to take in more natural wonders, I believe, as well as visiting the Eastern cities—what he sees in them I cannot say. Why, I have hedges in the garden older than most of those cities. I much prefer the European capitals, myself." She gave a polite little laugh. Lily's mother joined her.

"Then he is not planning to return soon?" Lily asked.

Countess Buckley's expression warmed slightly. "Not immediately, but there is no cause to worry. He will return in good time to pay you court—though I can see you are anxious over it."

Anxious. Yes, that quite described her feelings. "I would like to know that we will have time to become properly reacquainted before, well, before any final decisions are made."

"Lily, there is nothing to fear," her mother said. "The two of you are perfectly matched." She turned to the countess. "I recall my own anxiety before the Marquis of Fernhaven proposed. That is the way with women when a man of high station pays court."

"I quite agree. My, but that was a season. You with your marquis, and I with my earl. We were the talk of the *ton*."

"We had to coordinate the wedding dates carefully. It wouldn't have done to have the two grandest weddings of the season tripping over one another."

"Fortunately, we won't have that problem this time, but we will have to choose the date wisely . . ."

Lily began to tap one foot, the movement hidden by her skirts. If Countess Buckley favored the match, it had far more to do with her father's position and political connections than any virtue or talent Lily might possess.

She was really quite irrelevant to the whole scheme. They expected her to be one of those porcelain dolls—poised, beautifully dressed, and lifeless. Someone who stayed exactly where they were placed until the time came to show them off.

Was this what she had chosen?

So it seemed, if it could be called a choice at all. It was either this or finding herself a dutiful spinster daughter, spending the rest of her life accompanying her mother to interminable teas.

Like this one.

"So you see, Lily, there is nothing to be anxious about," her mother said. "Lord Buckley is a fine gentleman, and he will make you a fine husband."

The countess rose. "I have something for you that will be a comfort while my son is abroad." She lifted a locket on a slim gold chain and held it out to Lily.

"Really, Countess, it is not necessary . . ."

"But I insist." She took Lily's hand and pressed the locket into her palm, closing her fingers over it. The countess smelled of talc, and her hands were as cool and smooth as alabaster. "This is very precious to me, but I thought you should have it—especially with our expectations for the future."

Lily felt trapped by the woman's pale eyes. She dropped her hand back into her lap, the locket clenched in her fist.

"Really, darling," her mother said, "Your restraint is charming. Go ahead and open it—you needn't be modest with us."

Lily fumbled with the catch. A miniature portrait of a man that must be Lord Buckley gazed out at her, his face the face of a stranger. He had light blond hair receding from a wide forehead, his mother's pale blue eyes, thin lips, and a soft chin that was lifted with a superior air.

She swallowed and slowly raised her eyes to the countess. "Thank you."

"Oh, do put it on, Miss Strathmore. Don't be shy. I am sure Gerald would approve."

With a sinking sensation Lily glanced at her mother. Lady Fernhaven's gaze was bright and avid. She nodded encouragingly.

"I really don't think . . ."

"I will fasten it for you." Her mother took the locket from her daughter's hand and closed the chain about Lily's neck. The gold-encased portrait came to rest on the green taffeta, nestled between her breasts.

"There. You can wear it near your heart."

The weight of the locket dragged against her neck. So heavy for something so small.

What had she done?

Lily was quiet as the carriage took them home through the streets of Mayfair. Her mother was vexed with her—that much was clear in the way her lips were tightly pinched together, the way she avoided looking at her daughter.

At last Lady Fernhaven turned stiffly. "You could have been more helpful, Lily. Really, one would almost think you did not want this match to succeed. Making a mention of your botanical work after I specifically warned you—and accusing the countess of an interest in horticulture! I nearly thought she would see us out then and there."

Lily stared straight ahead. The countess was going to have to make some adjustments to her way of thinking about lady painters. Lily had a mind to show her some of the sketches she had done illustrating the differences in root structure between hybrid and climbing roses. How refined would she consider roses once she had seen them with their earthy parts on display?

Her mother shook her head. "We were fortunate I was able to divert the conversation. It was a very narrow escape."

"You think she approved then—despite my painting?"

"She would have never given you the locket if she had deemed you unsuitable. Still, it is a good thing you will be going abroad with your uncle. There will be far fewer chances for you to make a misstep that could jeopardize our plans."

"Mother, I need to tell you—"

"And speaking of plans, here we are." Lady Fernhaven pulled back the curtain as the carriage slowed.

Lily looked out the window. They were in an area of fashionable shops—nowhere near the Fernhaven residence. "Where are we?"

"Why, at the modiste's, of course. We need to have the preliminary fittings for your wedding gown so they can begin on it while you are away."

"You have chosen my wedding gown? But there is not even a groom yet."

"Really, darling, one must be practical about these things. He will call on you, and he will offer. It has all been arranged. And of course I have not chosen your gown—I have merely made a few preliminary selections. Do not frown so, it is hardly becoming. I want Madame Voisseur to see what lovely features you have."

A few minutes later Lily, dressed in her shift—and her frown—stood before the modiste. The quick, beak-nosed woman fluttered around her like a bird.

"So petite, the waist," Madame Voisseur said as she drew the tape tightly around Lily. "You have a lovely figure—it will look well in the beautiful gown. Your husband will be most pleased to see you coming up the aisle—a vision of beauty. And your neck, so slender. Marchioness, your daughter will be a beautiful bride." She pulled the tape around Lily's breasts, pausing to glance at the gold locket. "Such a lovely trinket. Whose picture does it hold, I wonder?"

Lily held her breath, trying to keep her chest very still. Would this woman never be finished?

"It is a portrait of her betrothed," Lady Fernhaven said.

Lily exhaled in annoyance. "Mother. We are not betrothed."

"Of course, darling. Open it and show Madame Voisseur."

The modiste craned her neck as Lily sprang the catch. "Ah *oui*. Very lordly. And the eyes—so remarkable. What a lucky girl you are."

Lily snapped the portrait closed. "I beg your pardon, Madame, but I do not think I can continue much longer."

"Certainly, *ma petite*. We will just measure here, and lift your arms once more. *Bien*. That will do for now."

This was impossible. Not just the fitting—the entire production. Lily felt like a moth that had blundered into the middle of a spider's web, and her mother was blithely spinning more plans, more sticky strands. If she remained, soon she would not be able to breathe, or move, or think. Lily touched the locket, felt its cold through the thin fabric of her shift. Already the paralysis was setting in.

The sky lowered and it began to snow on the way home from the modiste. Lily looked out at the shivering gray buildings and leafless avenue trees and imagined Tunisia: Palms capturing the red glow of sunset. Citrus and pomegranates. Ancient Roman ruins to explore and sketch. And sunlight, warm, pure sunlight on her upturned face. She should not go to Tunisia. But she certainly *could* not remain here as her last days and hours of freedom trickled away. It was simply impossible.

What right did James Huntington have to waltz into her life and do this to her? Why did his needs outweigh hers in the matter? Hadn't her uncle begged her to reconsider the decision to stay behind? Uncle Edward needed her artistic skills for his work. And she needed to be there, with the family of her heart, if she was to have the strength to face her future.

As soon as they arrived back at the Fernhaven residence, Lily summoned Edwin. "Did the morning post go out?"

"Yes, Miss. And the afternoon post as well."

Oh no. Lily began pacing. If only they had not stopped at the modiste . . .

"Are you perturbed, Miss, or are you simply expressing your distaste for the new carpet by treading upon it?"

"I am perturbed. I need to send a letter to my uncle. It is most urgent."

"Then I will arrange for a courier to go tonight."

She spun to face him. "Could you?"

"I have a nephew. He is young, but quite reliable, and in possession of a very fast horse. Would that do?"

Bless him. Edwin was the best ally in the whole world. "Oh yes! Thank you so much."

He bent stiffly at the waist. "It is my pleasure, Miss Lily."

Lily stepped into the drawing room and found a fresh sheet of paper. She dipped the pen and wrote—

I have changed my mind. Look for me at the docks on Wednesday. And don't forget to pack the folding easel.
                                                                 —Lily

Chapter 11

"That's the last of the supplies, sir." Sir Edward's head gardener, Higgs, nodded toward the wooden crates being hoisted aboard the sailing steamer *Sidonia*.

Good man, thought James. Capable and reliable—just the kind he needed if he were going to haul the Strathmores and their towering piles of baggage to Tunisia and back. When he had left Brookdale with the wagon of supplies, Lady Mary had assured him they were prepared for any eventuality. Any eventuality, he thought, except one that would require them to travel quickly.

He reached into his pocket for a silver coin. "Good work Higgs. Why don't you take the lads over for some refreshment. It'll be the last pint you drink on English soil for some time."

"Thank you, sir. We'll drink to quick success and a speedy return."

"Just keep it to one round. I want you all ready to board the moment the Strathmores arrive." Which had better be soon—the *Sidonia* carried the British Mails through the Mediterranean and would not wait for tardy botanists.

"We'll be just across at the Tarry Mermaid there and we'll keep a watch out. You won't be leaving none of us behind, sir."

Higgs beckoned to the other servants. "Come on, lads. The work's done for a bit."

James watched them pick their way carefully through the dockside crowd toward the tavern. They looked out of place here—men with earth seamed into their hands and green stains at their cuffs. Some of them were already as far from home as they had ever been. How would they fare plucked up and transplanted to North Africa?

"Mackerel! Fine fresh mackerel!" A fishmonger stopped his pushcart beside James. "Fish, gov'nor? Any fresher and they'd jump right out of me barrow."

James eyed the catch. "None just now."

The monger shrugged and continued down the dock, leaving behind a stench of things too long from the sea. The odor slowly faded, blending with the smell of tar and brine and sweat.

The ship that would carry them to Tunisia was tethered to the dock with stout hemp ropes. Amidships a walkway with railings ramped up the side. Most of the passengers had already made their way aboard and were now strolling about on deck or waving and calling out to friends and loved ones who had come to see them off. Puffs of black smoke rose from the twin stacks and several sailors were aloft in the ship's rigging. James flipped open his pocket watch and frowned. What could be keeping the Strathmores?

A hansom cab pushed its way along the crowded quay, headed toward the *Sidonia*. It was slowed by the press, halting now for a tearful group of women embracing farewell, then again by two sailors arguing in the street. It was too small to contain the entire Strathmore family, but they could well be arriving in two vehicles.

The cab halted nearby and the footman swung down to open the door and set the steps. He moved to the back and busied himself unloading luggage—hatboxes, valises, a polished black steamer trunk. Yet no one emerged from the cab. Perhaps the ladies had arrived first and were waiting for an escort before stepping out into the crowd. James strode forward to offer assistance. Setting one foot on the bottom step, he leaned into the open doorway.

"Hello, James."

It was a man's voice, one all too familiar. James's first impulse was to leap back and slam the door. It was involuntary, like that of discovering a spider crawling on one's skin. He grabbed either side of the door, steadying himself.

"Reggie! What the devil are you doing here?"

Reginald Huntington took the cheroot from between his lips and blew out a cloud of smoke. "Enjoying my privacy—that is, until you appeared. Tell me, coz, do you greet every arrival this way? Say, I'll give you a shilling to carry my bags."

James ignored the insult—Reggie was so full of them that it was useless to call him on each slight. It was the fact he had arrived with luggage that concerned James most. It left him feeling as if ice were slowly melting in the pit of his stomach.

"I didn't know you frequented the docks," he said. "Seems a little seedy, even for you."

Reggie curled his lip. "It seems perfectly appropriate for you. I only wish you had the sense to realize it, instead of persisting with your sorry fortune hunting."

The words stung even though James had endured countless variations on the theme. *Getting above yourself, James? Why James, you look almost like a gentleman on that horse borrowed from my father's stables.* He could only imagine what Reggie would say if he learned about his attraction to Lily Strathmore—former attraction, that is. It was time to shift direction and find out what his cousin was really up to.

"So, you've come to see me off—how thoughtful."

"See you off?" Reggie said. "'Bon voyage, coz, good luck stealing my inheritance?' I think not. You need to be watched—tiresome business though it may be. As you insist on going to Tunisia, despite my offer of better accommodations elsewhere, you leave me no choice but to come with you."

"Steal your inheritance?" James took another step up, blocking the doorway with his shoulders. "I have no plan to cheat you out of anything, and more to the point, I have no desire to be your traveling companion. You're not welcome here, Reggie. Go home."

Reggie mashed out his cheroot out. "You're hardly one to say where I can or can't go. I'm no felon—haven't shot the son of anyone influential lately." He patted the breast pocket of his jacket. "I have a ticket here that says my passage is paid. If you find my company so distasteful, *you* stay behind."

If only it were an option. England itself seemed almost too small to contain the two of them. The last place he wanted to be was confined on ship with Reggie. "What do you hope to gain by this? You're Lord Denby's heir, for God's sake. Why the obsession with one property when the entire earldom will be yours? Your father needs you—at least he would if you started acting like the heir and not a spoiled schoolboy. Go be a son to him. There's nothing for you in Tunisia."

Reggie laughed. "On the contrary, James. There is something I most decidedly want. The pleasure of seeing you fail. What good is my inheritance to me? I can hardly even borrow against it. Somergate would bring a splendid price—*now,* not someday in the future when my father has the courtesy to die."

James reached and seized his cousin's shirtfront, hauling him forward until their faces were inches apart. "How can you speak like that? Your father is alive and cares for you. Have you any idea how precious that is?" He slammed Reggie hard against the seatback. "You are a pitiful creature. I wouldn't be you for all the wealth in England."

Reggie wrenched himself from James's grasp and swept up his silver-headed walking stick, raising it to strike. "I need no lecture from you, orphan. If you lay hands on me again, you will learn that I can still give as good as I get. Now stand aside before I lose my patience. I have a ship to board."

James remained unmoving in the doorway, breathing hard, his fists doubled. He looked at his cousin in his fine coat and cuffs, knuckles white around the handle of his walking stick. How he wanted to wrench that stick out of his hands. But Reggie would not back down. Cornered, he was like a dangerous animal, and there was nothing James could do to prevent him from sailing, short of knocking him unconscious and tying him up. Tempting as that sounded, there were limits. He could not humiliate his uncle yet again by leaving the man's heir beaten and trussed up at the docks.

Slowly, one step at a time, James forced himself to back away and out until he stood on the rough wood of the dock, arms crossed, still struggling with his own dangerous impulses. A moment later his cousin descended and straightened his coat. He held his walking stick under one arm, looking for all the world like a bored aristocrat. Only his eyes revealed his fury. When he looked at James they shone like two hard black stones.

"I'll see you aboard, coz."

James watched Reggie ascend the ramp and disappear onto the Sidonia. Of all the blasted luck. He had expected their troubles would begin when they reached Africa, but his cousin's presence changed everything. Why did Reggie have to be the worm in every apple?

"Huntington! Huntington!" James turned. Sir Edward was waving from the doorway of a large coach. The botanist grinned and bounded down the steps as soon as the coach stopped. "We had a bit of a breakdown on the way. I was afraid the ship would depart without us."

Now that Reggie was on board James almost wished it had, but it was too late to change plans now. "You're in time, but only just. We'll have to look lively."

Look lively—it was a command he had used frequently as an officer. But as he watched Lady Mary emerge from the coach and carefully descend the steps one thing was very clear—this was not the army.

"Good afternoon, James," she said, opening her lace-trimmed parasol. "What a glorious day to begin our voyage. I trust the sailors were careful with the crates and baggage when they stored them."

"Everything is stowed safely. Higgs was a great help, just as you anticipated."

Lady Mary nodded a gentle I-told-you-so to her husband,

who had wanted the head gardener to remain behind to care for the collection at Brookdale. "I knew he would prove valuable."

Even as she spoke, Higgs hurried up and set the servants to unloading the boxes and luggage strapped to the roof of the coach. James stared up at the mountain of luggage. No wonder they had suffered a breakdown.

The other Strathmores emerged from the coach. Richard's eyes lit when he spotted the *Sidonia*, and Isabelle, with her golden hair and fresh beauty, caused a temporary work-stoppage on the docks. Mrs. Hodges came last, armored in dun-colored cotton and wielding a thick, black parasol.

James felt a wave of affection for all of them. He had come to them a stranger, and they welcomed him, not as a guest, but almost as a member of their family. A pity they would now have to meet his real family—at least its most notorious member.

James greeted them and was about to turn away when another person stepped out of the coach.

Lily.

What the devil was she doing here? Up until this moment he had pictured her in London with her parents in some grand home—all marble and stained wood and age-darkened portraits of men in powdered wigs. He had imagined her there, believed it with such conviction that his mind had difficulty accepting the reality now standing before him.

The breeze teased a strand of chestnut hair from beneath her bonnet. Somehow the sun seemed warmer and the raucous bustle of the docks faded. James stepped forward and reached up to offer his hand, steadying her as she descended.

"Good day to you, Mr. Huntington."

"And you. Here to see your family off?"

"I beg your pardon?"

"You've come to see your uncle and family off—you returned home to London for the season."

"No. I changed my mind. I'm going to Tunisia."

"What?" He scowled. "That's impossible. Out of the question." She was Fernhaven's daughter. There were a hundred—a thousand—reasons why she should not be here, not the least being that every time they had been alone she had wound up in his arms.

"Mr. Huntington." She looked over to the others and lowered her voice. "Mr. Huntington, I don't see that you have any say in the matter. I am my uncle's illustrator. I have every right to go."

"No. I forbid it. It's far too dangerous. Pirates along the coast, savage tribesmen, rough conditions—I can't expect a lady of your station to endure such hardships."

"Really." She narrowed her eyes. "I don't see that my *station* has anything to do with it. Might I remind you that my cousin, aunt, and Mrs. Hodges are traveling? You seem to have no objection to any of them. As for hardship, I'm well aware that Aunt Mary has packed all the civilized comforts. I have been in the field with her before."

"This is different." Apart from the fact he had no desire to kiss the other women in the party, he simply could not allow Lily on that ship with Reggie aboard. It was madness. If his cousin sensed that James had any feelings for her he would show no pity—to either of them.

"I see no difference." Her voice rose. "As my uncle's illustrator, I am a very necessary part of the expedition. I might remind you that *we* Strathmores were already planning to travel before you ever came into the picture. You did agree that my uncle's family was to be part of the expedition. I believe I qualify. Now, if you will excuse me."

James caught her arm and swung her back to face him. "You cannot sail with us. You must return to your parents. I'll have Higgs escort you back to London where you belong."

"Where I belong?" Angry tears welled in her eyes. "How dare you dictate where I belong!"

Her look of accusation tore him. How could he explain the menace his cousin represented, or the way that even now he wanted to pull her into his embrace and kiss her? He didn't know where to begin, and it wasn't necessary. The only thing that was important was keeping her off the ship.

"Miss Strathmore. The matter is decided."

She tugged herself out of his grasp. "Well. I shall keep that firmly in mind." She spun on her heel. "Mrs. Hodges, I would like to view the ship now before we board. Please accompany me."

James took a step after her, but it was too late. She had taken Mrs. Hodges by the arm, placing the parasol-wielding matron between them.

"Stand aside, let us pass." Mrs. Hodges pressed through handkerchief-waving well-wishers with Lily in tow.

He raked his hand through his hair. There had been a time when people actually obeyed him. The *Sidonia's* whistle shrieked, the blast echoing off warehouses and taverns lining the quay.

"Best hurry, Huntington," Sir Edward called. "We wouldn't want to leave our leader behind."

James was the last passenger to board. As soon as he set foot on deck the ramp was pulled away, the ropes cast off, and the ship's whistle sounded a final blast. Standing at the rail beside Sir Edward, he watched the paddlewheel churn the murky water.

"Bit of a rocky start, eh, Huntington? But we're safely off and in pursuit of your grandfather's flower. Makes the blood race, it does. We're all grateful that you allowed us to come along on this adventure." Sir Edward looked further up where Isabelle, Mrs. Hodges and Lily were standing. "And don't worry about Lily—she's a sensible girl and as worthy a traveler as you might find. A bit spirited sometimes, but then that's not always a bad thing."

James nodded. How had he managed to get himself in this situation? Searching North Africa for a journal that probably no longer existed; dogged by a vengeful cousin; responsible for the well-being of a family from the English countryside that traveled with enough baggage to fill a train; and most maddening of all, his heart unsettled by an unpredictable, and seemingly uncontrollable, botanical painter with sea-green eyes.

It was beyond absurd.

Lily glared at the water widening between her and England. The gall of the man! As if one kiss—well, two—gave him the right to order her about like a recruit in his own private army. Go back to London where she belonged? She had been very wrong about him, or actually, quite right at first and then foolishly let her guard down. He hadn't seemed such a tyrant back at Brookdale.

She was absolutely finished with people trying to manage her life. A dozen cutting remarks flew through her head—all the things she should have said to him when he was manhandling her on the dock. She ought to march right over and tell him that he—and his overbearing commands—meant *nothing* to her. She whirled, only to find the place at the rail beside her uncle empty. The coward had probably made for his cabin. No matter—he would have to wait to feel her wrath. She would be ready when the time came.

"Lily." Isabelle was watching a sailor high in the rigging. "When do you think they will set the sails? The masts look so odd and bare. But we are off! Let's explore the ship." She linked her arm through her cousin's.

"Explore?" Mrs. Hodges asked, "How can you think of exploring with the deck shifting and rolling so? I am going below."

"Yes, let's go below," Isabelle said. "I'm perishing to see our stateroom. I have read that the accommodations are quite fine."

"It would be nice to get settled." Lily followed her cousin to the stairwell, the teak door held open with a brass hook, and descended to the dining saloon, a bright room finished with white enameled panels and ornamental gilt work.

"Oh, this is lovely," Isabelle said. "I wonder which table is the captain's?"

They passed between the long, gleaming tables and went

through a set of double doors to the ladies' cabin. Private staterooms reserved for the female passengers opened into this social space.

"My, it's just like a fancy parlor. And look, a piano—won't Richard be jealous." Isabelle bounced down on a curved velvet couch set under the aft portholes. "How comfortable."

Looking out, Lily noticed the shore was well on its way to becoming a smudge on the horizon. She took a deep breath. She was here, on her way to Africa. There would be no changing that now—not by her, not by her parents, and most especially not by the overbearing man who had commandeered the expedition. Could it be that just yesterday she had feared she was developing feelings for him? How laughable.

"You're looking fierce, Lily. Whatever are you thinking?"

"I'm thinking Mr. Huntington had better not try and tell me what to do in the future. It's none of his concern."

"Goodness. If you glare at him like that, I'm sure he'll keep his distance—assuming that is really what you want."

"Of course it is." The more distance, the better, for all concerned.

"Well, there's not much distance on this ship, but you can always take refuge here, or in our stateroom." Isabelle scanned the gleaming wood doors lining either side of the room. "Look, number eight. That's ours." She jumped up and went to the door, then stopped short at the threshold.

"Let me look, Isabelle. Are you going to go in, or do you plan to stand there all afternoon?"

Isabelle stepped into their stateroom. "It's just—it is very small, don't you think?"

Lily entered, her gaze taking in the beds built-in on either side of the door, the delicate washstand and mahogany wardrobe. "It's charming. And it's a ship, after all. You've been reading too much promotional literature." The sun slanted through their porthole, the light illuminating the inlay of exotic woods paneling the walls. She thought the room very cozy—a secret haven.

"Well, I prefer the ladies' cabin. There is more room to

move and more company." Isabelle stepped out. "Look, they're about to serve tea. Come on, Lily. Father says the P&O line employs excellent chefs."

The ladies' cabin was filling up as passengers descended from the decks, and swirls of conversation filled the air. Lily and Isabelle chose a small table directly under one of the skylights where sunlight from the stained-glass edges threw colorful patterns on the floor beside them. A steward brought them cups of tea, setting them down carefully along with a plate of delicacies. Lily noticed the small railings edging the table to keep items from sliding off during storms and hoped the voyage would not become so rough that they would be needed.

Isabelle took a bite of her tea cake. "Delicious. At least the food is as advertised."

"I wonder if everyone else has settled in."

"Perhaps they're taking tea in the dining saloon. Should we go and join them?"

"And abandon your perfect cake? Actually, I prefer it here. Would you like to play a game to pass the time?"

"I brought a deck of cards, and I'm sure other ladies will join us if we ask." Isabelle glanced about the room. "Everyone looks friendly enough. Whom shall we invite?"

Lily followed her cousin's gaze. "What about that raven-haired lady in the red dress? She doesn't appear to be with anyone."

"She will do nicely." Isabelle stood.

Lily watched her cousin introduce herself to the woman and then lead their guest over. Isabelle had the gift of seeing everyone as a potential friend. She could enter a room and twenty minutes later everyone there would feel as if they had known her for years. It was charming to watch her in action.

"This is my cousin, Miss Lily Strathmore. She is a wonderful artist. Lily, let me introduce the Baronessa Maria Bellini."

The Baronessa made a little curtsy and favored Lily with a warm smile. "I am pleased to make your acquaintance." Her velvety voice held a charming accent.

"Won't you join us?"

"Yes. I will be delighted." She took the chair across from Lily. "And where are you bound? I am home to Sicily, myself." The hint of a shadow crossed her face.

"To Tunis. My uncle has arranged a botanical expedition there."

"Yes," Isabelle said, "We're going to collect a flower discovered ages ago by Lord Twickenham—his grandson, James, is guiding us. He's very handsome, and rather smitten with Lily, I think."

"Isabelle! I hardly think the Baronessa cares to hear *all* the details—and you're mistaken about Mr. Huntington. Weren't we going to play cards?"

The Baronessa's dark eyes twinkled. "It sounds as though you will be having an exciting time in store, and I am not at all surprised that Miss Lily has an admirer."

The Baronessa proved to be a skilled player and lively conversationalist, amusing them with stories of her recent time in London and how baffling she had found many of the English customs.

"I am invited to breakfast, no? I think on this word—it means to break one's fast. So I do not eat a bite. I arrive, but there is no food, and the morning has passed! Finally, when it is two in the afternoon, we sit to eat. This is breakfast? It is everything I can do to take the tiny bites and make conversation about dogs." She laughed. "I now know to always eat before going to one of these London breakfasts."

"My father calls that a late breakfast," Isabelle said. "It makes sense if you eat dinner at midnight and stay up until dawn, but in the country we must go to bed early and have our breakfast at ten."

Despite the pleasant company, Lily's thoughts kept wandering. She drew the jack of hearts in two succeeding hands. The stubborn set of the figure's mouth, the dictatorial look in his eye—James had obviously not expected to see her at the docks and had clearly been unhappy about her arrival. She remembered his hold on her arm as he tried to keep her from boarding. Why the change in his manner? The last time they had stood so close his touch had set her afire. Had she been just a pastime? An amusement while he waited to leave for Tunisia? He hadn't seemed like a rake, but she imagined the most successful ones probably never did—until it was too late.

So she was an inconvenience to him now. Well, he would just have to become accustomed to her presence. She refused to fade quietly into the background so as not to embarrass him. This was her voyage as much as his. She fanned her cards.

When the light from the skylights began to fade, a white-capped maid entered the cabin and lit the oil lamps mounted on the paneled walls. Lily set her cards on the table. "I expect it is almost time to dress for dinner. Thank you, Baronessa, for the lovely company. Will we see you in the dining saloon?"

"Yes, I hope to dine with the captain tonight. Have you seen him? He is very handsome, no?" Her smile was mischievous. *"Ciao, bellas."*

Chapter 12

While trying to change and freshen up for dinner, Lily was forced to admit their cabin was a bit cramped—at least for two women wrestling with crinolines and skirts while the floor gently rolled beneath them.

"We should take it in turns, next time," she said.

"I agree." Isabelle looked at herself in the mirror and gave her blond curls one last fluff. "But at least we are ready—and don't we look fine? Here, Lily, let me fasten your pearls before we go."

The dining saloon was brightly lit and full of the sound of voices. They stood in the doorway a moment, until Lily spied the table in the corner where the family sat. James was there too, of course. There could be no avoiding him. Not unless she intended to lock herself in her cabin for the remainder of the voyage—something he was probably hoping she would do. Well, she would not give him the satisfaction. She set her shoulders, determined to appear cool and unconcerned.

"My dears," Uncle Edward said, rising. "All settled in?"

"Yes, father." Isabelle sank into the chair he held for her. "Though our stateroom *is* rather small."

James drew out a chair for Lily. She slid into her seat, avoiding his gaze. It was wicked, but just before he scooted her chair in she sat her full weight down and lifted her feet off the floor. It was an old trick she usually reserved for Richard, but in this case she would make an exception. Let him exercise his muscles instead of his mouth for a change.

Uncle Edward unfolded his napkin. "The cabins are luxurious compared to twenty years ago when I first traveled the Mediterranean. We went by sail then, completely at the mercy of the winds. The trip could take months, and you were stuffed into a closet tween decks with a grubby porthole if you were lucky. Now it's pure luxury—skylights, carved wood. Real beds."

"And there is all that open sky and wind out on deck," Richard added, his eyes alight.

"My grandfather's letters tell of taking passage on an Arab dhow. They slept—" James halted mid-sentence, his jaw tightening as an elegantly dressed black-haired gentleman approached the table.

Lily wondered what it was about the man that would cause James to forget his story—and his manners. The stranger seemed perfectly inoffensive and was actually quite handsome, except, perhaps, for the faint suggestion of a sneer when his eyes found James. But that curl of the lip, if there had indeed been one, was quickly replaced by a bright smile as he drew up in front of their table.

"Aren't you going to introduce me—coz?" the man said, when the silence became awkward.

James leaned back, his eyes narrowed. The entire family waited. Finally, as if some internal debate had been settled, he pushed back his chair and stood.

"Allow me to present my cousin, Lord Reginald Huntington," he said in a flat voice.

Lord Reginald inclined his head, teeth gleaming as James performed the introductions—Sir Edward, Lady Mary, Mrs. Hodges—who glowered, but when did she not?

"Richard Strathmore," James said. Lord Reginald leaned forward to shake Richard's hand. "And his cousin, Miss Lily Strathmore."

"Charmed, I'm sure." Lord Reginald bowed briefly over her hand then turned to Isabelle. "And who is this beauty?"

James gave his cousin a hard look. "Miss Isabelle Strathmore. She has not yet had her season."

"Pleased to meet all of you. What a surprise to find my cousin aboard, and I might add, in such delightful company."

Aunt Mary said, "This is most extraordinary. Won't you join us for dinner, Lord Huntington? You are a member of James's family, after all."

James smiled tightly.

Lily wondered if the rest of their party sensed the tension between the two men. Beside her, James held himself with a rigid formality. She felt a perverse satisfaction at his discomfort. Perhaps she would cultivate Lord Reginald's acquaintance on the voyage if James continued to behave like a petty tyrant. Although likely one Huntington was trouble enough.

Their guest seated himself with a languid grace between Isabelle and Mrs. Hodges. "I say, the ship seems adequate, don't you think—in a cramped sort of way. It will do until I reach Tunis. Such an exotic destination."

"What a coincidence," James said, folding his arms across his chest. "That is our destination as well."

"A remarkable coincidence, indeed, and what fine luck to find you all aboard. The journey will be far more agreeable for it, I am sure." Lord Reginald gazed at Isabelle as he spoke. She blushed and smiled.

"I expect we will not see much of you, Reggie." James turned to the others. "My cousin prefers to keep to himself."

"But perhaps I will have to make an exception—you can't keep this charming company all to yourself. Two weeks is such a long time to languish alone in my cabin."

"I'm sure you'll manage."

"What I'll miss most is my daily drives—and my new team. I've a lovely pair of matched bays I just bought at Tattersall's. And not to brag, but I am considered a fairly notable whip."

This information was guaranteed to catch both Richard and Isabelle's interest. They began to ply Lord Reginald with questions about his horses and the goings-on in London, and he answered them readily.

Lily shot James a sidelong glance only to find him studying her, his expression serious. How could he not have known that his cousin had booked passage to Tunisia on the same ship? It seemed very odd, particularly seeing the way James had reacted when his cousin had sauntered up.

He bent toward her and spoke quietly. "I am sorry for ruffling your feelings this afternoon. Despite the way it appeared, I am glad you are coming along."

"Whether you are glad or not makes no difference to me, Mr. Huntington. I'm here to assist my uncle and your approval is no concern of mine." Her words were steady, but the linen napkin in her lap was wound tightly around her fingers.

"I think my approval does matter."

Her breath caught. "I refuse to let you order me about like some kind of underling. You may be in charge of the expedition, but you are not in charge of me."

The amber lights in his eyes glinted, and he seemed about to say more, but checked himself. Lord Reginald was watching them from across the table. "We can finish this conversation later."

"Well, I am finished with it now." She turned away and looked across the room. There was the baronessa, dressed in a bright turquoise gown, at the captain's table. At least she seemed to be enjoying herself—she caught Lily's eye and smiled. Lily tried to return the smile. Why was she so affected by the man seated beside her? Even now a part of her wanted to believe his words—but how could she when his actions earlier so clearly spoke otherwise.

"Ladies and gentlemen, dinner is served," the steward announced from the head of the room. White-coated waiters began to circulate, carrying silver trays piled high with oysters, poached fish, and pastries baked in the shape of seashells. Soon the table was covered with delicacies. Lily welcomed the distraction.

Across the table, Lord Reginald was sampling the fish. "Miss Isabelle, the halibut is divine—you must try some." He beckoned to the server. "And the sauce is just there. Madam, if you would be so kind?" He turned to Mrs. Hodges who passed the dish, frowning.

"Lord Reginald, I've met another couple also bound for Tunis," Uncle Edward said, indicating a thin man and serious-looking woman at the next table. "Doctor Fenton and his wife."

Aunt Mary nodded. "Yes, Mrs. Alice Fenton. We met in the ladies cabin. She told me they are traveling for the London Methodist Missionary Society. They hope to start a clinic in Tunis. Do you know them?"

"I'm *sure* I don't know anyone traveling for the London Methodist Missionary Society," Lord Reginald said.

"Lily and I spent the afternoon with Baronessa Bellini," Isabelle said. "There she is, at the captain's table. She is very charming."

"Baronessa Bellini?" Lord Reginald raised one thin eyebrow. "Now that is a name I have heard. I'm not surprised that she is leaving England after all the goings-on in London."

"Do tell." Isabelle leaned forward.

"Well," he said, giving the others a quick glance before continuing, "It seems Lord Severn—the Duke of Hamblin's brother—met her while traveling abroad and became completely smitten. He invited her to visit—and stay with his mother and sisters, naturally. Apparently he even broached the subject of marriage."

"Marriage to the baronessa? What happened?"

"A scandal, of course. Lord Severn is quite a catch, I'm told, and the English mamas with ambitions for their daughters were outraged by the imported competition." Lord Reginald leaned back, clearly aware he had captured everyone's attention. "The ladies of the *ton* went out of their way to make her feel unwelcome. Of course, that didn't stop them from rushing to copy her style of dress."

"She does have a splendid sense of fashion," Isabelle said.

"The poor dear." Aunt Mary said. "We must make sure she realizes the English are not all like those ladies she encountered."

Lily was not sure who she felt more sympathy for, the baronessa, or the daughters those London mamas would now offer up like bon-bons to the poor heart-broken Lord Severn. Thank heavens she would not be one of them.

"The baronessa is wise to leave London," Lord Reginald said looking at James. "She is not one of us. One should always know one's place."

"But that's hardly romantic," Isabelle said. "I had thought better of you, Lord Reginald. Some people believe that true love admits no obstacle."

James set his glass down. "My cousin has never been known for his romantic sensibilities."

Lord Reginald shot James a dark look, then returned his attention to Isabelle. "It wounds me to disappoint you—I only meant to say that sometimes a love that is impossible is the truest love. The baronessa, by recognizing her place and retiring the field, has given Lord Severn the greatest gift that love can offer."

"Oh yes, I do take your meaning," Isabelle said.

"Then allow me to make amends by offering you some of this heavenly lobster salad."

She laughed. "You may, sir."

Reginald turned to Mrs. Hodges, "If you would be so kind? It seems the lobster salad has fetched up on your shoals."

Mrs. Hodges passed the platter, her scowl deepening as Lord Reginald spooned a portion onto Isabelle's plate.

"Tell me, Miss Isabelle, have you read Thackeray's accounts of his journey around the Mediterranean?"

"Oh, yes, I adore Thackeray! I intend to keep a journal of my own while we travel."

Lily watched her cousin bask in the attentions of the darkly handsome Lord Reginald. He seemed perfectly agreeable, and yet . . . perhaps it was only the way James reacted to him, but seeing how he drew Isabelle's giggles and blushes made her wonder if he were the right sort of company for her cousin to be keeping. Aunt Mary, too, seemed aware of how raptly her daughter hung on his words. She sent Lily a look that implied they would discuss Lord Reginald Huntington later.

"I can hardly wait to be in London," Isabelle said. "Nothing of any interest ever happens in the country. We miss all the truly entertaining events."

"Then perhaps you did not hear that the Duke of Hereford's son was shot in a duel—reputedly in a place unmentionable in mixed company. It has been the buzz of London for weeks."

"Really? Who shot him?" Richard asked.

Lord Reginald arched his eyebrows. "I haven't the faintest idea. Perhaps my cousin would know. He was in town at the time."

The expression on James's face did not change, but Lily noticed that his hands had curled into fists.

Richard turned to James. "Who was it?"

"I don't pay much attention to the London gossips, but I believe it was a gentleman who took insult when young Hereford slandered the reputation of the man's sister. Not wise to provoke someone like that. Don't you agree, Reggie?"

Lord Reginald shrugged. "I would go as far as to say that it was unwise in Hereford's case. Miss Isabelle, would you care to sample the relish?"

"Yes please." Isabelle beamed at him.

"Mrs. Hodges . . ."

The matron's stout hand closed on the cut crystal bowl brimming with plum relish. She lifted it from the table and turned towards Lord Reginald. For just an instant the dish balanced on her fingers, then it toppled, nicking the edge of the table and spilling a cascade of burgundy into Lord Reginald's lap.

"Blast you, you clumsy woman!" He jumped to his feet, knocking over the chair. Conversation at the tables around them stilled as he brushed frantically at his trousers with his handkerchief.

"Slipped right out of my fingers," Mrs. Hodges said. "Dreadful mess."

"You are extremely correct, madam. A most dreadful, clumsy, stupid mess." He turned to the others. "You will excuse me. Goodnight."

"Perhaps we shall see you later, Lord Huntington," Lady Mary said.

And perhaps not, Lily thought, observing the thin smile that brushed James's lips as his cousin stalked from the room.

When the commotion died down, Uncle Edward turned to James. "You are not pleased to see your cousin aboard?"

"No. His presence is . . . unexpected. We are not close."

"I see how it stands between the two of you. And it was quite rude for him to bring up that shooting . . . er, well . . . at least you won't be holding the fact that Mrs. Hodges bathed the chap in plum relish against us."

"It wasn't right, him paying such attentions to Miss Isabelle," Mrs. Hodges said. "The way he kept *feeding* her—and her not even out yet. We're well rid of the scoundrel."

Isabelle thrust her chin out. "Lord Reginald was behaving with the utmost of good manners. You are all mistaken if you think him less than a gentleman. Besides, we can hardly avoid him—we are on a ship, after all."

"We will be polite to him, of course," Aunt Mary said. "But Isabelle, I am not certain he is the best company for you."

"My cousin, though superficially charming, is one better left alone," James agreed.

Isabelle dropped her gaze to her plate and pushed a forkful of fish about. "I understand."

Understand? Lily found it doubtful. It was quite unlike her cousin to give in so easily. She hoped Isabelle would show some good sense concerning Lord Reginald. Why was he traveling to Tunisia anyway?

After dinner the passengers went on deck to take the air. The faintest blue glow lingered in the west, the brightest stars newly visible, and on the dark coast a few scattered lights burned. Sails had been run up to catch the favorable breeze—they bellied in the light wind.

Lily walked apart and leaned against the railing, watching the last light leave the sky. She felt strangely suspended between worlds, struggling to find her equilibrium. James was no help—he was a large part of the problem. And her family—how could she confide in them? It was all so complicated. She longed for the time when her greatest trouble had been correctly rendering the sepals of *Rosa floribunda.*

As if her thoughts had summoned him, James appeared beside her. "I would like a private word with you, Lily."

He was standing uncomfortably close. The light from the ship's lamps brought out the planes of his face. She knew those features so well, after painting them, after . . . The heat rose in her cheeks and she hoped the light was too dim for him to make out her blush.

"If it concerns our time at Brookdale, I assure you I regret those indiscretions as much as you do. But like it or not, we are on board this ship together. We will simply have to put them behind us."

He was silent a moment, looking out over the dark ocean. "I see. Thank you for making it clear where you stand." He turned to her. "But that is not the reason I wish to speak to you."

Not what he wished to discuss? Lily frowned. Why didn't the man speak plainly?

James glanced about and lowered his voice. "It's Reggie. He is not—how shall I say it—the most honorable of fellows. To put it bluntly, my cousin has a certain reputation with young women. You must—"

"—not speak to him? Avoid him altogether? Confine myself to my cabin?" She turned to face him squarely. "Why? Does he insinuate himself into their family, kiss them on terraces and in conservatories, and then order them back home to London when they become inconvenient?"

She whirled to leave, but he was surprisingly quick. He grasped the railing, his arm barring her way. His body blocked the wind, and he was so close she could feel the heat of him.

"You misunderstand me. It's Isabelle that I'm concerned about. She is young and not prepared to deal with the likes of my cousin. You are older, and if any woman can put Reggie in his place, it would be you."

Older? He considered her older? Lily drew herself up, the top of her head at a level with his chin. Why was this man so blasted tall? "Thank you for the warning, Mr. Huntington. As her *older* cousin I will be on my guard. Now, if you will excuse me, I have had a dreadful day."

She pushed past, and he did not try to stop her.

A storm had come upon them late the first night, with winds that sang through the rigging and great foam-flecked waves that surged along the side of the ship and sent up jets of spray at the bow. Even now, three days later, the wind still blew in gusts, but the sun was warm on Lily's face and the waves had subsided. She sat near the aft railing, her sketch-book propped on her lap, making quick studies of the seagulls that followed the ship. They seemed so sure of themselves, soaring effortlessly, their calls harsh and exciting. Behind them the distant coast of Portugal was a dark line where the sea met the sky.

One old veteran of a bird landed on deck to beg for a hand-out. "You must be the one Richard was talking about at lunch-eon. Did you approve of the sardine he stole for you?"

Her cousin had been one of the few passengers unaffected by the tossing of the ship—one of the lucky few who could face a sardine with a smile. James had been another, she had glimpsed him in a greatcoat exiting the saloon on two occasions.

She herself had not felt particularly ill, but Mrs. Hodges and Aunt Mary had both succumbed, and Isabelle was still not her usual self. Lily ought to go check on her soon.

The bird tilted its head to look at her.

"Sorry, I've no food for you old fellow."

"But I do." The baronessa was approaching with a bit of cracker in her hand. She tossed it to the gull, who took it and scuttled a few feet away to enjoy his feast.

"Hello, Miss Lily. You are drawing Richard's friend, yes? May I see?"

"Certainly." Lily handed her the sketchbook. She remembered that once she had felt shy about showing her work to others. Now it seemed natural. It was what it was—like a heartbeat, it needed no excuse or apology even when the work was rough.

"How lovely your drawing is. Just a line or two from your pencil and a wing appears, a beak, an eye. It is a magic, I think. I wish I could do this. Then I would never forget the beautiful things."

Lily smiled. To never forget the beautiful things. That was what she wanted, too.

"I saw you also sketching the captain. He is an excellent subject, no? Despite that he is happily married."

They both laughed. The baronessa exaggerated her attraction to the captain, who seemed a decent, though unremarkable, fellow. She turned the pages of Lily's book and paused at a sketch of James sitting next to Uncle Edward. She tilted her head, dark eyes twinkling. "But the captain is not the only excellent subject aboard, I see. Mr. Huntington, he watches you with such eyes when he thinks you are not looking—and now I see you are watching him too."

Lily held her hand out for the sketchbook. "I hear we will be stopping in Spain, at Cadiz. Won't you be glad to take an afternoon off the ship? I certainly will."

The baronessa made a humming sound and did not answer immediately. Lily watched the seagull sidle closer, hoping for another tidbit. She would not talk about James. She could not.

"Yes, Miss Lily, to feel the solid land, especially after these last days when we could not come out on deck. I am grown weary of books and cards. They say the cathedral is very fine, and one supposes many handsome Spanish men will be lounging on the piazza smoking their cigars."

Lily smiled—she could not help it. "You and your handsome men! Think of the broken hearts you leave behind."

The baronessa's smile faltered. "I do. I think of it every day."

"I am so sorry. I did not mean—"

"I know, *bella*. You have a good heart—one that you should learn to trust. As for my heart," she shrugged, "It will mend. One day. But I am keeping you from your sketching."

"Not at all. It's high time I put it away. I promised Isabelle I would look in on her—she is still not feeling well and is resting in our stateroom."

"I think she must be recovered, for I saw her strolling at the front of the boat just a moment ago."

"Alone?" Lily reached for her satchel and pushed her pencils and sketchbook into it.

"No, not alone. She and Lord Huntington were conversing with the Fentons."

"Then you must excuse me, Baronessa."

"Of course. It was lovely to speak with you."

The seagull squawked and took wing as Lily rushed past. Her cousin's quick recovery was suspicious, especially if she was now passing time with Lord Reginald. Bother him. Aunt Mary had decided they all needed to keep a close eye on Isabelle where he was concerned—a task that had fallen solely to Lily the past few days, but it had not been difficult, until now. She recalled James's words, *has a certain reputation with young women*, and sped her steps. She would not let that happen to her cousin.

There Isabelle was, standing at the bow, her golden curls tumbled by the wind. She was smiling up at Lord Reginald, who was standing much too close.

"Isabelle!" Lily called. The girl made no response.

"Isabelle," she said again, coming up. "There you are. Good day, Lord Huntington. My cousin has been ill and should not be out on deck."

"I thought some air would help clear my head, and Lord Reginald kindly—"

"Yes, well, he will kindly excuse you now. We had better get you back inside. I suspect Aunt Mary is wondering how you are faring."

At the mention of her mother, Isabelle's stubborn expression faded. She looked at Lord Reginald. "I'm afraid I should go. It has been delightful."

He bowed. "The pleasure has been entirely mine."

Indeed. Lily took a firmer grip on her cousin's arm and

hastened her away. When they were some distance down the deck Isabelle pulled free. "What has come over you, Lily?"

"I was going to ask you the same. I thought you were indisposed."

"I felt better. And bored. You know that—"

"Listen to me. Lord Reginald is not proper company for you. There are certain types of gentlemen who do not have your best interest at heart. I fear Lord Reginald is one of them. Promise me you will not spend any more time in his company."

Isabelle made no response, only hurried ahead to the stairwell. Lily followed and pulled the door firmly shut behind them.

Chapter 13

Cadiz, Spain, March 1847

From her seat in the ship's boat, Lily could smell citrus blossoms and dust in the offshore breeze. The sailors plunged their oars into the sea, pulling briskly toward shore, and a drop of spray wetted her cheek, sudden coolness against her sun-warmed skin. Hills covered in olive and lemon groves held the town with its tall white cathedral in their embrace. Lily gripped her sketchbook. The distant sound of a bell echoed across the water.

"Picturesque, isn't it?" James had claimed the seat beside her for the ride across the bay. The sea wind ruffled his hair and he looked relaxed, free of the tension he had carried since the voyage began. He grinned at her. It made him look charmingly boyish.

"Yes," Lily said. "And after a week aboard, I'm more than ready for some time ashore, if only for a few hours." His mood today caught her off guard. Like the weather, it had brightened.

Not that she had been much in his company. Lily's eyes went to the lead boat where Lord Reginald's darkly elegant form was visible seated beside the baronessa. At least he was in the other boat. She suspected James's presence had much to do with that, and she was thankful. They were allies in this, at least.

Isabelle must be protected from Lord Reginald. She was too inexperienced to recognize her danger. She could not be allowed to make the same mistake Lily had. She must not.

But Lily knew Isabelle would not respond to ultimatums, so she had made a bargain with her cousin. She would not tell Aunt Mary about finding Isabelle in Lord Reginald's company, if Isabelle promised not to seek him out. Her cousin had grudgingly agreed, although it did not seem to stop her from focusing her attention on him. Lily noticed that Isabelle had barely taken her eyes off him since the boats had set out. Lily hoped Mrs. Hodges would recover from her seasickness soon. She did not relish playing governess for her cousin, particularly under these circumstances.

"Doesn't Lieutenant Mundy look as stuffed as his mailbag?" Richard asked, his eyes also on the boat ahead. A sailor behind Lily guffawed.

Mundy, the officer charged with delivering the Royal Mails, sat in the lead boat with his locked leather mailbag. He looked stiff and well-polished in his dress uniform. The brass buttons on his coat shone like miniature suns.

"Oh no, he is quite fine," Isabelle said. Lily wondered just who she was referring to.

The boats crossed the bay, heading for a broad expanse of beach where a knot of barelegged men waited at the waterline.

"Almost there," James said. "The *gallegos* will haul the boats onto shore."

The lead boat was run up on the sand. Timing his exit to avoid wetting his shoes, Lord Reginald jumped down and hurried up the beach to well above the tide line, leaving the others in his boat behind. He bent and whisked the sand from his trousers.

Their boat followed, heaving through the breakers. The unexpected movement shifted her against James—she felt the long length of his leg pressing against her skirts. He offered a steadying arm, and after fighting for a moment to keep her balance she took it. He was solid and warm under her hand, and though she knew better, she could not help feeling that she was protected in his company. She did not let go until the *gallegos* waded into the surf and hauled the boat to shore, then she edged away, smoothing her skirts.

Richard was first out. "How strange to be on land again. The entire shore seems to be rocking."

"I hope I shan't appear too clumsy." Isabelle resettled her bonnet over her blonde curls.

"I don't think you clumsy in the least, Isabelle." James leapt easily from the boat and offered his hand. Lily tried not to notice his agility, the lean strength of his body. This was not a man who had confined himself to billiards and ballrooms.

"May I assist you, Lily?" he asked, returning to the boat.

She looked at him, his easy grin, the amber lights glinting in his brown eyes. Where was the overbearing, dictatorial man that had so angered her? She felt for the resentment that had been her shield, but could not find it. The warm air, the fragrance of flowers—Spain was working some odd alchemy in her. Perhaps it wouldn't hurt to forgive. At least for today.

When she clasped his outstretched hand, the look in his eyes deepened. His grip was strong, steadying her as she rose and stepped from the boat. They stood together on the damp sand, her hand in his. The breeze blew a lock of his hair down over his forehead.

"Lily! James! Watch out," shouted Uncle Edward from the safety of the dry sand.

A wave frothed whitely up the beach toward them. James reacted instantly. Scooping her up into his arms, he sprinted ahead of the water.

"Oh," she gasped, clasping his shoulders. He held her firmly against him, his strong arms supporting her. Their faces were close, her lips almost brushing the line of his jaw. He smelled of sun and wind and salt. Her heart pounded in time to his steps as he carried her effortlessly up the shore and set her back on her feet.

"Forgive me," he said. "I did not mean to take liberties."

"There is no need." She found her balance. "It was a narrow escape. It would have been terribly uncomfortable to take in the sights in soggy boots."

"Most assuredly."

"And to promenade up the dusty streets with wet skirts . . ."

"Unthinkable."

"Then there was really nothing else to be done."

"Nothing at all." James offered his arm. "Since we have both escaped unscathed, may I escort you into Cadiz?"

Lily could hardly say she was unscathed. Oh, not touched by the water, but a wave of awareness had surely flooded her. It was hard to tell if he were similarly affected, but there was something in his eyes, in the curve of his lips that made her think he was. Her pulse jumped as she slipped her hand through the crook of his arm.

They strolled up the sand with the others, past the brightly colored fishing boats, to where the main street descended to the water. Uncle Edward stopped beside a flowering bush and was holding a branch up for inspection.

"Your uncle is glad to be ashore, I see. Not much scope for botanizing ship-board."

Lily laughed. "You might be surprised. He has directed the sailors to bring him any plant material they find floating on the waves, and I believe he has examined several different types of seaweed so far. Of course now that we're on land, I expect we will have to pull him away from every shrub and flower."

"Hardly a change there," Richard said, coming up beside them. "I wonder whether we can taste Spanish chocolate here. It is supposed to be a marvelous beverage."

"Donde esta chocolate?" said Uncle Edward, setting aside his branch. "We'll ask the first likely vendor."

"Is your uncle fluent in Spanish?" James asked.

"I think his vocabulary is limited to things that can be eaten."

They laughed together, and then he sobered. "I was concerned for you when the storm struck. I hope you were not ill."

"No, thank goodness. Not like so many others, although I admit to existing on tea and crackers."

"I saw you sketching occasionally."

"Did you? Well, it would take more than a few waves to keep me from that, and it did take my mind from the rocking of the ship. How did you . . ." Her words faltered as she felt him go rigid. His eyes were eyes fixed ahead of them.

Lily glanced up to see Isabelle walking with Lord Reginald, her arm entwined with his. The two were far enough ahead of the rest of the group to converse without being overheard, and Lord Reginald was speaking earnestly. Isabelle shot a quick glance back over her shoulder at the following group.

"Oh heavens. I've told Isabelle to stay clear of that man. She is acting so foolishly."

"We need to separate them." James had quickened his pace.

"Absolutely." They were in perfect accord about this, at least. "When the opportunity arises, I will attach myself to your cousin for the remainder of the afternoon. You can occupy Isabelle."

James scowled. "I will not have you . . ." he stopped himself. "Rather, I would prefer it if you did not keep company with my cousin. I will deal with Reggie myself."

"And how long until the two of you came to blows? I don't know what is between you, but it won't do to be scuffling in the streets."

He did not speak for a long moment. "It is true that Reggie is provoking, but I don't like the idea of you strolling about on his arm."

"Better me than Isabelle. At least I will not be blinded by his flatteries. You said yourself that if any woman was a match for him, I was."

"Just keep close to the others."

It was a command, but at least it was a sensible one. Lily decided not to protest. He was, at least, making *some* progress.

Ahead, Isabelle and Lord Reginald had reached the market, a square surrounded by tall white houses draped in scarlet bougainvillea. Women in black *mantillas* hurried past carrying their baskets. Vendors lounged behind piles of oranges and lemons and the briny scent of fish filled the air.

James leaned in and said softly, "We'll keep close and watch for our chance."

Lily nodded. Isabelle and her escort paused here and there, but she clung tightly to his arm, and they did not linger in any one place. At last Isabelle stopped at a table shining with glass beaded necklaces. She reached out to them, laughing as Lord Reginald took up brilliant blue and bright green strands. He dangled them in either hand, making them dance and sparkle in the sunshine.

"How pretty," Lily said, releasing James's arm. She stepped up to the table and ran her fingers over the display.

"Oh, yes," Isabelle beamed. "Lord Reginald says they sparkle like my eyes."

"But mere stone and glass could never capture the vibrancy I see. They are but a shallow approximation." Lord Reginald flashed his toothy smile.

"You are turning my cousin's head most dreadfully, Lord Reginald."

"I speak only the truth." He lifted a thin eyebrow. "Wouldn't you agree, James?"

"I agree that you are keeping her beauty too much to yourself. Isabelle, do walk with me. We wouldn't want Reggie to become too dazzled. Perhaps you would enjoy a glass of the fabled Spanish chocolate. The guide books recommend it highly."

Isabelle's eyes widened and she took a step away from James. "Oh no. It wouldn't do to leave the marketplace and the other passengers."

"Isabelle," Lily said, "He is not going to abscond with you. The café is just there. See? Richard and the baronessa are sitting on the patio. You can go and join them."

"I would hate to deprive Lord Reginald—"

Lily threaded her arm through Lord Reginald's. "I will accompany him. Go enjoy your chocolate."

"Very well." Isabelle turned to him. "I hope I will see you soon, my lord."

"As do I. Before you go, won't you take this trifle to remember Spain by?" He held out the blue necklace.

"Thank you, my lord." Isabelle took the necklace and curtsied. Then she turned, and without taking James's offered arm, set off across the plaza towards the café.

"I seem to have been outmaneuvered," said Lord Reginald

as he watched Isabelle go, James close behind her. "Would you care to see the sights with me, Miss Lily?"

"Very much so."

The travelers from the ship sampled chocolate and purchased curios, but soon they were making their way in ragged groups through the narrow streets toward the cathedral. As they walked, Lily could not help noting the family resemblance between Reginald and James—the clean-lined jaw, the expressive mouth. Lord Reginald's nose was thinner, his brows darker and more finely arched but it was obvious they shared a common ancestor. He was quite handsome—not nearly so much as James—but Lily could understand Isabelle's infatuation.

He noticed her gaze and offered a sly smile. "You find my face agreeable, I hope."

"I would find it more so if you did not flatter Isabelle so outrageously. She's very young."

"And thus easily taken in by unscrupulous gentlemen?" His dark eyes focused sharply on her. "I understand your concern—do you know why my cousin is traveling to Tunisia?"

"To locate a flower first discovered by his grandfather. He has sought my uncle's help in the matter."

"My grandfather as well." Reginald's lips thinned. "Then I see James has not confided his true purpose."

"And what other purpose might there be? Really, you make it sound so ominous. I assure you my uncle would never aid James if there were anything dishonorable about his motives." She looked him directly in the eye. "The only thing that strikes me as odd is your presence on the *Sidonia*. I don't believe chance brought you aboard. Why are you here?"

He laughed. "Ah, I see you are as clever as you are handsome, Miss Lily. But I think you may be too trusting. My cousin is no plant fancier. Are you certain he has not mentioned anything else?"

"I am certain you did not answer my question." Heavens, it was difficult to get an answer from this man. There was something very slippery about him. He was too glib and impossible to pin down.

"Did I not? My apologies. But we must hurry to catch up with your family—they have already entered the cathedral."

The white towers rose above them. They climbed the worn stone steps and Lily paused at the top to admire the view, wishing she had time to paint it—the houses with their brilliant flowers clustered above the half-moon of sand, the bay gleaming perfect cobalt.

"Are you coming?" Lord Reginald held open the small door that was set inside the tall, arched doors of the entry.

The air inside the church was cool and dim. Rows of candles glimmered before figures of saints, sunlight filtered through the stained glass in the nave to pool in multicolored patterns on the floor and walls.

Lily stepped up beside Lord Reginald and lowered her voice. "You were going to tell me the purpose of your journey to Tunisia."

"Certainly." He leaned toward her. "But you were telling me about this mysterious flower your expedition is pursuing. How did my cousin come to learn of it? Has he shown you the letters?"

"Really, Lord Reginald, you should ask him about it yourself."

He sighed. "James has always been so secretive and scheming, saying one thing while planning something else. I have tried to help him—the whole family has—but to what end? You have no doubt observed how little love my cousin has for me. That is how he repays kindness."

The doors opened behind them, silhouetting James and Isabelle. They halted nearby, both looking at Lord Reginald, but where Isabelle's face was soft, James's seemed carved of stone.

Lord Reginald shifted. "This hushed atmosphere is becoming rather oppressive. I shall wait outside until the others have finished gawking. Would you care to accompany me?"

"Thank you, but no. I will rejoin the others." She motioned to the front of the cathedral where her uncle and Richard, along with the Fentons, were admiring the carved and gilded altar screen.

"Good day, then. But beware of my cousin. He is not as he appears." Lord Reginald retreated, giving his cousin a wide berth. Well, she had kept him from Isabelle at least, even though the blasted man refused to answer any of her questions. He was too clever by half.

Lord Reginald was silhouetted for an instant as he pulled the door open, slipped through, and was gone.

"Come see," Uncle Edward whispered loudly. "We've found someone with the keys to the bell tower!"

The stairs spiraled up tightly, and soon Lily stopped trying to count the turns. Here and there the curved stone wall was pierced with a narrow opening to light the stairwell. Through them she could see the red curved tiles on the roofs of the nearby buildings. When at last the stairs opened onto the flat roof, the brilliance of the light was almost too much. Lily blinked and shaded her eyes, gazing south across the water.

"The coast of Morocco," James said at her shoulder.

Africa! She laughed for the pure joy of the moment and spread her arms to the sun and air, nearly certain she could take flight.

"You have a delightful laugh."

"Flatterer." She wrinkled her nose at him.

"Certainly not." They walked forward and leaned over the low wall. "Is that Reggie down there?"

"Why? Shall we drop something on his head?"

"Tempting. I don't suppose you have a large pot of geraniums with you."

Lily laughed again, shaking her head. She enjoyed this side of James. Far too much. "No. No geraniums, and no paints. How I wish I had my paints."

"I wish you did too. I would like to remember this."

"Yes," she said, knowing she would.

When they exited the cathedral, Lily linked her arm through Isabelle's. She did not see Lord Reginald lurking, but she was not about to leave anything to chance where he was concerned—there were too many winding streets and empty courtyards.

"Look here!" Uncle Edward plucked a stray bit of greenery from beside the street. "This appears to be a grass, but it is actually more of a sedge!" He held out his find for inspection, pointing out the differences to Dr. Fenton and Richard.

James, standing with them, met Lily's gaze. He raised one brow, the faintest question in his face, and she nodded. Isabelle was under her protection.

"Come on, Lily." Her cousin drew her forward. "It's too hot to stand out here. Let's wait for the others down by the water."

"A fine idea. Did you enjoy your Spanish chocolate?"

"It was lovely," Isabelle said flatly. They turned a corner and her cousin glanced behind her, then tightened her grip on Lily's arm. "I must speak with you."

"What is wrong?"

"I fear we have fallen in with the worst sort of man."

Anger flared through Lily. She pulled her cousin to a halt. "That scoundrel! What has he done?"

Isabelle stared at her. "He is not what he appears . . . and he is traveling to Tunisia for a terrible purpose."

"He told you this?"

Isabelle nodded. "His family made him leave England."

"Lord Reginald?"

"Not Reginald! He's here to help. It's *James*."

"James? No." Lily shook her head. "I am sure you misunderstood. Lord Reginald is the dubious one."

"No, it's James. Reginald told me all about him."

"And are you certain he is telling the truth?"

Isabelle set her jaw. "Reginald is a lord, Lily, and a gentleman. I believe him."

"Being a lord does not make him honest. There are lords who are the worst scoundrels you will ever meet. Tell me what he said."

"He told me James was banished from the country because he wounded the Duke of Hereford's son in a duel over a woman. And it isn't the first time. He had to leave England seven years ago, too." Isabelle swallowed. "James stole papers from his family just last month. He is using father and all of us to achieve his own ends. He's a dreadful villain. Whatever shall we do?"

Lily looked her cousin in the eye. "I am certain there is a good explanation for all this. Lord Reginald must have put things in the worse possible light. James has given us no reason to doubt him." Even as she spoke she recalled his stolen kisses, the feel of his lips on hers, and the forbidding look on his face when he tried to keep her from the ship. A seed of apprehension took root inside her.

Isabelle narrowed her eyes. "I know you fancy James. It has clouded your vision. Can't you see we are in danger?"

"The danger is coming from other quarters, Isabelle. Lord Reginald's attentions to you—"

"You're just jealous!" Isabelle's voice rose. "Because he is handsome and cultured and paying court to me instead of you." She pulled away. "Can't you understand that Reginald is here to protect us?"

"It can't be true." Could it? Did she see clearly where James was concerned?

"I'm going to denounce James tonight at dinner. Father and mother will know what to do." Her cousin began to stalk away, back held rigidly straight.

"Isabelle, wait!" Lily hurried after her. "Don't do anything foolish. You have no proof. Let me speak to James."

"As if he would tell you the truth."

"I promise I'll get to the bottom of this. We'll discover the true villain and expose him. But don't be hasty. Wait until we have proof—something to substantiate the accusations." She had to see the sense of it.

Isabelle chewed her lip. "All right. But we must do something before we reach Tunis—before it is too late."

Drat those Huntingtons—both of them! Lily's intuition told her James was not a rogue, but what if he was? And what if Lord Reginald were lying? Then he was every bit as bad as James had said, and her cousin—indeed the whole expedition—might be in jeopardy.

Lily held out her hand. "Come Isabelle, we must get back to the ship."

Chapter 14

Lily fastened her earring then brushed at a wayward strand of hair. She could delay no longer. They would arrive in Tunisia tomorrow, and she still had not confronted James with Lord Reginald's accusations. She reached for the other earring and turned her head in the mirror. But one couldn't just sit down to dinner and ask, "So Mr. Huntington, you haven't shot anyone lately, have you?" It just wasn't done. Why were the most vital questions always the most difficult to ask?

"Lily, are you finished yet?" It was Isabelle, knocking on the door of their stateroom. "The musicale is starting soon and Richard will never forgive us if we miss his performance. Let me in."

Lily dabbed lavender water at her throat and wrists. "Come in then."

Isabelle pushed into the room, then stopped, her eyes widening. "Oh."

"Do you think it too much?" Lily adjusted the lacy edges that framed the low neckline of her blue silk gown.

"No! It's perfectly stunning, except—" Isabelle frowned.

"Except what?"

"Well, it is bound to attract James Huntington's interest. Are you sure it's prudent with a man like that?"

"Yes, I think it is." Lily turned back toward the mirror. Why did Isabelle insist on condemning James before he even had a chance to speak on his own behalf? "I want Mr. Huntington's full attention tonight because I intend to get to the bottom of things. You were the one who insisted we settle the matter before we arrive in Tunis."

Isabelle clapped her hands. "Of course. Lily, you are brilliant. That gown will set him completely off his guard." She paused. "But do be careful."

"I will. I know how to handle Mr. Huntington."

Lily draped her wrap across her bare shoulders. Who, she wondered, had packed this gown for her? She would have a talk with Bess when they returned to England and, if everything worked out as she planned tonight, thank her.

The attendants were extinguishing the lamps in the dining saloon when Lily and Isabelle arrived. Candelabra burned at the head of the room and the pianoforte had been moved in from the ladies' cabin. The chief steward stood up and cleared his throat.

"Ladies and gentlemen, our musicale is about to begin. Tonight your talented fellow travelers have graciously agreed to provide us with the evening's entertainment. I am sure we can all look forward to diversion of the highest standard."

Isabelle hurried ahead and scooted into the last empty seat in front, settling beside Mrs. Hodges. Lily cast a quick glance around the shadowed room, but James was not there. Suppose he did not come? She wrapped her shawl around her shoulders and took a chair in an unfilled row near the back, sliding over to leave an empty seat beside her.

He had to appear, and when he did, she had to arrange for some way to speak with him privately. Isabelle would only wait so long before taking matters into her own hands.

And what if Lord Reginald's accusations were true? Lily didn't credit them—Reginald was obviously not fond of James, and his conduct with Isabelle spoke poorly of him—yet she could not quite dismiss them either. After all, what did they really know about James?

The buzz of conversation hushed as the captain rose and

made a brief speech about this being their last night all together and what pleasant company the passengers had been. Lily thought he sounded bored, as though he had mouthed the same words countless times. No doubt he had.

In the dim light, a warm, masculine presence slipped into the chair beside her. She did not need to turn to know who it was.

"Good evening, Lily." His voice was low.

"James." She did turn then and could not miss the appreciation warming his brown eyes. She took a deep breath and allowed her shawl to slip a bit further down her shoulders.

He leaned in, so close the warmth of his breath tickled her neck. "You look beautiful this evening."

Thank goodness the music was starting. She faced forward. It was not cowardice—she simply needed a moment to regain her composure. His response to her was more, well, vital, than she had anticipated.

In the front of the room Mrs. Alice Fenton stood in her dark, high-necked gown, clasped her hands tightly together at her bosom and began to sing "Abide With Me." Her voice, though reedy, followed the melody well enough.

Lily closed her eyes. Her plan was working—James was here and she had his attention. Now, to get him somewhere where they could speak privately.

Mrs. Fenton dipped a curtsy and hurried to her seat, replaced by a plump young woman who settled herself at the keyboard and began to play a Bach minuet. Lily found it difficult to concentrate. How could Lord Reginald's accusations of theft and violence be true? She had never sensed anything like that about James. On the contrary, she had sensed only—well, whatever it was she had sensed had nothing at all to do with Lord Reginald's accusations. He was a danger, but to her alone.

She folded her hands in her lap and tried to force her mind back to the music. What was that cologne James was wearing? Clove? Bay? Something familiar, but with a hint of wildness. She breathed it in. Would it be possible to love the scent of a criminal? She imagined such a person would smell vaguely sour—dishonest.

James leaned back in his chair and she felt the brush of his elbow against hers. It was the lightest touch, but he did not move away.

In front, Richard seated himself at the piano. The audience stilled. Into their silence he began to play, swelling the music to fill the room. The notes mingled with the gentle sea air, with the flickering light and shadows, with the collective breath of the listeners. Through the window Lily could see the vastness of the sea, still and shining.

She felt the gentle roll of the ship, the slow pulse of the music, and most of all she felt the pressure of James's arm against her own. It was steady, and close, and spoke to her in the language of possibility. She was compelled to listen.

Once the lights came up her mind would function more logically—once the music stopped and she was not sitting so close to James. He shifted and the contact between them deepened. She concentrated on keeping her breathing even, but she did not move away. To do so would be to admit that she was aware of his touch, and she could admit no weakness tonight.

Richard played the final chord, letting it linger then fade into stillness. There was no sound, no breath for a long moment, then the audience erupted in applause. The lamps were re-lit, and Lily saw the captain, his eyes shining, moving forward to shake Richard's hand.

James leaned close. His eyes were shining, too. "Would you care to take the air on deck?"

She nodded. "Yes."

The look in his eyes deepened.

The attendants circulated the room bearing trays of drinks. James stood and drew her to her feet, then tucked her hand into the crook of his arm.

"Champagne?"

"No. Thank you." She felt quite unbalanced enough. She needed to get out on deck quickly and let the night air cool her. Then she would ask him the hard questions and look for the truth in his eyes.

Just before they stepped out, Lily felt a prickle of unease.

She glanced up to see Lord Reginald looking at her from across the room. He raised an eyebrow, then his flute of champagne in salute. She turned away, but she no longer needed the night air to sober her. What if she were mistaken about James? How utterly foolish to trust him merely because of his eyes, his smile, his touch.

"Is something wrong?" James asked.

"No."

Yes, but it was nothing she could confide.

The soft air wrapped them both as they emerged on deck, the stars blazed undimmed by the quarter-moon riding low on the horizon. There was no wind, only the gentle movement of the waves beside the hull, the splash of the paddlewheel and low thrum of the engine. They strolled wordlessly along the railing.

Lily wished the deck would stretch for miles, that they could simply walk together without speaking until the night dissolved. They passed the ship's boats, lashed to their supports, and she recalled how James had looked as they had rowed to Cadiz. His laughing eyes, the way the breeze had tousled his hair—it felt as though she had always known him, and always would. That was what she wished for now, not questions and doubts. Not answers she was afraid to hear.

At the bow she slipped her hand free of his arm and faced out over the dark sea.

He broke the silence first. "Is something troubling you, Lily?"

How to begin? The words scrambled, and she could not sort them into the measured, direct questions she had rehearsed. It was not going at all as planned. "Isabelle . . ." she managed.

"I had been wondering. She hasn't spoken a word to me since we returned from Cadiz."

"You noticed, then."

"How could I not? When someone as sociable as Isabelle suddenly starts acting as though I've been caught stealing the silver."

"She . . . she is confused. I am sorry for her behavior, but there are reasons."

"Tell me." He set a hand on her arm. "Please."

Lily swallowed. The weight of his touch was warm, his eyes sincere. "Isabelle has heard some distressing things about you. It would reassure her greatly if I could tell her they are not true."

"She wouldn't have heard these things from my cousin Reggie, would she?"

"Who else? Who on this ship knows anything about you except your cousin? A month ago we didn't even know you existed—then you come riding out of nowhere and suddenly the whole family is following you to Tunisia."

"I see." He lifted his hand and set it on the railing.

Lily turned to face him. Now that the words were coming, she could not stop. "What is Isabelle to think when your cousin, whom you obviously hate, appears on the same ship headed to the same destination and begins telling her that you are the worst kind of villain? James, the charges he makes against you are far more serious than stealing the silver."

"And you believe him as well." The hand between them fisted closed, though his voice was controlled.

"No! That is . . ." She didn't want to, but doubt moved in her like the shifting surface of the waves.

"What did Reggie say?"

"He said that your family banished you from England. Because you shot a man in a duel over a woman." It hurt to say the words.

He gave a grim laugh. "He is quite right. Reggie, like the very best liars, mixes his falsehoods with a seasoning of truth. The woman is my sister. A lady, not a harlot—which is what young Hereford was publicly calling her before I challenged him."

"You were defending her? Your sister?" Something unclenched inside Lily. The stars seemed closer, the waves smoother.

"Yes. Caroline and I were orphaned when we were children. I was the only constant for her as we were growing up—and she for me. I have always taken care of her as best I could."

Lily took a deep breath. She had known there must be a reasonable explanation. But it still meant—her heart stumbled—he had faced the man with pistols.

"I don't think your sister would have liked your solution, especially if you had been killed or injured. What good is dueling? If you are successful it is a tragedy, and if you are not, it is worse." She closed her mind to the image of him bleeding in an open field. She hadn't even known him then, and it still sent a chill through her.

"I understand your distaste—but it was serious. If I hadn't challenged him my inaction would have been seen as agreement. Caroline's reputation would have been in shreds. I would rather lay down my life than allow her to be slandered by a drunken dandy."

"Well, I would have advised you to punch him in the nose on the spot and have done with it. Why risk your life—or his—by shooting at each other?" Her hold on the railing tightened. "You didn't . . . kill him, did you?"

"No. I'm a better shot than that. Though by unfortunate accident he was injured."

"Then you didn't mean to—"

"Kill the puppy? No. Frighten him, maybe, teach him a lesson. I let him take the first shot—he was shaking so badly he couldn't have hit the ground if he were aiming for it. His bullet was last seen heading in the general direction of the Thames. Then it was my turn. I aimed at him, letting him consider the graveness of his error. Then, just before firing I swung my aim wide. He lost his nerve and dodged—right into the path of my bullet as ill-luck would have it."

"Was it serious?" Something about his story seemed familiar.

"Let me just say he will be more comfortable standing than sitting for some time yet."

"Then it was you Lord Reginald was referring to that first evening, when Mrs. Hodges spilled the plum relish!" Lily was trying not to smile—the story was really not so laughable. It was just the relief making her feel giddy. She reached out and touched his arm. "Your sister is fortunate, to have you, even if you are a fool for putting yourself in danger."

"I'm the fortunate one." His voice had softened. "You'd like Caroline. She has strong opinions and a clever way of expressing herself. Sometimes too clever—she has cut far too many gentlemen down to size, but she is the best of sisters." He studied her for a moment. "The two of you are similar in many ways, though her hair is not quite so . . ."

"Untidy?"

"Exuberant. Beautiful." He brushed her cheek, where a lock had escaped.

Lily gazed into his amber-flecked eyes. He was not a murderer, and he had not been fighting over the hand of some woman. Her body responded to his touch, his nearness, even though her mind was still filled with questions. "Then I take it you were not exiled from England."

"The exile, if you want to term it that, is temporary and self-imposed." He reached and took her hand, almost casually.

She did not let her eyes drop to where they touched. Could he hear how loudly her heart was beating? He was missing his sister and wanted some contact with the feminine—that was all. No doubt he would release her as soon as she asked her next question.

"Then why are you traveling to Tunisia? What is your real reason?"

He did not let go, after all. If anything, the warm hand holding hers tightened. Back in the dining saloon the musicale had resumed—the notes of the pianoforte threaded the night air.

"My cousin has been very busy whispering into innocent young ears," James said. "We cannot let him spend any more time with Isabelle."

"Of course not. But we will make Tunis tomorrow. What more can he do?"

"More than I'd like—but this talk has made me forget myself. I did not intend to spend our time out here discussing our cousins. You look beautiful tonight, Lily Strathmore. Like a blue flame in the heart of the fire." His thumb moved against her palm, the slightest caress, but it was enough to send sudden sparks all through her. Possibility shimmered in the air between them.

"Wait! You did not answer my question."

"Which question was that?" His voice was low as he leaned toward her.

She was beginning to feel like the fire he had named her. This would not do—not at all. "Why Tunisia?"

"To find the valley, the flower."

"Yes, but what more?" If only he were not so close. She could barely keep her balance.

James set his hands at her waist. "What more? Much, much more."

She stared at his mouth, just inches from hers. "And how did you find out about it—the flower? Some family papers?"

"Yes, papers . . ." he bent his head.

"And your grandfather was a botanist too?" It came out almost a whisper.

"Mmm, a most passionate botanist." His mouth brushed her cheek.

"Did he discover the flower during his travels?" She was acutely aware of his breath feathering her skin, the strength of his hands as he drew her to him.

". . . a most passionate traveling botanist."

He kissed her then, and her heart leaped, her questions silenced by the warm lips pressed over hers. She was immersed in sensation—the silky air, the piano music faint and low, the ship carrying them south under a burning banner of stars. And James, his arms encircling her, the sweetness of his mouth, the heat where their bodies touched.

It was enough to be there—to feel his hands, smoothing the thin fabric of her gown. It was enough to lean in and feel his grasp tighten, molding her against him. The gentle motion of the ship rocked their bodies together, swaying in a dance of balance and desire. He kissed her slowly, softly, his lips questing against hers. Her doubts vanished even as her blood took fire.

"Lily," he murmured, fluttering kisses across her cheeks, along her jaw. His mouth dipped to her throat, lips pausing against her pulse as she trembled beneath his touch. His mouth brushed her bare shoulder then detoured down to follow the low neckline of her gown. The railing at her back was the only solid thing left in a universe of quicksilver stars and rushing waves.

She melted into him, breathing deeply of the sea-scented air. The thrum of the engines vibrated along her back and settled in her center. Lily suddenly knew that she was sure of this man, that she did trust him—with her honor and her safety. And perhaps, even with her heart.

Yearning for the taste of him, she tangled her fingers in his hair and drew his lips back to hers. He lightly traced the seam of her mouth, smooth and wet. She parted her lips for him. The first touch of his tongue sent heat streaking down into her belly, lower. Twining, probing, their coupled mouths gave and took from one another.

James slid one hand along her side, then up, curving around the fullness of her breast. Her eyes flew open as his thumb slid over the light material, finding the hardness of her nipple and circling it. Lightning ran from his touch, sizzling through her. He continued to caress her, softly cupping her fullness with his palm, thumb moving against the tight peak. Tongue stroking hers, his other hand held her hard against him. She closed her eyes and kissed him fiercely in return.

From the stern of the ship came the distant sound of applause. James lifted his head, glancing about the deck. "Come."

He led her down to the open deckhouse where sails were bundled. Walls enclosed them on three sides, shutting out the brightly burning stars. It was the easiest thing in the world to slip back into his embrace, to lose herself again to his kiss, his touch.

"Gods, Lily," he whispered, lifting his head. "You are beautiful."

She believed. She had to, his touch could not lie. The way his hands circled her hips, ran over the smooth silk of her gown, the way he kissed her as though he could never get enough—she *was* beauty, and passion, and flame. How could she be otherwise?

The low-cut gown slid from her shoulders, leaving her

bared, her corset pressing her breasts up into the night air—
into his hands, his hungry touch cupping and circling her.
Then his mouth, the hot thrum of his lips, his tongue curling
around her nipple, shooting a dazzle of sensation through her.

"Ah," she breathed, fingers tight on his shoulders as he bent
his head over her, relentlessly laving her with his tongue. Lily
arched into his touch, wanting more, wanting . . .

His hand smoothing along her thigh, coasting over the thin
material toward the burning center of her. There, between her
legs. The press of his fingers sent a jolt coursing along her
nerves. He stroked her, gently, insistently, and she was floating, nothing but a handful of sparkles tossed into the air.

Suddenly the motions stopped and James went rigid.

"Hush," he whispered, drawing her tightly against him,
stilling her.

Then Lily heard it too—footsteps moving down the deck
toward them. She pulled up her gown, suddenly acutely conscious. If someone were to discover them it would be a terrible scandal. Outside, the shape of a tall man was silhouetted
against the ship's railing. He paused, as if listening, and Lily
held her breath, clutching the taut muscles of James' arm.

The figure put his hand to his mouth and muffled a cough,
then placing his feet carefully he moved on, the sound of his
steps fading.

Heart pounding, Lily watched James step out of the deckhouse and glance about, then motion for her to follow. "He's
gone."

When she joined him he took her hands, his look intent.
The moon burning low was reflected in his eyes.

"Lily. I swear to you that I mean your family no harm. I will
do everything in my power to protect you." He raised her
hands to his lips and pressed a kiss into each palm. "Come
now. We must return."

She set her hand on his arm and let him lead her back
toward the dining saloon. He had not answered all her questions, but her heart was satisfied. She knew she could trust
him, difficult as that might be to explain.

The music swelled as they approached the stairs. He drew her to a halt, his grip warm on her arm. "Lily," he said softly. "I must tell you—"

"Well, well." The voice came from behind them.

They turned and James took a step forward, his body shielding her as a figure detached himself from the shadows.

"So, I am not permitted to pass the time of day with Miss Isabelle, but you may stroll the deck—rather intimately, I might add—with her cousin?"

James took another step. "Say any more, Reggie, and I swear you'll find yourself swimming home to England."

"Oh, I won't say anything—yet. But how like you, fortune-hunting with Fernhaven's daughter. You do have a way of worming yourself into these well-born chits' affections." He looked past James to Lily. "And elsewhere, no doubt."

She caught her breath. The man was unconscionable. James's shoulders bunched and he leapt forward. There was a dull thud and Lord Reginald sprawled hard onto the deck, hands covering his face.

"We should go, before he recovers his senses." James took her elbow and led her away. "I apologize for his words. I wish that I could have spared you, and your whole family, from making his cursed acquaintance."

"Was he spying on us?" She glanced over her shoulder, but Lord Reginald had disappeared into the shadows. "Will he . . . ?"

"Tell anyone? I don't think so. If he had observed us, I'm sure he would have run to summon witnesses. But I have no doubt he's guessed at more than he has seen." James raked a hand through his hair. "I'm sorry, Lily." They had reached the door of the dining saloon. "It is best I leave you here. Good-night." He caught her hand and pressed it to his lips, then turned and moved quietly away.

Lily waited for applause, then slipped inside and took a seat near the door. No one had seemed to notice her return. She wrapped her arms around herself and wondered how she could possibly explain to Isabelle the certainty she felt about James.

* * *

The next morning the *Sidonia* entered the Gulf of Tunis. Deep blue water lightened to turquoise, and to the west the distant purple shadows of the Dorsale mountains stood sentinel. The passengers gathered on deck, chatting excitedly and watching as the ship approached the coast.

"Look!" Uncle Edward pointed to the starboard side where toppled columns and crumbling walls crowned a hill. "The ruins of ancient Carthage!"

"Oh, it is too, too thrilling!" Isabelle said. "Just as described in the travelogue!"

"Founded by a woman," Lily added. "Or so the legend goes."

"Queen Dido of Tyre, wasn't it?" James leaned against the railing, looking more handsome than any man had a right to.

"Very good." She smiled at him. "Queen Dido was given a cow's hide and allotted just that much land—rather a poor gift if you ask me, especially for a queen. Fortunately she had ambition and common sense. She cut the hide up into hundreds of thin strips, fastened them end to end, and encircled the entire hill."

"Never underestimate a woman," Isabelle said.

"Never underestimate the practical value of sewing skills," Mrs. Hodges corrected.

"Yes, but her hill and all of Carthage did fall to the Romans." Richard turned to his sister. "They sacked the place."

"Not while Queen Dido ruled. It took Rome centuries." Isabelle tossed her head.

Lily was pleased to see her cousin engaging in the family banter. Maybe her words on James's behalf after the musicale had not fallen on deaf ears.

Her attention shifted back to the ruins and the gray-green hills descending to the sea. The light here had edges and planes that England never knew, a hard, brilliant quality that lay over everything. She wanted to capture it, feel it tangibly through her fingers, make this moment of arrival even more real by translating it onto the page.

"Excuse me, but I must fetch my sketchbook. I'll just be a moment."

When she entered the ladies' cabin, Lily paused. A woman in green sat alone on the velvet sofa. It was the baronessa, her hands folded and a wistful look on her face. She glanced up. "Hello, Miss Lily."

"Good day, Baronessa. There is a beautiful view out on deck."

"I am sure." She patted the couch beside her. "But I am glad to see you. I would like to speak a word before we part."

"Certainly." Lily sat down. "It has been a pleasure making your acquaintance, Baronessa. If you are ever in London again, please call upon me."

"I thank you for the offer, but it is most unlikely that I will return to London. There is nothing there for me now." She took Lily's hands. "It is of broken hearts I wished to speak— and men named Huntington."

Of course. The baronessa had not missed much with her sparkling dark-eyed gaze. Lily pressed her lips together in a rueful smile. "I know—I am well aware that James, that is, Mr. Huntington and I have no future together. It is a passing fancy, that is all."

"You and James? But you are mistaken. It is not about him I worry. Your James, he is a good man."

"He is not mine."

"No? But I think he is." She paused, letting the silence add its weight to her words. "It is the other one that worries. Lord Reginald. Tell Miss Isabella she does not want to learn what this man can teach. She does not want to know." The baronessa shook her head as she spoke, and Lily felt a bond of sympathy with this woman who had learned the hard lessons love can teach.

Lily leaned forward. "Know what? What do you mean?"

"He is full of shadows, and your cousin's brightness will not be enough to keep them at bay. Her heart is in danger. Perhaps more."

"I know. I will look out for her, I promise."

"That is well—I hope it will be enough." The baronessa

released her hands. "But I am keeping you." She leaned forward to give Lily a kiss on each cheek. "It has been a delight knowing you, *bella*. You have the courage to find what is in your own heart. I do not doubt it." With a rustle of skirts she rose and went to the door.

Lily leaned back against the burgundy velvet cushions after the baronessa had gone. *Your James*. If only he could be. But why deceive herself? What future could they have? Even now her wedding dress was being stitched for her marriage to Lord Buckley. Her mother and future mother-in-law were busy with arrangements. This voyage was just a dream, a season that would end too soon.

Besides, James had made no indication that he had intentions of a lasting nature. He had not spoken of the future. Only kissed her, caressed her until she felt as if her entire body were made of starlight. Her life was now, today, this week, this journey. She had paid dearly enough for it.

Lily went to her stateroom and began gathering art supplies. She would begin a fresh sketchbook to celebrate their arrival. As she rummaged in her valise a small brass box fell to the floor spilling out a length of fine gold chain and the locket Countess Buckley had pressed upon her. Bother! Lily had nearly left it behind, but her mother would certainly have noticed. She knelt to retrieve it and caught a quick glimpse of Lord Buckley's pale eyes before snapping it shut.

Even if James did speak, she was not free to give her heart in that direction.

She replaced the locket in the box and tucked it deep in a corner of her valise. She had no time for this. Her fingers tight around the fabric binding her sketchbook, Lily abandoned her room for the sunlight and air above.

James was still there, wind playing in his thick, brown hair. He leaned with casual grace against the railing, his form set boldly against the backdrop of the ruins, and she suddenly was on fire to draw him again, like this, to take hold of time and make it stand still. With a pang she realized that soon the day would come where she would not see him each morning at the breakfast table. At best they might cross paths in society, introduce their spouses and children and pretend never to have held one another on the dark waters of the Mediterranean.

She studied the line of his jaw, his lips. Lips she remembered on hers. Her traitorous heart knocked against the door of her ribcage, but she refused to answer. She drew in a shaky breath.

"Lily?" His gaze was intent.

"We are here at last." She summoned up a smile. "I can't wait to sketch Tunis."

"By all means." But he remained looking at her, a questioning light in his eyes.

She turned away, staring at the city now coming into view. Domes and square minarets rose against a painfully blue sky. The huge bulk of the mosque dominated the tangle of streets and buildings in the *medina*, and a short distance outside the old city the Bey's palace sprawled, surrounded by high walls. Near the palace were the European accommodations—more French than British. The party would stay in the hotel Le Palais before setting out.

Sketching the skyline, Lily tried to let the familiar rhythm of her work soothe her jagged emotions, but the lines did not flow smoothly—the buildings were too blocky, the shadows too deep. She could feel James near, his concern and his quiet strength. If only she could lean into him. Her pencil stuttered across the page.

The conversation around her abruptly ceased. Lily looked up to see Lord Reginald approaching, immaculate in his frock coat and pressed trousers. Immaculate, except for the dark bruise beneath his left eye.

"You're not welcome here, Reggie." James drew himself up to his full height. "Be on your way."

Lord Reginald shook his head, as if his cousin's words deeply saddened him. Then he turned to Isabelle.

"Oh, you have been injured!" She rushed to his side. "What has happened to you?"

Lily stiffened, but James signaled with a barely perceptible shake of his head. They could do nothing except wait.

Lord Reginald paused for what seemed an eternity, then spoke loud enough for the entire family to hear. "I was surprised on deck last night by an assailant who attempted to murder me. I drove him off, but he left me with this souvenir." He lifted his face, displaying the bruise to better effect.

"Oh heavens." Isabelle's eyes were wide. "Lord Reginald, you must have that wound tended. Mrs. Hodges, go at once and fetch a poultice. Someone, bring cool water and a damp cloth."

He sighed. "It's too late—the damage has already been done. I had the ship's doctor look at it. The disfigurement will heal in time, but little can be done for the loss of vision."

Richard stepped closer. "I would never have thought it that serious. We must tell the captain—it won't do to have a ruffian running loose on deck and attacking the passengers. Did you get a look at the fellow?"

Lily bit her lip, her heart flipping desperately between anger and fear. The man was an incorrigible liar—standing here in the midst of her family and eye-witnesses, spinning the grandest exaggerations. He deserved to be called out and exposed, except—except that would require explaining why she had been on deck, and with whom. It was a trap and Lord Reginald was baiting it with his outrageous lies.

"Did I recognize the assailant?" Reginald rubbed his temples and shot James and Lily a sly look. "I'm not certain—perhaps it was the force of his blow, but my recollection on that point is hazy. Although I understand such lapses are often temporary. You can be sure I will name the villain if the opportunity arises."

Isabelle placed her hand on Reginald's arm. "You ought to be resting, my lord. You have suffered greatly."

"Indeed," Aunt Mary said. "Blinded and bruised and with a loss of memory. Sir, you should not be standing here in the sun. You must go below and rest at once. Mrs. Hodges, do you have anything for Lord Reginald's ills among your medicines?"

Mrs. Hodges pursed her lips. "A double dose of castor and cod-liver as a general curative. A very potent combination. I'll fetch my dosing ladle straight away."

Aunt Mary stepped forward and plucked her daughter's

hand from Lord Reginald's sleeve. "I am certain that will be most helpful. Don't you agree, sir?"

"It will not be necessary." He showed his teeth, very white and even. "Perhaps another time—I was just about to go below. Good day to you all. Farewell, Isabelle." He bowed and turned away.

Lily let out a breath she had not realized she had been holding. She felt as though she had narrowly avoided being bitten by something poisonous. No wonder James reacted as he did when Reginald was present. The man was despicable.

"Goodness," Aunt Mary said. "He moves rather quickly for one so grievously injured."

"Well, I trust that's the last of him." Uncle Edward brushed his hands together.

"I wish I shared your optimism." James frowned after his cousin's departing back.

"Well I for one am comforted he will be close by," Isabelle said. "Lord Reginald is everything that is noble. It is *you*, Mr. Huntington, whom I'm not sure of. It is evident you do not want him in Tunisia. To what lengths are you willing to go?"

"Isabelle!" Aunt Mary's voice was shocked.

"Now, now, my dear girl—" Uncle Edward began, but Isabelle would not be quieted.

"This expedition is a horrible mistake." Her voice rose. "Can't you see that Reginald is the only one we can trust? Father, Mother, I must tell you that James is dishonorable—a complete scoundrel. To begin with, his family forced him to leave England because he was dueling—"

"Isabelle, I explained it to you," Lily broke in. "He was defending his sister. It was not dishonorable in the least."

"Quite right," Uncle Edward said. "I am fully aware of his actions prior to leaving London—his uncle sent a letter that made it all clear. Isabelle, you are mistaken. I think you owe James an apology."

She glared at them. "You have to listen. Lord Reginald told me—"

"My dear." Aunt Mary took her daughter's arm. "Quite

plainly, Lord Reginald is not fond of James. You must consider what he hoped to gain by such accusations. I do not believe the man is completely honest."

"How can you say such things!" Isabelle's eyes were bright with unshed tears. "Don't you understand?"

"Isabelle." It was James, and the concern written on his face only strengthened Lily's conviction that he was not the villain his cousin made him out to be. "I know how persuasive Reggie can be, but we are about to land on a foreign shore and it's imperative that we trust one another. I promise you that I take my responsibility to your family seriously. Let me answer to Reggie's charges, whatever they are."

Isabelle folded her arms. She sent a dagger of a look at her parents, but said nothing. Lily hoped her cousin would remain silent. Already other passengers had edged closer, attracted by the scent of impending scandal. Publicly accusing James, however false the charges, could only cause a scene.

Isabelle seemed to sense the truth of it and dropped her gaze. "I apologize, Mr. Huntington."

"No harm done," he said. "But in future, come to me with your concerns. Give me the opportunity to answer any questions you might have."

She only nodded, keeping her eyes fixed on the deck.

"Come, my dear." Aunt Mary wrapped her arm about Isabelle's shoulders. "We will retire to the ladies' cabin where it is not so bright. We are not accustomed to such an exuberance of sunshine. You will feel better soon. Mrs. Hodges, would you care to accompany us?"

"Of course. I am sure I have something that will restore her spirits in my medicine bag.

"Sorry about that, Huntington," Uncle Edward said when they had gone. "You were right about your cousin, I'd say. Imagine, telling Isabelle such lies." He peered at James through his spectacles. "You do know we trust you."

"Yes, and I thank you." James glanced at Lily, his eyes searching.

She met his gaze squarely. "Isabelle is the one who is confused, not I."

His look eased. "We must all take care. When we land it will be apparent how far from England we really are."

"We'll be on guard," Uncle Edward said. "If that rascal causes trouble he'll have to answer to me. I was considered quite handy with fisticuffs in my day, you know."

Richard grinned. "And if that fails, there's always Mrs. Hodges's tonics and dosing ladle."

Lily closed her sketchbook, picture unfinished. At least they would no longer be confined on a ship with Lord Reginald. She hoped Isabelle would see sense once she was away from his influence. The baronessa was right—he offered nothing but ruin and heartbreak.

The rising wind teased a strand of her hair loose, tickling it against her cheek. She tucked it firmly back under her bonnet, aware that James was watching her. Unable to meet his eyes any longer, she turned her attention to the bright bay, the city, the exotic land that awaited them.

Chapter 15

Lily closed her eyes and took a sip of tea. It was Aunt Mary's favorite blend, retrieved from somewhere in her satchel and provided to their hotel's maître d' with strict instructions on brewing and service. Its taste evoked rainy afternoons at Brookdale.

That in itself spoke well for the beverage since nothing else here was even remotely like England.

Sliced figs and sweet almond cakes accompanied their tea and the air was deliciously warm. The murmur of French spoken at the other tables on the hotel's terrace was punctuated now and again by shouted Arabic floating up from the crowded street outside. A pomegranate tree was flowering in the courtyard, and the scents of honeysuckle and jasmine hung heavy in the air.

Lily opened her eyes. This was it. This was what she had fought for and promised for—to be here in this strange new place with her senses alive to everything around her. She traced the intricate pattern of the tile tabletop with her finger. Even the furniture was different, decorated by artisans with a sensibility so alien to her own. Tunisia was everything she had dreamed of.

She should be content, not feel as though her heart were as fragile as that thin glass bowl holding figs. But oh, how could she be content when thoughts of James followed her constantly, when the memory of his touch burned through her, leaving her wanting more? And when she knew it was only ephemeral—a mirage that soon would vanish into the desert air.

"I hope James returns soon," Aunt Mary said. "It was good of him to see us settled before returning with Richard for the baggage. You don't suppose they have run into trouble?"

"Not to worry, my dear." Uncle Edward helped himself to another fig slice. "Huntington knows his way about foreign places. We all saw how he managed the bedlam at the docks this morning. Richard will be fine with him. We all will."

Her uncle was right. James had been quite resourceful. As soon as the family disembarked they had been met with a chaos of carts and conveyances. Drivers shouted at them in Arabic and broken French, pushing each other to get to the baggage and load it into their vehicles. It was all very unsettling, but James had quickly taken charge. His piercing whistle startled everyone into silence and, seizing the advantage, he quickly selected several drivers to transport them. With the newly appointed drivers' help, he was able to shoo the others away. Lily had to admit that he had been both commanding and impressive. And thoughtful—he had insisted on finding suitable transport for Dr. Fenton and his wife before they left.

Lily looked across the table at Isabelle. She hoped her cousin's opinion of James would improve now as Lord Reginald's influence waned. James was certainly not to be blamed if Isabelle insisted on considering him a scoundrel.

"Look, there they are now." Uncle Edward stood and waved an arm.

"Do sit down, dear. I am positive they have spotted us," Aunt Mary said. "Isabelle, would you be so kind as to fix them each a plate?"

James chose the chair beside Lily, which, for such a simple thing, gave her more pleasure than it ought. She tried not to smile too broadly, but she was suddenly filled with delight. Tunisia truly was a splendid place.

"Tea?" Aunt Mary poured out a cup. "The French know nothing about brewing a proper pot. It is fortunate we have our own supply."

"You brought tea, mother? In your luggage?" Richard shook his head. "I can only imagine what else you have in that mountain of crates we unloaded. The best silver? A harpsichord?"

"Don't be foolish." She handed him a cup of tea. "I would never risk the best silver on an outing such as this. I brought the travel silver, of course, and a few other items to maintain a minimum of civilized comfort. If you disdain such comforts we can always have Mr. Huntington procure you a native gourd. You can drink your tea from that."

"Richard can sleep in the dust if he likes," Isabelle said. "I'll take mother's cots and pillows, thank you very much."

Lily nodded. "And the tea service and the portable writing desk."

James winked at Richard. "Just the minimum to maintain civilized comfort."

Richard leaned his elbows on the table. "Civilized indeed— we'll hardly know we're not in Sussex. James was telling me how he had to eat lizard in the East Indies."

Isabelle wrinkled her nose. "Did you really, Mr. Huntington? How disgusting."

"It tasted rather like partridge, actually. And since it was pressed upon me by a local warlord and his armed henchmen, I thought it unwise to refuse."

"Not much different from a London dinner party," Lily said, "where you must either pretend to enjoy what is served, or if it is unspeakably awful, feign a dizzy spell and retire to the drawing room."

"Just like you did last October when Count Karlov served his infamous jellied boar's head," Richard said. "How was it prepared? The lizard, I mean, not the boar."

Aunt Mary placed the teapot firmly in the center of the

table. "I think we have had enough of this topic. James, how did the baggage fare?"

"Yes, yes," Uncle Edward said. "Is everything in order? What about the botanical equipment?"

"Everything arrived intact. Our supplies are being loaded into one of the hotel's storerooms as we speak. Richard was a great help, and has agreed to take on the responsibility of overseeing the baggage when we set out."

Richard nodded as he refilled his plate.

"When will we set out?" asked Isabelle, setting up straight in her chair.

James frowned. "That depends on how soon we can obtain travel permission from the Bey. Having a letter with his official seal will allow us to travel unimpeded. Without it, we would have to negotiate passage with every local official and tribe."

"How long will it take to get such a letter?" Aunt Mary asked.

"Difficult to say. If it's too long, we'll have to go without it and pay whatever bribes are necessary. We want to be out during the flowering season. Isn't that right?"

Sir Edward nodded. "It's imperative. Our time is limited if we are to locate the valley and your grandfather's flower."

"Before we depart I should like to go to the native market-place," Aunt Mary said. "What do they call it?"

"The *souq*," James said. "In the old city."

"And we must see the truly *old* city," Uncle Edward said. "We will never have a better chance to explore the ruins of ancient Carthage."

James leaned back in his chair. "I'm certain we can arrange that. I've already been solicited by half a dozen would-be guides. One even offered to sell me tiles from the ancient mosaics. He claimed to have gone up to the ruins at night and pried them loose himself."

"Pried the tiles loose from the mosaics?" Lily asked. "How criminal! Did you report him? He has to be stopped. Those mosaics are treasures of antiquity, not souvenirs for tourists to cart home."

James just smiled, a reaction she found infuriating. Didn't

he realize what a serious problem this kind of vandalism was? Why one might just as well condone cutting up the paintings of the great masters into postage stamp size souvenirs. Selling the tip of the *Mona Lisa*'s ear, or a bit of shell from Botticelli's *Birth of Venus*.

"Something must be done." She thrust forward in her chair. "They need to post a guard. The mosaics must be in tatters if the locals are selling pieces to tourists."

James was still smiling. "Lily, he was lying."

"Lying? How can you possibly know that?"

"The mosaics are in the Bey's palace."

"But I thought . . ."

"They were moved so that people like my friend in the street couldn't get to them."

Lily picked up her napkin. "They aren't in Carthage any longer then?"

"No. They are well protected in the palace."

"Oh." She bit her lip. They could easily go to Carthage, but it was unlikely she, as a woman, would get an invitation to the palace. "I wish . . ." She stopped in mid sentence. She should be relieved that the mosaics were protected from thieves even if it meant that she would not have an opportunity to view them.

Aunt Mary set down her teacup. "We should see to the unpacking."

"Certainly, my dear." Uncle Edward rose and pulled out his wife's chair.

James did likewise for Lily, then offered his hand. She took it, her fingers sliding beneath his. He gave her that particular smile, the one that lit his eyes with warmth and carved a line in his left cheek. They walked together, allowing the rest of the family to go ahead.

"Lily—you started to say something at the table. That you wished for something. What was it?"

She shrugged. "It's not important. I was only going to say that I wished I could view the mosaics. I'd imagined we would see them when we visited the ruins. I was disappointed, that's all. I'm glad they are protected."

"It is disappointing. I've heard they were marvelous examples of ancient Roman art."

She smiled at him. "No matter. There is so much to see and experience here. Really, I have nothing to complain about."

"Nevertheless." He paused. They had come to the top of the stairs. He bowed and lifted her hand to his mouth and she felt a thrill of longing at the brush of his lips. There was that smile again and something else—something playful and mischievous dancing in his eyes.

James walked the morning streets of the *medina*, making his way through the narrow lanes of the old city. The dwellings here stood tall and close, forming walls that overshadowed the street. Their tiled windowsills and brightly painted doors spoke of a secret life inside.

He had come early to hire mounts and pack animals for the expedition. In India, the best time to walk the city had always been in the early morning when the air was still cool. Old habits died hard. Besides, he smiled to himself, he had plans for the afternoon.

An arch piercing the wall yielded a glimpse into a sheltered courtyard where children played games with balls and counters. They stopped their game, whispering and giggling as he passed. Further down, two old men wearing robes and white beards studied him silently from where they squatted in the early sun, drinking coffee from tiny cups. A tantalizing whiff of cumin and mint drifted from an open doorway.

It was temping to linger here, but there was no time to waste—not if the arrangements he had made over the last three days were to amount to anything.

He continued to the *caravanserai*, located just outside the city walls. Here he would find the mounts and pack animals they needed for the expedition, and men to handle them. James searched for the best animals, and when he found them sought out their owner, a fat, round-faced old merchant who seemed to enjoy the ritual of negotiation as much as he did striking a profitable deal.

"Camels also, yes sir? You must have camels. Their strength and endurance is superior to horses and mules and my nephew and his sons are the finest drivers in all Tunis." The merchant waved for more tea—the mandatory minty blend, served in hammered metal cups—then resettled his bulk more comfortably on the piled rugs.

James shook his head. "We are heading west, not into the southern desert, but I will remember your nephew and his camels should I need them in the future."

His host nodded. "But even if you travel west, you still lack a guide, yes?"

"Perhaps. If he is familiar with the area along the *Wadi* Medjerda."

The merchant's smile creased his eyes behind his wide cheeks. "A moment." He turned his head and bellowed into the tent behind him, "Khalil! Come here!

"You are in most fortunate luck, sir. My own son by my second wife has spent much time in that very place!" He paused. "Of course, so knowledgeable a guide commands a high fee."

A man ducked under the hangings, his nose a prominent beak, his face weathered by the sun and wind. James was glad to see he was lean and agile, lacking his father's impressive girth. The man listened as his father spoke in Arabic, then turned to James and bowed. "My name is Khalil," he said in French. "My father says you are heading west. I know the Medjerda valley well."

"And the mountains above it?"

"Not so well." His answer was quick and honest. "But I have hunted there on occasion and know the tribes that hold sway."

"The Berbers. Perhaps I will hire you." James thought of his grandfather's tragic adventures in those mountains. Had the Englishman employed a guide, or had he struck off optimistically in search of rare blooms with just his companion Mercer and a few bearers?

Khalil smiled slowly. "Be warned. My father will try and empty your purse for my services."

The merchant grunted and glared at his son. "To leave your family, your ailing child? No. It will not do."

"My 'ailing child' is already begging to go out and play with the other children." Khalil glanced at his father.

"Very well." The merchant waved a large, fleshy hand. "Bargain for your own fee, if you wish to remain a pauper. I only am trying to see to your welfare."

And to his own coffers, James thought as he and Khalil quickly settled on a price. "We will be leaving soon—two days, perhaps. I'll send word."

"All will be ready, sir."

At the entrance of the tent James turned. "Have you seen a dark-haired Englishman about in the last several days?"

Khalil shook his head. "No, I have not."

The old merchant looked at the wall of the tent, but then he had said almost nothing since his son had insisted on negotiating his own fee.

Inside the city walls once again, James pulled out his pocket watch, the burnished weight of it comfortable in his hand. It had belonged to his father. The bargaining had taken longer than he'd intended—he would have to hurry if he was to make it back in time.

He looked at the roads branching through the city from the gate. If he took that one along the city wall, then cut back through the marketplace, he could make up time. The huge dome and towers of the central mosque would provide a consistent landmark.

The street he had chosen followed the wall then branched and branched again, each time becoming narrower as it entered an area of dilapidated houses and shops. Paint peeled from around doorways and he had to negotiate his way around piles of debris in the street. Men sitting on the ground outside shops and rundown coffee houses ceased their conversation as he passed, their gazes hard and unsmiling. Hostility hung in the air. James quickened his pace trying to catch a glimpse of the central mosque between buildings.

The street branched again, neither lane looking more promising than the other. He stopped and looked back the way he had come. There was no one there, no one following him—it must be his surroundings that made him feel so edgy. He reached instinctively for his pocket watch, then stopped himself. This was not the kind of neighborhood where it was advisable to display wealth of any kind, and besides, he didn't need his watch to tell him that too much time was passing.

He selected one of the two equally unlikely paths and started down it when from afar he heard the tower-flung cry of the *muezzin* calling the faithful to prayer. The mosque! It came from the left. Following the sound, James turned down a narrow track between two buildings—a path which grew wider and more traveled as it approached the market. He breathed deeply. It was a relief to emerge into the busy *souq*.

He stepped nimbly around a spice merchant's wares—vibrant powders heaped in metal bowls, curls of cinnamon bark, kernels of fenugreek and gnarled knobs of turmeric root adding their pungent smells to the air. Women wrapped head to toe hurried past, clenching their headscarves between their teeth to leave their hands free for bundles. He halted as a young boy ran past, chasing an escaped chicken.

But there it was again, that premonition that someone was watching him. He turned slowly, but nothing seemed out of place in the busy market, except—had that man in the dun-colored robes turned away too quickly?

James forced himself to slow—meandering, stopping to look over a display of brass trinkets, a rack of scarves. Yes, there could be no question. The man was following him. Bloody hell. He didn't have time for this. James turned and looked him directly in the eye—the game was up. The man in the dun-colored robes started forward, reaching into his robes as he came in a motion that screamed danger. Another man that James had mistaken for a beggar followed.

Unarmed, James turned and ran, hot anger flaring inside

him as the market crowd parted before him. Not today. He would not be stopped today.

He wove a path through the booths, darted down the street of the cloth sellers, then turned into the area where the leather-workers displayed their wares.

Ducking into the door of a shop, James crouched behind a rack of tanned hides, heart pounding from effort and adrenaline. The sound of running footsteps approached, then stopped outside. James looked for something—anything—he could use to defend himself. Supple leather hides, soft boots, sheepskins. Why couldn't he have concealed himself in a knife maker's shop?

Voices sounded outside, questioning. He could not hope that his hiding place would go undiscovered for long.

Then he saw it. Lunging to the wall, James snatched the coiled black whip from its peg. This chase would have to end sooner or later. He stepped back into the street. Sooner was better.

"Were you looking for me?" He let the whip uncoil at his side.

The two men spun and charged together. Before they could close the gap, James slashed forward with the whip, sending it snaking around the legs of the dun-robed man. Yanking with all his strength, James sent the man down hard on the street, then stepped forward to meet his remaining attacker. The man was on him in an instant, hands reaching for his throat.

He twisted aside and jabbed the handle of the whip into the man's stomach. The ragged man let out a whoosh of breath and James grabbed a handful of the man's robe, pushing him hard against the plaster wall of the leather worker's shop.

"Why are you following me? Who sent you?"

His captive squirmed, his dirty turban knocked askew. "We mistook you for another man."

James shook him. "Try again—and this time, the truth."

A shift of the man's eyes was the only warning. James released him and whirled as the other man lunged, the knife in his hand glinting in the sunlight. There was the sound of tearing cloth. James caught the man's wrist and twisted. With a cry, his attacker dropped the knife to clatter against the cobblestone pavement.

His assailants exchanged a look and took to their heels. James followed for several steps before reason tethered him.

Cursing, he opened the tear in his sleeve to assess the damage. Just a scratch, but it stung like the devil. He bent to pick up the whip and coil it. Handy, that. If he had been caught unarmed . . . Sweat trickled down his back. He would have to heed his own advice and be more careful when he went out.

A thin, nervous-looking man stuck his head out the door of the leather shop and eyed first James then the whip.

"Doctor Jones?"

James handed him the whip. "No—you must have me confused with someone else."

An hour later, changed and freshly shaven, James knocked at the door of Lily and Isabelle's suite. Lily opened it immediately, smiling.

"You're late. After three days of plotting and secret arrangements you're late! Won't you tell me where we are going? Please, James." She gave him her most winsome look. In her gown of gauzy white cotton she looked deliciously beautiful.

"Just a little longer then all will be revealed. The carriage awaits, and I am here to escort the lovely Misses Strathmore."

Lily's smile faded. "Isabelle has decided to join her parents and Mrs. Hodges for tea with the Fentons this afternoon. She asked me to convey her regrets."

"Still avoiding me? I'd hoped her feelings would have softened by now."

"Give her time—and don't worry. There's no need to let Isabelle spoil your surprise. Let me fetch my parasol." Lily stepped back into her room then joined him in the corridor.

"Don't forget your sketchbook."

She patted the small case that contained her sketchbook and pencils. "Why? Are we going somewhere picturesque?" Her blue-green eyes sparkled at him.

"Perhaps."

Her eyes widened.

"Or perhaps not. Let's collect Richard and be on our way—the carriage is waiting outside."

It was a perfect afternoon—the sky a dome of turquoise, a light breeze stirring the palm leaves, and Lily beside him in the open barouche. James felt like a boy setting out on a merry picnic to the seaside—carefree, joyous. The anticipation in Lily's eyes only added an extra keenness to his pleasure.

"Where are we going?" Richard leaned forward from the seat opposite. "Surely you'll tell us now?"

"You'll just have to wait and see." James grinned.

"Lily, I can't believe we're keeping company with such a scoundrel."

She twirled her parasol. "I couldn't even get the secret out of Uncle Edward. He knows, doesn't he?"

"Of course," James said. "And your aunt, and Mrs. Hodges. It's a grand conspiracy, really."

Richard leaned out of the barouche, trying to see where they were headed. "Do you think he's taking us to the grand mosque?"

"Could it be?" Lily turned to face James. "I didn't bring any veils. Perhaps you would be kind enough to snatch a bed sheet off a clothesline for me. Something that matches my eyes." She covered her face with her sleeve, but even then her eyes spoke her smile.

He loved her in this mood, the easy banter between them. James raised a brow and said in his most unctuously flattering voice, "Something that matches your eyes? How is that possible? Can one match the color of the sky? Can one match the color of the sea at dawn?"

"Well, actually, with a good grasp of color theory and the right paints—"

Richard gave a snort of laughter. "I think brown muslin. Mud brown."

"You don't mind converting then?" James said. "It is the only way they will allow us to enter the mosque."

Richard looked thoughtful. "It has advantages, you must admit. We can take several wives each."

"Ha," Lily said. "Richard, you can begin with Anne Riding. That would keep her from chasing you about the dance-floor at any rate. And for James . . ." She tapped her lips with one finger. "Someone equally troublesome, I would think."

"How about Isabelle," Richard said. "She's been troublesome since birth."

James shook his head. "I don't think Isabelle would have me."

"No, probably not." Richard cocked his head and looked at the two of them. "Lily, then. Granted, she can be every bit as troublesome as Isabelle, but at least she chose you over a stultifying tea with the Fentons. Of course, you will spend the rest of your days seated on a stool holding a pot of tulips while she paints you. Dreadful thought."

James fought to keep his expression light. It was not a dreadful thought at all. And if it were possible to take Lily Strathmore for his bride he would make damn sure he held far more than a pot of flowers—he would have the artist herself right there amidst her brushes and paints. He looked at her, he couldn't help it, and something of his thoughts must have shown, for she blushed and quickly glanced away.

"Really, Richard, you do go on. After traveling all this way with two such *troublesome* females, I doubt James intends to set up a Moorish household with Strathmores as wives one and two. In fact—oh, isn't that the palace?" Her attention focused ahead of them.

"The Bey's palace?" James kept his voice neutral. "It would appear so." The driver turned to the right and they followed the street bordering the palace walls.

"What was it like inside?" Lily asked.

"Yes," Richard said. "You and father did not tell us nearly enough about your meeting there."

"Beyond the fact that we had permission to travel," Lily said. "Are the floors paved in precious stones? Are there fountains flowing with wine?"

"No, but there were silken carpets woven in deep scarlet, and the Bey wore a ring with a ruby the size of a quail's egg."

She sighed. "I wish we could have gone."

"Women are not allowed in the palace," Richard said, giving her a smirk. "Unless you want to join the harem."

"Actually," James said as the barouche slowed to a stop, "In some instances women are allowed." He vaulted lightly down onto the street and held out his hand. "This instance, for example."

Lily glanced at him. "James!" She set her hand in his and he could see the excitement beginning to light her eyes.

"Splendid," Richard said. "I was disappointed when you and father left me with the women the other day. You don't suppose we'll get to see the harem building, do you?"

"No," Lily said, her voice almost a whisper. "We are going to see . . . However did you manage it?" The joy in her expression nearly undid him.

"What?" Richard looked from one to the other. "What are you talking about?"

"The mosaics! We are going to see the Roman mosaics."

James nodded. The look on her face was worth all the effort it had taken to arrange this. "Come." He held out his hand.

An arched door in the wall swung inward. "Welcome, James Huntington and guests," a young, turbaned man said. "I am Ahmed, your escort, showing you the wonders of the palace. Please, be welcome."

"We are honored to be your guests." James let the young man usher them into a courtyard filled with an orderly planting of orange trees. Fruit and flowers mingled together in their branches, and the sun sparkled off a fountain in a square pool at the center.

"How enchanting." Lily took a deep breath of the scented air. She looked more beautiful than he had ever seen her, framed against the glossy leaves. He had a sudden, ridiculous urge to sketch *her*, but no markings he made on paper could hope to capture the essence of the woman who stood in front of him.

Their guide waved them forward. "Shall we go? There is much to see. The hall of the mosaics is this way." He led the party to an arched door, the lintel inlaid with blue and yellow tiles.

Inside, the air was cooler and the light dim after the bright courtyard. The room soared two stories, supported by inlaid columns. A balcony ran around the upper perimeter and windows high above let in shafts of light.

"Here are the great artist's treasures of my homeland," Ahmed said, gesturing to the richly patterned mosaics set in the pale marble floor. "They are nearly two thousand years old, dating back to when Rome ruled here."

James watched Lily closely, wanting to savor her every reaction. For a moment she stood unmoving, then slowly began to walk between the mosaics. Her eyes traveled over each work of art as she paused to admire the details—but there was something more in her expression. Joy? Thankfulness? Pleasure at seeing the mosaics? He did not know—only that when she looked up at him, her eyes alight, something inside him gave way. It was all he could do not to gather her into the center of his embrace.

"James," she said, voice filled with emotion. "They're more beautiful than I ever imagined."

"I'm glad they please you." If his quest failed, if they had to leave Tunisia tomorrow, the entire adventure would be worth it, just for this moment. Just to see the joy in her eyes.

She held out her hand to him and drew him to the edge of the tiles. "Look here—see the vines twining up out of the blue vases. There are angels, or cupids, in the branches—and what is that exotic bird?" She leaned closer. "It would be impressive if it were painted, but to think they achieved the pattern and depth with tiny squares of glass."

"You like this one?" Ahmed gestured. "Come, I will show you the rose lady." They followed him down the great hall. "Here she is. With the sun shining upon her, she is shown in all her beauty."

Sunlight beamed down from the upper windows, slanting onto the mosaic before them. The colors of the tesserae deepened and brightened like a thousand tiny jewels.

"Spectacular," Lily said. "Look at her basket of roses—it glows. Why, she could be in any garden in London, gathering blooms on a bright summer morning. I think we are not so different from the ancients who made these."

"Except for their taste in clothes," said Richard. "I don't think you'll find anyone picking roses in London so dressed— or should I say, undressed . . ." He bent forward for a closer inspection. "Can you imagine anyone in Society picking roses with just a wisp of drapery over her thighs? She'd better mind the thorns."

"It's a good thing you play the piano so well." Lily took out her sketchbook. "Otherwise I'd think you completely devoid of artistic sentiment." She turned to Ahmed. "Don't you have any of heroes slaying wild beasts to occupy his simple mind while I sketch?"

Ahmed grinned. "I have better than that. I will show him the mosaic of the wild beast devouring the hero. It is over here . . ."

James watched the two make their way across the hall, then wandered among the mosaics. He needed to put some distance between himself and Lily if he was to allow her the space and time to sketch.

She shared the rose lady's light, her pencil driving across the page, the rest of her perfectly still, blue-green eyes narrowed in concentration. She glowed, her dress illuminated, her face radiant. Then she paused to turn the page and glanced up, sending him a quick smile before returning to her work.

Forcing his gaze away, he continued to stroll the room, describing a slow orbit around her until Richard and Ahmed returned.

"Lily," her cousin said, "You don't intend to spend all afternoon here, do you? Ahmed says the palace stables hold the finest horses in all Africa, and there is a garden with a reflecting pool and a parade ground, and the walls of the harem compound to see."

She glanced at the mosaics laid out down the hall and bit her lip. "Well, I was hoping . . ."

Richard frowned. "Ahmed, are they really the fastest horses in Africa?"

"Oh yes, without a doubt. No others can compare."

James stepped forward. "I'll stay with Lily. I had a chance to see some of the palace on my earlier visit."

"Do you mean it? I will not be long, I promise."

"Off with you then," Lily said. "I can see that you won't be happy until you have beheld the horses."

"If you need refreshment," Ahmed said, "I have prepared a room with food and drink upstairs." He indicated the flight of stairs at the far end of the hall. "Now come, Richard. We will pass near the harem on our way. You may look at the outer walls, but no higher, for to glimpse a concubine of the Bey is to forfeit your eyes." The two young men walked down the hall in animated conversation.

As the door closed behind them, Lily looked at James. "I dare say we won't see Richard for some time. He really is over-fond of horses. But won't you be dreadfully bored?"

He strode over to where she stood beside the rose-woman and held out his hand. "No," he said. "I don't imagine that I will."

Chapter 16

He could see the warm color rise on her cheeks. She glanced down to her sketchbook and then back to him. The look she gave him made his blood quicken.

"Tell me, James, what outrageous bribes did you pay in order to arrange for our presence here this afternoon?"

"Outrageous bribes? I wouldn't go so far as to call them outrageous."

Lily smiled. "Outrageous or not, I thank you." She swept her arm to encompass the room. "For all of this."

"It was nothing—" he started to say, but before he could finish she leaned forward and kissed him lightly on the cheek. The sudden unexpected gesture said more than any words of thanks ever could. He looked at her, her smiling eyes, her lips slightly parted—how easy it would be . . .

As if sensing his thoughts she took a step back, hand going to her hair. The air between them was heavy with awareness—they were alone. She glanced about, her eyes fixing on the balcony that ringed the hall. "I would love to see the mosaics from above. It would provide an excellent change in perspective."

"Then by all means." He held out his hand to her and after an instant's hesitation she took it, allowing him to lead her to the stairs. They climbed in silence, her slender hand in his.

"Look," she said, going to the low railing of the balcony.

"They are like paintings from here. One can hardly see the individual bits of colored glass and tile."

Directly below them lay a mosaic of Neptune driving a chariot over the waves, his hair in wild locks, a long blue scarf draped over his arms. Lily studied it a moment. "Would you like to know what I see?

James nodded. "Very much."

"The scarf shows the movement of the chariot. See how it billows back? And it echoes the stripe of blue along his horses. Whoever conceived this design had an excellent model. Look at Neptune's face, so full of intent and purpose. And his form, perfectly proportioned. See how the artist used darker tesserae to bring out the muscles of his . . . chest." She halted, blushing.

James watched the transformation from artist to woman. Neptune was as unclothed as the rose woman she had sketched earlier. "The Romans' code of dress was rather more relaxed than our own. Do you think them immodest?"

She looked down again at Neptune.

"No," she said at last, "not immodest. They seem more idealistic. Here is a male figure so well-formed that he can represent a god. And the rose woman—a female whose unadorned beauty rivals that of her flowers. But tell me, what do you see?"

James looked at the images arrayed below. "There," he pointed. "A warrior carrying a woman." In the mosaic, the woman's naked breasts were pressed hard against the warrior's bronzed skin, her arms clasped around his neck—he was bearing her where he would. James recalled standing at the bow of the *Sidonia*, Lily in his arms—how she had responded to his kisses and melted into his embrace.

He straightened and stepped towards her. "It seems the Romans were less idealistic about love."

"I think not. See how her arms are wrapped so tightly around the warrior's neck. Perhaps he has just returned after a long absence and we see them in that moment of reunion. He is not bearing her anywhere she does not wish to go."

James caught her hand. "Come then. Let us see what refreshments have been provided—or would you rather I tossed you over my shoulder and carried you in the Roman fashion?"

"Oh . . ." Her eyes opened wide, but she met his gaze and did not look away.

He led her to where a door stood open midway down the gallery. The room inside was furnished with a low, silk-draped couch and two backless chairs. The inlaid table beside them was set with an array of refreshments, and from the arched, open windows beyond came the sound of the fountain splashing in the courtyard pool.

"How perfect." Lily was looking everywhere but at him, though she made no move to pull her hand away, and he did not release her. "Like something from the Arabian Nights. I feel as though we have stepped into a fable."

He did not have to carry her off—she would come willingly. This day would be about her pleasure, and he had far more than gazing at mosaics in mind.

James drew her inside and closed the door.

It was perfect—an ideal setting for an afternoon of slow, sweet kisses. "If this is a room from a storybook, then you must be the Persian princess. Take your ease, my lady." He seated her on the couch, then poured two goblets from the moisture-beaded flagon on the table.

"What is it?"

He tasted. "Chilled honey-wine."

She took the goblet he held out, and sipped. "It's very . . . unusual. But quite refreshing."

He took a swallow, letting the cool liquid soothe his throat. "What else do you desire, my princess? Tangerines, pistachios, honeyed dates?"

She leaned back into the silken cushions and inhaled. "A tangerine—as the scent of citrus blossoms is filling the air. Peeled and segmented, please, as befits my rank."

He selected one and drove his thumb in, peeling the rind away in one curving whole. Juice trickled between his fingers. "It's quite messy. I wouldn't want it to drip on your gown."

"How shall I eat it, then?"

"Allow me to assist you." He went to his knees before her and held out a slice, lifting it to her lips. Her gaze flew to his face, then to his fingers, holding the succulent tangerine slice. After a brief hesitation she opened her mouth. He placed it against her lips, then slid it slowly inside, letting his fingers brush the softness of her lips. Where would this game lead them? Her eyes closed—he could see the shiver of sensuality and awareness flow over her. Heat tightened his groin.

"Another?"

She gave him a sidelong glance. "They are delicious. But be careful—I could become accustomed to such luxuries."

"Then it would be my pleasure to indulge you." He brought another piece to her waiting mouth.

This time she leaned forward and flicked her tongue against his fingertips, then slowly licked the juice from them. He nearly groaned aloud at the sensation.

"My turn." With a teasing smile, she took a slice from him and placed it against his lips. A rush of tangy citrus filled his mouth. He opened and took her finger in, savoring the sweet juice with his tongue. She drew in a sharp breath.

"It tastes delicious from your fingers," he said, "But it would be better still from your lips."

Her eyes heavy-lidded, she parted her lips, allowing him to set the last slice of tangerine between them, the fruit partially exposed. His heart pounding, James leaned forward and opened his mouth over hers. It was the sweetest kiss he had ever tasted—the cool, wet tangerine, the hot moistness of her mouth. He let his tongue lightly touch hers.

"James." Her voice was a sigh of pleasure.

He brought his hands to cup her face and brushed his lips against hers. She trembled at the touch and laid her hands on his shoulders.

She tasted of oranges and honey. His lips quested at the corners of her mouth, finding the sweetness and savoring it, keeping his kisses light. He slid his fingers back into her hair, thumbs tracing the delicate curves of her ears. She swayed forward, the curves of her breasts brushing his coat.

Slanting his mouth over hers, he opened his mouth and let his tongue smooth along the line of her lips. It opened, granting him access to the warmth, the wetness, her tongue lightly flicking against his, eager to join in the dance. Heat spread out from their fused mouths, slid through his veins like honeyed fire. She was so beautiful, so responsive.

"Wait," she breathed, pulling back. "You have pleased me well. Come, join me on my throne." She patted the cushions.

He shifted, settling beside her and taking her hands. Lacing his fingers through hers he said, "I would like to please you more."

Her eyes met his, curiosity and desire flaring in their depths. "Yes."

She lifted her hand and set it against his cheek, slipping it in a soft arc over his face, then around to the back of his neck. The feel of her fingers brushing against his hair incited such yearning, such desire. He pulled her to him, one arm curving around her waist. His lips quested along her jaw, nibbling at the soft skin of her neck, tasting her, and her head fell back as she arched into him.

Lifting a hand to her breast he cupped her and brushed his thumb across the peak. A soft moan rewarded his caress. Slowly he drew her down onto the cushions, supporting her until she lay against the bright silks. The heat of her blazed along his side.

He pressed his mouth to her temple, scattered kisses across her forehead, her cheeks. She smiled up at him. Holding her gaze, his fingers rested on the top button of her dress. She nodded, and slowly he unfastened the row of buttons, the backs of his fingers lightly brushing against her breasts as he worked down to her waist. Her eyes widened, but she made no move to stop him. The cotton dress opened, sliding back from the silk of her chemise, leaving only the thin fabric molding to her curves.

"Lily," he murmured, folding back her dress to expose the skin of her throat and shoulders. He lightly traced her collarbone, felt her pulse leap beneath his touch, then dipped his head, tongue following the curve of her neck, tasting her clean, faintly salty skin. Her body intoxicated him—he wanted to savor her, inch by inch, touch her as he had dreamed of so often during these last weeks.

Gently, he dipped lower, breathing against the skin of her chest, licking softly. His lips met the edge of her chemise, coasted along the smooth fabric, up the curve of her breast. She drew in a deep breath, her heated, silk-covered skin rising to his lips. He bent his head, placed his open mouth over her nipple.

Slowly drawing his tongue across the taut peak he let the moistness penetrate the silk. Soon the thin layer of fabric was all but transparent, wet and clinging. His warm tongue caressed her, making her gasp and sink her fingers into his shoulders.

He moved his hand to her other breast and lavished the same attentions upon it, fingers alternately plucking and stroking. Hands and tongue slowed, teased, then without warning he sucked fiercely at her nipple and tightened his fingers about the nub of her other breast. She shivered beneath him, sighing in pleasure. Her hands moved to grip his head, fingers threading through his hair.

At last he levered himself up and returned to the warm richness of her mouth. Tongues darted and tangled, melded together. Her arms encircled him, coaxed him against her. He complied, letting her pull him down until he lay firmly against her, pressing her into the cushions. Every inch of him was aware of her beneath him. He slid one leg between her thighs, pushing lightly upward until he touched the heat of her. She was still for one startled moment, then her body seemed to take over, rocking slowly back and forth against him.

Urgently, he ravished her mouth, his erection pressed against her hip, fanning the flames higher. He knew he needed to pull back. They were already going further than he had intended—almost further than he could bear.

Somehow she had tugged his shirt free of his trousers, her hands now stroking his back, palms skimming his taut muscles. James moaned against her lips. It was one thing to caress her, to feel her responses, to explore her rising sensations together.

But he would not be able to control himself if she insisted on turning the tables this way.

"James," she whispered.

He lifted his head to look at her, her lips moist from his kisses, her eyes darkened with emotion and desire. Gods, but she was lovely.

Gathering his strength, he began to roll off her, but she tightened her arms around him.

"No," she breathed, staring dreamily at him, a half-smile on her lips. "Show me more."

He gazed down at her, measuring her words.

"Please."

He considered her a moment more, then relaxed, watching her smile deepen as he curved his hand over her shoulder and brushed his thumb over her collarbone. He bent his head to nuzzle her neck, nipped lightly, hands smoothing her curves, gliding over the silk. It was the work of moments to unfasten her chemise.

He pushed it back to her shoulders, baring her soft skin. Raising up on his elbow, he gazed down at her full breasts with their dark pink aureoles, the nipples puckered in arousal.

"You are so beautiful," he said softly.

She studied him, no trace of apprehension in her look. Concealing the speeding of his heart, the love and desire that swept through him, he bent and blew softly on the peak of her breast. She let out a soft moan, fingers tightening on his shoulders as he blew again, openmouthed, letting her feel the heat of his breath, his desire, then curled his tongue beneath her nipple, stroking the sensitive flesh.

Now he gave his hands free rein. They roamed across her legs, down, dipped below her petticoats and drew them up, slowly exposing her to his touch. His fingers curved around her smooth calf, drew tiny circles behind her knee, echoed by the circling of his tongue on her breast. His hand moved higher, pushing the spill of white cotton and silk up her thighs. He drew his palm from her knee along her inner thigh and her leg fell open, responding to his caress.

Her hands moved restlessly, slipped around to caress his back, sweetly distracting. She had unbuttoned his shirt and was tugging at the fabric bunched beneath his coat.

"I want to see you," she said.

He paused. This was not in his plans, but the impatient entreaty in her eyes swayed him. Raising himself up, he shrugged out of his coat. She pulled his shirt down, then stopped, the white linen crumpled halfway down his arms, falling off his shoulders.

It was his turn to be exposed. Her eyes devoured him.

"You are beautiful, too," she murmured, then finished stripping off his shirt. She placed her hands flat against his chest.

The heat of her touch made him breathe in sharply. He started to dip his head, to kiss her again, but she pushed him back.

"Let me just . . . look at you," she said.

Heart pounding, he did. First her gaze then her hands swept over his broad chest, following the hard planes of his muscles, teasing the light dusting of hair, pulling gently. Then she set her fingers to his nipples and his whole body tensed as she caressed.

She took his breath away. She so boldly, so playfully, embraced her passionate self.

He was lost, and knew it.

When she slid down, leaving a trail of kisses, and tentatively took his nipple between her lips he had to close his eyes, clench his hands, trying to contain his reaction. Her tongue flicked against him and sent his desire spiraling.

With a deep groan he pulled her up, fastened his lips on hers, and feasted on the sweetness of her mouth. He had to end this soon, before he lost all control.

His hand moved down her body, dipped under her skirts to rest on the soft skin of her hip, just above her drawers. He began to draw little spirals with his fingertips, each caress moving lower, charting new territory. Lily's breathing quickened and he could feel her attention focused there, where his hand gently cupped her.

Her drawers fastened with a ribbon. Tugging, he loosened

them, let his hand slide down against her heated skin. He brushed his palm over the curly tuft of hair between her legs and she shivered. He gave her a moment to adjust to his touch, then began to stroke—a slow, almost infinitesimal movement of his fingers, softly fluttering against her.

She gasped against his lips. Her thighs opened for him as he rubbed gently, parted her, explored her folds, then coasted up to her tight nubbin and brushed lightly. A low cry sounded in her throat. He swallowed it and continued to enjoy her mouth.

His finger went to her entrance then slowly, slowly he penetrated her, thumb still circling her most sensitive spot. She was fiery velvet, soft and wet. He played her, coaxing sighs and moans from her like a master musician bent over his instrument, using all the skills at his command. Mouth fused to hers he began to increase the pace, tongue thrusting in time to his finger, thumb teasing her, coaxing her, winding her tight, tighter.

Her fingers tangled in his hair, pulled hard, holding him against her as she tensed, shuddered. A cry of pure pleasure tore from her and she arched against him. He could feel her pulsing against his hand, hard, then subsiding.

Lily fell back against the cushions, letting the languorous aftershocks ripple through her. She'd had no idea.

But James obviously had. She opened her eyes to see him gazing at her, the amber lights in his eyes sparkling. He looked at her searchingly.

"Yes," she smiled up at him. "Oh, yes."

Some deep emotion streaked through his expression, gone too quickly for her to catch. He gathered her close and she lay her head on his chest, feeling completely relaxed as he stroked her hair, twined a strand about his finger. His heartbeat thudded under her ear and she smelled the sharp, masculine tang of him.

"Thank you." His voice vibrated through her.

"For what? It's you who has given me this whole wonderful afternoon." Tears now ached in her throat.

His arm tightened around her and she nestled in, soaked up the sensation of being held so intimately, skin to skin, his fingers playing in her hair. She splayed her hand over his chest, felt the rise and fall of his breath. Perhaps she dozed. He shifted beneath her, held her a moment longer, then sat.

"Time is passing," he said.

"Of course." She lifted onto her elbows, watched him don his shirt, remembering the feel of those strong, smooth muscles under her hands. Already yearning to feel them again. She wanted him again, lying beside her. He had given her such pleasure.

He shook his coat out and donned it, then bent to press a lingering kiss against her lips. "I'll be back in a moment."

She nodded, watched his tall form move to the door, silhouetted briefly as he left.

Sitting up, she waited for a sense of shame to descend, some shock at her behavior, but none was forthcoming. Instead she felt light inside as though she had swallowed a star and it was still glowing within her.

He had evoked such sensations in her—so very different from that other time, the awkward grappling in the garden with her art tutor. James was so different—so splendid. And now they were lovers, after weeks spent thinking of him, capturing his image under her hand, dreaming about his kisses. She already wanted more.

Lily buttoned her dress and began re-pinning her hair into its coil. What now? She could not deny the way he made her feel so breathlessly, perfectly alive. They were here together in this exotic land full of orange blossoms and warm sun. England seemed so far away.

England. Her thoughts skittered away, but too late. Always it remained like a worrisome dark cloud on her horizon. James had made her no promises, offered no alternatives for the future. He had only kissed her, delighted her with dizzying new sensations. He was charming, no doubt, but his intentions remained a mystery. It was foolish to expect more. Whatever they had only existed now, for this one perfect moment. She stood quickly and shook out her skirts. The bargain with her mother could not be erased by an afternoon of kisses.

"Lily." James was back. He held out a spray of orange blossoms, a grin tugging the corners of his lips.

She took it and breathed its rich perfume. Oranges would always remind her of this day. A bittersweet thought. Gathering her sketchbook and pencils, she turned. "Let us go."

He nodded then reached for her hand. Their fingers remained clasped as they descended the stairs. When they reached the bottom she forced her fingers to let go, determinedly going to sketch a nearby mosaic of an elephant.

When Richard and Ahmed returned, full of apologies for losing track of the hours, she had managed several quick sketches. The mosaics were every bit as lovely as before, but her heart was not in her work. How could it be with him in the same room, smiling when she glanced over at him? It was a relief to close her sketchbook, to bid Ahmed and the Bey's palace farewell, to leave the courtyard filled with blossoms and light behind.

Back at the hotel, James escorted her to her room. "I'll see you at dinner." He took her hand and raised it to his lips, lingering.

"Yes, at dinner. It was a lovely day, James." Closing the door, Lily sighed deeply. The end of a lovely day.

"You're back." Isabelle jumped up from the writing table. "I've a surprise for you."

"Oh?"

"Letters from home! The mail packet just arrived. Here, these are yours."

"And who have you heard from?" Lily took the stack her cousin thrust at her.

"Charlie Thomas, for one. But his correspondence is so boring and immature. He prattles on about nothing much for simply pages, and his hand is a dreadful scrawl. I could barely finish reading it." Isabelle glanced over at her. "Aren't you going to see who they're from?"

"Of course." Lily stood, holding the letters loosely for several heartbeats. She began to flip through them and her hands stilled, halting on the creamy envelope addressed in a familiar curling script. Throat dry, she moved to her bed and sat. The vellum was napped and velvety. She ran her fingers over it.

"Well?"

"Don't hover, Isabelle. Please."

Her cousin flounced back to the desk, and Lily slit the envelope and unfolded the pages.

My Dearest Lily,

Wonderful news! Lord Buckley is positively disposed to a union and is expected home by June. Such a perfect time of year for a wedding. Your father has agreed that Fernhaven chapel will be entirely suitable. I think white peonies, don't you? The countess and I are drawing up the guest list next week. It is so exciting!

Do make sure to wear your bonnet and keep out of the sun. Use that cream I sent with you, and be careful about what you eat. Travel can be so taxing. Tell your uncle to wind up his trip and have you home by mid-May. We must have time to finish fitting your wedding gown!

Your fondest,
Mother

Lily smoothed the creases her tight fingers had left on the paper.

What had she done? How could she have spent a dreamy, honey-soaked afternoon with James, when this was her future? A small, wounded sound escaped her.

Isabelle looked up sharply. "Is everything all right?"

Lily swallowed. "Perfectly."

She walked to the window and looked out over the inner courtyard of the hotel. The sky was pale blue deepening to indigo in the east.

She was as wanton as she had feared these many years.

Hadn't she allowed her young art tutor to have her? And wasn't she allowing—no, she thought back to the Bey's palace—wasn't she *encouraging* James to take liberties even though he had given her no hint that he contemplated a future with her? She already missed his touch. It was wicked.

She was wicked, for there was no repentance in her.

Lily folded the letter in careful squares and reached for the small brass box she had brought with her. She tucked the letter in beside the gold locket—the locket that had remained unworn since the day Countess Buckley had fastened it about her neck. Quickly, firmly, she closed the lid and pushed the box back out of sight.

The dining room of the hotel Le Palais was full, the chandeliers overhead sparkled brilliantly, and a babble of English and French conversation filled the airy space, blending with the clink of crystal and cutlery. It could be England, except for the exotically arched doors and windows and the delicious air wafting through. It had rained earlier in the evening, and the air was heavy with fragrance—jasmine and orange blossom. Lightning still flared over the mountains to the west.

"Lily." James eyes followed her as she entered and he bent low over her hand.

"Good evening." Her pulse fluttered wildly at his touch, even as she fought to still her emotions. It was not fair to James—or herself—to continue on like this. She pulled her hand away.

"Are you well?" Concern darkened his brown eyes.

"Quite," she said, moving past him to take the seat beside her aunt.

Uncle Edward leaned forward. "So, Huntington, how was your trip to the marketplace? Find us a guide?"

"A fellow named Khalil. How are your preparations going?"

"Very well. Indeed, I would say they are virtually complete—if such a state were possible."

"Good." James smiled, but there was something hard in his expression. "After this morning's work, we'd do well to depart as soon as possible. Tomorrow, early. I've already spoken to the servants about it."

"Yes, yes. No more waiting. Our flower awaits. And after the recent rains, the blooms should be spectacular."

"Oh," Isabelle said, looking startled.

"What is it, my dear?" her mother asked.

Eyes cast down, Isabelle replied, "Um, it is only . . . I seem to have trod on the lace at my hem and ripped it. May I retire to the ladies' lounge and make repairs?"

"Of course." Aunt Mary made to rise. "I will accompany you."

Isabelle stood hastily. "Really, I can manage. Lily, will you come?"

It was a relief to be removed, however temporarily, from the sweet torment of James's presence. Entering the lounge Lily crossed to a brilliantly tiled basin, dampened a towel, then sank down on a silk-covered chair near her cousin and draped the cool cotton across her eyes.

"Lily, are you quite sure you are all right?"

"A little tired," she murmured, thankful for the quiet. Her head was pounding—desire and guilt and anger at herself a potent mix pressing against the inside of her eyelids. Whatever was she going to do? She should have remained in England, but she had not and there was no way to return now. Perhaps she could stay with the Fentons here in Tunis—but that would raise questions she could not easily answer. Just entering the dining room and seeing James there had sent the heat rising in her face. She must avoid arousing her aunt's suspicions. She had insisted on coming despite her own better judgment. There was no turning back now.

Isabelle seemed to understand her desire for silence. Lily could hear the rustle of her gown, the snap of her reticule. And then, curiously, the rasp of pencil on paper. Removing the towel she glanced sharply over at her cousin.

"What are you doing?"

"Nothing." Isabelle quickly tucked a scrap of paper into her reticule. "Shall we return?"

"Is your gown mended already?"

"Yes. I thought I heard it tear, but it appears there was no harm done."

Lily glanced at her cousin's handbag. She had only suspicions, nothing definite to confront Isabelle with, short of snatching the reticule and searching through it. That would only destroy the shaky trust they had been rebuilding since arriving in Tunis, and she had too much on her mind already to add one more thing to the clamor in her head.

Still, she watched her cousin closely during dinner—and tried to keep her attention from straying to James. Something inside her twisted each time she met his eyes.

"Had tea with Doctor Fenton today," Uncle Edward said. "Seems they are having some success raising support for their clinic, but not as much as they'd hoped."

"It is difficult to effect change, especially for the poor," Aunt Mary said. "I wish them the best of luck."

"Wish us luck too," Richard said. "I'm not sure we have enough room on the mules for all the unnecessary baggage."

"We have no unnecessary baggage." Aunt Mary frowned at her son. "They are necessities. You will realize that when you rest yourself on the excellent camp stools I found in the *souq* yesterday."

"Hmph. Ought to hire out a dozen more mules, the amount of provisioning going on," Mrs. Hodges said. "Carpets and teapots and pillows and such. A bathtub."

"Really?" Richard looked appalled.

"It does fold up," Aunt Mary said. "Proper hygiene is of especial importance."

"But mother. A bathtub?"

"How splendid," Isabelle said. "Richard, you simply must find a way to transport it."

James nodded at the young man. "He will. I have every confidence."

They were leaving then, bathtub and all. Lily felt a pang.

She would miss Tunis. It was a city of such contrasts—whitewashed walls accented by bright blue shutters and grill-work, intimidating Arab faces showing a constant, friendly courtesy to their party, the music everywhere, jangling strings of an oudh, a pipe's reedy wail down a palm-lined street. She had not drawn a fraction of the things she wanted to sketch in the marketplace.

And every step closer to their journey's end also brought them closer to London.

"More sherry?" Uncle Edward asked her.

"Please."

Mrs. Hodges drilled her with sharp gray eyes. "Indulging, Lily?"

Lily took the glass of amber liquor and turned it restlessly between her palms. James was looking at her. The light burnished his hair. Why couldn't it be like this? A future with him in it, seated across from her at dinner, talking together, sharing a life. His lips curved. The look he sent was full of promise.

She could not bear it, but she could not resist it either. He had captured her with his warm eyes, his strong arms, his touch . . .

"Lily, how is your mother?" Aunt Mary asked. "Isabelle said you received a letter from her today. I trust all is well in London."

Lily's fingers tightened on her glass, the cut crystal sharp against her fingers as she forced herself to respond. "My mother is well. She sends her regards." She swallowed the last of her sherry and set the glass carefully down on the table-cloth. "I must retire. Please excuse me."

"May I fetch you anything, dear?" Aunt Mary's eyes looked worried.

"Thank you. But I just need to rest." She did not look at James.

"I'll come too." Isabelle hurried to her side and accompanied her out of the dining room. Halfway across the marble foyer, her cousin halted. "I forgot my bracelet. Go on, I'll catch up."

Lily nodded, but paused just inside the corridor that led to their suite. Glancing back she saw Isabelle stop a servant, draw something from her reticule and pass it to him, then hasten to the dining room. What was she up to? Could she still be in communication with Lord Reginald?

It would be difficult to slip the leash, but Lily had done it herself just that afternoon.

"Here it is." Isabelle hurried up, flourishing the silver bracelet.

"Wait." Lily turned to her. "What was all that business with the note?"

"What note? I had to fetch my bracelet. Are you sure you're feeling well? I'll send the servant for a tisane."

"Tell me. It's Lord Reginald, isn't it?"

"Heavens no. I am utterly weary of everyone bringing him up." Isabelle linked arms with Lily. "Come, cousin. We both need our rest tonight. I'm so thrilled—we are heading out at last!"

Chapter 17

They headed west from Tunis, traveling over a quarried stone road built by the ancient Romans. The city gave way to orchards—pistachios and dates, then groves of lemons, their starry blossoms scenting the air. James ranged along the party, encouraging the stragglers, keeping an eye on the riders and pack animals. It did not take long to notice that Lily became engrossed in conversation with her cousins or guided her horse away from him whenever he approached. She had not met his eyes all morning.

Yesterday she had taken tangerines from his fingertips and shivered with pleasure in his arms. He had thought it so clear, the connection between them. Now it was as if a door had swung shut. She was without a doubt the most aggravating woman he had ever encountered.

At least they were on the move. With a hundred small things to occupy his attention he could retreat into the familiar rhythm of travel—a recalcitrant mule that balked whenever they had to cross a bridge, an argument between two of the drivers, a bundle gone missing. Still, no matter what occupied him, he was constantly aware of Lily's presence.

Just before luncheon they gained the Medjerda River, swollen and muddy from the night's rains. James called a halt by its banks in the shade of an olive grove. The men raised a small pavilion and in short order the Strathmores were sipping tea and eating sandwiches, for all the world as if they were on a country picnic in Sussex. Lily had settled herself between Isabelle and Mrs. Hodges, the latter of whom had produced a hank of brown wool and was knitting what looked to be a long stocking.

"Off to a good start," Sir Edward said. "Don't you think, Huntington?"

James accepted a sandwich and dropped down beside Richard on the patterned *kilim*. "We're making decent progress, but at this pace I expect at least three more days of travel."

"Your calculations include time for botanizing, I hope. This is an advantageous time to be in the field." Sir Edward suddenly set down his cup and stood. "I say, that is a most unusual flowering shrub growing over there. If you'll excuse me."

Lady Mary shook her head as he disappeared into the grove. "My husband is in his element now. I fear we shall have to find him and put him bodily on his horse when it is time to depart. Edward does tend to lose track of time when he is collecting."

"He really should have a keeper," Richard said.

Isabelle laughed. "Remember when he got lost in Farmer Dobb's fields? He missed supper entirely and returned home completely covered in burrs."

The siblings exchanged tales of their father's single-mindedness, but James's focus was on Lily. Her eyes were closed, her face tilted to the sunlight. He studied her features. High cheekbones and round chin, the slight downward arc of her nose, and full, lush lips. Passable enough features, by any standard.

He found them beautiful.

He ought to speak to her. Yesterday the words had left him. The feel of her, the scent and taste of her skin, the way she had shivered with pleasure at his touch, made conversation impossible. Words had been unnecessary. Everything important could be said with a kiss, a caress. It had seemed enough.

But perhaps she needed more. Uncertainty might be the reason for her distance today.

He finished his tea and rose. "Lily, would you stroll with me? We can recover your uncle."

There was hesitation in her eyes.

Mrs. Hodges glanced over. "It'll do you good, miss. You'll be back on a horse again far too soon. We all will. Take the chance to move about while you still can."

"Go, my dear," Lady Mary said. "Tell your uncle we are starting to pack."

Lily pressed her lips together, then stood. "Very well. I think Uncle Edward went this way." She marched off into the grove, angling to parallel the stream.

The light under the trees was silvery and the tang of ripening olives filled the air. James let her lead the way—he needed seclusion before he spoke.

"Oh, look," Lily said.

A great tree grew near the edge of the river, its branches hanging down like a pavilion. They walked beneath it, parting the low-hanging branches to stand under the dome formed by it boughs.

"It seems as if it has grown here forever with its roots in the river." Her voice was wistful. "Like a fairy tree out of a dream."

He placed a hand on her arm and turned her to face him. "Yesterday—was that a dream too? You've been so distant since we returned from the palace."

"No," she said, looking at the ground. "Not distant, just thoughtful."

"And what thoughts are those?"

"I'm not sure you would understand, Mr. Huntington."

"So I'm Mr. Huntington today?" He let his hand drop from her arm.

"Isn't it better that way?" She met his eyes. "We will not always be free as we are here. When we return to England things will be different for us. There will be certain . . . expectations. My parents . . ."

She trailed off, seeming on the verge of tears, but whatever those tears were for, it was clear that the "expectations" were that he would be Mr. Huntington to her. Of course she was right. She was the daughter of the Marquis of Fernhaven, and he—he was the orphan of a second son. Not exactly the match of the season, at least not for her. Her truth stung, but he admired her diplomacy. After yesterday he had begun to entertain foolish notions about a future for the two of them. She had saved him the embarrassment of speaking those thoughts aloud.

"What passed between us meant nothing to you, then?"

"Nothing? No, Mr. Huntington. It showed how weak I am. It showed I am more susceptible to a grand gesture than is good for me. It means I must raise my defenses, or drop them altogether, and I have no way of knowing which is the right course of action—if there even is such a thing."

He could see the hurt in her expression and softened his tone. "Then I have only added to your confusion."

"You *are* the confusion, you foolish man!" She laughed through her tears and gave him a most unladylike shove backwards, but he caught her hands and held them, drawing her forward.

"If I am to become Mr. Huntington when we step out from beneath this tree, then I will be James to you now, one last time."

Her eyes widened, but she did not resist as he pulled her to him, a hungry desperation rising. He dipped his head to fasten his lips upon hers. Gods, he would never get enough of holding her, of kissing her.

She sighed and leaned into him, mouth warm under his. Her hands slipped up to curve around his neck, holding on.

Everything else blurred except the heat between them, the urgent dance of their tongues, the press of two bodies close together. How well she fitted against him, soft and perfectly female. It made him wish to have her unclothed beneath him, her skin again his, their bodies moving together. He wanted to undress her, to kiss her beautiful full breasts, to hear again the sounds of pleasure he had drawn from her yesterday, and to join her in that wave of ecstasy.

She was as eager as he, it seemed. Her questing hands were tugging at his coat, pulling it down. Lips still locked together,

James shrugged out of the garment. He could not keep his own hands from skimming over the delicious curve of her breasts, circling, then settling at her hips and pulling him firmly against him.

Their breaths mingled, fast and desperate as he deepened the kiss, as if he could claim her by making her senseless with desire. He would make her his own and the world be damned.

She stiffened suddenly in his arms.

Blast it. Someone was pushing through the branches. James stepped back, leaving Lily holding his rumpled jacket.

"I say, what a marvelous specimen of a tree!" Sir Edward's head appeared through the thicket, followed by the rest of him.

"Ah, hello Uncle," Lily said, a stricken expression on her face.

Sir Edward's gaze went to the jacket in her hands. "Well. This is most irregular, my dear."

"No . . . not at all," she said, cheeks still flushed with passion. "I thought I spotted some unusually shaped seed pods in the upper branches. James offered to climb up to obtain a sample and I, um, I offered to hold his coat while he scaled the tree."

"Seed pods?" Sir Edward squinted upward. "A pity I left my field glasses back with the horses. But they won't be needed if we can obtain a sample. Capital idea, Huntington. We'll make a botanist of you yet."

"No doubt," James said, rolling up his sleeves and approaching the trunk. "Or a raving lunatic." Why was it that the most tempting fruit was always just out of reach?

The next day the expedition followed the road beside the river. The Medjerda continued wide and swift, still swollen by the rains.

"Mr. James." Khalil pointed back down the road, to where sunlight winked off white cloth, illuminating a flurry of movement. James turned in the saddle, shading his eyes with one hand. Horsemen, riding fast.

"What do you think?"

The guide shook his head. "I do not know. They are riding swiftly. Perhaps they are being chased."

"Or chasing someone." James looked over his own party. Large enough, certainly, but not prepared for violence. He glanced behind them. The figures were closing quickly, a band of about ten men, robes flapping. He could hear the sound of their hooves in the distance.

"Off the road!" James shouted, pulling his horse's head around. He waved the Strathmores into the surrounding field, then reached for his pistol. He prayed he would not be called upon to use it—but if they tried to touch Lily . . . . He concealed the gun under his coat.

The servants struggled to turn the mules—one animal balked at crossing the narrow ditch that ran beside the road. Its load swayed precariously as the men pushed and cursed. Finally it dashed ahead, spilling a clamor of canteens and pots onto the ground.

Then the riders were upon them, the jingle of their harness cutting over the heavy thud of hoof beats. James, last to leave the road, placed himself squarely in front of the Strathmores. He could smell the lather of the horses, hear the animals' labored breathing.

The band did not slow. They swept past, dark faces turned briefly toward the party. An unlucky pan, left behind, spun and clattered, crushed under the booming hooves.

James's scalp prickled. For an instant he had thought he recognized a familiar, black-haired form among the riders. There was something about the way the man sat his horse that native dress could not quite disguise. James blinked twice, but when he looked again he could see nothing that would distinguish one robed figure from the others, and then the riders reached a bend in the road and vanished.

Could Reggie have somehow gotten word of their departure and followed them?

The expedition collected itself and returned slowly to the road.

"What the devil?" Sir Edward glared in the direction the riders had gone.

James glanced at Khalil, but the guide shrugged. "I do not know, sir. None of them were related to me."

It felt like a close call, even though the riders had done nothing to threaten them. He uncocked his pistol. He needed to be more careful here outside of Tunis. The Strathmores' welfare was his responsibility.

"Khalil—take the rear for a bit. Keep a sharp eye out and warn us if anyone approaches. Everyone, if we're threatened form up close, with the women behind."

They were more vulnerable than he liked—a caravan of luggage and women and botanical equipment. Too many complications. He looked over to Lily.

Far too many complications.

They rode on for an hour more through orange groves and past wheat fields before coming to an ancient stone bridge spanning the river. A swarthy man in striped robes stood at the head of the bridge, casually holding an ancient musket. Behind him ranged five other men, with long, wicked blades tucked in their sashes.

James raised his hand, halting the party. His horse shifted restlessly beneath him. "Move out of the way," he said in French.

The leader sneered. "For you to cross, one hundred *dinar*."

Behind him James heard Sir Edward's sound of outrage.

"Ridiculous." Khalil had ridden up from the rear. "Even my father would not charge so much. This is the Bey's road, and you have his letter. There is no charge to travel. I will tell him."

The two natives spoke angrily in Arabic, their voices growing louder as they exchanged what could only be insults.

"What is he saying?" James asked at last.

A frown lined Khalil's face. "I will not repeat what that flea-bitten dog says, except that he insists now the price is two hundred dinars."

James studied the ground in front of him. Fresh tracks led straight over the bridge and beyond. He bent low in the saddle to look, and then dismounted to examine something on the ground. He picked it up—the butt of a stubbed-out cheroot.

"The ones who came before us," he said to the man on the bridge. "Did they pay?"

"No." The bandit's thumb stroked the gun barrel. "But you do not pass."

"On whose command? Yours or the foreigner's?"

His opponent shifted his eyes to one side and sucked his teeth. "Three hundred dinars," he said. Behind him, the other men stepped forward, their hands gripping the hilts of their swords.

James looked back. Sir Edward's face was flushed with rage. "Huntington, we outnumber them four to one. It's outrageous for them to stop us."

"It is—but consider what we have to lose if we try and force our way across." His gaze rested on Lily for a heartbeat, then Isabelle, Richard, the men from Brookdale. Which one would he be willing to endanger? They were all here because of him. "We can't afford to take risks. There must be another way."

"Yes," Khalil said. "There is a ford, though it brings us some distance from our chosen path."

James swung himself into the saddle. "Take us there."

The men on the bridge laughed—a raw, harsh sound like the conversation of crows. James did not look back. It would be harder going off the main road, but the bridge was closed to them.

The river path was overgrown with branches, and the party was continually molested by small black midges whose bites were painful all out of proportion to their size. James dropped back to listen every so often, but could hear no one following.

Conversation within the party dwindled as the path rose and grew rockier and the animals labored. The underbrush made it hard to see the river, but he could hear it, rushing louder. Finally the path widened again, sloping down to disappear under the muddy wildness the Medjerda had become.

Khalil sent a doubtful glance at the river, "It may be a difficult crossing. The rains."

"Oh my," Lady Mary said, looking at the water seething before them. "It is quite a torrent."

James slung down from his horse to study the opposite bank. It would be possible—but not easy. The men and mules waited, as far back from the river as they could, and he could see the drivers were reluctant.

"Fetch a rope—a long one," he said, stripping off his coat. "I'll go across and secure it to that tree."

"It is too dangerous," Sir Edward said. "Have Khalil go instead."

The guide backed up, holding his hands in front of him. "Allah have mercy. I cannot swim."

"I didn't expect you could." James handed his coat to Richard.

"Let me go," the young man said, adventure lighting his eyes. "I can swim splendidly."

"I have no doubt." James rolled up his sleeves. "You may have the chance to demonstrate your skills if the water is deeper than it looks, but stay here for now. I'll need you to help guide the others across." He took the rope and tied one end around his waist.

Lily was looking at him. "Be careful." Her voice was low.

He gave her a wink. "I can swim splendidly, too."

His horse snorted as he urged it into the river. The muddy torrent rose to the animal's knees and then its withers. The water was cold and swift, but he was nearly halfway across. The current was every bit as strong as he had feared. Each step toward the far bank also pushed them downstream. He could feel the animal struggling.

And then it lost its footing as the bottom dropped away.

"James!" He heard the shouts behind him. The horse lunged, and lunged again, the animal's powerful muscles surging against the downriver pull.

The rope was sodden and heavy around his waist, the length of it dragging behind them, and the water buffeted his hips. He could hear nothing but its angry rushing. Finally the horse's feet found purchase and a moment later they splashed out of the river.

The watchers on the far bank let out a cheer, and he turned to wave, dismayed to see how far the current had pulled them. The others would have to start further upstream. He made short work of securing the rope and saw that Khalil had done the same on the opposite side. That would help.

Richard did not hesitate to urge his mount into the water, and shortly the young man joined him. "That wasn't so bad."

"It may be harder to convince them." James nodded at the native men whispering together. "Stay here and help get people ashore. I'll take the other side."

Thank the gods for his horse—a solid dun that did not balk at re-entering the water. The return trip was easier, and with the rope to guide them they avoided the deep water. James rode up to Sir Edward.

"I think we should try and get the men across next," James said. "Give them less time to think about it—since they don't have the benefit of horses."

The botanist nodded and James gestured Khalil and the men forward. It took some coaxing, some appeals to their manliness, and some outright threats, but one-by-one the bearers entered the river, clutching the rope, and cursing or praying as they were inclined. Richard, good lad, had ridden his horse several yards out. He encouraged and shouted, and helped them up the muddy shore until they had all arrived safely. The mules followed in a jangling, braying pack.

James let out a breath. The most difficult part was over.

"Who's next?" He turned to the Strathmores.

"Richard gets to have all the fun," Isabelle said, kneeing her mount forward. James followed her partway across, but the girl was a born horsewoman and was in no danger, though the current pulled fiercely at her skirts. She gave a triumphant cry as she gained the far bank.

Lady Mary was next, followed by Mrs. Hodges. There was a difficult moment when Mrs. Hodges's mount halted halfway, but she prodded the animal forward before James could reach them, and made the rest of the crossing without mishap.

"Go along then, Lily," Sir Edward said. "I'll come right behind you."

"Of course." She smiled brightly, but James could see the anxious set of her shoulders, her tight grip on the reins.

Her horse pranced nervously and nearly shied as it entered the water. James rode over. Of them all, he knew Lily was the least-experienced rider. Too much time spent sketching flowers instead of riding through fields of them. He urged his own horse beside hers, trying to shield her from the brunt of the current, and she gave him a grateful glance.

When they reached the middle of the river something skirled past in the water, startling the horses. Lily's mount let out a shrill whinny and reared wildly. The movement, combined with the current dragging at her, proved too much. Lily fell from the saddle with a splash.

"James!" she cried, reaching as the water tore her away.

"Grab the rope!" He kicked free of the stirrups and leapt after her. Where was she? He lifted his head above the fierce water, panic clutching his heart.

There—she was in the deep water, but had caught the rope, and now clung one handed, her skirts streaming out behind her.

"Hold on!" He did not know if she heard him. Her head dipped under as she fought to reach the line with her other hand.

In a heartbeat he had her, one arm slipping around her small form, lifting her up, the other hand joining hers on the sodden rope.

"James!" she screamed, her eyes wide.

He looked. Lily's horse had gone down and the current was bearing it directly toward them.

"Hold on!" he shouted, and let go of the rope.

The water closed over their heads, dragging them with it. He tried to stand, but as quickly as his feet found purchase they were dragged out from under him. He could barely keep his own head above water. Lily had it worse, but he would not let go even when the water upended him.

A sun-bleached snag thrust out into the water some distance below the ford. James threw his arm around the branchless trunk before they could be sucked under, and then drew Lily to him. "Put your arms around my neck."

Her hair was plastered to her face, dark against the pallor

of her skin. She locked her arms around him and clung so tightly he could scarcely breathe.

Using the fallen tree for support, he inched them toward shore. Soon the water came only to his waist, then his thighs, his knees. He pulled Lily into his arms and stumbled onto the bank.

When they got there he let himself sink down, rewarded by the feel of solid ground beneath them. He looked into Lily's face. It was pale, her lips almost blue. Spasms of coughing wracked her.

"That's my girl," he said, holding her shoulders until the coughing subsided. "Everything's fine, love. Everything's fine."

She clung to him then, and opened her eyes. "I thought we were lost. Did we make it across?"

He smiled down at her. "Yes. We made it across."

"Lily!" Richard shoved his way through the underbrush, his face frantic, his clothes dripping. "Are you all right?"

She drew in a deep, shuddering breath and James felt her relax suddenly in his arms. "Yes. I am."

Her cousin's expression lightened. "You should have heard Isabelle scream when your horse went down."

The others were shouting to them and making their way down the shore. James lifted Lily and stood with her in his arms. He could not let go. Not yet. The feel of her against him—warm, breathing—was too precious, the twine of her arms around his neck all he needed.

"James," she whispered into his ear, "I believe we are on solid ground. You can put me down."

Evening was laying long shadows across the hills when at last they straggled back onto the main road. The westering sun deepened the cinnamon-colored soil to a rich orange and gilded the limbs of cork oak growing beside the river.

"Where are the ruins you spoke of?" James asked Khalil. "The animals are tired."

"Not much farther." The guide pointed to a small rise ahead. "Just the other side."

"Take some men ahead to set up camp. I'll see to the rest of the party."

By the time they reached the camp set in the ruins, lanterns were burning and the tantalizing smell of lamb kebabs wafted from the cooking fires. The tents were standing, rugs and cushions strewn about the interiors where oil lamps winked and glimmered.

"Here we are," Richard said.

Lily dismounted before anyone could offer help, and looked about curiously. "Wherever *here* is. It makes a lovely composition."

Firelight flickered against stone walls, bits of geometric carving running along the top, visible where the stone had not crumbled away. Fluted columns stood sentinel at the edge of the rise, barely silhouetted against the fading light. Beyond, a few early stars twinkled. James swung down to assist Lady Mary.

"Thank you." She smiled tiredly at him as he steadied her.

Sir Edward moved slowly over to them. "I'm a bit stiffer than I'd like. Nothing a good night's sleep won't cure, though."

The accident at the crossing and the long road had left them all feeling subdued, but dinner revived the party considerably and they lingered over cups of tea. Richard excused himself and went to squat with Khalil by the open fire, likely after a cup of Turkish coffee. During their trips to the *souq* he had become a convert to the dark, heavily sweetened brew served in tiny cups.

"Your son is going native," Sir Edward said to his wife.

"At least he is not drinking out of a gourd."

"Don't the ruins seem mysterious?" Isabelle glanced into the shadows. "Especially in the moonlight."

"Worth exploring, I'd say," Richard said, approaching. "I don't feel sleepy at all."

James looked over the camp. Why not? The men would be on watch. The family needed something to take their minds off the near-tragedy of the afternoon. "If you enter the ruins beware," he said in a stage whisper.

"Why?" said Richard and Isabelle together.

James raised his hands above his head, curling his fingers. The light from the fire cast his shadow, huge and grotesque, on the ruined wall behind them.

"Evil djinns."

"Rubbish," Mrs. Hodges said.

Everyone else laughed.

"Do you feel up to going, Lily?" Isabelle asked.

"Of course I do. I'm quite resilient when it comes to falling off horses, although I'd prefer to fall onto a pile of folded linens or a mound of hay and not into a raging river next time."

James offered his hand, smiling.

"Go along then." her uncle said. "Roman ruins by moonlight. Perfectly splendid! We crossed the Mediterranean for adventures like this."

She let James draw her to her feet and he folded his hand over hers. Life was too precious and uncertain to be locked away for the future.

"Do take lanterns," Lady Mary said.

"We will," Richard said. "If there's a djinn to be found, I don't want to walk past it in the dark. They grant wishes, you know."

"Really." Isabelle tossed her head. "There's no danger . . . Is there?" She looked to James for reassurance.

"Giant spiders," Richard said. "The ghost of Hannibal."

"Ha." She drew her shawl more tightly around her shoulders.

"It should be safe," James said. "Khalil scouted the area before we arrived."

"Come on," Richard tugged Isabelle's arm. "Do you think that's a skull over there?" Without a backward glance he headed deeper into the ruins, his sister close behind.

James glanced at Lily. "Which way?"

She looked back at the fire, then seemed to come to some decision. "Up there." She gestured to the pillars cresting the top of the hill.

They set off, Lily stepping nimbly over the rubble while James guided them around larger obstacles. The lantern light picked out fitful details—an arched doorway, lichen staining a tumbled wall, the handle of a broken ewer protruding from the soil. They gained the rise, the bright splashes of the fires below seeming very small. Old Roman columns rose around them poised against the night sky.

"In the darkness they seem almost new," Lily said. "As though we've been transported back thousands of years."

Looking out over the dark valley, James could almost believe it was true. "I can hear the legions tramping down the road."

"And the rumble of chariot wheels. What was this place, do you think?" She turned slowly, examining the tumbled stones.

"A villa, a private retreat, perhaps." He set the lantern down, shrugged out of his coat and laid it on a nearby block of granite.

She sank down with a sigh. "It was a long day."

"I'm happy to reach the end of it with everyone intact. Are you sure you suffered no harm from our plunge in the river?"

"I'll be perfectly all right, thanks to you. If you had not caught me . . ." She looked at him, her eyes shining in the lantern light.

"Someone else would have." His heart clenched as he re-lived that moment when she had slipped from the saddle into the current. "Richard would have enjoyed rescuing you, I'm sure."

"Perhaps. But then I would never have heard the end of it. I'm glad it was you, James. I am always glad of you." Her last words were nearly a whisper.

He heard them all the same. She was staring up at the column beside them, the stars crowning it. The look on her face was wistful, filled with a melancholy yearning James recognized all too well.

He sat down beside her and took her hand—the same hand he had clung to as they tumbled beneath the muddy water. He traced each of her fingers with his own.

"When your horse went down today, Lily . . ." he shook his head slowly. "I could not live with myself if I let any harm come to you."

"I feel the same. It was very foolish of you to leap after me." She looked at him. "And very brave."

She reached up to trace the line of his jaw, one finger tentatively coasting over his lips. He closed his eyes, only to open them when he felt the warmth of her lips. A quiver raced through him. Softly, gently, she moved her mouth against his. James sat very still, letting her lead the way. Her hand cupped his face and she leaned in toward him, deepening the kiss. So, their embrace under the tree had not been their last after all.

When at last she broke the kiss she smiled up at him, eyes shining. "James," she said. "You are my James and my Mr. Huntington all rolled into one."

"Lily." He reached for her, She leaned into his touch, came willingly into his arms and lifted her face toward him.

"Kiss me," she breathed.

Her words were a spark kindling suddenly to a blaze. When he leaned down to press his lips to hers, she responded urgently. Life burned brightly through his blood and he had to touch her, skin to skin, he had to taste her and know that she was real and here. And his.

Need hurried his fingers down the row of buttons at her back, loosening her dress until he could slip it off her shoulders, his palms hot on the bare skin of her arms. Her corset thrust her breasts up, the thin silk of her chemise doing little to shelter the tight pink tips. James brushed his hand over her, heard her gasp deep in her throat as he tightened his fingers on the nub.

Her hair was falling loose, unruly and dark over the paleness of her chemise and skin. She looked like a goddess of the night. Passion shone from her eyes, and her mouth was soft and moist from his kisses. She untangled her fingers from the sleeves of her dress, then reached and laced them into his hair, pulling his mouth back to hers.

An answering wildness rising in him, James took her lips and swept his tongue into her mouth. He would kiss her so deeply, so thoroughly that she would never forget, never call him "Mr. Huntington" again. Not with the brand of his kiss seared on her lips. She arched against him, lips parting wide, yielding to his advance.

Without releasing her mouth he tightened his arms and pulled her onto his lap, turning her, nudging her legs until she was straddling him. Heat flared between them and he lifted his hand to cup her breast again, greedy for the feel of her.

"Ah." She flung back her head, exposing her neck to his

mouth, seeming oblivious to her wanton position, lost in the heady pleasure of the night. Even through her skirts he could feel the heat of her there, at the juncture of her legs. She pressed against him, her womanly softness so close to his throbbing erection.

James moved his mouth down, one hand pulling her chemise away as he dipped his head. His lips found her taut nipple and he wrung another gasp of pleasure from her. She shifted on his lap and heat speared through his groin. It was easy enough to gather her skirts in his hands and pull them up, knuckles skimming the soft skin of her legs as he bared her even further.

She was unbuttoning him too, he realized as the cool night air over his shoulders was replaced by the heat of her touch. The breath rasped in his throat as he slid his hands up her thighs and curved under her tight, rounded bottom. He could lift her, unbutton his trousers and let her hot, wet, warmth enfold him as she slid down his cock. He could have her here and now. He was sure she would not refuse him.

James let out a stifled groan. Much as he wanted her he knew this was not the place. She deserved better than a hurried coupling braced on the stones of an old ruin. He needed time to coax her and build her pleasure, comfort and luxury to lead her to a place of passion she would never forget. He pulled her against his chest, holding her still against him, summoning all his willpower.

"Mmm," she said, her mouth vibrating against the skin of his neck. She pressed her lips there, then the soft heat of her tongue flared over his skin. Gods, she was irresistible.

It did not help his resolve when her hands drifted low between them. Her touch found his hardness, her palm smoothing against the strained fabric of his trousers.

"Lily," he managed.

"Yes?" Her voice was throaty with pleasure. "I am so curious about you. When you touched me in the Bey's palace—is there an equivalent pleasure? Let me just . . ."

How could he tell her no? Every nerve in him was centered there, where she was unbuttoning his trouser flap. This was too dangerous, but he could not stop her. He would do anything to feel her touch him, yes, like that, her hand stroking the sensitive underside, then wrapping around him.

"You are so hot and hard and yet the skin is so . . . soft. And," a teasing note entered her voice, "you seem much larger than any of the marble statues I have viewed."

He laughed. "Sculptors don't show the aroused male state—at least not the sculptures on public display."

"Then I arouse you?" A brush of her fingertips along the ridge of his cock caused him to shudder with pleasure.

"Far more than is good for you." He drew her hands away, removing the utter distraction of her touch. The night settled in around them, the faint echo of Richard's laughter drifting up from the ruins below. It was time they returned to the camp.

Lily seemed to feel it too. She tugged her skirts down, then slipped her arms through her dress and pulled it back over her shoulders. Still, she did not leave her position on his lap. Her voice held that teasing note again as she leaned forward.

"Can you do up my buttons as quickly as you undid them?"

"Of course not. I am closing away your delights. It's to be expected that the process will be slowed by regret."

"Well," she leaned against him and linked her arms behind his head. "I am quite comfortable here, so you may take whatever time you need."

Whatever time he needed. A lifetime would not be enough.

When he had finished with the buttons he pulled her hard against him and ravished her mouth with one last kiss. Let her remember that as she lay in the canvas hollow of her tent, the wild fitful light of the stars above singing her to sleep.

Chapter 18

Lily urged her mount up the rocky track, leaning forward to help the mare scramble up the incline. The afternoon sun lay hot across her shoulders and insects droned from a nearby stand of trees. After three days of following the river the expedition had turned into the hills, leaving cultivated fields for open, rocky slopes and thickets of oaks and evergreens.

Ahead, James guided his horse around a tumble of stones, his lean figure easy in the saddle. She could not stop thinking about him. Paging through her sketchbook this morning it had become so clear—James in half-profile sitting beside the evening fire, James speaking with the Arab drivers, his face serious, his face smiling. Even when she had been trying to shut him out she could not keep from drawing him.

He was nothing at all like she had thought him to be back on the Southampton docks. What an admirable leader he was, commanding respect without being harsh. Everyone had come to rely on him. He was intelligent, sometimes sweet, and his flashes of humor . . . He fit well with this family of her heart.

Yesterday, clinging to the rope while the river tried to pull her under, it had not mattered at all what her future held. She had nearly had no future. So why had she been so determined to hold to a course she detested?

Suddenly the sky was too bright, the wind too gentle. She wanted to laugh and weep at the same time.

"I love him," she whispered.

She had been a fool not to admit it before.

Because her future did not allow it she had pretended it was not happening, that she was not falling beautifully, hopelessly, in love with James.

There was no way she could wed Lord Buckley now. Not when her heart had veered in an entirely different direction. Marriage to him would be a sham, one she would regret each bitter day for the rest of her life.

The horse's hooves clattered over loose scree as she guided it around the stones. There must be room in some corner of the empire for two wayward hearts. She would begin a life with James somewhere else, and as long as he was beside her she would be content.

Ahead, Uncle Edward drew rein and leaned precariously over. "*Orchis italica!* A perfect specimen. Higgs, bring my trowel and the Wardian bottle."

The head gardener rummaged through the equipment and removed a bulky specimen jar. Drawn by her uncle's enthusiasm, the party gathered, watching as Uncle Edward carefully excavated around the base of the small pink flower.

"The jar is hermetically sealed after the specimen is placed in it," he said, carefully taking it from Higgs. "Ingenious, really. Revolutionized collecting. Now the entire plant can now be safely transported. No need to rely on seeds or delicate cuttings. Here we are." He lifted the orchid. Bringing his hand lens to bear he inspected the leaves, and then moved on to the myriad small petals making up the conical flower head. "Fascinating. On closer inspection, one can see that the petals do indeed form an anatomically correct male figure."

"Really, Edward!" Aunt Mary drew Isabelle back.

"Sorry my dear." He tried to tuck the plant away, but Richard leaned forward, catching his father's arm.

"It is, by Jove. Who would have imagined?" Richard grinned

as his father nestled the plant into the jar and closed the lid tightly.

Lily tried to look uninterested, but she wondered. Did it really look like, well, what her uncle had implied? She glanced about casually, hoping to spy more of the low-growing pink blooms beside the path. James caught her eye and she felt heat rise to her cheeks.

When the party rode on, the trail flattening out into a broad valley, James brought his horse next to her.

She glanced over. "Whatever will my uncle find next?"

His eyes laughed down into hers. "Who would think a flower could be so indiscreet? Exposing itself right beside the trail."

"Obviously not a native English plant."

His grin held a touch of wicked humor. "I assure you the resemblance was not as striking as you might think."

"It's in the eye of the beholder, I suppose. Though I didn't get a good look, I suspect the proportions are not quite accurate." She recalled the feel of his hard body against her, the heat of him in her hand—what she had felt could hardly be classified as a blossom of any sort. She glanced away and smiled secretly to herself. If he wished to further instruct her in the ways a man and a flower differed, she would not refuse him.

His voice grew serious. "Khalil says the village we are seeking lies ahead. Someone there may be able to point us to the valley we seek."

"Then we are close?"

"Very close." He guided his mount even nearer. "Lily. If we find what I hope to, then everything will be different. And I would ask you something important."

She looked up at him, hardly able to breathe.

Yes.

She wanted to shout it, but before she could speak he caught her hand and raised it to his lips. The feel of his soft kiss lingered there as he released her and spurred his mount up the trail.

Lily gazed after him, a wash of heat spreading through her. What did he wish to ask her? She hardly dared imagine, but the possibility made her spirit soar.

The village, when they reached it, was no more than a collection of small houses built of stones scavenged from roads and ruins. Goats bleated at the approaching travelers and children clustered to whisper and stare. A delegation of men waited beside the dirt track.

"Stay here." James slid to the ground. "Khalil and I will see if we're on the right path."

They went forward, exchanging greetings with a craggy-faced old man wearing dark robes. After an animated discussion, James returned.

"The headman is curious about what brings foreigners to his village." He opened the flap of one saddlebag and removed a leather wallet. From it he drew several folded sheets of paper. "I want to see if this is familiar to him."

"Capital idea. Show him the drawing," Uncle Edward said.

"What drawing?" Richard asked.

Isabelle prodded her mount up beside Lily. "What is it?" she asked with more interest than Lily would have expected.

"I don't know. It looks like a letter." Was it the one Lord Reginald had questioned her about in Cadiz?

"The map," Isabelle said. Her horse sidled nervously beneath her.

So, James had had a clue to their destination all along, one that his cousin had wanted to lay his hands on. But why?

"Buried treasure," Isabelle whispered.

Could it be? No wonder Lord Reginald had been so eager to learn of it. It would explain James's words, as well. If his fortunes were about to be changed . . .

They watched James lift one of the sheets and show it to the headman. Lily's breathing quickened. The man gestured toward a peak visible in the distance, and James nodded, a quick grin flashing across his face. It seemed they had found their way at last.

They followed a narrow track out of the village, winding higher into the foothills. The air felt cool and the sky overhead was the color of ripe plums. She had never seen James so happy—joking with the men, riding off the trail to bring back cuttings for her uncle. And when he looked at her—her blood caught fire, for his eyes held a sultry promise she could not misread.

The sun was low when James halted the party to make camp in a fold of meadow. Lily could not resist the bold light and stark lines of the ridges. She set her easel up a short distance below the tents and began to paint. The shadows here were nearly cobalt against the spice-colored earth.

One of the men was whistling and the smell of frying onions floated down from the cook fire. Tomorrow they would reach the valley, and the whole camp seemed to share James's excitement.

He came toward her, hands in his pockets, his hair tousled by the breeze. A wide smile lit his face when he saw her watching him. "The best of evenings to you, Lily. Your aunt asked me to tell you the bathing tent has been set up and will be at your disposal after supper."

"A bath—how divine. I could use a good soak."

He sniffed the air. "You certainly could."

"Wretch. You need one more than I do." Lily tucked her brushes away. "Please, do me the favor of standing downwind."

"If that's your opinion then perhaps I ought to visit the bathing tent after supper, myself."

"I'm afraid you'll find it occupied, and the tub is hardly large enough for two."

"Are you quite certain about that?"

Oh my. The sudden memory of him rising over her, naked chest gleaming, made her feel giddy—and bold. "If you appear there will be nothing for you but to scrub my back. It's so much easier with help."

His expression grew intent. "If I appear, I will do far more than scrub your back."

Goodness. Was that a threat or a promise? The way he looked at her made it difficult to think of a properly witty retort. She swallowed. "We'll just see about that."

He raised a roguish eyebrow and then broke into a grin.

"Supper is almost ready. If you want to be fed before you are bathed, you'd better hurry."

The water was pleasantly hot. Lily lay back in the bath with a sigh and wiggled her toes in contentment. Lamps shed a soft, golden glow inside the tent and the scent of lavender and roses wafted up in the steam. They may have all laughed at Aunt Mary, but Lily was thankful for the small luxuries that existed only because of her aunt's insistence—and this was no small luxury.

She supposed James was not coming—not that she had really expected him to. It would have been daring in the extreme. He had been teasing, of course. But with the flickering lantern light, the breeze moving against the tent, her own nakedness, it was easy to imagine that she was waiting for a lover. She closed her eyes and slid deeper into the water.

The sound of footsteps approaching outside roused her. She held her breath, listening as the tent flap whispered open.

"Lily?" His voice. He had entered the tent, but could not see her, screened as she was by the silken privacy hangings.

She closed her eyes and remained very still. He had come. She almost did not answer, but a wild and careless excitement thrummed through her.

"I'm here," she called softly, the knowledge of her choice making her tremble.

She heard the hush of silk. Then silence.

James stood there, one hand holding back the curtains. The linen of his shirt outlined the muscles beneath and his open collar showed the sun-darkened skin at his throat.

She met his eyes. Being exposed to his gaze made her feel reckless, wanton. She lifted one knee above the water, the skin glistening where droplets ran down, and watched his attention focus there.

"You are perfect, Lily." His voice was low as he stepped forward.

The look in his eyes took her breath—desire tempered with a tenderness that made her feel cherished beyond compare.

The lamplight burnished his features and sparked glints of gold from his hair.

He stood over her a moment and she knew the translucent water provided no concealment. She resisted the urge to cover herself with her hands. The naked passion revealed in his face was ample reward for her boldness. Then he knelt beside the tub and lifted his hand to her cheek, a touch light as the finest sable brush.

She smiled at him. "Have you come to wash my back?"

"Yes." He leaned forward, grazing his lips against hers. She sighed and felt him smile against her mouth.

"How many times I have dreamed of this," he murmured, then kissed her.

The wetness of their mouths echoed the sensations of the water buoying her, lapping her skin. He deepened the kiss then nudged her head back to rest against the tub's rim, her throat exposed to his questing lips, his tongue flicking against the smooth, moist skin.

"Shall I get out?" It was difficult to speak. The combination of his kisses and the water moving gently around her body was intoxicating.

"No." He breathed the words against her neck. "I'd rather . . . assist you . . . with your bath." Each pause in his words was punctuated by a kiss, making delightful shivers course through her.

He stood and stripped off his coat, rolling up the sleeves of his shirt to bare tanned, muscled forearms. Taking up a washcloth, he settled on the low stool beside the tub. "Let me begin with . . ." he directed a lazy, dangerous smile at her, "your arm."

He drew the rounded bar of soap slowly down from her shoulder to her fingers, and then retraced the slick path with his palm. The wet washcloth followed, sending rivulets of warm scented water tickling down her skin.

He turned her hand over and rubbed his soap-slick thumb lightly against her palm, then laced his fingers with hers, sliding them gently back and forth. She stirred, sending ripples against the side of the tub.

He lavished the same attentions on her other arm, leaning over, his linen-clad chest just above the naked peaks of her breasts.

"I must do a thorough job," he murmured.

Letting his fingers skim lightly over her body, he moved down and lifted her ankle. Lily lay back in the water and let the sensations wash over her—the smooth slip of soap, his warm, strong hands, the rougher nap of the cloth. Her breath caught as he worked his way up over her knees to the soft skin of her thighs. Where would he stop?

Her center began to pulse with anticipation of his touch. She had not forgotten how he had made her feel the last time he had touched her there.

Her nipples tightened and puckered, lapped by the water.

Finished with her legs, James slid the soap between his palms, working up a lather. He leaned forward and placed his palms flat against her collarbones, his touch smooth and firm. With excruciating slowness he drew his hands down. She nearly forgot to breathe as he slid them over her breasts and traced her curves. He cupped her in his hands and brushed his thumbs across the slippery, sensitive peaks. Pleasure streaked through her as he caressed her, his hands slick against her skin.

The wet cloth was almost too rough. At her gasp he drew back, cupped water in his hands and let it trickle over her, gently rinsing her body.

"I believe it is time to scrub your back," he said. "Lean forward."

She did, wanting his hands on her, wanting him to touch her everywhere. He worked with his bare hands, smoothing across her shoulders, following her spine down then coming to rest on the curve of her hips. She held her breath, released it on a sigh as he leaned forward and set his lips to the back of her neck. Bent forward she felt both vulnerable and adored.

"If you'd care to rise?" He reached for one of the thick white towels and held it ready.

Frustration stabbed through her. The juncture of her legs throbbed, still waiting for his touch. Did he know what he was doing to her? From the wicked light in his eyes, she suspected he did. Lily stepped, dripping, from the tub, and let him enfold her.

He rubbed her skin with the soft nap, turning her, lifting her clean, wet hair and drying it.

"I have a gift for you," he said.

"Really? What does one bring to someone just out of her bath?" Suddenly modest, she clutched the towel to her when he would have let it drop to the floor.

He handed her a parcel. "Open it and see."

Lily untied the string, folding back the wrapping to reveal a swath of blue-green cloth shimmering in the lamplight. She shook it out—a length of dusky sea woven of supple, silky fabric.

On a whim she let the towel slide and instead wound the sumptuous length of cloth around her. It clung to her thighs, her hips, outlined her breasts. She felt transformed—not a proper English lady at all, but some wild, sensuous spirit.

"Gods." He stared at her, fire in his look, and then stepped close. "I also brought you this." A simple teardrop turquoise pendant set in silver dangled from his hand. "I found it in the market in Tunis." He fastened it around her neck, his fingers brushing her skin. The stone settled between her breasts. "Now I believe you are properly dressed."

"For what?"

"For being carried off to my lair, of course."

"I wasn't aware you had one." Her voice came out in a whisper.

"Yes. For what I have in mind, I definitely need a lair."

"And a captive?"

"A willing one. Are you willing?"

For answer, she covered his mouth in an urgent kiss. When she finally pulled away they were both breathing raggedly. In one smooth motion he caught her behind the knees and lifted her into his arms. They were out under the stars almost before she realized he was moving. James strode quickly up the slope, surefooted in the darkness. She clutched his shoulders.

"Is this the way to your lair?"

He didn't answer, but Lily could see the white flash of his smile. They rounded a tumble of rocks and he knelt, laying her down in softness.

Rustling, the clank of metal on stone. Light blossomed from a shielded lantern to illuminate a sheltered hollow walled off from the camp by a tumble of boulders. The light revealed the unexpected wealth of the cushions and coverlets she rested on, gold and garnet fabric shimmering in sharp contrast to the rough, elemental backdrop of rock.

Above them Lily could see the night sky filled with constellations and between them farther stars, glowing faintly, and behind those soft lights, even dimmer stars stitched to the darkness.

She reached up and touched his face. The way he looked at her made her feel poised on the edge of a warm, cherishing sea. His features—she had traced them so often that his face was more familiar to her than her own.

She had dreamed of this, lying in his arms, the two of them removed from the world. Yet all the world, everything that mattered, was here, cradled in cushions, the solid embrace of the stones, the pulse of the earth beating with impossible slowness beneath them.

He slid down beside her and their lips met, lingered, opened. The thin fabric was hardly a barrier between them—she felt the strength of him over her, wanted him closer. She drew him close, reveling in the feel of his body pressed against her.

"I want to see you," she breathed. "All of you."

He knelt, pulled off his coat, and then drew his shirt over his head in one motion. The soft glow of lamplight lay over his chest and broad shoulders. His hands went to his waist, and he stripped his trousers off. Lily's breath caught. Against the backdrop of the night he looked like some elemental god formed of fire and darkness. His manhood, freed from the restraints of clothing, rose up.

"May I . . . touch you?" His body was so different from her own.

He nodded, his eyes hooded. She reached, wrapped her fingers gently around the shaft, amazed again at his heat, his smoothness. He tensed.

"Does it hurt?"

"No." He spoke through gritted teeth. "It pleasures me."

Watching his face, she tightened her hold, stroked her thumb over the top. She didn't think it possible, but he grew even larger under her caress.

"Stop." He was breathing fast. "It's my turn."

Laying her back on the cushions, he ran his hands over her silk-wrapped body, loosening, unwinding, revealing a bit of thigh, the curve of her shoulder, then her hip. Each new discovery was rewarded with a kiss. Her skin burned, sensitive to his every touch. Finally she lay naked on a swath of sea-green. He moved his hands to her hair, combing through the long tresses with his fingers. She curled her arms overhead and sighed.

James studied her. "I've wanted to see you like this."

She felt unfettered—free to follow her heart at last, to accept the sweetness life had to offer. To give herself to him, body, heart, and soul.

He kissed her lightly, his lips feathering caresses over her throat, her arms, her breasts, down the curve of her stomach. Nudging her legs apart, he kissed her thighs, her knees. He left her breathless and tingling, her skin so sensitive she could almost feel the cool starlight washing over her.

"More," he said, kneeling between her legs. He bent and brushed his hands over the curls between her thighs. Lily sighed at the touch. At last—just when she thought she could wait no longer. His kiss touched her thigh, another her hip, then one even closer to where his hands were playing. Lily's eyes opened wide. Surely he wasn't going to kiss her there?

But to her delight he did—his lips moving, then his tongue lightly touching her. She gasped at the intimacy as he roused sensations she had never dreamed of. The flick of his tongue there, probing against her softness, made her writhe against the silks. He gripped her thighs in either hand, opening her even more, savoring, tasting her. Something began to tighten in her—she remembered the feeling, the tension and desire.

"Not yet," he said. "There is more—so much more."

He rose over her and guided himself to her entrance. She could feel the blunt tip parting her folds. Slowly he eased partway inside, and then stopped. He was over her and around her and within her all at once, her body opening to accommodate his hard length. He pulled back, and she clutched his shoulders. All her concentration was centered on the feeling of him between her legs.

He entered her, pulled out, each time sliding a little deeper. His face was taut with desire, but he led her slowly until she rocked her hips up against him.

"Don't stop." His even stroking was winding her up again. The stars brightened overhead.

"Lily," he murmured, dropping his head to take her lips again. Their tongues joined the rhythm of their bodies. She held tightly to him, hands splayed across his back, legs wrapped around his hips.

Held on—even as her senses flew apart, lightning sheeting through her, coursing through her limbs. She was dimly aware that he, too, had tensed and was shuddering above her. They were two stars streaking across the sky, fiery tails burning the night around them.

When at last they fell back to earth he shifted off her and drew her against him. She had not known it could be like this—shaken, amazed, she was touched to her very core.

"Ah, Lily." He pulled a coverlet over them both and held her tightly against the shelter of his warm body. She was not sure, but as sleep rose up to claim her she thought she heard him whisper, "My love."

The night breeze brushed Isabelle's skin, making her nerves tingle. For a moment she fought the urge to slip back into her tent, but she could not turn back. She took a hesitant step forward, all her senses alert, then another, and another, until she was moving quickly away from the camp. It was for her family's protection, after all. Someone had to save the expedition.

Not that she didn't long to see Lord Reginald again.

How wearily the days had dragged since she had last seen him. The knowledge that he was following them was her only comfort. He was truly the most perfect man—dashing, kind, yet with an air of mystery that had drawn her to him from the first. His aristocratic features and elegant ways, not to mention the marked attention he had paid her, made her heart skitter with delicious emotion. Here, out in the wilds, she had often imagined him atop a promontory, mounted on a spirited Arab stallion and watching over her, protecting her from afar as he had promised.

Her fingers smoothed the note in her pocket, the note she secretly re-read several times a day, even though she knew the words by heart.

> *Dearest Isabelle—what would I have done without your courageous actions? You have saved the day. Meet me the evening after you reach the village that James spoke of. I will come to you.*
>
> *—R*

She glanced about once more, then hurried down toward where animals were tethered. There was a sentry on watch there, but Isabelle had given the matter much thought.

"Who goes there?" The voice was louder than she had expected.

"Tom! Must you rouse the whole camp?"

"Miss Isabelle! Beggin' your pardon. I didn't know it was you." The gardener's son doffed his hat.

"No matter. I'm quite recovered." Isabelle straightened her shoulders and stepped closer. "Tell me, Tom, has everything been quiet down here this evening?"

"Aye, miss." He cast a glance at where the horses were tethered, placidly lipping the night-dark grasses. "They were restless a wee bit ago, but everything is calm now."

"Good." She kept herself from looking out into the night. "Then perhaps I won't trouble you too much."

"What, miss? I'm sure it won't be no trouble at all."

She clasped her hands together. "Well, it's just that the roof of my tent is sagging. I think some of the ropes are not tight enough. I knew that since you helped put it up, you would know just what to do."

"That I do, and terrible sorry to hear it caused you trouble, miss."

"Yes, well, if you fixed it now, then it would be all taken care of." Isabelle gave him her sweetest smile.

"Right away, miss." Tom turned toward the camp.

There, it hadn't been so difficult. Her lips curved into a secret smile as she gazed up at the stars—impossibly bright. Tonight was made for something more, something special, she could feel it in the warm dark air stirring about her.

Would Lord Reginald kiss her? She had thought he was going to twice before, but it seemed his gentlemanly instincts had not permitted him to do more than lean toward her, his black eyes dark with secrets and promises, his elegant fingers brushing a path down her cheek before he turned away. Tonight, though . . .

"Miss?" Tom's voice made her start.

"What is it?" Could he not just go?

"I should be escorting you back. Wouldn't like to leave a lady unprotected."

She mustered up a smile. "Nonsense. I found my way down here, after all. And the night is so beautiful, I crave a few moments of solitude."

Tom wrinkled his brow as she spoke, then shook his head, as if the ways of the gentry were beyond him. "If you say so, miss."

This time Isabelle watched until his figure had completely disappeared up the hill. At last! She raised her hand to her face, gently touching her own cheek. Lord Reginald was out there in the night, waiting for her. She could feel it.

A noise made her whirl—the crunch of dry leaves underfoot, the snort of a horse. There, in the shadows of the trees beyond.

Her heartbeat quickened as she glided forward, just like some heroine in a book, her pale gown swirling, the starlight glimmering in her hair. In the darkness beneath the trees the air was still and fragrant. Isabelle turned, but could see no one. Her heart raced furiously, her entire body taut and listening.

Despite the pitch of her nerves she did not sense his presence until a large hand covered her mouth, muffling her involuntary shriek. Strong arms pulled her back against a tall, masculine form. They encircled her, pinning her arms against her body. For an instant mindless panic engulfed her, but just as quickly the fear was transformed into pure joy. Lord Reginald! She would never mistake his scent—cloves and tobacco smoke and something else, something so warm and enticing that she did not know what to call it. He had come to her! It was impossibly romantic.

Isabelle tried to turn, to drink in the sight of him, but he would not let her. Nor did he lift his hand from her mouth, only drew her with him deeper into the shadows.

"Mmmf," she said. This was not precisely how she had imagined their reunion.

"Hush." The command was a mere breath feathered against her neck, immediately replaced by the brush of his lips.

The intimate sensation was almost enough to make her forget her discontent. Yet it was hardly a fitting welcome— even under the unusual circumstances. She dreaded to think what Mrs. Hodges might say of a young woman who allowed such familiarity. Why, Lord Reginald hadn't even wished her good evening. How could he notice she was wearing the necklace he had bought her if he wouldn't let her turn around? She needed to face him, to see the brilliant white of his smile, to hear him murmur her name, to recognize her own longing reflected in his dark eyes. No, this was not how it was supposed to be at all. She wrenched her head in a very unladylike manner, trying again to turn in his arms.

For a moment the pressure of his arm eased, but before Isabelle could seize the advantage he had caught her tightly again. His hand brushed upward over her stomach and, shock of shocks, settled over her breast!

The nerve of the man! Where were the tender words and sweet kisses? He might enjoy playing the wicked savage, but she needed the gallant gentleman she had come to adore aboard the *Sidonia*. His thumb began to stroke against her. Really, Lord Reginald was taking the most outrageous liberties. Without thinking Isabelle kicked back with a move she had perfected on her brother in more innocent times. She was rewarded with a muffled grunt.

The hand dropped from her breast, but Lord Reginald did not release her. She was preparing a second kick when another figure moved out of the darkness.

"Tie her hands," the man behind her whispered. His voice was rough—no sweet lover's murmur. The night was suddenly too dark.

He dropped his hand from her mouth and Isabelle drew in a deep breath. Someone would hear her if she screamed. But he was too quick. In an instant the hand was replaced by a length of cloth, pulled back and tied roughly behind her head. The other man had hastened to do his master's bidding, prisoning her hands behind her with rough rope.

Now she struggled in earnest, half in fear, half in rage at the betrayal and humiliation. She was strong for her size, and landed one more good kick, her hair coming loose and falling down about her face, but the two men hauled her to a tree and quickly wound the rest of the rope around her. Lord Reginald was careful to stay behind her the whole time. The coward! The utter scoundrel! Could he possibly think she had not recognized him?

"That should keep her occupied." A low laugh accompanied the words. "Now drive off the horses and signal the others." The two men moved away, leaving Isabelle swallowing against the gag. Tears burned down her cheeks, the rough fibers cutting into her wrists as she struggled in the rope's embrace.

Chapter 19

James sat upright, the sound of a gunshot pulling him instantly awake. Shouts carried up from camp along with the sound of clattering hooves. In a heartbeat he was up, scrambling into his clothes, pulling on his boots.

Beside him Lily stirred, then sat, clutching the wrinkled sea-green wrap to her. Her eyes were dark with questions and alarm. "What's happening?"

"I'm going to find out." He set his hand over hers, the brief contact waking a fierce protectiveness in him. "Stay here where it's safe."

Her eyes flashed. "No! My family is down there." She rose to her knees, the length of cloth only emphasizing her nakedness. "I'm coming with you."

James bent and took her face between his palms though every instinct screamed for haste. She had to understand. "Lily. Stay here. Put out the light and wait for me." He planted a fierce kiss against her lips, then was off, leaping boulders and sliding down the steep gravel slope.

Below, a tent was burning, casting a wild, fitful light over the camp. Panicked horses were running loose, equipment and belongings scattered over the ground. James sprinted past the bathing tent toward a confused knot of servants.

"You there!" he shouted as he approached, "All of you. Go

as a group to the Strathmores' tent. Arm yourselves with anything that can be used as a weapon." The men remained where they were, looking fearfully into the darkness as if they did not understand.

"Go, damn you!" James seized one of the Sir Edward's servants by the jacket, and pushed him in the direction of the Strathmores' tent. "To your master." The man stumbled in the proper direction and the others followed, several bending to seize stout sticks of firewood from the pile beside the fire.

James cursed himself for a fool. What had possessed him? How could he have allowed this to happen! He turned toward his tent.

"James!" Richard bolted up, his face pale. "Are we going after them?" Fear and excitement mixed in his young eyes.

"Who did you see? Is anyone hurt?"

"I don't know—those bandits came out of nowhere. They drove the horses right through camp. I never thought we would actually be in danger this trip."

James winced. He had chosen the worst of nights to let down his guard. "Go to your father, and take anyone you can find with you. I'll join you shortly." He gave the younger man's shoulder a squeeze. "Go now."

James sprinted in the opposite direction. There would be ample time for regret later. Right now he needed to secure the camp and retrieve Lily.

A jagged rent in his tent greeted him when he arrived. Someone had hacked at it with a blade. He pushed his way inside. "Bloody hell."

The flickering oil lamp showed his cot tipped, the mattress slashed. Clothing was flung on the floor and his saddlebags were upended. He gritted his teeth. How obliging of him to leave the tent vacant so the thieves could do such a thorough job of plundering.

A soft gleam from the table caught his attention—his gold pocket-watch. It stood untouched where he had left it.

An icy premonition threaded through him.

What kind of bandit would ransack a tent and leave something so valuable behind? James turned in a circle, breath rasping in his throat. There—he could see the silver handle of his pistol protruding from beneath the cot.

The letters! Where were his grandfather's letters?

He dropped to his knees, tossing aside a coat, a smashed stool. There was the wallet they had been in, gaping wide, empty.

"Reggie!" The name left a taste like bile in his mouth. Who else would take those items and leave the valuables? It had to be Reggie.

James snatched his pistol, tucked it into his waistband and rushed out of the tent, half-expecting to see his cousin retreating into the darkness.

"Damn you!" he shouted into the empty dark.

Reggie would be riding for the valley at this very moment, leaving the chaos of the camp and its scattered horses behind. By the time James followed there would be nothing left but a trampled meadow of purple flowers. He doubled over, his hands on his knees.

Why had he dropped his guard when he was so close? Without the journals, how could he speak for Lily? How could he promise her a future? With the wealth the journals could bring, he could be Mr. Huntington to everyone and James to Lily. Without them he would be James to everyone and Mr. Huntington to her.

In one night he had lost everything—everything he wanted, everything he hoped for. Everything he loved.

James turned and sprinted toward the paddock. He had to stop Reggie. Surely there was at least one horse left for him. He would ride hard—unencumbered by folding bathtubs and Wardian bottles. He was twice the horseman Reggie was, and he needed this more. Cold purpose filled him.

"Sir! Sir, wait!" One of the servants was running after him. "Sir Edward—he has been wounded! Come quickly."

James turned on the man. "What the devil are you saying?" He hadn't realized he was shouting until the servant stepped back, fear in his eyes.

"Please, sir."

James took a ragged breath and lowered the pistol he held in his hand. "Tell me what happened—and be quick about it."

"They found Sir Edward lying face down and carried him back to his tent. He don't look good, sir."

James closed his eyes. This couldn't be happening. Not now. With every beat of his heart, hope was slipping further away.

The night seemed colder, the stars obscured. He glanced toward the paddock, toward fortune and respectability and hope. Toward a vanished future. His foolish quest was over before he had even caught sight of the cursed valley.

"I'm coming."

Lady Mary looked up as he entered the tent, her face streaked with tears.

"Thank goodness, you are here, James!" She knelt on the floor beside Sir Edward, who lay prone and ashen on his cot. He was so still and white that for a moment James thought he was looking at a dead man.

"What happened?" James laid a hand on Sir Edward's forehead. A large bruise discolored his temple and the skin was broken, though the bleeding had stopped.

"We had retired and Edward was writing up his notes when we heard horses and shouting. It sounded as though we were being attacked. Edward grabbed his gun and rushed out. It was so foolish of him. Then I heard a shot. They found him like this." Lady Mary covered her face with her hands. A moment later she looked up, eyes filled with tears. "He had just been saying what a lovely holiday this had been."

Before James could find words to express his remorse, Isabelle burst into the tent. Her hair was tumbled around her face and her dress was torn. She took one wild look about, her gaze going to the still figure on the cot.

"Father! Oh no!" She flung herself down beside her mother and began sobbing uncontrollably.

Lady Mary looked up at James. "He . . . he will be all right, won't he? As soon as he wakes?"

James felt for Sir Edward's pulse. It fluttered weakly against his fingers. He had seen injuries like this before. Sometimes the men recovered completely. Sometimes they woke missing pieces of their memory. Sometimes they never woke at all.

"We must get him to a doctor. We'll head back to Tunis at first light."

There could be no hope of overtaking Reggie now. James fought down a wave of helpless anger. It was not Sir Edward's fault.

"Here, now. What's all this?" Mrs. Hodges stepped into the tent. She stopped, pursed her lips, then immediately began issuing orders. "Isabelle, your wailing is doing your mother no good. Pray, control yourself. You there," she gestured to a servant, "fetch more blankets and hot water—and tea. Mr. Huntington, bring a chair for Lady Mary at once."

James fetched the chair while Mrs. Hodges assisted Lady Mary to her feet.

"Oh, Rose," Lady Mary said.

"Courage, dear. Your Edward is made of strong stuff—a little knock to the head will not slow him for long. And Mr. Huntington will get us back to civilization with all speed." She gave James a piercing look.

"Of course." He stepped back.

"I will remain here." Mrs. Hodges gave him a brusque nod. "I expect you are wanted elsewhere."

"Yes." He needed to get to Lily. "I'll look in on you later."

James ducked out of the tent, leaving Isabelle's muffled crying and the strained murmur of women's voices behind. The tent fire was out, and he could see the dark shapes of the men he had posted silhouetted against the flickering light of torches. A horse neighed near the paddock.

If only it were as easy to mend the invisible damage he had done. Despair clawed him as he turned toward the bathing tent. Where was Lily now? Huddled and afraid in the bed he had made them? Was she already regretting everything that had passed between them?

If not now, then soon.

Something glinted on the ground near his feet—a small brass box, probably belonging to one of the ladies. It rattled as he pocketed it. He would find the owner later. Right now he had to get Lily properly clothed and back to her family.

Inside the bathing tent everything was untouched. The water in the tub stood cold and still. His coat, one sleeve darkened with water, sagged in the corner.

Lily's clothing was folded neatly. The silk of her chemise sighed against her dress as he lifted it. He brought the cloth close to his face and inhaled her scent. He had touched heaven and stolen a piece of it. It already seemed a lifetime ago.

What had he gained from his audacity? He had ruined the woman he loved, allowed her uncle to suffer grievous harm, and had shown a complete and utter disregard for his responsibilities. He had lost his chance to save Somergate and win the wealth and respectability he needed to offer for Lily. An ill night's work, indeed.

"How can I ever make amends?" Anguish tore the words from him.

"Handing me my dress would be a good start."

Lily stood at the entrance of the tent, barely concealed by crumpled sea-green fabric. He looked away.

"You could have at least left me with some shoes. What's been happening? I saw that a tent was on fire."

"You didn't stay."

"Of course not. How could I, when my family might be in danger? When *you* might be in danger." She folded her arms across her chest.

His gaze slipped past her to fasten on the tent door. Staring resolutely at the rough canvas, he swallowed. "Bandits attacked the camp and your uncle has been hurt. I accept full responsibility. In the morning we will transport him back to Tunis. I cannot tell you how deeply I regret that my conduct tonight has led to such disastrous results." He handed her dress out to her. When she took it he stepped back a pace. "I must see to my duties. Go to your family—they are worried about you."

Her hands trembled. All color had left her face. How he wanted to take her into his arms, comfort her and beg forgiveness. He crushed the impulse. What right did he have? Hadn't he already caused enough grief?

James stepped past her. "I will leave you with the privacy I should never have invaded."

They left the meadow at dawn—only the creaking of leather and the jingle of harness breaking the quiet as they headed down the trail they had climbed yesterday with such high hopes. Four men on foot carried Sir Edward, lashed to a stretcher fashioned from tent canvas and poles. Lady Mary followed close behind.

James pushed them as hard as he dared, but it was not nearly fast enough. Sir Edward remained unconscious. The bright daylight revealed the gray pallor of his face.

They passed the village, the single street now empty. The locals would celebrate their good fortune when they discovered the abandoned baggage. He wondered what they would make of the folding bathtub. There was no time for luxuries now.

It was past mid-day when they stopped to water the animals at an ancient stone cistern. James led his mount up and let it lip the cold water. Beside him Richard was doing the same. The young man's face was streaked with dust and sweat and James knew he looked no better. If only there was some way to make more speed. He wished he could sling himself into the saddle and ride hell-for-leather to Tunis. This slow plodding was maddening when everything in him called for swift action.

"If only we could go faster," Richard said, echoing James's thoughts. "I can't stand watching father like that and not being able to do something."

James looked at the young man. They might not be able to move Sir Edward any faster, but perhaps they could shorten the distance to a doctor.

"Are you up for a fast ride to Tunis to fetch Dr. Fenton?"

Richard's eyes lit. "Yes. Absolutely. I'd do anything."

"Your mother has to agree to it. And remember, speed is important, but arriving in one piece even more so."

"I understand."

Lady Mary was seated on a crumbling stone wall near her husband. Mrs. Hodges had insisted the servants assemble luncheon and light a fire for tea.

"It's all very well to press on, but we must remember to maintain our strength," she said, handing Lady Mary a sandwich.

Lady Mary took the offering, but made no move to bring it to her mouth, only sat, staring wearily at nothing.

James cleared his throat. "If we sent a rider ahead, they could reach Tunis far faster than the main party. I'm sure Dr. Fenton would agree to meet us on the road if we sent someone to guide him."

Lady Mary looked up. "Anything that might bring aid to Edward sooner."

"Richard and Khalil will go."

"No. I cannot allow it. I . . . I couldn't bear it if anything happened to my son. This place has proven dangerous enough."

"Dr. Fenton knows Richard. He would come right away. Even a few hours could make a difference. Khalil has proven himself trustworthy—he will see Richard safe." James reached and took her hand. "I would not risk him unnecessarily."

Lady Mary looked to Mrs. Hodges, who gave a short nod. "Let him go, my lady. It is something the boy needs to do."

Taking a deep breath, Lady Mary straightened her shoulders. "Then be careful, Richard."

"I will." Richard wrapped his arms around her and she leaned against him. "I'll be back soon, Mother. Don't worry."

A few minutes later, he and Khalil were mounted and ready. With a last wave, they spurred their horses and galloped toward Tunis.

Dinner that night was subdued. The fire seemed less cheerful, the flames struggled to take hold among the branches. Isabelle huddled close while Lily wrapped herself in her cloak, head down.

James took a sip of tea and glanced at the weary faces

around him. He had pushed them to the edge of endurance. They were exhausted from a sleepless night and an endless day of travel. His gaze shifted to the tent where the bundled figure of Sir Edward lay. At least they were all still alive.

"We should make Tunis in another day-and-a-half if we can continue this pace." He had meant to sound encouraging.

Lady Mary looked at him. "You think Richard could be there by this time tomorrow if all goes well?"

"He will. Don't worry."

"James is right, Aunt." Lily said. "Richard is a fine rider and the road is straight from here. He may reach Dr. Fenton even sooner than we expect."

Lady Mary gave her a wan smile. "I'm sure you are right, my dear."

"Too much fretting going on, I say." Mrs. Hodges marched up to the fire. "This family is made of sterner stuff." She turned her fierce gaze on each of them in turn, not sparing James. "Too much fretting and not enough resting. Come, my lady. Come, Isabelle. Your beds are waiting." She planted herself solidly, hands on hips.

Thank God she had come along—she was keeping the Strathmores together with little more than the force of her will.

Isabelle rose. "Please excuse me." Her voice was thin. James realized that he had not heard her speak more than ten words since last night.

"I too am quite weary." Lady Mary joined her daughter. "Goodnight."

James stood. "May I escort you to your tent?"

"Thank you, James, but we can manage," Lady Mary said. "Rest while you can. We do appreciate all you have done for us."

His throat tightened. All he had done for them, indeed. Dragging them to Tunisia on a foolish quest, exposing them to his dangerous cousin . . . there was too much, altogether, that he had done. "Good night, then," he said, but his voice hardly seemed his own.

They followed Mrs. Hodges, but Lily lingered by the fire. James turned reluctantly to face her. He had wronged them all, but Lily most of all. He had to say something, had to make some attempt to set things right.

"Lily," he began, "I am aware that certain things have passed between us. Things that, if known, could compromise your reputation."

She turned her head away. How could he begin to make amends? He wanted her to smile at him again. James paced, hoping he could find the words. "I am deeply shamed by my conduct. What passed between us . . . well, I want you to know that I will do my duty as a gentleman even though I have not behaved as one."

The silence that followed his speech hung heavy in the darkness. How hollow his offer had sounded. He shoved his hands into his coat pockets, wishing his words unsaid.

"I thank you, Mr. Huntington, for your offer and devotion to duty." Her voice was blank. "I, however, do not believe that shame is the emotion I wish to form the foundation of my marriage. You may keep your shame, and your duty, and your regrets." She stood and drew her cloak more closely about her. "I am weary, sir, and concerned for my uncle's life. You will excuse me if I do not speak further of your . . . offer."

James stood alone in the flickering firelight. He bent to stir the embers with a stick, then straightened suddenly and hurled it into the darkness. What a fool he was. He hadn't intended to make his offer until the words were already spoken—and so clumsily. He hadn't realized how much he had wanted her to accept, until she refused.

He extinguished the fire and made for his tent. Exhaustion had finally found him. When had he slept last? He couldn't remember—but he was not sure he would be able to find any rest now. *You may keep your shame, and your duty, and your regrets.*

It seemed he had learned nothing.

The night seemed to press in on him. A gleam of brass on the table caught his eye. The box he had stumbled over last night—he still hadn't returned it to its owner.

A weary curiosity stirred as he picked it up. The metal was

hammered into raised designs, flowers and leaves twining around the lid. There was no lock—the catch opened easily at his touch.

Inside lay a gold locket and a creased sheet of thick vellum.

He took the locket by its chain, lifting it out of the box. It swayed and turned, catching the lamplight. He thumbed it open. A miniature portrait of a pale, weak-chinned man stared out at him, the features unfamiliar. A nephew of Lady Mary's perhaps? If so, there wasn't much of a family resemblance.

He set the locket aside and unfolded the paper. It was a letter.

"My Dearest Lily," he read, then continued, a horrible fascination dragging his eyes down the page. The phrases leapt out at him. *"Lord Buckley . . . perfect time of year for a wedding . . . finish fitting your wedding gown."*

Bloody, bloody hell.

Lily was betrothed. Had been all along.

He was on his feet, clutching the letter. How could it be possible? When he had held her, she had been planning her nuptials. When he had made love to her under the stars, she kept the image of her betrothed clasped in a golden locket.

He felt sick. He had loved her. He had even offered to marry her. With tight, controlled motions he refolded the letter and placed it back in the box.

Hollow anguish speared him, the emotion all too familiar. He should have known better. Hadn't those he had loved always abandoned him? His parents, Amanda . . . Lily.

Numbly he lay back on his cot. It took a long time for the morning to come.

Lily watched James as he rode at the front of the party. He would not speak to her—would not even look at her.

Was what they had done so terrible?

It had been wonderful. All she wanted was to be enfolded in his arms again, to know there was some surety in the world, something true and solid. She had thought she had that with

James. But now, after his grim and loveless proposal by the fire, it seemed a lie.

Her uncle was gravely wounded, possibly dying, and the man she had thought she loved had not offered her one word of comfort. James had become so rigidly formal. He had not spoken to her except to mouth empty words about shame and duty. She dashed an angry tear from her eye with the back of her hand. Confound the man.

It felt as though they were traveling further and further apart with every mile they rode. Yesterday had been dreadful. And today was a hundred times worse.

Well, this was how it would be. If he wanted distant formality, she would do her best to oblige him. She would pretend her heart was not breaking, take tea and wear a brittle smile. She would ride onward, trying not to be so desperately afraid each time she looked behind her at the stretcher bearing Uncle Edward.

She could not bear to lose both of them.

They rode through groves now, and the warm, sweetly perfumed air only underscored her mood—the beauty and pain of the world side-by-side. Lily had thought she would always love the smell of orange blossoms.

"Stop! Stop the horses!" It was Aunt Mary, her voice high. "He is stirring, I swear it. Oh, Edward . . ." her voice dissolved in tears.

Immediately Lily was off her horse and beside the stretcher. She took Isabelle's hand and squeezed it tightly.

"Make way, now," Mrs. Hodges said, brandishing a canteen. "Give him some room. He has to drink something."

Aunt Mary took the canteen and coaxed water into her husband's mouth. At first it dribbled out, as it had before, only a small movement of his throat marking that he had taken any liquid at all.

Then, suddenly, he was gulping. She let him drink a moment more then carefully pulled the canteen away.

"His eyelids fluttered. Oh Father!" Isabelle cried.

"My love," Aunt Mary whispered over and over, stroking his face. "Come back to us."

A moment later, Uncle Edward opened his eyes. He looked around blearily. "Here now, what's all the fuss?" His voice wavered, and then gained strength. "Where are we? Did we find the flower? Where's the specimen jar? I have such a terrible headache."

The family erupted with joy. Isabelle clung to Lily. Even Mrs. Hodges was wiping her eyes. Lily could not help glancing at James. He was smiling, his expression full of warmth and relief.

Until he looked at her.

Now she was crying too, tears of joy and grief mingling on her cheeks.

When the party made ready to ride on, Uncle Edward waved his hands in protest. "I can ride, I'm certain. Just give me a hand up, a little boost. I can manage it."

"Out of the question," James said. "We'll wait until a doctor says you're fit."

Despite her uncle's brave words, he looked pale as he slumped back onto the stretcher. He did not make any further insistence on riding.

By late afternoon they crossed the bridge where earlier their way had been barred. It was deserted. The horses' hooves thudded hollowly over the stones.

"We'll make camp in the groves ahead," James announced. "Doctor Fenton should meet us somewhere along the road. And tomorrow we'll reach Tunis."

"High time," Mrs. Hodges said. "I'm ready to leave this blasted wilderness behind. The steamer back to England couldn't arrive too soon for me."

Lily glanced at the silvery rows of olive trees, the curving river and stone road. It was hardly a wilderness. Though she wanted her uncle to be safe and well-cared for, part of her ached at the thought of leaving. This journey had freed something within her—something lush and open, something that chafed and rebelled when she thought of returning to London.

But there seemed no hope of recapturing what she and James had shared. She was not sure she knew him anymore—if she ever had. Returning to England, to everything known and predictable, was the only course left to her.

She slept fitfully that night. Just before dawn she heard riders clatter into camp—Dr. Fenton and Richard, accompanied by a half-dozen men.

"You must have ridden through the night!" She heard her aunt say.

"Of course, my lady," Dr. Fenton said, "When I heard of how grievously injured he was, I came at once. Has there been any change, any at all, in his condition?"

Lily took a deep breath of the cool night air. The breeze rustled the trees reassuringly, like a mother hushing her child. She pulled the blankets up around her chin and slept.

Late morning sunbeams slanted into her tent when she woke. Lily could hear easy conversation, the clank of cooking pots, all the sounds of a morning camp. No hurried packing or urgent voices. She took a deep breath and sat up.

When she emerged from her tent she was immediately aware of James conferring with her uncle. Uncle Edward was sitting up, his color improved. James, however, still seemed drawn and haggard, a brittleness about his mouth, a rigid set to his shoulders. His gaze moved impassively over her.

Anger and hurt warred in her. Anger won. How dare he act as though she were invisible?

James nodded to her uncle, and then strode to the center of camp. He lifted his voice. "Everyone, gather round, please. I have something to say."

Two of the servants lifted Uncle Edward's stretcher and set him next to James. Lily remained where she was and crossed her arms, watching as the party clustered around James.

"Dr. Fenton arrived last night. He has pronounced Sir Edward out of immediate danger." He held up a hand to still the cheering that followed his words. "The party is a half-day from Tunis, and though we did not find the valley or the flower we sought, we can be glad that we are all returning safe." His look grew distant. Lily caught her breath. "I will be leaving you here in the capable hands of Richard and Dr. Fenton. Thank you, all of you, for coming on this expedition. I wish you an easy journey home."

He shrugged off the questions that followed and made straight for Lily. Now he saw fit to approach her—now that he was about to abandon them?

"So, you are leaving us."

"Yes."

"You will not see us back to Tunis? Not stay to make sure my uncle makes a full recovery?"

"I will not."

His curt answers were infuriating. She wanted to grab him by the lapels and drag him close—shatter the distance between them. "Then this is how a gentleman discharges his duties. By running away."

Something flashed in his eyes. Fury? Despair? He made to turn away, then swung back to her. "I had felt obliged to offer for you," he said stiffly.

"Obliged!" Lily narrowed her eyes. "Is that what I am? An obligation? Some burden to carry until you can safely discard it? Well, I wouldn't have you—even if you begged me to marry you."

"No." His voice was icy. "I don't suppose you would." He reached into his pocket and pulled out a small brass box.

Her box.

"I see you recognize it. I found the items within very . . . enlightening. And luckily for me, I won't be forced into a marriage with a woman I now despise." Contempt laced his voice. "I wish your future husband joy of you." He thrust the box into her hands and strode to his horse.

"James, wait!" She followed him. "It's not what you think."

His eyes were hard. "What I think doesn't matter. Goodbye, Miss Strathmore." He slung himself into the saddle and spurred away, dust pluming up behind as he galloped back the direction they had come.

He truly did despise her.

Covering her mouth with one hand, Lily watched as his figure grew smaller and smaller in the distance.

Away from her forever.

She forced herself to remain standing. Her family was watching. She could not let them know how much she hurt.

She could see Isabelle's mouth moving, but no sound emerged. Aunt Mary came toward her, and it was as though she swam through the air, she moved so slowly. Lily could not feel her aunt's hand under her elbow, could not taste the water in the battered metal cup. Could not remember how she had ended up mounted again, following Richard as they clattered down the old Roman road to Tunis.

She could feel nothing. Nothing at all.

Chapter 20

London, England, June 1847

Lily sat on the chintz-covered settee, awaiting her first visit from Lord Buckley. *Her future husband.* The words rang oddly in her mind. She glanced again at the clock—half past two. The appointed hour had arrived.

She ought to be feeling something, she supposed. Anticipation, curiosity, fear. She had traveled so far to end up sitting here in her mother's parlor, waiting for a suitor she barely knew. Lily laced her fingers tightly together and glanced at her mother.

Lady Fernhaven was seated near the window. "Now, darling, try not to look so anxious. Though I daresay you are excited about finally seeing Lord Buckley." She gave a little sigh. "I really cannot blame you. Who would have thought you'd do so well for yourself? A future countess, only think of it!"

Lily had been doing just that.

It was high time she started using her head again. Her heart had proved an unreliable compass, poor bruised and bewildered thing that it was. A useless organ, altogether. To think she would have followed *that* man anywhere.

Since her return to England, Lily had simply passed each day as it came. There was nothing else to be done. Even painting seemed too much of an effort.

"When Lord Buckley comes in, I would like him to sit next to you on the settee." Her mother smiled. "I am certain he will be quite taken with you. And I have noticed that your travels agreed with you. You have a certain air about you now."

"Whatever do you mean?" Lily asked, not quite sure she wanted to hear the answer.

"It's just . . . oh!" Lady Fernhaven rose to her feet, her attention drawn to the window. "The Buckley's carriage has arrived. I have instructed Edwin to show them straight in." She bustled over to Lily. "Do try and smooth your hair—and smile."

A few moments later the butler opened the parlor door. "Lord Buckley and Countess Buckley."

Lord Buckley stepped inside, his mother on his arm. He was shorter than Lily remembered, and his waistcoat bulged slightly over his stomach, but he was otherwise unobjectionable.

"Welcome, welcome." Lily's mother beamed at their visitors. "Lord Buckley, we are so pleased you have returned to London. Lily has been greatly looking forward to your visit."

"Yes." Lily smiled wanly.

Lord Buckley released his mother's arm and bent over Lady Fernhaven's hand. "How good to see you again. You are looking as lovely as ever."

"You are too kind, my lord. And here is Lily."

Lily curtsied and offered her hand. He took it, bowing perfunctorily.

"Miss Strathmore." His pale blue eyes skimmed over her. "A pleasure, to be sure."

She kept herself from frowning as Lord Buckley turned back to the older women. One would expect a man to give his future intended more than just a cursory glance.

"Shall we be seated?" Lily's mother motioned Lord Buckley to the settee. "We'd be delighted to hear of your travels. Do make yourselves comfortable."

"Certainly." Lord Buckley guided his mother to the settee and settled beside her. Lady Fernhaven's brows drew together.

Lily was just as happy to take the nearby chair. She could see the garden from here.

The countess turned to her son. "Do tell them about your trip. The story of the pompous majordomo." She turned to Lady Fernhaven. "Gerald wrote me faithfully—he always does—and related the most charming anecdotes of his travels."

"Such devotion," Lady Fernhaven said. "Lily includes lovely sketches with her notes home. They say a picture is worth ten thousand words, you know."

Lord Buckley sniffed. "Actually, they say a picture is worth one thousand words, isn't that right, mother?"

"I do believe you are correct, but if she sent ten sketches that would equal ten thousand words. So Lady Fernhaven would also be correct."

"I suppose so. If she actually sent ten." He turned to Lily. "Did you?"

"Pardon me?"

"Did you send ten sketches?"

"Well, no. Not ten."

Lord Buckley nodded. "There you have it. Miss Strathmore's sketches are not worth ten thousand words." Apparently satisfied that he had made his point, he launched into a long tale of his travels.

Lily leaned back in her chair. It was insufferably tedious, but this—not orange blossoms and kisses beneath the stars—was the stuff real lives were made of. She forced her attention back to the room, to Lord Buckley's voice. It was becoming clear that her marriage would not be a silent one. Perhaps, under some circumstances, a picture *was* worth more than ten thousand words.

"What an entertaining story!" Lily's mother said at last. "The majordomo certainly got what he deserved, I do say. And you tell it so well."

"I was there, after all," Lord Buckley replied, "And I consider myself a keen observer, particularly when people make fools of themselves—as they so often do."

"Not everyone is as sensible as you, dear boy," the countess said.

"I am sure." Lady Fernhaven smoothed her skirts. "Shall we take a turn about the garden? The roses are at their very best."

"An excellent plan." Lord Buckley stood and, somewhat to Lily's surprise, offered her his arm. "May I escort you, Miss Strathmore?"

The two of them led the way, their mothers following at a distance, heads close together in conversation. The scent of roses hung in the warm summer air and the blooms were ripe and heavy, but there was no toga-clad maiden to gather them.

"Do you enjoy traveling, Lord Buckley?"

"Yes, I do. I welcome the freedom it brings, the new vistas. And when I travel I prefer to travel in comfort. There's nothing like a well-sprung coach. Why, mine is so smooth I can sip a whiskey without spilling a single drop."

"Admirable." Lily glanced down. "I don't suppose you bring a portable bathtub with you?" She blinked away the image of lantern light dappling canvas walls.

"Why would I want with such a thing when the hotels I frequent are fully equipped with every modern convenience?"

"My aunt brought one on our expedition in Tunisia."

"What an absurd and foolish extravagance."

"Yes," she said. "It was."

Lord Buckley drew a fine handkerchief from his pocket and dabbed perspiration from his forehead. "Mother says you paint, as I recall. Landscapes, is it?"

"Sometimes—but my main work is botanical illustration. My uncle, Sir Edward Strathmore, is a respected botanist. I provide all the plant studies for his scholarly papers."

Lord Buckley frowned. "Miss Strathmore, you will find that I am a man that speaks plainly. It is my nature and a virtue, though there will be times when it may not appear so to you. I must say I do not approve of women dabbling in the sciences. The fairer sex should tend to the domestic spheres for which they are best suited. It is where their talents lie."

She removed her arm from his. "My talents lie in botanical

illustration, Lord Buckley. And I assure you, I am well-suited to it."

"Yes, I had heard that you were a bit . . . reclusive. All to the good, really. And I'm sure you can manage a household properly. Mother would not have recommended you, otherwise."

Lily swung to face him, but he merely smiled at her, seeming not to notice her annoyance. The angry words died on her tongue. Why bother? She had not lifted a brush since leaving Tunisia. There was one thing she must know, however, before continuing any further.

"You do not object to a woman painting flowers—so long as she tends to her other responsibilities. Do you?"

He thought for a moment. "No, if they are painted for the sake of decoration and beauty. These things properly belong in the sphere of women."

"Then you would not forbid me to paint?"

"I did not say that I would forbid you. Now come along." Lord Buckley offered his arm once more. "It wouldn't do to let Mother see us at odds. Our first lover's spat." He gave an odd little laugh.

The matter was settled, then. Lily took his arm and they resumed walking, their footsteps loud on the carefully raked gravel.

At length he cleared his throat. "Would you accompany me to the theater tomorrow?"

"I will." It would be pointless to refuse.

"Very good. Look, Mother is beckoning to us." He led Lily toward the countess.

Lily slipped her arm from his and paused. Cupping her hands around a full-blown yellow rose, she inhaled deeply. For one moment she was drenched in the scent, the feel of sunlight, the soft petals yearning against her hands.

Ahead, the mothers smiled expectantly.

Lily let out an impatient breath and yanked her thoughts back to the breakfast table. She had been thinking about *him* again. James Huntington. She was better off without the scoundrel. True, she hadn't told him about her mother's plans for Lord Buckley. And she should have, considering what had been between them.

But he was equally at fault. If he had had taken the time to discuss the matter instead of riding off into the wilds like a tribal Bedouin she could have explained. If he had made his offer for her something from the heart and not empty words dragged from his lips by guilt or obligation, then everything could have been different.

Her tea had grown cold. Lily swirled it then set it back down, untouched. She did not have much of an appetite. The last two weeks had been filled with a flurry of dinners and balls and outings with her mother and Countess Buckley and sometimes even Lord Buckley himself. She sighed.

Lord Buckley was not the suitor she would have chosen for herself—but that did not make him unsuitable. To her mind, his imperfections were precisely what made the match tolerable. She was not exactly a prize herself—not with her secrets and tattered virtue. If it were possible to love Lord Buckley then Lily doubted she would be able to go through with the wedding.

But she could not love him. She did not even pity him. He was getting what he valued—an outwardly respectable bride from a highly respectable family. She could not expect more from this arranged match. It was too much to ask that he care about her or her skills, beyond the fact that she was able to play the role of aristocrat's wife.

And the other duties. Lily shivered. She could not imagine his soft hands on her, his fleshy lips pressed against hers, although one of her primary obligations, her chief one in fact, would be to bear Lord Buckley an heir. Still, many women who did not love their husbands managed to fulfill that responsibility, and ultimately there would be children to compensate.

At least she was not carrying James's child.

She had not considered the consequences of her night with him, not until the morning her courses had come. She had removed her nightgown and stared blankly at the small red stain, then wrapped her arms about herself and cried, silently.

But that was done with. Lily took up her fork. She pushed her eggs to one side of the plate, then back again.

Her mother glanced up from perusing the society pages. "More kippers, darling?" she waved toward the chafing dish. "You have not seemed quite yourself recently. Not that it behooves a lady to eat overmuch at breakfast. But do have something more."

"Yes, mother." Lily took a slice of toast and spread it with strawberry preserves.

Lady Fernhaven continued to look thoughtfully at her. "It is your nerves, I imagine. But don't worry darling, the time is almost right for Lord Buckley to make his offer. His attentions to you are not going unnoticed. These things take time, after all. We do not want people to form the wrong impression—which a hurried courtship and marriage can unfortunately convey."

"Of course not." She took a small bite of toast and then set it aside. "Mother, since things are progressing so well with Lord Buckley, couldn't I make a brief visit to Brookdale? I haven't seen Uncle Edward and the family since we returned."

"Your aunt did write to tell us your uncle was fully recovered, did she not? It is best you remain in London. Especially with Lord Buckley almost brought to the point. You must be ready when he pays that important call—it will be one of the most significant moments of your life! When you are Countess Buckley you may have your uncle and the entire family to visit at your home whenever you wish—with your husband's permission, of course."

"I would be gone no more than two or three days." Lily tried to keep the pleading note from her voice. She had felt so alone since returning to England. She missed them all dreadfully.

Lady Fernhaven tightened her lips. "I will hear no more on this subject." She picked up the paper and returned to her reading.

Lily stared out the window. It was a perfect day, warm and golden. She wished the clouds would mass and cover the sun. It was far too bright.

"My goodness!" Lily's mother exclaimed. "Lord Severn is getting married. Who would have imagined it—and to a foreigner, no less. A Baronessa Bellini."

Lily looked up. "Did you say Bellini?"

"Yes, it is rather a thrilling tale. The page says—

"Word has just reached this author's ears that the dashing Lord Severn has returned to London. And, what is more, that he has brought a fiancée back with him! Well may you inquire, dear reader, what lady has managed to snare the heart of the ton's most fascinating bachelor.

It is none other than the charming and spirited Baronessa Bellini, who, as you may recall, spent the winter here in London and was seen once or twice on Lord Severn's arm. Who would have suspected the depth of their attachment?

After a lover's tiff last March, witnessed by unnamed sources, the baronessa sailed for home on the Peninsular and Oriental line. Lord Severn set off in pursuit, following his lady love back to Italy to beg her forgiveness on bended knee. He won it. And her hand as well, it seems."

Lady Fernhaven folded the page and tapped it against the table. "I do not recall meeting the lady, myself. Was she at the Wembly's ball, do you think?"

"I made the baronessa's acquaintance, mother. She sailed with us on the steamer that took us to Tunisia."

"Really?" Lady Fernhaven raised a well-manicured brow. "What was she like? Did she seem suitable? One never knows with those foreign titles if a person is truly up to standard."

"She is a lovely person. Warm and . . . discerning. And quite fashionable as well."

"I suppose a certain continental flair in dressing is to be expected. And her choice of fiancé shows impeccable judgment." Lady Fernhaven nodded.

Lily hoped the baronessa had made the right choice in Lord Severn. After all, she had been so wrong about James. But anyone could make a mistake. Hadn't Lily done so herself? James had been handsome and kind and honorable—or at least had appeared to be.

Her mother laid the paper aside and took a sip of tea. "Lord Buckley is escorting us to a picnic this afternoon. And the weather is so lovely for it. We shall have a splendid time."

"Oh yes, a perfectly splendid time." Lily wasn't sure she could bear another outing. Perhaps she was developing a headache. She drew her brows tightly together. Yes, there it was now.

"I am not feeling quite well, Mother."

Lady Fernhaven gave her a sympathetic look. "Nerves again, darling? Go and rest. I hope you will be recovered in time for the picnic. It would be a shame to miss such a pleasant afternoon with your suitor."

"Yes, a rest will do me good." Sleeping seemed the one thing she excelled at these days.

The butler entered the room, bearing a silver salver piled with correspondence. "The morning post has arrived, my Lady."

"Very good, Edwin." She riffled through the stack. "My goodness. Well, Lily. You have certainly cultivated the right acquaintances lately. An invitation . . ." she held it up proudly, "to the betrothal ball of Lord Severn and the Baronessa Bellini. Well done, darling! We shall attend, of course. Everyone will be there."

Chapter 21

"James! You're back!" Caroline dropped her fork with a clatter and rose from her chair. "Why didn't you let us know you were coming home? We've been so worried since the Strathmores returned without you."

He caught his sister up in an embrace. "Caro—it's good to see you!" He held her close for a long moment, then set her back on her feet. "Hello, Uncle. I see I have arrived in time for dinner."

Lord Denby rose to greet him. "Welcome home, James. I must say it is good to see you have returned in one piece. Did you just arrive in England?"

"No. I had urgent business with Sir Edward and went directly to Brookdale." He smiled at his sister. "I was only there long enough to finish my business before I came racing back to see you."

It was true. He could not have stayed another day at Brookdale Manor even if he had a mind to. A weight had lifted from him upon seeing Sir Edward in good health, but the manor held too many reminders of Lily for him to linger.

Lord Denby rang for a servant. "I'll have another place set. Do join us."

Caroline folded her arms. "I'm not sure he merits it, the way he disappeared without a word to his family. What happened,

James? Your last letter said you were leaving Tunis, then we get a note from the Strathmores saying there had been an attack and you were not with them—that you had ridden off into the wilds. Alone!"

James swept her up again—he couldn't resist.

"I'm certain you're ruining my gown," she said. "Put me down, you oaf, and come sit. I want to hear everything."

When they were at the table his uncle lifted his glass. "A toast James, to your safe return."

"To safe returns." James drank.

"And how goes your work with your charitable societies, Caroline?" he asked when his plate had been set before him. "Are you still intent on founding a school on Malta for the orphans of British soldiers and sailors stationed there?"

"Of course. Did you think I'd given it up for needlepoint in your absence? I will happily talk for a week or more about the work, but not before you tell us about your adventures. What happened?"

"Yes, James. How fared you in Tunisia? Were you successful?"

"I can hardly rate it a success. The expedition itself was a disaster." James paused for a moment, trying to push thoughts of Lily from his mind. No matter how he tried, how much he knew that she had lied to him from the start, he would never be able to forget the feel of her body against him as he held her beneath the stars.

"Go on," Caroline said, her eyes full of questions.

He gathered himself and continued. "At least I can confirm that grandfather's stories about his adventurous youth have some basis in fact. The flower he found does exist and truly *was* an undiscovered species. I brought back a specimen for Sir Edward, who was overjoyed at the sight of it. He's now working on a monograph to present to the Royal Horticultural Society. The working title is *'Primula mercerium:* A New Species Discovered by the Huntington/Mercer Expedition of 1792 and Collected by the Huntington/Strathmore Expedition of 1847.' Catchy, don't you think?"

"Mercerium, eh?" Lord Denby said. "After your grandfather's companion who died in the valley."

"It seemed . . . appropriate."

"Indeed. And with the publication of the monograph your grandfather will have much of what he wanted—recognition for his early explorations in Africa and his discovery of a new species. I do not think it was easy for a man of his temperament to give up the adventurous life and accept his role as holder of the family title. I understand that far better now that I have taken up his responsibilities."

James looked at his uncle. "I never knew he gave up anything for the sake of his title."

"No? Consider that he was suddenly responsible not just for himself, but for producing an heir, managing the estates, the well-being of the servants and tenants, not to mention his responsibilities with the peerage in Parliament. He put the care-free life of the adventurer behind him, not because he wished to, but because he had to. His role was scripted before birth and he had to play it whether or not he was suited for the part. Not everyone has the luxury to do what they wish with their lives."

It was an unexpected thought, that family duty and obligation had kept his grandfather from his true passion. James took a sip of wine.

"But what about you James?" Caroline asked. "Were the journals in the valley?"

"No. There was nothing of the journals in the valley."

She frowned. "Oh, how disappointing. You would have looked dashing striding around Grandfather's old estate ordering your minions about and pruning things."

"A pity," Lord Denby agreed, "But with the passage of so many years, the loss of the journals is not wholly unexpected."

No, not unexpected. James closed his eyes. It had not been difficult to find the valley after leaving the Strathmores in the care of Dr. Fenton. They had been so close when the attack occurred. The boulders stood, just as his grandfather had sketched them, surrounded by a sea of wild orchids. Trampled earth and overturned rocks told that Reggie had been here before him, but James searched anyway.

There was nowhere else to go. His heart still reeled. How could Lily have deceived him? Each kiss, each caress, each smile had been a lie. When she had cried out beneath him and held him as if the entire universe were shattering—it had all been a lie.

Now everything was broken. Even if he could recover the journals and win Somergate, what would it gain him? He had lost the only thing he truly wanted—no, damn him, he had not lost it, for it had never been his.

So he combed the rocks, crawling in the crevices, turning over boulders. There was nothing. He expanded the scope of his search on the chance the box containing the journals had been carried somewhere and discarded. When darkness fell he slept, exhausted, at the base of the rock outcropping while his horse nipped tender shoots and watered at the small spring.

He spent days searching the valley and the lonely hills, with no companions except the flowers—the ubiquitous purple orchids that carpeted the valley, and a small yellow flower that twined among the rocks, scenting the air with its delicate fragrance. Each morning the sun rose, chased shadows across the valley, then set—he did not count how many times. It could have been five or fifty. It made no difference to the ache and loss he felt. Only when his supplies were almost gone did he think to leave.

On the last morning, in the cool before dawn, he made tea and took his battered tin cup to the top of the boulders to watch the sunrise. Steam bathed his face with each sip. The strengthening light brought the vivid purple of the orchids to life and it seemed he was on an island in the middle of a lake of flowers.

Here, in this valley, his grandfather had fought for his life and lost his closest friend. Here James had come to search hopelessly and grieve his broken heart. Yet beauty dwelt here, full and complete and untouched by human joy or sorrow. The flowers and grasses waited for the rains, then bloomed heedlessly, and the pink and gold of dawn painted the clouds in hues for which no words existed.

He stood watching, transfixed, as the sun rose above the horizon. Rays of light burst into the sky—yellow light picked up and reflected by the yellow flowers that clung to the rocks.

It was then that something shifted inside him and he knew he must return to England.

The journals might be lost, but his grandfather's flower was here. It had been with James always as he searched. For days he had been walking among the un-catalogued blooms that both his grandfather and Sir Edward had tried in vain to collect. His own ambitions had been crushed when he parted from Lily, but beauty remained. He would carry it back with him to honor his grandfather, and for Sir Edward, his friend who saw in every leaf and flower the wonder James had glimpsed in the morning sunrise.

And he had done it. He had finished the work started by his grandfather so many years ago. It was enough. It had to be.

James forced his thoughts back to the present. "Reggie didn't come back with the journals, did he?"

Lord Denby looked at him in surprise. "No, he would have sought to claim the inheritance by now if he had. Were you expecting him to? I thought you said the journals were lost."

"No. I said they were not in the valley."

"James!" Caroline said. "Speak plainly. Did you find the journals or not?"

"Well, I found something, though they can't properly be called journals. When I decided to bring back specimens of the flower, I returned to the nearby village. The villagers there had scavenged the goods we had abandoned in our hurry to get Sir Edward back to Tunis, and I hoped to recover some of the expedition's plant collection bottles.

"I must have looked the fool, pantomiming the shape of the bottles, but somehow I made my intent known. The headman kept nodding and repeating a word I did not understand. He motioned to one of his men, who soon returned with Sir Edward's bottles and I paid him well for them.

"I packed them away and was about to return to the valley when I was struck by how old the villagers' dwellings looked. They must certainly have stood when Grandfather explored the area. Were these the descendents of the bandits who had attacked him? Had their fathers and grandfathers looted the remains of his expedition? I returned to the headman.

"'Book,' I said, trying both English and French. 'Pictures.' I was miming again, doing everything I could think of to communicate. I squatted down and drew an open book in the dust, and endeavored to show a flower sketched on one of its pages. Not my best work, I assure you. How I wished then that I had not lost my guide and interpreter.

"The headman and others spoke to each other. I couldn't understand what they were saying, but again one of them left. I had nearly given up hope when he returned with an ancient little man dressed in stained robes. The old man's face was lined and weathered and he leaned heavily on the younger man. 'Book' I said again, pointing at my sketch and miming someone reading and writing in a journal.

"The old man paid very little attention. Instead he tottered forward and tugged on the chain of my watch."

"'Father's watch?'" Caroline asked.

"Yes. Before I could stop him he lifted it from my pocket and held it swinging and sparkling in the sunlight. He looked up at me and then proceeded to pet the watch.

"I looked to the others in hopes that they would take him in hand. 'Book' I said yet again, and the old man stopped petting the timepiece long enough to fish up his sleeve and retrieve several tattered pieces of vellum. He had these."

James brought out an envelope and handed it to his uncle.

Lord Denby opened it and carefully removed four pages.

"Extraordinary." He gestured a servant over. "Turn up the lamps, and fetch my quizzing glass."

"What are they?" Caroline shifted in her seat, trying to get a better look.

"Sketches," James said. "The first is of the rock formation in the valley where the flower grew. The second two are of plants that must have grown locally in the region. The last is the mosque in Tunis. Its square minarets are unique."

"Yes," his uncle said. "But how in blazes did the old fellow get them?"

"I can only guess. Perhaps he had a hand in looting Grandfather's camp. Or maybe he found where they were hidden some time later. The leather bindings and most of the pages must have been used for other purposes, but these drawings would interest even an illiterate."

"Do you really think these are from Grandfather's journals?" Caroline asked.

"I believe so. They are of subjects that would have interested him."

"Then you did it James!" She turned to their uncle. "Didn't he?"

Lord Denby was still scanning the pages with his glass. "Remarkable. If these can be established as pages from the lost journals, then they could be very valuable pieces of paper, indeed. May I keep them for a few days? I can make no promises, but I would like to consult the family solicitor."

"Do whatever you like with them," James said. "I'd prefer to put pages—and the whole Tunisia adventure—out of my mind."

"A capital idea," his sister said. "I know just the thing. You may take me riding tomorrow in Hyde Park. Along the Serpentine, preferably. I have a new . . ."

As James stood from the table, Caroline's eyes dropped to the place where his watch chain would ordinarily have been.

"James! What did you give him for those pages? Not Father's watch."

He was silent a moment, then shrugged as if to ease a weight he carried. "I gave what was required. Good night, Caro, good night, Uncle. I must go."

At the gate to Hyde Park James reined his horse to let an open carriage pass. It was filled with ladies decked in lace and finery. A fluffy white lapdog braced its paws on the rear seat and yapped at him. The park beyond teemed with the cream of society strolling, riding in open barouches, or mounted on horseback.

Was Lily here somewhere walking the paths with her intended? He had a powerful urge to turn his horse about and head back the way they had come. If they met, what would he say? "Miss Strathmore, such a pleasure. Really? I had no idea. Congratulations. You make a lovely couple." Just the thought left his chest tight and his head swimming.

"Come on, slowcoach. Accompanying your sister to the park on a sunny summer day can't be that unpleasant." Caroline was looking back over her shoulder at him.

"Of course not." He would not run away. He had already lost too many precious years with his sister when he had been in India.

James straightened in the saddle and kneed his horse forward. Caroline deserved better than to have him run off whenever some chit got under his skin. If he saw Lily, he would simply ignore her. She would probably prefer that. And if cornered? Well, he could always turn the conversation to billiards or fowling guns.

He took a deep breath as he passed through the gates. The sun slanted golden and lazy through the leaves and ahead Caroline sat easily on her gray. Her saddle, worked in silver, had been their mother's.

There was a painting of their mother standing beside the saddle and as children they had often examined the portrait, imagining what life would be for them if that kind-faced woman with the dark hair and eyes had been there for them. They had entertained one another with stories of the places she would take them—to the seashore, the market, or to watch the Morris dancers on the village green.

Now it seemed almost as if the woman in the painting had returned and rode beside him. Caroline was no longer the adolescent he had left behind. In fact, she was certainly of an age to be considering marriage. The thought made him feel unanchored all over again.

"Goodness, if you rode that slowly in Tunisia no wonder it took you eons to return home." She shot a smile at him.

"You're just trying to goad me into racing—don't deny it." James glanced around. "I'm afraid the path is too crowded, sister dear. You wouldn't want to trample anyone."

Caroline peered ahead, her smile fading. "Oh wouldn't I? I see one gentleman ahead who simply begs to be trampled. The ever-vexatious Viscount Briarly."

"Miss Huntington! I say, Miss Huntington!" It was a young fair-haired man driving a curricle toward them, seemingly heedless of the pedestrians he sent scattering out of his path. When he drew abreast he pulled his horses to a stop and sprang out, sweeping his coattails back in a flourishing bow to Caroline.

"My dear Miss Huntington, how good to see you. I was disappointed you did not attend the Dalton's supper party. You haven't been avoiding me, have you?" He straightened and shot James a dark look.

"Viscount Briarly. Allow me to introduce my brother, Mr. James Huntington."

"Not the Dastardly Dueling James Huntington! Beg your pardon, but that is what some wits have called you." He chuckled, then rushed forward and pumped James's hand. "So pleased to meet you. I didn't mean to slight you sir. It is only that your charming companion steals my sense, leaving me witless in every situation."

"I assure you, my lord, one cannot steal something that does not exist," Caroline said. "If you would be kind enough to release my brother's hand, we really must be going. Good day." She bestowed one of her winning—and entirely false—smiles on the hapless young man before urging her horse forward.

Another of Caro's victims, James thought. "You showed him no mercy. Poor man. Is it true you've been avoiding him?"

"Ha. Wouldn't you? Poor man, indeed. He fancies that I fancy him. Absolutely delusional. The more I try to set him straight, the more doggedly he pursues me."

James noticed the viscount staring longingly after Caroline's trim figure before whipping up his horses again.

"Would you have me speak with him and put it more forcefully? I might succeed—after all, I am the Dastardly Dueling James Huntington."

Caroline laughed, but then her eyes grew serious. "I can look after myself. You needn't act like a father bear, you know. When the right suitor arrives I expect that I shall know it—and until then fools like Viscount Briarly approach me at their peril."

James frowned. "Is there anyone, Caro, who you might consider as a suitor? I know your dowry is not overlarge, but I do have some funds from cashing in my commission."

"Are you implying that you'll have to *pay* someone to take me off your hands? A bride of my surpassing beauty and wit?"

"Of course not! I was only wondering." Wondering if he would lose her soon. Someone would enter her life, someone courageous enough to breach her defenses. And then—then he would wish them well and all the happiness in the world. He swallowed. "The stretch ahead is clear—first one to that maple tree is the best rider in all England."

Almost before the words were out of his mouth, Caroline had spurred her horse past him. He thundered along just behind her, content to ride hard, if only for a handful of moments.

"I win!" she crowed, turning her horse in a circle around him. "You owe me a forfeit."

"I do? Not my dessert again."

"Silly." She sobered. "No, James, you must tell me the truth. What happened in Tunisia?"

James turned to look at her, the bright eyes, brown as his own, the wide lips, capable of engaging smiles and spiteful words, the curiosity and affection written across her face.

"What do you mean?"

"You must tell me," Caroline said, "about a certain Miss Lily Strathmore who was mentioned rather frequently in your letters, but who has not been spoken of once since your return."

"There is nothing to mention."

"James." She gave him a penetrating look. "What happened? You seemed absolutely stricken when I mentioned her name just now. You may as well tell me."

"Because?"

"Because if you don't I will have to call on Miss Strathmore myself and ask her. I'm your sister, James. I want to help if I can, and provide a nice absorbent shoulder to cry on if I can't. What happened?"

"Let's go to the blasted Serpentine, then. I'll tell you as we ride."

It took the better part of an hour for Caroline to coax the sorry story out of him—minus certain details, of course. There were some things that could never be revealed. They were riding back through Mayfair when he finished.

"So you rode away, back to the valley? James, you deserve so much better." Her voice was soft with sympathy.

"Better than a woman who's betrothed to another, at any rate." His lips twisted. "But enough of this. That story is over."

"And we are home." Caroline drew rein in front of Twickenham House. "Come in and have some tea. Or whiskey, if you prefer."

"Tea with whiskey—there's a thought. Don't look so sad, Caro. The sun is out, Grandfather and Sir Edward have their flower. Everything has turned out for the best." He followed Caroline into their uncle's residence, trying to believe his own words.

In the parlor, James settled into a comfortable chair and let her pour.

"Are you really going to take whiskey in it?" she asked.

He made a face. "With my tea? I'm not that badly off. Lemon will do."

She set the teapot down. "Are you planning to attend Lord Severn's betrothal ball tonight?"

"No. I intend to put my feet up—or maybe take a bath and read something moody. Horses couldn't drag me there." Lily would almost certainly be attending. With her fiancé— if he wasn't already her husband.

He took a swallow of tea, wincing as it burned the back of his throat.

"Be careful, the tea is just off the boil. Here, have a drink of milk." Caroline quickly filled another cup and thrust it at him. "Or a tea cake. Stop laughing at me. I'm sure the frosting will be quite soothing."

"Doubtless. Tea cakes are universally known for their healing properties."

She frowned at him, but there was laughter in her eyes. "Better than dry toast, at any rate. When was the last time you had a tea cake?"

"When I was twelve and knew no better."

"Ha. They are one of the chief delights of English society." She bit into the pastry. "Mm. Delicious. Speaking of bad tastes, you should be glad you weren't here yesterday afternoon. Reggie came by and proceeded to have a terrible row with Uncle. Worse than their usual, it seemed."

"He seems to have become even more bitter than he was as a youth. I suspect he was somehow behind the raid on the expedition's camp."

Caroline nodded. "I wouldn't put it past him. He has always been supremely self-centered, but it has grown worse with the years—there is something darker about him now, more desperate. And when it comes to you, James . . ."

"What of me?"

"Just the mention of your name is enough to drive him into a jealous rage. I don't know why it has to be that way with him, but it is. Somehow he blames you for the problems between himself and Uncle, although I don't see why. He brings it on himself. Take yesterday for example—he was literally shouting in the study."

"Really? What about?"

Caroline raised her brows. "As if I would stoop to eavesdropping. What do you take me for?" She smiled and took a sip of tea. "Besides, the study door is too thick. Even when they raised their voices I couldn't make out what they were saying, but I'm positive I heard your name several times. It did not sound as if

Reggie were very pleased. Afterwards he sought me out. After making his usual insulting remarks he mentioned Miss Lily Strathmore. Curious, don't you think? He said he was planning to attend the ball to ensure that there were no unfounded rumors circulating about the two of you—which I naturally took to mean just the opposite." She opened her mouth to say more, then gave him a worried look. "James, is it that serious?"

"What?"

"You just ate a tea cake."

He forced himself to swallow, then took another gulp of tea. "I can't imagine what Reggie thinks to gain. Even if he suspected that Lily and I had formed an attachment, what bearing could it have now? It's over."

"Who knows what our cousin plans? Perhaps he thinks he can get at you through Miss Strathmore—or maybe he doesn't intend to go at all."

James rose, brushing cake crumbs from his trousers. "I should be off. Will you have enough time to get ready? I trust you have a suitable gown." He went to the door and turned. "I'll call for you at half-past seven."

"For what?"

"The betrothal ball. Don't be late."

No matter how things stood between them, he couldn't let Lily fall prey to whatever plot Reggie had hatching.

Chapter 22

"Welcome, *bella*." The baronessa took Lily's hands—her eyes alight with happiness, the gold-embroidered satin of her gown enhancing her radiance. She brushed a kiss over each of Lily's cheeks. "And this handsome couple—these are your parents?"

Lily introduced them, though her stomach was in knots and had been all day. What if the baronessa mentioned James? She had been far too perceptive on the *Sidonia*. Even though Lily's connection with James had been severed, it would still provide fodder for the gossips—especially in light of her impending engagement to Lord Buckley.

"My fiancé, Lord Severn," Baronessa Bellini said, smiling up at the dashing blond gentleman at her side.

"Well met, Miss Strathmore. Maria has told me how much she enjoyed your company aboard the steamer."

"It was entirely mutual, and it is a pleasure to meet you, as well." Lily edged forward as she spoke—not difficult with the press of well-wishers in the receiving line behind her. The safety of the ballroom lay just a few steps ahead.

"But where is the so handsome gentleman that is keeping company with you?" the baronessa asked.

Lily froze. Please—not here, not now. She fixed the baronessa with an imploring look.

"Oh, you must mean Lord Buckley," her mother said. "He will be joining us shortly. He has been in Lily's company frequently, I must say."

Baronessa Bellini's brows drew together. "I see." Though her look said clearly that she did not.

Lily spoke through the tightness in her throat. "Lord Buckley has been calling on me since my return. He has my parents' favor—but please, do not let me keep you from your other guests."

The baronessa took Lily's hands again. "We will speak together soon. So much has occurred since last we saw each other, no?" She gave a gentle squeeze then turned back to the next well-wishers who were already offering congratulations to Lord Severn.

Lily felt weak as her parents led the way into the ballroom between two huge marble urns overflowing with white roses. She trailed behind. Thank goodness her mother had assumed the baronessa had been referring to Lord Buckley.

Out on the dance floor couples swirled like petals scattered over moving water, the gaslights glowed brightly, and white-liveried servants circulated with flutes of champagne for the guests. Lily took a deep breath and willed her heart to slow. It had been a close thing, but no damage had been done. And tonight, at last, she would see Uncle Edward and Aunt Mary. That alone was worth a day's anxiety.

She scanned the crowd. Her aunt had written to say they would be spending a few weeks in London so Sir Edward could prepare for the Royal Horticultural Society's upcoming meeting. Lily was certain they would not refuse the baronessa's invitation. How she longed to see them again—even if it meant introducing Lord Buckley.

"Lady Fernhaven!" The shrill tones of Lady Wembly, one of her mother's closest friends, interrupted Lily's thoughts. She turned to see the violet-clad matron bearing down on them.

"And the Marquis of Fernhaven, of course. How good to see you. Where is that girl of yours? Come here, let me take a close look at you. Hmm, the sun in Africa did not seem to have permanently scorched you. Wear your bonnet without fail, child, or you'll wind up freckled as a shepherdess." She held Lily at arm's length. "But what a lovely necklace—it matches your eyes perfectly, I declare."

"Thank you." Lily reached up, fingers tracing the teardrop pendant. The stone was warm where it lay against her skin. What matter that James had given it to her—it was only a piece of jewelry, after all.

Her mother nodded. "Lily brought it back from her travels. See how it complements her gown. I saw it on her dressing table this evening and I insisted she wear it."

"It's darling. A perfect choice," Lady Wembly said. "Now tell me, Lady Fernhaven, what do you think of the profusion of white roses used in the décor?"

"Lily," her father said, "Would you honor me with a dance?"

She mustered up a smile. "Of course. Unless you would prefer to stay and discuss the decorating scheme with Mother and Lady Wembly."

"I think I will leave that to the professionals." He offered his arm.

They stood at the ready, waiting for the music to begin.

"It will be lovely to see Uncle Edward again," Lily said. "I'm not certain I will believe he has fully recovered until I set eyes on him."

"I was quite concerned, myself, about what occurred in Tunisia. You never speak of it."

"It was . . ." Lily took a breath, "difficult, I suppose. But all that is in the past."

His look grew even keener. "I hope so. You have not seemed yourself since your return."

She was astonished. Her father's work in the House of Lords kept him quite busy during the season. They rarely saw him, except at the dinner table. She did not know what to say. That he had noticed either meant she had been more out-of-sorts than she thought, or that he paid more attention to her life than she knew.

She was touched. Some impulse made her want to confide

in him, to explain what had happened between herself and James—how he had broken her heart. Lily bit her lip, afraid the words would slip out. It would only hurt her father, and there had been more than enough hurt already.

"Well," he said. "There has been much to occupy your mind."

"Yes, there has."

She would miss him, she realized as he swept her into the opening of the dance. Even if she was no longer a child who could seek comfort in his arms, they could at least dance together.

Lily felt considerably better when they had finished. Her cheeks were warm, and a tendril of hair had unwound from her careful coiffure to tickle her neck.

Her father glanced down at her. "I see Lord Buckley has arrived. Shall we make our way over to him?"

"Of course." She lifted her chin. "He was to meet us here." There was no point in delaying.

As they approached Lord Buckley extracted himself from the circle of gentlemen he had been conversing with. "The Marquis of Fernhaven, how very good to see you. A great deal going on in Parliament this season, I understand. And Miss Strathmore. You are looking well." He bowed perfunctorily over her hand.

Lily's father turned his considering look on Lord Buckley. "Lord Abernathy wanted a word with me. May I leave Lily in your hands?"

"You may, sir, without fear." Lord Buckley transferred her hand to his arm. "Some refreshment, Miss Strathmore? You look a bit . . . over-warm."

"I was dancing."

"Enthusiastically, it would seem." He made it sound eminently undesirable to show enthusiasm for anything. "It is certainly a crush in here. I suppose Lord Severn must be pleased. society has approved his match to that Italian."

"That *Italian* is Baronessa Bellini, and she is a friend of mine."

He frowned, his gaze skating over her. "I shall fetch you

some refreshment. Would you prefer lemonade or champagne?" He peered into the crowd.

It was clear he was not going to discuss her friendship with the baronessa or apologize for the way he had referred to her. At least not now. Lily sighed inwardly. "Lemonade, please."

Over the course of their courtship she had noted that Lord Buckley somehow managed to spend very little time in her company. She did not doubt it would take him a rather longish time to return with her lemonade. Not that she minded. It was a match of convenience after all.

"I shall return shortly." Lord Buckley stepped away from her. She watched him go. The man walked as if his shoes were too tight.

"Good evening, Miss Strathmore." The voice came from directly behind her, making her heart jump. Lily whirled.

"Gracious, Lord Reginald, what are you doing here? Do you relish startling people?"

He was hovering uncomfortably close, dressed in impeccable black, even his waistcoat subtly embroidered with black silk. Lord Reginald made her a bow, dark eyes gleaming as they swept over her. "At one time I did enjoy startling people, but now it bores me. Besides, it was you who startled me, Miss Strathmore. What an unexpected pleasure. You have returned safely from your travels. Was the expedition everything you had hoped for?"

"Not entirely. And when did you return to England, Lord Reginald?"

"I've been back for some time. I can't neglect my projects for too long, no matter how stimulating travel may be. But is my cousin James here?"

She frowned. "I have no idea where your cousin is—not that it is any business of yours."

"Really?" He adjusted his diamond stickpin. "It was my impression that James was rather taken with you. I had supposed you returned the sentiment—wrongly, I am glad to know. Excellent judgment on your part, Miss Strathmore. My cousin was serving his own interests—as usual."

She searched his face. "What do you mean?"

"Just what I said, but if you would have it more bluntly—he was using you, Miss Strathmore, using all of you—"

"I say, Huntington," Lord Buckley interrupted, returning with the beverages. He handed her a flute of champagne and turned back to Lord Reginald. "I didn't know you were acquainted with Miss Strathmore. Are you keeping well?"

"I am. I was about to ask Miss Strathmore for a dance." Lord Reginald watched Lily's fingers close about the champagne flute, obviously not missing the fact that Lord Buckley was her escort. "If you don't mind."

"Of course not. It is a social event, and we are here to be social. Any understanding Miss Strathmore and I might have certainly does not preclude her from dancing with a proper gentleman such as yourself." He placed his hand in the small of Lily's back.

She took a small step away from him.

"An understanding?" Lord Reginald raised one thin brow, a speculative look crossing his face. "I had no idea."

Lily shook her head, but Lord Buckley continued. "Nothing announced yet, but it would be mutually advantageous for both of us."

At that moment she could not decide who she loathed more—Lord Reginald for his knowing smirk or Lord Buckley for discussing the merits of their upcoming engagement in front of her as if she did not exist.

"Go ahead, Miss Strathmore," her escort said. "Be gracious enough to grant Lord Huntington a dance."

Wordlessly, Lily proffered her dance card. At least she would be able to pursue her conversation with Lord Reginald without interruption. What had he been saying about James?

Lord Reginald filled his name in with a flourish. "Good to see you again Buckley. Miss Strathmore, I shall return to claim my dance at the appointed time." His smile held a predatory edge.

She nodded coolly. It was unsettling, facing Lord Reginald

again. It made her realize how reassuring it had been to have James beside her during their previous encounters.

"I'm glad you found some congenial company," Lord Buckley said, "but we really should join Mother. She was speaking with the Duchess of Carstairs just a moment ago."

"As you wish." Lily raised her glass to her lips. She really would have preferred lemonade. Frowning, she deposited the flute on a tray carried by a passing servant.

"Good gad, what a crush," Lord Buckley said as they were forced to detour around a group of giggling young ladies. "I feel as though I'm swimming against a current." He led her to where the crowd thinned.

"Lily! Lily Strathmore!" It was Uncle Edward, emerging from the crowd to lift her in a buoyant embrace. "Splendid to see you, my girl."

She smiled back at him. "And you, Uncle." More than she could say.

"Lily!" Aunt Mary hurried forward. "I hoped you would be here this evening. Wasn't the news about the baronessa a surprise? How wonderful for her."

Lily nodded, her throat tight with emotion. "I've missed you all so much. Are you well?"

"We just arrived in London today. But do introduce us to your escort." Aunt Mary looked at Lord Buckley.

Lily turned to him—there was no avoiding it now. "Lord Buckley, allow me to present my aunt, Lady Mary Strathmore, and my uncle, Sir Edward Strathmore."

Lord Buckley bowed. "A pleasure to meet you. We were on our way to join my mother, Countess Buckley. There are some people she wants Miss Strathmore to meet, and it wouldn't do to keep Mother waiting."

"But I have exciting news to tell Lily," Uncle Edward began.

Lord Buckley cleared his throat. "Miss Strathmore will certainly be able to spend some time with you later this evening. Please excuse us. We really must be going."

Glancing back as Lord Buckley led her away, Lily saw her aunt lay a hand on Uncle Edward's arm. He looked crestfallen.

She vowed to find them again as soon as she could escape the countess.

Countess Buckley was seated on a divan, chatting with a regal, gray-haired lady whose piercing gaze darted around the room.

"There you are, Gerald," the countess said, bestowing a smile on her son. "Say hello to the Duchess of Carstairs. And this is Winifred's daughter, Miss Lily Strathmore. A lovely girl, isn't she?"

Lily performed the obligatory curtsy. "A pleasure," she murmured.

The countess turned back to Lord Buckley. "I was just telling the duchess about your travels, and what a faithful correspondent you are. Now that you have arrived, perhaps you would relate that little story about the pompous majordomo. He tells it so well," she assured the duchess.

Lord Buckley launched into his story, one Lily had already heard more times than she would care to. She glanced back into the crowd, hoping to catch sight of her family. What was Uncle Edward's news? Had he heard from James?

Dancers scribed patterns on the floor, colorful gowns contrasting with the formal black evening kit of the gentlemen. On the rose-draped dais a string orchestra played, the music rising over the general hubbub of conversation.

A figure entering through the ballroom's grand entrance sent her hand to her mouth.

James Huntington.

She would never mistake his broad shoulders or sun-streaked brown hair. His eyes met and locked with hers for an instant, and she was transfixed. The lamplight flared and the crowd seemed to surge around her.

Then he looked away. He bent his head and smiled warmly at the woman on his arm, a young lady with cascading brown curls and a winsome smile. She laughed at something he said, reached up to brush a lock of hair out of his eyes, then took his arm again, leaning close.

Lily's corset felt unbearably tight. Her fingers locked

around the turquoise pendant as if to tear it from around her neck. He meant nothing to her! Nothing! She gritted her teeth.

". . . isn't that so, Miss Strathmore?" Countess Buckley was smiling expectantly at her.

Lily wrenched her attention back. "Yes, of course," she guessed, hoping no further response was needed. She had no idea what she had just agreed with.

The countess nodded with satisfaction. "I knew you were a sensible girl. See, Gerald, it is as I told you. Now go along and have a dance. You young people needn't spend the whole evening hovering about us."

"On the contrary, Mother. We could imagine no better company."

The duchess smiled at Countess Buckley. "Your son is a rascal." She turned her sharp gaze on Lily and her escort. "Go on. We have private matters to discuss."

Dismissed at last, thank goodness. Lily curtsied and then turned to Lord Buckley. "Please excuse me. I must find my uncle."

He patted her arm. "Admirable devotion to your family, I must say. Isn't that Sir Edward there by the refreshment table? I shall take you to him."

"It's really not necessary. I can rejoin you shortly."

"But I insist." Lord Buckley held out his arm. "I am your escort this evening. I shall see you properly escorted. And then, as Mother suggested, we will have our dance." He sounded resigned.

Lily's steps slowed as they approached. There was Uncle Edward, but oh dear, he was speaking with James—the man who despised her. Well, the feeling was entirely mutual.

"Come along," Lord Buckley said. "You did say you wanted to speak to your uncle, did you not?" He towed her through the press.

A wide smile crossed Uncle Edward's face as he spotted her. "There you are! At last I can tell you my news. And wonderful luck—see who is here."

James stood motionless. His hand was folded over his companion's, his jaw set. His eyes, flaring nearly amber, did not leave her face. Lily's nerves twitched at his nearness.

"Miss Strathmore." His voice was cold as he bowed. Rising, his gaze rested for a moment on the pendant lying against her skin. Did his expression falter? No doubt it reminded him of things he would rather forget. When his eyes went to Lord Buckley his features hardened again. The young woman at his side gave him a questioning glance.

Lily forced her voice to remain steady. "Mr. Huntington, have you made Lord Buckley's acquaintance?"

"I have not."

"Then allow me to introduce you."

The two men eyed one another. Lord Buckley seemed very pale and round next to James.

"A pleasure," James said tersely.

"Mr. Huntington, is it? Any relation to Lord Reginald Huntington? Why, we were speaking with him not more than a quarter-hour ago. Miss Strathmore promised him a dance."

"Did she?" James raked her with his gaze. "Reggie is my cousin. How splendid of Miss Strathmore to indulge him."

Lily stiffened. He was despicable. "I think it should make very little difference to you who I dance with."

"Quite right," Lord Buckley said. "Well, I am happy to make your acquaintance."

James turned to his companion. "Let me introduce my sister, Miss Caroline Huntington. Caroline, this is Miss Lily Strathmore."

"How do you do," Caroline said.

"Your sister?" Curiously lightheaded, Lily met the woman's interested gaze. Of course, she could see the resemblance now. "Your sister, Caroline. A pleasure."

"Miss Strathmore, I was hoping to meet you. James has told me so much about you." She glanced quickly at Lord Buckley, as if afraid she might have misspoken.

What had he told her? Lily doubted it was anything good.

"My brother says you are a talented botanical artist. I very much admire Miss Anne Pratt's illustrations. I have a copy of her *Flowers and their Associations*. Is your work anything like hers?"

"Lily's work is much finer," Uncle Edward said.

"Do you have an interest in painting?" Lily asked.

Caroline laughed. "I'm interested in nearly everything, although I have very little time for the arts at the moment."

Lord Buckley turned and addressed James. "So, friend of the family, are you?"

"Yes." James glanced at Lily, then back to Lord Buckley. "And you? It seems I have seen your face somewhere before."

Oh, the odious man! He knew perfectly well where he had seen Lord Buckley's likeness. How cruel of him to remind her.

"Huntington is a friend of the family," Uncle Edward said, clapping James on the shoulder. "A very good friend indeed. He has just returned from Tunisia, and although it seemed our expedition had failed, James has redeemed it. He succeeded in bringing home the previously uncollected flower we had been seeking!"

Lily felt suddenly rooted to the spot. "He what?" James had abandoned them and ridden off into the wilds of Tunisia . . . to collect the flower? How could it be? Her gaze flew to him, noting the faint lines of weariness about his eyes and mouth. He returned her look, no hint of warmth in his expression.

"He found the valley and collected the plant," Uncle Edward said. "Brought back two living specimens. It's extraordinary, makes everything worth the trouble, even that little bump to the head."

James gave a mirthless grin. "It was the least I could do."

"You went back to the valley?" He had not abandoned the expedition. He had become it, single-handedly accomplishing what the rest of the party, with their equipment, and sketchbooks, and folding bathtubs, had not.

He had done it—without telling her a thing.

Lily's anger flared. James had ridden off after that last dreadful scene and let her think he was running away. He could have at least said something! But rather than staying to exchange a few simple explanations he had galloped off.

Uncle Edward glowed with enthusiasm. "You must come to our townhouse, Lily, and paint the specimen. I have nearly finished the final version of the monograph, and your illustrations are vital. Wait until you see it. An entirely new sub-species!"

Lord Buckley frowned. "Surely there are better-qualified men who can draw the thing? Miss Strathmore has other, important, matters to concern her at this time."

"Such as?" James spoke with such deadly quiet that they all turned.

"Such as assuming her place in society," Lord Buckley said. "I suppose expeditions and such are very well for some people, but the *ton* has obligations, and Miss Strathmore is well aware of the fact."

Uncle Edward blinked at him. "Lily is one of the finest illustrators in the country. She has always drawn my specimens."

She spoke quickly, ignoring Lord Buckley's frown. "Of course I'll come, Uncle. In the next day or two, I promise. And Isabelle is here also? Is she well?"

"It would do her good to see you, my girl. And Mrs. Hodges has been asking after your welfare."

Lord Buckley cleared his throat. "Yes, well, it's been a pleasure meeting all of you. But speaking of dances, I believe ours is about to commence. Come along, Miss Strathmore."

She hung back a moment. "I will visit as soon as I can. Give my love to Isabelle and Richard."

"I will. And your specimen awaits you, my girl. Extraordinary, I must say."

Lily let Lord Buckley lead her back into the crowd. She could not help glancing at James. He was watching her, his brown eyes unreadable. It was beyond time to remove herself from his presence. Things could never be easy between them now. A pity—his sister seemed quite likeable.

The floor was terribly over-crowded and Lord Buckley was forced to hold her closer than usual to avoid contact with the other couples. It took nearly the entire dance to traverse to the opposite side of the ballroom.

He released her as soon as the music reached its end and

dabbed at his forehead with his handkerchief. "Thank goodness that is finished. You have several more dances promised, do you not? You are welcome to them, I must say. Would you care to take the air on the terrace?"

The warm June night carried the scent of roses and an underlying hint of London's soot. Lily walked beside Lord Buckley, keeping her gaze resolutely on the flagstones.

"Miss Strathmore, I know this is hardly the place, but I have an important question to ask you." There was something in his voice that made her glance sharply up into his pale blue eyes.

She froze. He could not possibly be thinking of proposing? Dear heaven, not now. She looked around at the other guests strolling the terrace. Not here.

"I would like," he continued, "to ask if I may call upon you Wednesday afternoon. I have a serious matter I would like to discuss with you."

Lily let out a breath. Of course he wouldn't propose here. Thank goodness. "Certainly. I shall look forward to it. Please, let us return to the ballroom." Only four days!

He guided her back inside. "There is Lord Huntington now. I will leave you to the pleasure of his company. I'm certain Mother has been wondering what's become of me." He bowed, exchanged greetings with Lord Reginald, and was gone.

"Your paramour seemed in a hurry to depart," Lord Reginald said, "Though I am happy to have you to myself for a moment. And what luck, I believe the next dance is a waltz." He held his arms out and Lily stepped reluctantly into his embrace.

Once the music began she went directly to the point. "Tell me, Lord Reginald. What were you doing in Tunisia?"

He regarded her, his expression calculating. "I take it my cousin did not see fit to enlighten you as to our mutual purpose in traveling to Africa?"

"No, he did not. Unless you, too, are interested in botanical discoveries?"

Lord Reginald gave a bark of laughter. "Not I—unless they are immediately profitable. And certainly less so than my grandfather, who left a substantial fortune to the descendant who returned to a certain valley in Tunisia and recovered his damnable journals. James and I were after a fortune, not a flower. Your uncle, your entire family, were the means to that end. In short, Miss Strathmore, he used you for his own purposes." His look suggested he knew what other uses James had made of her. Black eyes glinting, he guided her through a turn.

Lily followed, barely paying attention to the dance. Fury kindled inside her. So that had been the game. And James's heroic act of retrieving the flower? Just another excuse to make for the valley, this time without the awkward encumbrance of the expedition to hinder him.

"Did he find what he was seeking?" she asked.

Lord Reginald shrugged, but the movement lacked his usual nonchalance. "I don't believe he did. A fitting end, if you ask me. You should have heeded my earlier warnings about him, for I can see that you and your family did not escape entirely unscathed."

No, they had not—even though Uncle Edward seemed quite recovered.

"You said you shared the purpose of finding the journals. You didn't stay in Tunis, then, did you?" The peculiar, threatening incidents that had beset the expedition began to form a picture she did not like at all.

"I headed for the valley, but since James had taken my grandfather's letters and did not see fit to share, I was at a considerable disadvantage."

"So that's why you followed us."

"Me? I merely wanted to ensure the Earl's estate remained intact, not parceled out to poor relations right and left. I am the heir, after all, and I am not above protecting what is mine by right."

"I see." Memory rose—she was picking her careful way down the hillside, clutching a length of turquoise cloth around her, her heart hammering in her throat and the only light to guide her cast by a tent engulfed in flame. "To what lengths would you go, Lord Reginald? Would you raid a defenseless camp? Strike down an innocent man?" She could hear the sharp edge in her voice, the rising inflection.

He stepped back, his expression going flat and hard. "Miss Strathmore. Are you accusing me of something nefarious, in the middle of Lord Severn's ballroom? Before you take that dangerous path, consider how much attention you wish to draw to your recent travels with my cousin."

They had given up any pretense of waltzing now. An odd stillness began to spread out from where she and Lord Reginald stood. Glancing about, Lily saw the curious stares, quickly averted, heard the sudden whispers. He was right, blast him. This was not the time or place to make accusations. Frustrated, she glared back.

Lord Reginald gave her a thin smile, sharp as a blade. He took a step forward, arms raised to resume dancing. Then his eyes focused past her, his gaze sharpening.

"Speak of the devil." An incongruous smile curved his lips. "I regret I will not be able to complete our dance. Good evening, Miss Strathmore." He slipped away, leaving hardly a ripple in his wake.

Hands balled at her sides, Lily could only stare. She felt certain that somehow he had been behind the raid on the camp, possibly even the one who had struck down her uncle. Certain, but without proof.

The dancers swirled past, giving her a wide berth. She had to leave the floor immediately or become the talk of the evening—if it wasn't already too late. Lily turned hastily and took a step, only to collide with a tall man who could have been granite for all he yielded. Strong arms encircled her, and before she could draw breath, she was waltzing again.

With James—and he looked furious.

Chapter 23

"What the devil were you doing with Reggie?" James had been ready to launch himself at his cousin, but that snake had slipped away again, leaving Lily the object of whispers and stares.

He bared his teeth and swept her into another turn. If only she didn't feel so damnably good in his arms.

"I was dancing with your odious cousin—before he rudely abandoned me. I suppose I ought to thank you for coming to my aid, though I assure you it is not necessary for us to finish the dance. Escorting me to the edge of the floor will be quite sufficient."

That had been his intention before he had taken her into his arms. His gaze traveled over her face, snagged once more on the pendant she wore. The one he had given her the night they had lain together under the stars.

"Lily, what did Reggie want? And what did you say to him?" His cousin's interest in the Strathmores should have ended with the ill-fated expedition.

"I don't see that I need to tell you anything, Mr. Huntington." Lily wore an exceedingly stubborn look. "I'm afraid I'm not in the habit of confiding in men who *despise* me."

Despise her? Had he really used that word? Thinking back he supposed he had. Finding the locket, exhaustion, worry over

Sir Edward and the failure of the expedition had not inclined him to kindness or diplomacy. And she *had* betrayed him.

A nearby couple lurched precariously close. He pulled Lily hard against him and spun her, adroitly moving them out of harm's way. Her breasts grazed against him, her hair brushed the skin of his throat, and she smelled of softness and lavender. Gods. If things had been different . . . if *she* had been different.

He stiffened and set her back to the regulation distance.

"Whatever we may think of one another is irrelevant. You know how proficient my cousin is at stirring up trouble, and for some reason he seems intent on deviling you. If you value your reputation and your fiancé's affections, I suggest you confide in me."

"And if I refuse?"

"Then you are far less intelligent than I have given you credit for."

She looked away and was silent for several moments. Finally she spoke. "I learned quite a bit from your cousin—especially about your reasons for going to Tunisia. I hope your next quest for a fortune does not involve duping innocent parties into aiding you."

That stung. Trust Reggie to put things in the worst possible light.

"Regardless of what you may think, your uncle was fully aware of my reasons for traveling to Tunisia. He was more than happy to lend his assistance, especially since he would likely make a new botanical discovery."

Her eyes flashed, brilliant turquoise. "I don't see why you concealed the matter from me. After all, we were . . ." She trailed off, color rising in her cheeks.

"Yes. That is entirely the problem, isn't it?" He remembered all too well. Even now he was acutely aware of his hand resting on her body just where her slim waist curved into the sweet flare of her hip. "I didn't explain everything to you because I hoped . . . well. It's no concern of yours now, since according to your fiancé, you have important matters to attend to—such as your upcoming wedding. Now, tell me what Reggie said or there will be no wedding." Society would chew her up if rumors about them began to circulate.

"Mr. Huntington, I would thank you to loosen your grip on my hand before you do permanent damage."

He had not realized how tightly he was holding her.

She told him then how she had accused Reggie of being behind the raid on their camp and of his threats to her. It was as serious as he had feared, but there was something more behind his cousin's threat. Something that James did not understand—yet.

"Why would he seek you out? Reggie doesn't expend effort unless he hopes to gain something. Could it be there is still something between him and Isabelle?"

Lily shook her head. "He didn't even ask after her. It was as if she had completely slipped his mind—or never existed for him in the first place."

The couples in front of them had bunched together. James spun Lily and she followed his lead easily, avoiding the crush. "Whatever Reggie has on his mind, it seems you're in jeopardy until you and—what is his name?—are wed."

"Lord Buckley."

"Yes, Buckley."

"And what right do you have to assume that we are to be wed?"

He scowled. "Only that you carried his picture with you to Tunisia, and that your mother sent you a chatty letter discussing the progress on your wedding gown, and that you appeared here tonight with him and let him drag you around and tell you that you are not to paint your uncle's specimens."

Her face flushed. "He did not tell me I could not paint them. In fact, I distinctly told my uncle that I would."

"Buckley is not your husband yet, is he? He doesn't have the authority to rule you, but he—" James winced and missed a beat of the dance.

"I would thank you not to mash my foot again, Miss Strathmore."

"You were making a fool of yourself, and it was the only way I could silence you. It's obvious to me now that you are consumed with jealousy because I refused your oh-so-moving proposal of marriage in favor of Lord Buckley—who, despite his shortcomings, is a lord and a gentleman."

James could feel the blood throbbing at his temple. "Gentleman or no, your fiancé is a pompous ass by any standard, and I can't think of a couple who deserve each other more."

He had brought her to the edge of the dance floor. "Good night, Miss Strathmore."

He turned and strode for the exit without looking back.

"Out early, sir," the groom remarked as James swung into the saddle.

"Or late, depending how you look at it." He turned his mount through the gate in the old stone wall. The morning air was cool, the cobbles of the quiet street still wet with dew.

A few more hours and the scene would be entirely changed—cart vendors and sweepers would dodge around the elegantly dressed Mayfair residents crowding the street on their way to see and be seen. He planned to be on the outskirts of London by then.

A good hard ride and then a visit to the gentleman's boxing club. Anything to dispel his restless thoughts.

Lily. How easily she threw him into turmoil. He had thought he'd gained some measure of peace in the valley, but seeing her again—and meeting that Buckley fellow—was enough to drive a man mad. James spurred his bay into a canter and leaned forward into the wind.

When he returned to his lodgings several hours later there was a note waiting. *"James. Urgent business. Your presence is needed. My library, one o'clock.—Lord Denby."*

He ran his hand through his windblown hair. It was nearly one now—the boxing club would have to wait for another day. He threw on a coat and headed out.

Striding down the thickly carpeted corridor that led to his uncle's library, James heard voices raised in anger.

"That's impossible. I told you before, I won't stand for it." It was Reggie—a very angry sounding Reggie.

James paused before the partially closed door, then pushed it open. His cousin was standing, a scowl on his face, at one end of the long table. Catching sight of James his look grew even blacker and his lip curled with disdain. Taking a seat, Reggie leaned over to the bespectacled man at his right and the two began a hushed conversation.

"James. Come in, sit down," Lord Denby greeted him. "This is my solicitor, Mr. Clark." He indicated a white-haired gentleman with a stiffly starched collar.

James nodded a greeting. "My apologies. I was out riding and didn't receive your note until I returned." He cast a quick glance over the assembled gentlemen. "I'm afraid I haven't brought a solicitor of my own. Should I send for one?" The question was only half in jest.

"No, at least not yet. Hear me out before you decide whether that will be necessary." Lord Denby's tone was dry. "I have asked you and Reginald to be here today so we can conclude the matter of Somergate. I do not want to see the estate—so favored by my father and one of our older family holdings— escheat to Kew Gardens."

Reggie made a sharp movement of protest, but Lord Denby held up his hand. "As my heir, Reginald, you are well provided for, and James and Caroline have fewer assets than befits their status." He pinned Reggie with a sharp gaze. "I am aware there is no love lost between you and James—it is one of my deepest regrets that the two of you cannot be brothers in spirit if not fact. Frankly, I am reluctant to make him and his sister dependent on your charity when the title passes into your hands."

"I would not accept–" James began.

"If you think—" Reggie spat, but neither of them got any further.

Lord Denby lifted his voice, overriding them. "As executor of the will, I have examined the pages James brought back from Tunisia and concluded that they were indeed the last remains of my father's lost journals. James has satisfied the terms of the will and I am authorized to award Somergate to him. Since it would otherwise go to Kew Gardens, Reginald, you are losing nothing." His look silenced Reggie's protest. "Solicitor Clark and I have been through this carefully."

Mr. Clark nodded from his place beside the earl.

His cousin narrowed his eyes. "And I say the 'pages' he has returned with are a blatant forgery concocted by him and Miss Lily Strathmore, who is known for her artistic skills. There is nothing to prove they are genuine. Grandfather's gift was conditioned on the recovery and publication of his journals. Since that condition has not been—and cannot be—satisfied, the estate can never go to James." Reggie sat back.

Shuffling through the papers in front of him, Mr. Clark pointed out some text to the earl.

Lord Denby gave a short nod. "Actually, your grandfather's intent was to honor his fallen friend, Mercer, and to secure his own position as discoverer of a new species of flower. The publication of the journals was to have accomplished both objectives. Sir Edward Strathmore is preparing a monograph that establishes your grandfather as the discoverer, and James has named it *Mercerium*, after the fallen comrade. If the recovered pages are included in the monograph then I am satisfied that the terms of the will have been fulfilled. Somergate is to be awarded to James."

"And I say James has failed to return with the journals and the property goes to the crown." Reggie was on his feet, fury vibrating through his lean frame. "The whole scheme you have cooked up is ludicrous. Besides, Kew Gardens is bound to challenge this obscene perversion of the will. Even if you give Somergate to James it will be tangled up in the courts until his children's children are old men and women. Come along." He motioned to his solicitor, who scrambled to gather up papers on the table before him. "I will not stay and listen to this nonsense any longer."

As Reggie stalked past, he shot James a murderous glare. "You will never get that property," he hissed.

The room was silent until the door had closed behind the two men. Then Lord Denby leaned forward, worry in the lines about his mouth. "Well, James, I am sorry. That did not go as smoothly as I'd hoped. I hadn't anticipated Reginald would be so adamantly set against you inheriting Somergate. It's not as though the property would go to him." He shook his head. "I would like you to inherit it, but I'm afraid it may not be as straightforward as I had wanted. At least you know where I stand."

James met his uncle's gaze. "Thank you. It means a great deal. As for the estate . . ." He shrugged.

It was ironic to think he might actually end up with Somergate now that any hope of bringing Lily there was gone. The image that had grown in Tunisia was of the two of them there together. Without her it would just be acres of dirt.

"Don't assume you won't inherit, either," Lord Denby said. "Mr. Clark and I agree that our interpretation is sound." He sighed. "I am committed to seeing you get the place even if it puts Reginald and myself at odds."

"You don't need to do that."

"Yes, James, I do. It is past time. I am the earl now, and must do what I think is best for the family."

"Thank you, Uncle. Good day." James rose and bowed.

"We will keep you apprised. Don't worry."

James gave a tight smile. "I won't."

He strode back down the corridor, hands clasped behind his back. Caroline would certainly have an opinion about this, and she would want to know the details—if she didn't already. The staff doted on her and related all the choicest gossip almost as soon as it occurred. He turned the corner, heading for his sister's rooms.

"Well, coz. Going to gloat?" Reggie uncoiled from a shadowed alcove and moved to block his way. "I'd hold off on that if I were you. Probably forever. There is no way you're going to be master of Somergate."

"That remains to be seen." James kept his voice even.

Convenient of his cousin to waylay him—it saved him the trouble of trying to track Reggie down later. "Since you're here, why don't you tell me what the devil you meant by abandoning Miss Strathmore on the dance floor. Or even dancing with her for that matter. I warned you months ago to keep your distance. She is none of your concern."

"On the contrary. The time the two of you spent together in Tunisia is very much my concern. I was thinking of what would result if that connection were made public. Poor girl. She's engaged, you know?" He sent James a sly glance. "Ah, you do know. And don't argue that you don't care—you came running last night to protect the lovely Miss Strathmore, even though she has rejected you for another. You make such a pathetic hero."

"There's nothing pathetic about it. It has to do with honor—obviously a word you have little acquaintance with."

Reggie smiled. "That ridiculous sense of honor will be your undoing. I will not hesitate to drop a few choice words in the proper ears regarding Miss Strathmore's conduct with you. I saw more than you know. The *ton*—in particular one Lord Gerald Buckley—will be very interested to find out about her doings while abroad. She will be ruined, James, and you will be the one who ruined her. It's too rich, really."

Blood thundering in his veins, James started toward Reggie. "You wouldn't dare." But he knew his cousin too well.

Reggie took a step back and lifted one brow. "I wouldn't? James, I would. Unless . . ."

"Unless what?" James held himself back, jaw clenched.

". . . unless you agree to deed your interest in Somergate to me."

Blackmail. Of course. It was all about the estate. It wouldn't be enough for Reggie to tie the property up in court—he wanted it for himself.

Hot anger flooded James. It was not losing the estate to his cousin, though that galled, it was the knowledge that he had been the instrument of his own downfall. Had he left Lily Strathmore alone, as he knew he should have, she would not be in jeopardy, and he and his sister Caroline's places would be secure. Defeat had never tasted so bitter.

His cousin watched him, an avid gleam in his black eyes. "Consider it. Poor Miss Strathmore, shunned at every gathering, the disdainful looks and hurtful whispers following her wherever she goes. Her fiancé would certainly abandon the match—who wants another man's cast-off?—and she would have no hope of making another. She would be ostracized. No more waltzing with gallant gentlemen." Reggie shook his head. Then his look lightened and he gave James a mocking smile. "Perhaps you should refuse my offer. Let her be ruined and then make her your mistress. She would be pathetically grateful, I'm sure."

"No!" The echo of his voice reverberated down the hall. "Damn you Reggie. Damn you to hell. You can have the estate." Lily's future, however she had chosen to spend it, had to be protected.

"Come, coz, give me your oath. I know it will bind you while my solicitor prepares the formal documents." His cousin smiled. Every slight, every taunt, every loss James had ever suffered at his cousin's hand was in that dark-edged smile. He shook with the desire to take Reggie by the collar and beat him senseless, but he could blame no one but himself for this predicament. This was the price he must pay.

"I swear I will deed Somergate to you, but you will have no right to it until *after* Miss Strathmore has married Lord Buckley." She would be safe once she was married. "And Reggie," his voice grew softer, full of leashed menace, "if even a hint of scandal attaches to her name, I will hold you directly responsible and you will pay. Dearly. I swear that, as well."

There. James closed his eyes to block out Reggie's look of triumph. It was done. All that was left was to warn Lily.

James handed his hat to the butler. "Sir Edward is expecting me." The botanist had requested he come look over the final proofs of the monograph.

"Yes sir. He is in the study. Shall I show you in?"

"Thank you, that won't be necessary." James appreciated the informality of the Strathmore's household. Even here, in London, they did not stand on ceremony—which was well for his purposes today.

The faintest hint of a smile on the butler's face reminded James that even the servants here felt as if they were part of the family. He had been welcomed as part of that extended family himself, and he would be glad of it—if it were not for Lily. As things stood, he would finish his business and then distance himself. This was her family, her refuge. He would not intrude after today, but the matter with Reggie demanded he see her one last time.

He started down the corridor, glancing behind him as he went. The butler had disappeared back toward the kitchen. Good. James stepped quietly past Sir Edward's study and made his way to the sunroom where the specimens of *Mercerium* were kept.

If Lily were not here he would have to find another way to speak with her. They could not meet in public—that would only play into Reggie's hands. This was the safest place he could think of.

The door was open, sunlight spilling onto the carpet. His heartbeat sounded loud in his ears. Quietly, he stepped up, pausing in the doorway. Lily was inside, painting. He studied her profile, the wisps of hair blazing chestnut in the sunlight, her lips slightly parted in concentration, her hands, firm and capable, guiding the brush over the paper.

She looked up, brush arrested in mid-air. It struck him that she looked far more vital here than she had at the ball. Her eyes were brighter, her face more open.

She set the brush down carefully. "Good afternoon, Mr. Huntington." Her look held an edge of wariness.

"May I see it?" He indicated the page on the easel.

She hesitated, then nodded and moved aside so he could stand before the painting. "It is your flower, after all."

There it was, the modest flower, yet somehow it seemed

lambent, the petals glowing yellow with an inner radiance. Lily had made studies—they were fanned out on the table—root and stem, tendril and leaf, all exact, all possessing that sense of something more she put into each image she created. There was the wild beauty James had glimpsed in the valley. Looking, he could almost feel himself standing on that rock waiting for the new day to spill light into the valley.

"Yes," he said softly. "Though you can barely tell from this well-traveled specimen, the rocks where I found it are washed in its fragrance. Like the smell of early light, or promise . . ." He shook his head, "I can't describe it. But you have." Memories of his time there, that instant of peace, rose in him.

She smiled at him and he felt his heart tighten. This would be far worse than he had thought if a smile from her still had the power to wrench his emotions so completely. Damn Reggie for his scheming, for making it impossible for James to avoid her. How could he forget Lily when he had to look into those sea-green eyes knowing how she had betrayed him—and that she was promised to another.

Her smile wavered. "I'm glad my painting finds favor with you. As the first to collect the flower, you may be surprised at the notoriety it will bring you in horticultural circles."

"Notoriety is what concerns me, Miss Strathmore. I have learned what Reggie is up to." He hated having to bring this up, reminding both of what had passed between them.

"And what is that?"

"He claims to have observed us in compromising circumstances. I can buy him off for a time, but I don't trust my cousin at all."

Her hands stilled. "Blackmail, then? If it's money he's after—"

"No. I have something he wants more than money. He will keep silent until it becomes his own. After that, we have only his word, which counts for nothing." She looked at him, her eyes wide with understanding. "It would be best if you could move up the date of your wedding. The sooner you and Buckley are married, the safer you will be."

She raised her face to his, her eyes flashing. "Are you saying that Reggie will ruin me? Unless you give him whatever he wants?"

"To put it bluntly, yes. Once you are married, though, the danger to you becomes far less. Lily, I urge you—"

"Yes, I know. But what of you? What price must he be asking? I cannot have you pay it for my sake. What we did in Tunisia we did together." She stared at him, a challenge in her eyes. Her body swayed toward his—almost imperceptibly, but he was so attuned to her presence that he caught the slight movement immediately.

James forced himself to take a step back. It was either that or catch her up into his arms and kiss her fiercely and he could not go there again. His heart would never recover.

"I bear the brunt of the responsibility, and I will pay the consequences. What I stand to lose is little compared with your future." His words were stiffer than he intended, but it was the only way he could hold on to the shreds of control slipping from him.

Lily wrapped her arms around herself. "You seem overly concerned with my future. Especially as you hold no place in it."

He felt the hollowness begin to rise again. "Leave this to me. Your part is to finish what you began. Marry your intended—but do it soon. " He swallowed. "And now, I must call on your uncle. I trust we will not need to meet again. Good day Miss Strathmore."

James was barely aware of leaving the room, of passing a white-faced Isabelle in the hall outside, of collecting his hat and gloves from the butler. The whole encounter had left him feeling emptier than ever.

Chapter 24

Even though Lily was expecting it, she still jumped when the butler knocked.

"Lord Buckley has come to call, Miss Lily. He awaits you in the parlor."

She rose from the chair, and then slowly sat again. "Thank you. Edwin. Tell him I will be down shortly."

Her gaze went to the window. It was a fine day outside. She wished she could snatch her pelisse, call for her maid Bess, and go for a long walk, but Lord Buckley's carriage rested at the curb. There was ultimately no escaping this moment—it was time to face the question that had been looming before her since she had first agreed to the arrangement.

Lily stood and began pacing, her skirts swishing with each step. She had thought she was ready. And now with Lord Reginald threatening her, the sooner she was wed, the better. Her reputation was at stake. By marrying Lord Buckley it would remain intact. Even James was urging the match.

James. Her hand went to her mouth. She had wanted him to kiss her, and for a moment she had imagined he might, but it was only her imagination. He had pulled away. It was clear he had been thinking of other things—her reputation, his responsibility. He still loathed her, and would hate her still more after his cousin had extracted a price for his silence.

Still, she could not banish the image of his warm brown eyes, nor the surge of pleasure she had felt when he had admired her painting. She knew she had done an excellent job with the flower. His approval should not matter to her.

Lily folded her arms and stared at the twining pattern on her carpet. Why was she thinking of James when Lord Buckley awaited her below to formalize their arrangement? It was beyond foolish.

This was her chance to see that the mistakes she had made in Tunisia did not bring ruin. It was not just for her. Her family's standing could be jeopardized and Uncle Edward's discovery tainted by association.

Lord Buckley did not love her. She knew that. She was not sure he was even capable of such emotion, at least for females other than his mother, but he was not such a horrible match. Nothing more than she deserved.

Lily straightened her shoulders and pulled open her door.

As she entered the parlor, Lord Buckley moved from his careful pose beside the marble fireplace and took her hand. "Miss Strathmore. You look charming today," He was staring at the top of her head.

"Thank you, my lord. Shall we sit?" She indicated the chintz-covered settee.

Lord Buckley dropped her hand. "Of course. Though perhaps I ought to kneel." He gave his odd little laugh as he settled beside her. "I had hoped to find you at home yesterday. I did promise to call upon you on Wednesday, do you not recall?"

Her gaze darted to the door. "Did you receive my message? I would have liked to be here, but it was imperative that I finish the illustration for my uncle's monograph. He is presenting it quite soon."

He frowned. "I must make it clear that I do not approve of this scientific illustration nonsense you are involved in. A future countess has her standing to think of. This type of thing reflects poorly on the entire family." He patted her hand. "Not that you should stop dabbling. I simply ask that you limit

yourself to decorative painting. Science is a man's work. We
wouldn't want to cause an unnatural imbalance."

She stared at him, unable to frame a reply. Over the last
three days she had spent nearly every waking minute at her
uncle's, first making careful pencil studies of the flower, then
applying paint to paper. It was as if she had finally woken
from a stupor of the senses and come fully alive again. Now
Lord Buckley was asking her—no, commanding her—to
abandon the work. He wanted her safely swaddled in a cocoon
of what was ladylike and acceptable.

Most women of her acquaintance welcomed that kind of
life. They found everything they wanted there. Just look at her
mother. Why should Lily be any different? She could almost
hear her mother's voice telling her to accept and be patient.
Once established as a countess she would soon learn to
manage her husband. *Apply yourself to being agreeable, and
then slowly introduce the desired change—quite simple, darling.* Lily shivered.

Abruptly, her attention returned to Lord Buckley. He had
obviously taken her silence for acceptance and was in the
process of getting down on one knee.

"Wait!" She held her hand up. "Lord Buckley—"

"Now Miss Strathmore. No need to act the shy debutante
with me. We are both of an age that can see past such fool-
ishness." He straightened his trouser leg where it had bunched
at the knee. "It has long been our understanding that this
moment would come. I trust that I can provide you with every
comfort. Give me your hand."

It would cause such a scandal if she refused him. Yet even
now he called her Miss Strathmore. And he had never even
tried to kiss her. Lily held out her hand. It trembled.

Seeing that, he let out a soft tsk. "My goodness. You women
are quite ruled by your emotions. Your sex needs the firm
guidance of a man to steer you through the troubled waters
of life. Miss Strathmore, let me be that man." He cleared his
throat. "Will you marry me?"

She closed her eyes. This was the bargain she had made,

the promise that had freed her to travel with the expedition, to love, however briefly, and to look into her own soul far more deeply than she ever had before. It was time to seal the bargain.

Her heart beat frantically, like a moth against a windowpane. "Lord Buckley . . . It would make me, that is, I would be . . ." The words froze in her throat.

"Yes?" he said encouragingly, his pale blue eyes staring directly into hers. He held her hand lightly, too lightly. The silence in the room was tangible, pressing her into the cushions.

She glanced toward the window. The sun glinted off the summer green of the ancient elms that towered over the garden, daisies flung at their feet like bits of light.

Her chest felt constricted and she could not draw breath. Surely she was not fainting! If only she could breathe.

Look into your heart, bella. It was suddenly so clear.

Snatching her hand away, Lily jumped to her feet. She dragged in an uneven breath. Sound returned in a rush—the rustle of her skirts, the thrum of her pulse, the sound of hoof beats passing in the street outside. Lord Buckley was still on his knees, dismay in his pale eyes.

"Lord Buckley, I cannot marry you, and—and someday we will both be thankful for it." She felt dizzy with relief. "Please excuse me."

Her stride was light as she crossed to the parlor door, leaving him gaping behind her like a beached fish. "But Miss Strathmore—the arrangement. Won't you even look at the ring?"

She had found her wings and they would carry her away from Lord Gerald Buckley, out of the parlor, out of London as quickly as possible.

It did not take long to pack her valise.

Lily's mother flung open the bedroom door. Her face was flushed, her lips tight. "Lily! What have you done? Edwin informed me that Lord Buckley departed a short time ago, and that he did not look much pleased. I have a terrible suspicion . . ."

"You are looking over-warm, mother. Please, sit down." Lily waited until her mother had settled in a nearby wingback. She had nothing to be ashamed of. And though seeing the pain and disappointment in her mother's face was difficult, it did not compare to the prospect of an empty life as Lord Buckley's wife. "Lord Buckley called today, as you surely know, to ask me to marry him. I refused."

The echo of Baronessa Bellini's words came back to her. *You have the courage to look into your own heart.* It had taken her far too long to do so. But in the end, she had. She had made her choice and would stand by it with everything she was.

Her mother swayed. "But how could you? After we had planned everything so carefully? How could you be so ungrateful? What of your dreams of marriage? Of holding a title in your own right?" She drew out a silk handkerchief and pressed it to her mouth.

Lily's throat was tight. "I am sorry to grieve you, but those were *your* dreams, not mine." She sank to her knees beside her mother. "I don't expect you to understand, but it was the only thing I could do. I only regret I did not see that sooner."

Lady Fernhaven clenched the silk tightly and made no reply.

It would take time. And would be easier for all of them if Lily were gone. "I am leaving London," she said. "Today."

"You cannot simply leave. Where will you go? To Brookdale Manor? You cannot hide there forever."

"I don't expect to—but I need to be there now. Edwin is seeing to the carriage, and I will be departing in a quarter hour. I will send word soon." She hesitated and nearly reached for her mother's hand. Lady Fernhaven kept her gaze averted.

"Goodbye, Mother." Lily rose and retrieved her valise. She closed the door quietly behind her.

Before she could quit town, there was one stop she needed to make.

"I won't be long," Lily assured her maid as the carriage drew up in front of the Strathmore's townhouse. "Just the time it takes to speak with my uncle and collect my brushes."

Bess sighed. "Very well, miss. I'll wait here, if you don't mind."

The sudden departure had left Bess in a state, poor girl. A half-hour in which to pack for a trip out of London had been short notice, but the maid had risen to the task. As Lily opened the carriage door Bess leaned her head back against the cushions and closed her eyes.

Sir Edward was in the study. He glanced up from his desk, his smile fading as he saw her expression. "Lily. Whatever is the matter?" He was up from his chair and wrapping his arms around her before she could even frame a reply.

Closing her eyes, she leaned into him for a moment, then straightened. "Uncle Edward, I have come to ask a favor. I would like to go to Brookdale for a time."

"Of course, my dear. We'll be traveling home next week after I present the monograph. You are more than welcome to join us. You always have a place with us—I trust you know that."

"I do. Thank you." She swallowed, grateful beyond words for his solid, accepting presence, for that fact that he would not press her for answers. "I need to go there now. I have . . . I have rejected Lord Buckley's suit."

"Oh dear. I see. Well!" A smile warmed his face. "If it is any comfort, we were quite concerned, your aunt and I, about his suitability—that rubbish about your being unable to paint specimens because you needed to assume your place in society. Indeed! I should have known you would come to your senses. You had us worried, though." He sobered. "I suppose your mother disagrees. I can see how it might be a bit, er, uncomfortable for you in London just now. By all means, Lily. Go to Brookdale."

"Thank you. I'll await you and the family there, although I'm sorry I will miss the monograph's presentation."

He patted her hand. "I understand. Perhaps I should send Richard with you? Or Mrs. Hodges?"

"I will not be responsible for making either of them miss your triumph. I'll be fine. Bess and I have made the journey many times. I'll just gather up my supplies and go."

"Safe travels then, my dear."

Lily kissed her uncle on the cheek, and then hurried down the corridor to the sunroom. She began tucking supplies into her satchel—sketchbooks and paper, pans of paint, her brushes. Afternoon sun slanted in through the mullioned windows, pricking the air with dusty glints of light. She would not reach Brookdale until after dark, but the roads were safe and well-traveled. It was the first step on the journey of her own life. She would no longer have to worry about Lord Buckley. Or Reginald.

Or James.

She placed the last brush with the others in her satchel and took a final look around her. She had everything she needed.

Footsteps sounded in the corridor and Isabelle burst in. "Lily! Father said you were here, but about to leave London. Whatever is going on?" She folded her arms and planted herself in the doorway. "I won't let you leave until you tell me everything."

With an exasperated laugh, Lily set down her satchel. "Everything? I think not. The long and short of it is that I refused Lord Buckley's offer."

"You did? Your mother must be furious." Isabelle beamed at her. "I'm so glad. Now you are free to marry James."

"Whatever put that idea into your head? I will do no such thing. Besides, he has not asked." But he had, of course. She seemed to be making a habit of refusing offers of marriage. Lily picked up her bag. "I must go. Bess is waiting in the carriage."

"Wait." Isabelle stretched her arms across the doorway. "You can't mean to leave London just like that. What about James?"

"You seem to have had a change of heart. Wasn't it you who so questioned his motives that you nearly refused to leave the steamer in Tunis? Well, I have changed my mind as well."

"I was wrong about him. I started to realize it the day he rescued you from the river. And then . . ." She shook her head. "Lily, where have you been? He brought back the flower! He stayed behind even though we all left. If only you had seen father when James returned with the flower. I was wrong, and so are you if you think poorly of him."

"I do think poorly of him. In fact, I believe I dislike him as much as he despises me. He was more than pleased with the idea that I would marry Lord Buckley. In fact, he encouraged me to do so."

Isabelle dropped her arms. "Are you certain?"

"Absolutely." Lifting her chin, Lily stepped past her cousin and headed for the door.

"But Lily . . ." Isabelle trailed behind her.

Lily paused in the foyer. Fishing a letter from her reticule, she slipped it in with the others awaiting the afternoon post. "It is all for the best, believe me. Give my love to Aunt Mary. I will see you at Brookdale."

Chapter 25

His supper tasted like ashes. James shoved the plate away and stood. It was useless. He could not stop thinking of Lily as Buckley's wife. The man did not know her, could never appreciate her passion. From what he had overheard, it sounded as if Buckley did not even approve of her painting. How could she choose that?

He paced to the door then back to the table. Exactly seven strides each way. His mind went back to his own proposal to her in the wilds of Tunisia. Would it have been different if he had spoken of love instead of duty?

A knock sounded on the door, interrupting his thoughts.

"Mr. Huntington!" Two women stood on the step.

"What the devil?" James blinked in surprise.

"You make a very poor butler, Mr. Huntington. Do invite Miss Isabelle inside. She has something for you." Mrs. Hodges marched across the threshold with Isabelle in tow, scanning the small room that passed for James's parlor. The fire still burned in the grate, and he was glad to see that the remains of his supper had been cleared away. Isabelle looked about her curiously.

"What is wrong? Tell me," he said. The hour was far too late for a social call.

Isabelle glanced at Mrs. Hodges.

"Go ahead, girl, give it to him. Then we can explain."

Isabelle drew a letter from her reticule and held it out to him. His name and address were written across the envelope in Lily's angled hand.

James took it slowly, schooling his body, his face, to reveal nothing. The last time he had read a letter concerning Lily it had nearly destroyed him.

"Open it," Isabelle breathed.

Had Reggie already acted to ruin her? No, he wouldn't—not before he had gotten his hands on Somergate. And how could the letter contain any worse than what James already expected—that Lily would marry Buckley and be lost to him forever? He lifted a gleaming silver opener from the nearby desk and slit the envelope. The paper rustled as he drew it forth.

Mr. Huntington,

I am writing to inform you that I am leaving London. It is no longer necessary for you to protect me or complete the bargain you have made with your cousin.
　　　　　　　　　　　　　　　　—*Lily Strathmore*

His fist closed around the paper. "What has she done?" He rounded on his guests. "What in blazes has she done?"

"Mind your language, young man," Mrs. Hodges said, "And be assured, Lily is well and safe. She has gone to Brookdale."

"Why?" A hot rage flashed through him. If Reggie . . .

"That's what we've come to tell you, isn't it?" Mrs. Hodges fixed him with a mind-your-manners glare.

"Please, sit. I am sorry for my poor hospitality. Mrs. Hodges, allow me." He drew out a wingback chair, the faded upholstery barely noticeable in the gaslight.

"That's better." She settled herself and removed a ball of yarn from her bag.

He turned to Isabelle, perched on the edge of her chair. "What happened?"

"Lily left London just this afternoon."

"I don't understand."

"Lord Buckley proposed and she refused him! She has been wonderfully brave. I'm sure her mother is in a state right now with all her plans in tatters."

"I thought she had already accepted him—that they were engaged and had only to set the date of the wedding."

"No," Isabelle said. "Lily's parents forbade her to paint unless she married—and married well. You know what not painting would do to her. At any rate, Lord Buckley was courting her, but . . ."

Not everyone has the luxury to do what they wish with their lives. He recalled his uncle's words from the other night. Had Lily found herself in a similar trap, forced by social expectation and duty to her family to marry a man she did not love?

"Why didn't anyone tell me?" The crackling flames in the fireplace echoed his rising emotions. This could change everything.

Isabelle's clear green eyes rested on him. "Lily didn't speak much about it to anyone, and mother told us not to bring it up, that it was altogether too depressing and would only serve to make Lily miserable. Then, after she came back Lily was like a different person. I never saw her open a sketchbook the whole journey home from Tunisia. And after you stayed behind, well, it did not seem to concern you anymore."

He swallowed a curse.

She smiled at him. "I think, though, that now it definitely *does* concern you. That's why we brought the letter straightaway. You may not catch her on the road, but you'll arrive at Brookdale only a few hours behind her. You will go after her?"

He gave a short nod. "Immediately."

Mrs. Hodges tucked her knitting away and stood. "Then it's settled. Proceed to Brookdale with all speed. Come along, Isabelle. We have another matter to attend to."

"Let me fetch you a cab." He started for the door.

"We'll be fine," Isabelle said, "But you had best hurry."

James watched the two women leave, then snatched up his

coat. Lily had been pressured to marry, but she had refused Buckley's suit. She had refused it!

He must see her. There were so many things that needed to be said.

Lord Reginald rapped the head of his walking stick sharply against the carriage wall. The vehicle dipped as his driver swung down and in a moment the man appeared at the window.

"Yes, sir?"

"What's the blasted delay, Jenks? Why are we stopped in the middle of the street?"

The man swallowed. "Your lordship, there's some to-do ahead, blocking the way. An old gel with a parasol. The cabs ahead of us can't move, neither."

"Then deal with it, you idiot. Drive around or over—I shouldn't have to tell you how to perform your duties. Especially if you want to continue doing them."

"Yes, your lordship." The man bobbed his head and scuttled back to his perch.

Reginald tapped his long fingers against the carriage seat. Competent help was impossible to find. His staff had grown lazy while he had been away enduring the hardships of Tunisia.

What an utter waste of time that had been. He curled his hand into a fist. Even the letters he had taken from his cousin's tent had proven useless.

Although the whole wretched pursuit *had* given him a new leverage point against James. Namely one Miss Lily Strathmore. He couldn't imagine what his cousin saw in the chit; however, it was satisfying to see her slip through his cousin's fingers. And using her to take Somergate from James was the sweetest revenge on both James and his father—the two people who most deserved it.

The carriage jolted and Reginald leaned forward. Why weren't they moving? He raised his cane again, but before he could land a thwack against the wall, the carriage door was flung open and a woman climbed inside. Golden hair, a flurry of lavender skirts, an impossibly wide hat, and fire in her bright green eyes.

"Isabelle Strathmore. How unexpected." For once he was at a loss.

Isabelle plumped down on the seat opposite and adjusted her hat, for all the world like she was about to take tea with the Queen. She had spirit, he had to admit that. It had been amusing, watching her stand up to her family for all the wrong reasons. It was a pity he had not had the time or opportunity to make other use of her.

"Lord Huntington, your actions have compelled me to seek you out."

"Really? Still flinging yourself at me? I assure you, my dear, I have moved on to other pastimes. You would do well to follow suit."

Her gaze locked with his. "I assure *you* that I have not the slightest interest in renewing our acquaintance. I am here on my cousin's behalf."

Interesting. His conversation with Miss Lily seemed to have borne fruit in unforeseen ways.

"Then I assume it is the redoubtable Mrs. Hodges out there menacing traffic with her parasol? The woman is a loose cannon. You'd best go and see to her before she gets trampled under some impatient lord's carriage wheels."

"Meaning your own?" Isabelle gave a sniff. "In good time, sir. I have some things to say to you."

Reginald folded his arms and leaned back. "Have your say then and be gone. I hardly have time to indulge the whims of a spoiled child."

There, that earned a response. Her jade-colored eyes narrowed. "This is not a whim, any more than your threats against my cousin are. I have come to inform you that if you damage Lily's reputation in any way, I will tell everything I know about your misdeeds in Tunisia."

"And what do you imagine those might be? Taking in the

Mediterranean sights? Showing kindness to a misguided young woman? Do enlighten me."

A spark of fury blazed in her eyes. "Did you honestly think I would not recognize you that night at the camp? I *know* you were responsible for that bandit raid and the injuries to my father. I know it was you beneath the trees, disguised as a native."

Reginald shrugged, concealing the tension rising in him. "There is no evidence to indicate I was ever there."

"Isn't there?" She leaned forward. "What about the information I so foolishly provided you about the expedition's plans? And your note?"

"A love note forged by an overly romantic young woman? I'm afraid that story has been heard too many times, my dear. Allow me to point out that your own involvement will be made clear, and I do not believe your reputation could withstand the scrutiny."

A curious smile curved her lips. "No, I suppose it would not. But if you must be the ruin of someone, I am far more deserving of that ruin than Lily. If exposing you means my downfall, then so be it."

Alarm shot through him. The girl was annoyingly tenacious, and her words rang with conviction. It was just possible that she could carry it off. It was past time for him to take the initiative.

"My dear Isabelle." He made the name a caress, leaning forward until their faces were only a few inches apart. "I think you have forgotten what a very compromising position you have put yourself in just now. Your reputation can be easily ruined, yes, but I don't think we need to bring Tunisia into it. You are alone with me in my carriage, after all."

Her eyes widened, but she held her ground. "You do not frighten me, sir. In fact, if I were to scream, I'm certain we could draw many interested witnesses. There would be only one course open to you."

Despite himself, Reginald slid away from her. "Are you suggesting—"

"Marriage. Your family would force you to do the right thing. We would be shackled together for life—and I would spend every moment of it making you regret it. You caused my father grave injury. I would not forget to pay you back during the course of our unhappy union."

Damn the chit. She was not bluffing, it was clear in the determined set of her shoulders, the way her fingers clenched around the handle of her parasol. And even though a part of him wondered what it would be like to try to tame her anger, to break it and turn it to his advantage, the thought of being forced to marry this willful, spiteful girl was more than he could imagine.

"It wouldn't take much effort on your part. I don't think I could endure a future with such a foolish, naïve girl." He all but flung open the carriage door. "Do us both the favor of taking your leave before I have my driver throw you out."

"Not until we come to an understanding." Isabelle continued giving him her frank, clear-eyed stare.

A cold fury gripped him. The audacity. "What sort of understanding could we possibly arrive at?"

"That you cease blackmailing Lily and James and comport yourself like a gentleman where my cousin is concerned—and that you never speak of Tunisia again."

"And if I refuse?"

"If you refuse, then I will scream."

Reginald glanced out the half-open door. There were enough casual strollers that Isabelle's tactic would draw a great deal of unwanted attention.

His unwelcome guest gave him a tight smile. "And if you agree now, but later Lily's reputation is tarnished, then I will tell everything I know and present the court with that note written in your hand. You do recall it, don't you? It begins *Dearest Isabelle . . .*"

Blast her.

"Your logic is unassailable. It appears I have no choice. However," Reginald leaned forward, "if we are keeping secrets, one more will do us no harm." Before she could react he drew her to him, taking her dewy lips in a hard, demanding kiss.

When he released her there were tears shining in her eyes. She gathered her skirts and reached for the door, her voice unsteady when she spoke.

"To think I loved you."

His gaze found hers and held, mocking both of them. She had taken her revenge on him, but she would not escape unwounded.

"To think I did not."

Chapter 26

Sweat lathered the bay's shoulders and James could feel his mount's sides heaving. He needed to slow down, to walk the beast. They both had been pushing hard. Reining in, he swung his leg over the side and slid to the ground.

The quiet country night descended around them. Crickets creaked in the hedgerows and above him the sky was laced with stars. James threw his head back and took a deep breath of the clean air, willing his racing heart to calm. Brookdale lay just ahead.

Lily. Could it be different between them now after everything that had happened? He wanted her safe, protected from Reggie, from anyone who would harm her or use her to their own ends. But more than that. He wanted her for his own. Would she refuse him? Would he be able to bare his heart to her scorn and rejection?

He honestly did not know and that frightened him most of all.

James re-mounted the bay, letting him walk. As they crested a rise in the road, he could just make out the sheen of starlight on the glass panes of Brookdale's conservatory a mile ahead. Lights showed in a few windows, both upstairs and down. He urged the bay on.

They clattered into the stable yard some minutes later. James swung down and was met by a groom who took the reins, sparing him only a curious glance before leading the horse away.

James ghosted up the stairs to the front entrance. If it were locked there were plenty of other ways to enter, but as he expected, the latch lifted and the door swung silently open. He slipped inside and just as quietly closed it behind him. It was best if he attracted as little attention as possible. There would be more than enough speculation about Lily's arrival without his appearance adding to it.

Soft-footed he made his way up the stairs to the bedroom wing. He did not know which room was hers, but there, part-way down the corridor, a line of light showed from beneath a door. Reaching it, he hesitated and rested his hand on the knob. There was no sound from within.

He took a breath and pushed the door open.

Lily was sitting before the fire, chin resting in her hand as she stared into the flames. The thin cotton of her nightdress was almost transparent, backlit by the ruddy light. Her unbound hair spilled in dark curls down her back.

The door snicked shut behind him and she glanced up.

"James?" she whispered, her hand going to her throat. She sat immobile for a moment longer, then leapt to her feet and snatched an embroidered oriental robe from the foot of her bed. She thrust her arms into the sleeves. "What are you doing here?"

He could not take his eyes from her, the way the green silk clung to her curves, the defiant expression on her face. She was magnificent. "Gods, Lily. I could ask the same of you. What have you done?"

Her eyes narrowed as she tugged the sash tight around her waist. "It must have been Isabelle—the post could never have gotten to you so quickly. Well, it won't work. I refuse to return to London to play the pawn in the plans and schemes everyone has for me. Please, leave my bedroom at once. Leave me in peace."

"You think it's as simple as that? That Reggie will not follow through on his promise to ruin you if you leave town?"

He took a step closer to her. "Why the devil didn't you accept Buckley?"

She lifted her chin. "I know you thought us quite well-matched. I'm sorry to disappoint you—and my mother will be happy to commiserate. There is nothing you can say that will make me change my mind. In fact, you can just get back on your horse and ride away—you excel at that sort of thing. You have followed me here to no purpose."

"On the contrary." His blood was pounding. He stepped forward until he was standing before her. She stood her ground, glaring at him, her chest rising and falling with her rapid breaths. He reached out and stroked her cheek lightly with one finger. The softness of her skin nearly intoxicated him. Her lips parted at his touch, but she made no protest. "I have every purpose."

He could not stand it any longer. He leaned over her and brushed his mouth against hers. She gasped. Desire flared through him and he reached for her, his hands closing over her silk-clad hips and drawing her close. Her body molded to his, the hiss of silk against the rougher cotton of his coat loud in the stillness. She fitted against him so perfectly. The smell of her, the taste of her . . .

The crack of her hand across his face stung like the devil. "Lily! What—"

"I see." She pulled roughly away. Her tone was bitter. "Now that Lord Buckley has no more claim on me, you think I am easy prey. I will not be your wanton or your mistress, Mr. Huntington. Please go now." Her voice broke on the last words and she turned away from him, arms tightly folded across her body. "Just go."

"Lily," he made his voice gentle, "I did not come for that. It is time, past time, for us to be honest with one another. Look at me." She had to listen to him.

He let out his breath when she finally turned back to him and raised her head. "Have your say, then."

He swallowed, and then slipped to his knees before her. His cheek throbbed where she had slapped him. Courage was in knowing fear and facing it. She had to know how he felt, no matter the consequences.

She stared at him, the firelight leaving half her face in shadow, picking glints of flame from her hair.

"I lied to you." The words rasped from his throat. "I lied when I offered for you in Tunisia. It was not out of obligation. From the beginning of our journey, from the first time I met you, there was something that drew me to you. When I told you I despised you, that was a lie. I despised myself for having nothing to give you. I had hoped by recovering the journals that I would inherit an estate and have some chance of winning your family's favor."

She drew in a sharp breath, but he held up his hand. "You are more precious to me than breath, or light, or journals, or even one small, undiscovered flower. Lily, I love you. I always have."

With a sob, she came to stand before him. "James . . ."

He held out his hands, palms up, and could not suppress a shiver when she placed her own above them. Heat spiraled out from where they touched. He closed his eyes, then opened them and sought her gaze. "I have no fortune. No title or lands. All I have to offer is myself. The strength of my hands and body, my mind and spirit. And my love. A love that will remain true to you, cherish you until my dying day—whatever answer you give me here tonight."

Her eyes were wide and dark with emotion. The hands clasped over his tightened.

James drew in a shuddering breath. "Lily, is love enough? Will you marry me?"

She remained silent for a heartbeat. Two. He was steeling himself to rise, to somehow find his way out of the house and back to London.

"Yes," she whispered. Then, more strongly, "Yes." She knelt beside him, eyes bright with unshed tears. "I love you, James."

He was breaking apart. His heart did not know how to contain so much joy.

"Lily," he breathed, and drew her into his arms. With a soft sigh, she leaned into him and slid her hands up to his shoulders.

Their lips met and it was as though the weeks of self-doubt and recrimination had never been. Her touch made him whole. He moved his mouth gently over hers, re-learning the warm contours. It was she who pressed forward, parting her lips, coaxing his mouth open and exchanging her breath for his.

He spread his hands across her back and pulled her against him, yearning to feel each curve of her body imprinted on his. The silk robe slid beneath his palms and her unbound hair brushed softly over his hands. The feeling was achingly familiar. He could swear he scented the heavy richness of orange blossoms.

She leaned back and gently cupped his cheek. "I'm sorry."

"No. I brought it on myself. I should have spoken my heart to you so much sooner."

Her lips curved. "We are equally guilty of that. But no more recriminations, James. Kiss me."

He tangled his hands in her hair and gladly complied, sliding his mouth over hers and tasting her sweetness. At last. He stood, drawing her up with him, and moved them, still joined in their kiss, to stand beside the bed.

"Lily. My beautiful one," he murmured. "Be with me."

"Always," she breathed.

His hands made quick work of the sash about her waist. The rich silk robe slipped off her shoulders with a single tug. "I want to see you."

"And I you." Fingers brushing his neck, she untied his cravat and pulled it off, then began slipping the buttons of his shirt free. The look on her face was intent, serious, and her hands explored each inch of his chest as it was revealed, leaving trails of fire on his skin. He didn't know if he could burn any hotter, but each touch left him desiring her more.

"I could paint you like this," she said, "All firelight and muscle and smooth skin. Perfectly male. Perfectly beautiful." She leaned forward, trailing kisses across his chest.

"Enough. Now you." Before the words were out of his

mouth he had half the buttons of her nightdress unfastened. She took the fabric from his hands and pulled it off over her head. The firelight caressed her body and he touched her, tracing the patterns of light over her warm, soft skin. She sighed and he pulled her close against him.

Lily could not open her eyes. It must be a dream and she was nodding asleep by the fire. But no, the intimate touch of his hands moving over her naked breasts was real. She gasped—the heat of his mouth closing over one nipple was most certainly real. Her eyes flew open and she set her hands to his shoulders.

His hands moved lower, curving around her hips, smoothing down her thighs, while his mouth moved to suckle her other breast. Heat sparked between her legs and she did not know how much longer she could wait for him this time.

She did not have to. As if sensing her need, he swept her up and laid her gently on the bed. "James," she said, holding out her arms. She wanted him lying beside her—over her, the weight of him pressed against her. Inside her.

"Patience, love." He smiled at her. "I don't think you want these in your bed." He sat on the edge to pull off his boots.

"I want you in my bed. All of you. But I will allow you to take your boots off."

"And my trousers, shall I leave those?"

"Please." She was blushing, she could feel it, but even so she watched as his hands unfastened his trousers, allowing his manhood to spring free.

She reached and brushed her fingers over it. "Hmm. I think it needs further study, but you certainly do not resemble any flower I have ever seen."

"How much study?" His breathing sped when she smoothed her thumb over him.

"Years. Decades."

In one smooth motion he swung himself onto the bed and straddled her, knees on either side of her thighs, hands beside her shoulders. A fierce light burned in his eyes as he looked down at her.

"Lily. You are the flower that deserves the utmost exploration." He bent his head to her mouth again and she arched against him, yearning for the feel of his skin against hers. It was a thrilling, yet somehow comforting sensation. He must have felt her desire, for he slowly let himself down, straightening his legs over hers until his body pressed against hers everywhere. Her legs opened of their own volition, parting under his until she could feel the tip of him there.

"Not yet," he said against her lips. "I want you so much, but not yet."

Before she could question why, he had slid down her body, his hands moving along her legs, pulling them wider. The feel of his mouth there, at her center, drove all her questions away. There was only soft heat and desire and the sound of her own sighs. She was becoming one of the flames flickering in the night. Oh, what he did to her—she hardly knew she could feel this way.

"Now." His voice was rough with desire. "Now, Lily."

"Yes." She took him back into her arms.

His manhood was there, between her legs, sliding in deeper, deeper, until he was completely inside her. Her arms tightened around him and he went still. She had never felt so complete.

Slowly at first, he began to move in her, but she needed him closer. Lily wrapped her legs about his waist and arched her hips to meet him, welcome him. Each stroke echoed like a poem, an ancient meter of desire and love, lost and found with each new generation. She clung to him, pressing kisses against his neck and shoulders as he held himself above her and they obeyed the rule of their hearts.

Lily clenched around him and cried out. Shouting her name, James let the wildfire rush through him, let it burn away all the loneliness and despair he had carried so long.

The aftermath was like floating, both of them coming slowly back to earth, two petals borne on a languid breeze, whirling, coming to rest at last, side-by-side, on a disheveled bed in a quiet manor house in the middle of the English countryside.

Outside the stars turned, the wind rustled in the hedgerows, the whole huge breath of the night continued, waiting for dawn. All was well.

James lowered himself. They lay on their sides, legs still intertwined. The flickering light showed traces of tears on Lily's face.

Her smile was tremulous. "I feel touched, known so deeply. I've never been so close to the wonder. Even painting, I grasp it for a moment, and then it's gone. But you . . . James." She buried her head against his shoulder and he pulled her in close.

The wonder. He knew it too, knew that with her by his side it would always be within reach. The world might intrude, the everyday making of their lives might push the fierce intensity away at times, but in the scent of her, the feel of her in his arms in the fire-shot dark, he would know.

Lily opened her eyes. The fire had burned low in the grate, but there was enough light to see James propped up on one elbow. He was looking at her so tenderly it made her heart ache. He said nothing, only traced her face, and smoothed her unruly hair back with a gentle hand.

A deep, unshakeable happiness lodged in her. He loved her, had followed her, had the courage to bare his heart just as she had finally looked into her own. She laughed softly.

"What is it?"

"My reputation is secure, James. Even if your cousin announces our liaison from one end of town to the other, it will not matter, because we are going to marry."

He grinned at her. "Poetic justice. You're right, there's nothing Reggie can do. Not a thing." He dropped a kiss on her nose. Another on her cheek. Then her mouth. "Wait. I nearly forgot." He slid from the bed.

"What?" She watched him, the muscles pulling taut under his skin as he bent, hunting for his trousers. He was all sensual, manly beauty, and he was hers. One day soon she was going to lie him down on rumpled cotton and capture that lean, hard body on paper. Of course, he might insist that she be naked at the time too. In which case, it was unlikely that she would complete the sketch within a reasonable amount of time. But she would enjoy trying.

"I didn't finish this properly before," he said, kneeling beside the bed. He brought his closed fist up, and then slowly opened it, uncurling his fingers like a flower opening to the sun. The ring he revealed had a blue stone that glinted and winked—a sapphire, surrounded by the pale fire of tiny opals.

"It's exquisite," she said softly.

"No more than you are." He slid it onto her finger. It fit perfectly, fit as though she had always worn this ring. "It is one of the few things I have that belonged to my mother. Nothing gives me greater joy than seeing you wearing it." Emotion darkened his eyes, and she was lost in their flickering depths.

She breathed his name as he bent to kiss her, showed him her love with every touch and caress, gave herself to him as the stars faded into dawn. Her lover. Her love.

Chapter 27

Essex, England, August 1847

The pealing of the bells could be heard for miles when they left the church. The matched grays pulling their open carriage trotted effortlessly down the road, and larks swooped over the passing fields, singing as if their hearts were breaking with joy.

Lily knew that joy. She glanced over at James, who was handling the reins with a steady touch. He looked impossibly handsome, the warm sunshine striking tawny highlights from his hair and making the amber lights in his eyes dance.

He shot her a sidelong grin. "Well, wife of mine. I think we carried that off splendidly. The church was certainly full, at any rate."

"Yes, full of my weeping relatives. Aunt Mary must have gone through at least three handkerchiefs. And Mrs. Hodge's eyes looked suspiciously bright, don't you think?" Even Lily's mother had unbent enough to wish her daughter well. She had turned to her husband and said, "At least Lily is marrying. I had begun to despair of even that," then smiled at her daughter, taking the sting from her words. And if James was not her mother's first choice in a husband, he was certainly Lily's.

"I think Mrs. Hodges's state had more to do with her allergy to orange blossoms. At least that's what she claimed." He bent and nuzzled her hair, knocking her chaplet of white flowers askew. "I much prefer them to roses, myself. And Caroline thought they were most becoming."

"I'm glad your cousin did not grace us with his presence. Though in some ways we are here because of him."

"I might have preferred a less painful style of matchmaking. No, Lord Denby sent Reggie off to inspect the properties in Wales—urgent business, I'm sure."

She shook her head, banishing all thoughts of the dark rogue. "Now tell me, where are we going? You have been very mysterious about the whole subject, although I shouldn't complain. The last time you were so secretive I ended up being treated to the most delicious tangerines. Are you taking me somewhere to feed me citrus?"

"Definitely." He grinned. "Most definitely—but not yet."

They had spoken long and deeply about what their future would hold. She had assured James that if he wanted to take up his career in the military again, she would happily go with him. Her home was with him—the true home of her heart. Together, she knew, they could take any path and flourish, but he had shaken his head and declared himself finished with the army.

Between them they had a modest income, enough for a house in town or a spacious cottage in the country. James was as eager to leave London as she was. Lying curled together late at night their talk had ranged over where they could live and what they wanted to turn their hands to. He wanted to tend the land, he said, happy to boast muddy knees and rough hands. It could be a simple life, that of the country gentry.

For her part, Lily wanted only an airy, north-facing room where she could paint. Sir Edward was eager to have her continue illustrating for him. In fact, the *Mercerium* monograph had been wildly successful. She had been asked about her paintings so many times recently she thought perhaps she might assemble a book highlighting her best illustrations.

"You'll know where we're going when we get there," James said, placing his free arm around her shoulders. "But it will be some time yet. Rest, my love."

She did, lulled by the steady movement of the carriage and the warm sun. They passed through a village—she was dimly aware of the horses' hooves striking sharply off the cobblestones. Later, shadows flickered across her face and she heard the susurration of wind through poplar leaves.

When the carriage slowed she roused. Long rays of sunlight slanted from the west as James guided the horses down a wide lane. Ahead she glimpsed the edges of a building through the greenery surrounding it.

"Are we there?" She rubbed her face and took a long breath.

"Nearly." A mischievous grin tugged the corners of his mouth.

She scanned the roadside and sat upright. They had almost drawn even with the building—a small cottage with flowers blooming in the dooryard.

"It's lovely, James."

"Yes, it is." He took the reins in a firm grip, but instead of pulling the horses to a stop he urged them on to a quicker pace.

Lily swiveled, keeping the cottage in sight as they passed. At his low chuckle, she glanced over at him. "You laugh, but I believe I could be happy there—as long as we were together."

"I'm glad you think so." He guided the horses around a turn, then drew them to a halt and gestured. "Look. Could you be happy here as well?"

Ranks of beeches lined the drive, their tall branches stretching into the clear air, rustling a welcome. In the field beyond a white horse lifted its head and cantered away down the gentle rise. She watched it go, tossing its gleaming mane. Then her eyes were drawn past, to a brighter sparkle.

A fountain played high from the middle of a small lake, throwing clear drops into the air. She could not hear the splash from where they sat, but imagined its watery music. Ornate steps led up to a series of terraces, large pots planted thickly with flowers adorning the walkway.

And presiding over it all—the house. Except it was not a house, or a spacious cottage, or even a manor. It was a mansion, four stories rising from the lush green lawns and terraces, the roofline sporting turrets and dormers and fanciful ironwork. The stone façade glowed warm gray in the westering light, and the windows winked at her.

Lily leaned forward. There, on the far edge of the building—was it possible?

"The conservatory," James said, following her gaze. "It was my grandfather's pride." He clucked the horses into motion, smiling widely as she took it silently in. Was this their new home? How could it be? "The folly is just over there," he pointed, "and the wilderness walk and grotto. And here we are." The carriage swept up the drive and he halted them just before the doors. He leaped down and held out his arms to her.

She closed her eyes, afraid if she opened them again it would all disappear. Surely this place was a dream?

"Come, my lady." His voice was laughing and tender. Lily opened her eyes, but before she could step down from the carriage he had taken her into his arms.

"I am quite capable of walking," she said, sliding her hands around his shoulders to keep her balance. Being clasped in his embrace reminded her of the beach at Cadiz, of the long, long journey that had taken them, at last, to where their hearts belonged.

He dropped a kiss on her forehead but kept striding up the stairs. "I know. You are quite capable of so many things. But let me do this."

The doors swung open at their approach and James carried her into a golden-lit entryway. His boot-heels clicked over the marble floors then were muffled by a rich blue and burgundy carpet.

"Welcome to Somergate, my love. Welcome home." He gently set her on her feet and placed an achingly sweet kiss on her lips.

She leaned into him. "But how?"

"Reginald renounced his claim, and with some prompting from my uncle and his solicitor, Kew Gardens agreed that the property was fairly won—but I did not know it for certain until this morning." He reached into his pocket and drew out a large key made of gleaming brass and ornamented with flourishes. "Lord Denby gave me this, just before I took my place by the altar, and told me the staff were prepared and waiting for our arrival." He gave her a lopsided smile. "Between that surprise and the sight of you walking toward me down the aisle, I was hard-pressed to keep from shouting aloud and dancing over the pews."

"I'm glad you were able to restrain yourself. Though it came as a surprise when you whirled me off my feet after we kissed." The memory made her laugh aloud. The look on her mother's face at their improper behavior had been priceless.

"Ah, Lily." He enfolded her in his arms. "With you at my side, I am capable of anything."

"It seems as though you have your work cut out for you. This is a bit more than we were imagining." She gazed around the spacious entry, then caught sight of the painting at the top of the stairs. Recognition made her gasp aloud.

It was the portrait of James—the one she had painted a lifetime ago in the conservatory at Brookdale.

Slowly she walked up to it, feeling his strong presence at her shoulder as he followed. Those features, so known now, so beloved. How could she have guessed that he would come to mean so much to her? "My husband," she murmured, reaching to trace the lines of paint.

She paused, struck again by the look in the portrait's eyes— the shadowed loneliness, searching for completion. Her heart ached to see it, then ached with happiness as she turned and cupped his face in her hands. His warm skin, his smile, a hint of a dimple in the left cheek. And his eyes.

No trace of sorrow remained there. Pure joy danced in those warm brown depths. He had found what he had been searching for, it seemed.

"You are what I've needed my whole life," he murmured, then kissed her.

Lily's blood sang as his mouth moved fiercely, lovingly, over hers. She embraced him, pressed herself against his hard, lean body and pulled him close.

They were, both of them, home.